ENCHANTED CANYON

ENCHANTED CANYON

YESTERDAY'S TOMORROW

"Somewhere between now and then"

BY

TRUMAN ROCK

An Adventure Between Two Times

A Love Story in Time

A Story That Cheats the Trickster That Is Time

Order this book online at www.trafford.com
or email orders@trafford.com

Most Trafford titles are also available at major online book retailers.

Printed in the United States of America.

ISBN: 978-1-4669-1189-5 (sc)
ISBN: 978-1-4669-1190-1 (hc)

Library of Congress Control Number: 2012900849

Trafford rev. 05/07/2012

 www.trafford.com

North America & international
toll-free: 1 888 232 4444 (USA & Canada)
phone: 250 383 6864 ♦ fax: 812 355 4082

ACKNOWLEDGMENTS

Again to Joseph Kennedy, my cousin, for his help rough-drafting my
handwritten pages and for his timely suggestions.

Again, also, to Patricia Serio for typing all the rewrites.

To my editor, Connie Pollock, for such an excellent job with
Enchanted Canyon.

The cover design and illustrations are by the author,
with assistance from TLC Publishing, Roseville, California.

Enchanted Canyon is dedicated to the memory of Skip Spotts Jr. of
North Platte, Nebraska, my hunting buddy and friend.

DEDICATION

Enchanted Canyon is a moment that reflects stories and places the author experienced during hunting trips to western Nebraska. *Enchanted Canyon* is dedicated to the memory of my hunting partner Skip Spotts Jr., who passed away in 2008 before this book was completed. It is also dedicated to his wife Cathy.

Skip was a friend, a hunting partner, and a fellow veteran of the U.S. Navy. He and I spent many a cold day out on the Frenchman Hunting Preserve, thinking we were hunting deer, when it was all about developing a friendship. Whether we produced a deer or not, there were always stories about old Fort McPherson, the Nebraska Sand Hills, the Oregon Trail, and very old abandoned farms and ranch steads, each making the Nebraska hills come alive for me. It was never just a deer hunt. For me it was a life exposed.

The photo is Skip and me after a day of hunting. Skip is on my left, and I am the wild-looking one with sunglasses.

A Moment with the Author

YOU MUST WRITE it as if you dreamed it, that's where living one's life comes in. If you have never traveled, never visited ancient places, even touched remnants of ancient past civilizations, never loved or lost, never won, or received a gift beyond your expectations, or gifted from your heart, then it's difficult to have your words form pictures and have weight.

After all, that's what writing fictional stories is about. "Bringing it together," creating characters and imagined lands, and setting down daydreams. If what develops as a story seems to be real, then the words have weight. It is my attempt at these weighted words that produced *Enchanted Canyon*, now a memory for me.

PART ONE

An adventure between two times

A story that cheats the trickster that is time

PROLOGUE

"YESTERDAY"

An Ancient Luminal Flash Ship's Voyage to Earth

There is only one of me in all of time and in the entire universe, thought Siren, captain of the luminal flash ship E-DON, as they began to drop from light speed. Her abstract thinking echoed again, *All of time, one of me.*

The luminal starlight in the command center gave everything a blue glow. Occasionally a chime sounded, short tones followed by longer tones. Talking was not the norm as the ship soared in orbit.

Siren noticed a light coating of dust on some equipment. The environment officer smiled. "Nice touch."

Siren nodded. It did connect all of this stellar travel with home. Obviously it was intentional. Dust, what a subtle thought.

She felt something, like billowing storm clouds building and signaling change. The E-DON had just made a seventy-light-year crossing, an eclipse of a day in Siren's time. Nothing in the universe is a single journey, there is always a starting and then a truth or a deception that defines the next step.

The sleep ships of old, she thought. *Hundreds of years of travel lost to time. What they had tried to outrace, to cheat and bypass, had itself passed them.* She touched her chest where her heart beat, feeling a kinship with those other captains and crews, aboard ships that lived forever in eternal sleep heading for yesterday's dawn, a thousand years of tomorrow. *Somewhere out there . . .*

With her hand still at her heart, she gazed out upon the universe, considering the sleep ships and the E-DON being at their destination when they arrived and awoke. Here she was, her craft about to drop from luminal speed, arriving at her stellar destination and finding no evidence that she had overtaken any of the earlier, more primitive sleep star ships. *Had they not survived the crossing?*

She dropped her hand from her heart, setting it on her command seat's armrest. She had marveled at the E-DON's crossing, which had been launched after a beacon from the Sleep Ship T.K.K., more than thirty-three thousand years away. The images recovered from the returning beacon so excited everyone on Siren's planet Edon that a decision was made to send the newest star ship in pursuit, and the advanced star ship had crossed the universe in one day. Siren was excited about meeting those from her world, thirty-three thousand years back.

Sometimes these feelings overwhelmed her, especially now that she was the captain of the first luminal star ship. Her take-charge attitude often overrode her womanly nature. Certainly she had chosen this important position, which required a certain professional distance from her personal emotions. But there were always those moments when she boiled over with loneliness and the simple desire to be just a woman loved by her man.

Siren possessed a quality that caused everyone to notice her. Other women found themselves lacking when they compared themselves to her, so Siren had few female friends. Men longed for her, but they also, in comparison, found themselves falling short and did not approach her, fearing rejection. This added up to a lonely life for Siren.

In reality, Siren was no different from others who lived on Edon. The exceptions were that she was the daughter of the world's mother, a way-knower and Edon's next mother, and she had achieved the lofty position of star ship captain.

Siren had the high brow of her family, and her granite-gray eyes spoke of the mysteries she had witnessed. Her prominent cheekbones and slightly tapered eyes gave her an exotic appearance. She wore her rich, deep chestnut hair swirled atop her head or loose to brush her shoulders. Either way it always shimmered with a quiet red flame. Her alabaster white skin at times reflected a bluish hue, as if washed in a full moon's radiance. Her lips were as soft and plush as her full breasts, so much so that anyone who gazed too long at either feature might forget what they were saying to her. Those who stared into her eyes might experience a fright, seeing in there such a fierce determination of purpose that they backed off, fearful of taking the chance of getting to know her.

Siren's reverie was shattered by the flight officer. "Captain, we are reversing reflectors to drop out of light speed. We are right on course."

The engineer smiled. He had rigged up two computers, one looking back and one scanning the pulse stars. Siren admired the engineer's ingenuity. *Advanced science always required a degree of improvisation.*

Star travel like this was so new to everyone. How lucky her home world had been. The star closest to it—just half a light year's distance—had produced technology that allowed luminal ships to evolve in a way that made journeys of great distances possible.

Siren stood, her eyes surveying the command room. She pondered her planet's decision to travel to the world the ship T.K.K. had found. Thirty-three thousand years' distance in time—what would that produce? Did the T.K.K. repair and continue? Did it remain, and, if so, did the crew survive? Survive? A colony without support? Siren thought that would have been very difficult, to say the least.

She wrapped her arms around her torso. She needed a close contact at this moment, a small comfort that being in command never offered. In a flash, she glimpsed the warmth of a man's embrace. Again, her daydream moment was interrupted.

"Captain," the ship's navigator announced, "the ship is slowing and has transcended luminal speed." Siren glanced at the fore and aft screens. A beautiful brilliant light in the forward screen signaled that they had made the crossing, the star system they were heading for was in sight. Wow.

"Reflectors are reversed and we are thirty-eight light minutes out at sub-light speed, captain," the navigator continued. "Right on target. The three pulsing beacons have confirmed that our position is correct."

Siren turned to her command officers and saw in their faces a sign of accomplishment. "Open all emergency frequencies and have a signal broadcast on every possible frequency in case there is an automated receiver response from the T.K.K.," she ordered.

"Yes, captain," came the response in chorus. The crew was excited about being so far from home and preparing to orbit in a new star system.

The assistant flight commander spoke up. "Thirty-three thousand years—is it possible anyone or some piece of equipment will hear us?"

"We have to try," Siren intoned. "We have to try!" she repeated. "We can't just go out like a flame."

The engineer, a woman as lovely as Siren, announced, "Reflectors are retracted and stowed."

Siren nodded, and the engineer continued reporting the standard in-flight data. Siren's eyes were fixed on the blue-white, almost blinding, light from the star her ship had searched for, found, and approached for a rendezvous with a thirty-three-thousand-year-old question. The probe from the ship T.K.K. had indicated the star—an "M" class clustered with five known worlds of inhabitants—was now in front of them. She wondered about the crew of the T.K.K. *For sure the crew's influence would have advanced the civilization there.* Siren absorbed the light of the star before her and let it warm her soul.

"Captain, the ship has settled into sub-light speed. We are twelve light minutes out from the system. Will we orbit the Twins?"

Siren gave the command for orbit preparation. "Yes, the Twins will be fine. Navigation, light up the system and show me the five planets the probe indicates are inhabitable and especially the Twins."

"Yes, captain." The larger screen lit up projecting the solar bodies of the system they were heading for. Instantly everyone gasped.

"Holy E-DON! Captain, this is all so different. Look! The Twins are gone and only rubble orbits in their stead."

"What happened?" one of the navigation officers blurted. No one responded, still in shock after seeing the Twin planets gone.

Siren's second flight captain said, "A round-trip journey of one hundred seventy light-years is a long time exposed to change."

As the E-DON crew members surveyed the system before them, it became obvious that the Red planet, fourth from the sun, was desolate and absent its water and its heavy atmosphere of one hundred seventy light-years ago. The White Pearl, second from the star, was eight times its original heat, and the third planet out from the star was now blue, not green. The planet looked flooded, compared to the way it had looked one hundred seventy light-years back.

"Head to number three," Siren ordered. The Twin planets, fifth and sixth from the star, were now orbiting asteroid rubble.

The silence in the command space of the luminal ship reflected the silence of deep space. Siren caught her breath. "What's happened. Any life signs? Any technology?"

"No, captain," the probe officer replied. "Nothing is vibrating."

"Not even the third world?" Siren asked.

"Nothing artificial," came the response. "Nothing is making any noise, but it should have life. Good atmosphere and the temperature is in our range."

"Someone should be home," Siren murmured. Coming back to her command behavior, the captain said briskly, "Thank you, navigation." Then she gave another order again, "Orbit the third one."

"Yes, captain."

"Send out a scout to survey the other worlds."

"Yes, captain."

"Excuse me, captain, we are in orbit," the sub-commander spoke.

"Navigation," Siren ordered, "play the tapes of the probe sent out from T.K.K."

Siren watched the screen. Mars looked like a soft, ripe orange-red fruit dotted with azure oceans and puffy white clouds. Next the Twins, one was a land with a few oceans and another water world with a smattering of islands and white clouds. The smallest one, with pearl-white clouds filling the sky, showed no ground features. Last, the green planet, three, showing lakes, oceans, and land masses, with its lush emerald growth on the surface.

"Captain, we are in a fixed orbit at number three."

"Thank you," Siren answered softly, belying the intensity of wonder and apprehension swelling in her soul.

CHAPTER 1

She walks in darkness, like the void of space.
Her voyage in time, in time for her to love.
She is the song that eludes memory, but strikes the heart's notes forever.

THE NEBRASKA SAND HILLS
1859
THE STAR SHIP E-DON ORBITS ABOVE

ON PLANET EARTH, near a cow town in Nebraska, North Platte, to be exact, in 1859, a few cowhands and townsfolk saw a quick flash of colorful light in the sky. It faded quickly, and they returned to what they were doing.

A few miles out of town, as the gentle prairie breeze blew the cottonwood leaves against the tree line next to the windmill water tank, two trail hands, Slim and Dakota, stopped for a smoke.

"Hear how dry them leaves are?" Dakota said.

"Going to be an early winter, look at all them ants and the prairie dogs packing in the chow," answered Slim, whose wind-worn complexion had been tanned by the hot summer's sun and frostbitten by winter's snow. Slim slung his left foot, encased in sharp-toed boots, from the stirrup and shot it across his saddle horn.

His horse whinnied. "Shush!" Slim whispered to his mount, and the horse calmed down, its withers flinching. Out of Slim's shirt pocket came a cloth bag of cut tobacco. He opened it with his teeth, pulling on the string, and retrieved a cigarette paper, which he cradled between his two forefingers. He shook out a measure of tobacco into the paper, pulled the drawstring shut with his teeth, and using two fingers and the thumb of his left hand, he rolled his cigarette. He licked the paper, finishing the job of a custom smoke, and he planted it between his time-worn lips.

Dakota, who also exhibited range-worn brown skin and was in need of a haircut and a shave, not to mention a bath, had cut a chaw and was giving it hell as he worked it into a pliable mass that he could cheek and begin spitting.

Spitta! Dakota's sun and wind-parched lips puckered and out shot a tar-colored mass that splattered atop an anthill that both riders were staring at as they took a break from fence riding on the North Platte range. "Look at them fuckers squirming in my spit!" Dakota mumbled as he watched the ants struggle in the sticky juice.

Slim pulled a tin bandage box from his other shirt pocket, opened it, and took out a wooden match, the kind you could strike anywhere. Raising it to the just-rolled cigarette hanging from his lips, he popped his thumbnail on the match tip and it flared in a yellow-orange sulfurous flash.

Instantly he moved the flame to his cigarette and drew in. The cigarette's end glowed red as his eyes caught another flare of light up in the sky—a brilliant sort of rainbow in an unusual shape. Even thought there was not a rain cloud in the sky, there was a tremendous clap of thunder that shook both riders to the seat of their britches. Both horses bolted. Slim went flying off into the sandy prairie grass, and Dakota, nearly swallowing his chaw, held his seat. He caught the reins of Slim's horse and settled it down.

Getting up, cigarette still lit and clamped between his lips, Slim grumbled, "Goddamn! That's the first time ol' Jebb has ever thrown me!" Dusting off his jeans, he remounted.

"What the fuck was that?" Landing in his saddle, he added, "Have you ever seen a round rainbow? Where is all the gold?"

"In the center," Dakota joked and spat.

Looking back into the western sky, neither rider saw any more evidence of what had just spooked their mounts and had momentarily dazzled their squinted eyes. But the luminal ship E-DON was now in a stationary orbit over North Platte, about a hundred miles above Earth's surface.

*   *   *

"Captain, we are in stabilized orbit. We are viewing many settlements of various sizes, however, there seems to be no electronic chatter or other com noise. If the old ship's crew were stranded here, there is no evidence."

CHAPTER 2

If it weren't for winter, how would you know summer was at hand?
Were it not for a pocketwatch, you would never wonder where time went.
It would all just be sun-up, sunset, day in and day out.
Where does the summer go?

CALIFORNIA
NOVEMBER, 1992

FALL AGAIN, COOLER days and colder nights, trees flaring in gold and red, fiery leaves rattling in the rustling breeze—Traver was relieved. The long days of summer heat were behind him, no more of that get up at 5 a.m., grab a cup of coffee, go out to the field, pack and cut fruit for shipping and drying till 4 p.m., go into the house for a shower, eat, and sleep. Then repeat, for seven days a week. Now he was preparing for a deer-hunting trip to Nebraska.

The pungent smells of summer—of ripe fruit, freshly disked dirt, weed and grass aromas—had given way to the acrid aromas of the busy LAX airport, jet fuel and fast food, lightened by the occasional and delightful fragrance of French perfume on a passing female passenger.

But his destination, the sand hills of Nebraska, with their quietness and stillness, with the scent of cedar trees and the absolute aloneness of where he deer hunted, crowded his senses. This was so attractive to him after an intense summer of work. He couldn't wait to leave California.

Deer hunting didn't always mean that a buck was shot. That sassiness of thinking reflected Travers's life experiences. Looking at his large hands, calloused from the summer's farming, he saw all sorts of memories surfacing as instant flashes in his thoughts as he sat in the terminal at LAX. He was a fit older person, though not the figure he cut as a combat Marine in Vietnam. He still had that military haircut—high and tight—but his hair was now silver instead of the black of his youth. That thousand-yard stare remained a part of how he evaluated a situation. And yet those soft brown eyes could be the quality everyone remembered. His lips did not move in idle chatter, his graying mustache covered his upper lip, nothing special, just a run-of-the-mill mustache.

He had a youthful complexion that hid his years. His six-foot-two-inch height was commanding and he never slouched. He had been called antisocial and corrected the speaker. He was choice social. He had been accused of being non-aggressive. That always made him chuckle. They should have been in Vietnam with him. But these comments, usually made by women, showed how unlikely he would be to create a deep relationship with the speaker.

He had always felt comfortable in not rushing into a relationship. It usually turned out that the goal of his interest had a fantasy image of herself reflective of what TV suggested a woman should be. He looked at romantic relationships as assets, but he knew that his heart was a better judge of female character. He did not have a lot of girlfriends, but those he chose to date all had that special something—that honest view of self he valued. So Traver Wells was just one of the few men satisfied with where he was, a man still searching for that very special partner.

Traver looked about the waiting area LAX Terminal 3. *What a mixture of people all heading somewhere.* The PA system blared, "Flight 87 is now boarding, Gate 38-D. First class and special needs passengers first, please." He stood up, grabbed his carry-on, and picked up the trash magazine he had bought at the coffee shop on his way to the waiting area. He had considered leaving the magazine, but he had not read it completely, and the article about two children from 1862 found on a national historic Civil War battlefield back East had caught his interest. A boy twelve years old and a girl six, wearing clothes in the style of the 1860s, were discovered wandering and dazed. *How did this occur and who determined they were from the 1860s?* The possibility of this being true interested Traver, and he hoped the article wasn't a bunch of crap. He had some feelings about time travel and was hoping it was really true.

After he gathered his stuff and lazily walked over to 38-D, he handed his boarding pass to a handsome gal. Their eyes connected for a moment, she smiled, her lips parted, and she wished him a pleasant flight, handing back half of the boarding pass. He took that extra moment of eye contact and thought how he would enjoy getting to know this gal.

As he had grown older, he had become comfortable living by himself and had begun to enjoy flirting with women more than dating them. If he wanted to be quiet, he could do so without being continually nagged, "What's the matter?" He smiled inwardly. *What's the matter? Equals, Nothing!* He truly did not miss that irritating behavior by a gal who thinks she can discover something very valuable to tease their date with.

Still looking at the ticket agent attendant, in that space of a millisecond, Traver wondered if she would exhibit some of those behaviors that he disliked so much? He clutched his half of the boarding pass and tramped down the jetway. The jet fumes were so strong that he sneezed and then coughed. *Boy, will I be glad to get out of the airport and all the pollution!* Sometimes he thought that the technological advancements that produced all the junk in the air weren't worth it. Maybe a slower life and simpler technology would be better. That's why he enjoyed sitting out in the cold, open canyons, sipping hot, black coffee and hoping no deer would come along to interrupt that. *I don't need to kill a deer to have a great hunt.* Out in the Sand Hills he lost track of time.

The clot of passengers began to disappear as passengers found their seats. He entered the plane's hatchway, and two flight attendants greeted him and pointed out row six for him.

"Ahhh . . ." Traver flopped down, totally relaxed, in the business-class seat of the Boeing 737 Mid West Express Jet. Embraced by soft leather, he closed his eyes, forgetting the long drive from Fresno, the crazy traffic on the 405 in L.A., and the T.S.A. hassles. All that behind him, Traver was ready for three hours of napping. Relaxing and reading for enjoyment, perhaps starting a letter or two, and having a few Pepsis. His eyes were closed but his ears were absorbing the activity of passengers loading, storage bins banging closed, seat belts snapping shut, and the various levels of talking. Suddenly, his nose was tickled by a delicate fragrance. It had to be a woman. He grinned. *Well, some men in California had a tendency to smell good.* He focused on that faint and fragile scent. It brought up memories of a warm Florida evening, a mixture of rain shower, orange blossoms, and a touch of magnolia. That led to thoughts of the smoked mullet at the Sea Breeze restaurant out on the 22nd Street causeway and its crab cakes with Tabasco sauce and lemon. Then he was snared back to the fragrance, no doubt belonging to a goddess. *What was that scent?* Maybe it was an exotic scent he had smelled at Penney's perfume counter the other day when he had gone to the mall to shop? He always enjoyed seeing the fine-looking gals there trying on different scents. One attractive blond there had blue sparkling eyes with a glimmering hint of emerald. She had requested Opium perfume. She was smartly dressed in a western shirt that showed off her breasts, faded jeans that accented her rear, and polished Western boots lifted her to at least five-eight or five-ten. Nope, this scent wasn't Opium, but he had smelled it when he was a kid in Florida at his uncle's place. He began to think of his home as a young kid growing up.

"Excuse me, you are in my seat." A soft feminine voice spoke with a warmth that complemented the fragrance he had scented. His eyes opened, and his head turned. There stood a striking woman in a gray business suit, rather chesty with a well-developed physique. He looked up to her face, crowned by brown hair and accented with dark eyes, red lips, and a smile that undid every bit of structure he had. Immediately, Traver thought this girl was surely a dream. He would wake from a nap quickly. A second or two passed. No dream. She was standing there, boarding pass in hand, looking at him.

"I am?" Traver stuttered and got up. She looked at her ticket. "Business Class, C-6, aisle," she said. He pulled out his boarding pass: Business Class, C-6, window.

He smiled. "Sorry." He scooted into the window seat and sat back down, buckling his seat belt, looking back at her and smiling.

"Thank you." Her eyes held him a moment before she sat down in the aisle seat he had just occupied.

Jeee, how lucky can I get? A hot chick to visit with on the flight to Omaha. He leaned over, said "Excuse me," and reached to the pouch on the seat in front of her for his trash magazine. She smiled. "You don't believe all the stuff that's written in there, do you?"

Traver grinned. "I do and I don't. For example, look at the headlines." He opened the magazine to the article "Children from Civil War Battle Grounds Show Up from the 1860's."

"Well, that's interesting," she said. "I think that's possible."

He said casually and grinned, "Or it's a crock of shit!"

"How so?" she said in a rather genuine way.

"How so?" he repeated. "Dimensionally I suspect anything is possible, but I wonder how a physical property can transcend dimensions or planes? It's like, did the two time dimensions, the 1860's and today, touch and the children pass from one to the other or did something cause their physical makeup to change and reassemble in the future?" He paused and looked over at her. "What makes it sound phony is the article says the government has the two children in a secluded place. Well, if two children from the Civil War were found wandering around a battlefield in today's time, someone other than a trash magazine would surely know about it. You know, like WOLF News."

"I know what you mean," the lady said. "The headline is a grabber, but the story turns out to be very questionable at its conclusion."

"Your seat belt, sir." The cabin attendant touched Traver's shoulder.

"Oh, yes, thank you." He turned to continue his conversation, but the C-6 aisle goddess had closed her eyes, her hands clasped and resting in her lap. He observed her for a long moment. Her curly dark brown hair had hints of gray, her cheekbones were a bit pronounced, and her lips were perfect. Under her business suit jacket her ample chest was rising and falling with each inhale and exhale. Discreetly Traver glanced at a bit of her thighs as her skirt had hiked up past her knees. *Strong leg and thigh muscles, this lady was in very good physical shape.* Traver respected that, wondering for a moment what she did for a living.

As the passengers settled down, the intercom came active with a flight attendant going through the emergency procedures. Traver peeked to see if the lady had opened her eyes. No, she was still in the same position. *Maybe I won't get to visit with this goddess if she sleeps the entire trip.* He didn't like that thought.

His thoughts were going everywhere, things popped up and as quickly disappeared. He thought about the two Civil War children. He was sure the picture in the magazine was posed with present-day models. The article mentioned how calm the children were regarding where they had come from and where they had found themselves.

Where HAD they come from? The article said the 1860's. He thought that was probably literary license. What would these two kids be thinking? Were they on the battlefield or in a home not far from the battlefield?

Traver felt like he was on the battlefield, the roaring jets sounding like the booming of cannons. He heard small arms fire snapping and popping, as seat belts were clicked open, and the slam of an overhead bin sounded like a rifle shot close by. Quickly he became part of the article.

He felt himself behind a fallen tree, with his men on either side, firing and reloading their rifles. This was not an easy battle and lots of men were being hit. Cannon fire was becoming more accurate. He frantically thought it was time to shift their position because soon a cannon might acquire their range. BOOM! The ground behind them exploded. He yelled as he was thrown against a log. The plane lurched Traver out of his dream. He was being shaken and he yelled again. He was now being shaken very hard.

"Sir! Sir!"

Sweat was running down his armpits, his breathing was fast, swirling in his thoughts was cannon fire.

"Sir!"

His eyes fluttered open. The lady in the seat next to him had her hand on his shoulder and she was shaking him and her red lips were forming the words, "Sir! Sir!"

"Yes!" Traver gasped. "Yes, I'm okay." He leaned forward and brought his hands to his face. "Jesus! That was too goddamn real!" He felt the woman's hand leave his shoulder. He raised his head and turned to look at her. "1 was dreaming. It sure seemed real." He sat up straight and ran his fingers over his hair.

"It felt like I had been hit with cannon fire."

The lady pointed to the trash magazine in my lap. "The article," she said, smiling.

"Most likely," Traver agreed. "It sure felt like a battlefield action." He looked around and then whispered to her, "Did I yell real loud?"

A beautiful smile broke across her lips and a small chuckle came from her. "Loud enough to startle me from my dream."

"Oh," he said, a little embarrassed.

"It was pretty loud, and I heard those two old ladies say that you were probably drunk."

"Drunk?" Traver looked shocked. "I haven't had a drink in, oh . . ." He looked at his watch. "Minutes!" He grinned at his joke. "I don't drink, but if you do, may I share a drink with you for all the trouble I've caused you? I'll have a Pepsi."

She looked at me an extra moment. "I'll have a rum and Coke, thank you. Lots of lime."

She reached her right hand over to me. "I'm Donna Williams."

He took her hand. "Traver Wells."

"Traver?" she said and squeezed his hand. "Traver," she repeated, "it's good to meet you, sir."

He sensed that fragrance again. It was as if she had heated up and that caused her fragrance to radiate out in profusion.

"Donna," Traver said. "What's that fragrance you are wearing?"

"It's kerosene, hydraulic oil, and toilet water."

"Well, by God," Traver played along, "you wear it well."

"Actually it's a gardenia-jasmine mix. It's not too strong, is it?"

"Yes! That's it!" He thumped his armrest. "No, no, I mean, it's actually just right! It's quite nice, just a hint now and then." He was quiet a moment. "Hey, what did you mean by all that kerosene and hydraulic oil stuff?"

Smiling, she said, "I'm a pilot in the military, Air Force, and I was teasing you."

"You're a pilot?" he answered with a hint of surprise.

"I sure am." She reached her hand to me again. "Actually it's Colonel Donna Williams." I took her hand again and held it a bit. "Warrant Officer, U.S. Marines, retired," Traver said, squeezing her hand rather firmly. Her eyes began to sparkle. "A War Horse!" She pulled back her hand, which felt warmer and softer as the seconds ticked by.

"You stationed at Offutt?" he asked since their flight was ending at Omaha.

"Not yet. Just been transferred there from Travis Air Force Base in California." She took her hand from his to grab the drink the flight attendant had brought, and she took a sip. "Ummmm, good!" Donna continued, "My new job is flying a DC-9 Looking Glass."

"Looking Glass?" he asked. "That's still in operation?"

She focused on his eyes. "You know about Looking Glass flights?"

"Mostly over in the east. I don't think Russia and China are that much of a threat nowadays. I operated with Looking Glass in Vietnam."

"What do you do now?" Donna asked as she took another sip of her drink.

"I farm now. I'm on my way out to my buddies to hunt deer. Sort of makes working my ass off during the summer all worth it to be able to hunt during the fall."

"The cabin is warm today." Donna said, putting down her drink and leaning forward to take off her jacket, thinking, *The plane's not too warm, it's this man next to me that's heating me up.*

Just that morning, as she was toweling dry after her shower, she had that empty feeling of not having a special man in her life. Being divorced had not bothered her so much. But this man sitting next to her was stirring her emotions big time.

Donna took a deep breath. How long had it been since she had that feeling? A couple of years, she decided. When she got divorced she put her hormones on hold and put her energy in her career and helping her children get through college. Right now, however, her hormones were making a jail break. It had been so long that she experienced deep sexual feelings that she felt a little clumsy responding to this man. *Respond? I need to bang his brains out! And my brains, too!*

As she leaned forward to remove her jacket, he lifted the back of her collar and helped ease her out. "Whew, that's better!" she exclaimed.

Traver thought it was indeed better, for Donna's breasts were large and just so beautiful tucked away in her blouse. He was a breast lover, and Donna's breasts were breathtaking. Her nipples began to press through her blouse, and he became disconnected from the world around him as he focused on the hardening points. *A couple of great C's.*

"Do you dream often when you're sleeping?" he heard her asking, as if from a distance.

I'd like to dream about her breasts.

"Uh, no, I don't," he said. "Only when I've eaten a lot of food late and when something distracts me."

"Distracts you?" she asked seductively. "That could get to be a problem."

"It sure could." He sighed and sipped his Pepsi. *Well, here goes the hunting trip. I'm going to see if I can get a date with her.*

I was going to ask her for her phone number and where she would be staying in Omaha when she said, "Traver, are you staying in Omaha before you head out for deer hunting?"

"No," he said quickly. "I plan to pick up a rental car and get on the road."

She sipped her drink and turned to me. "Do you suppose I could hitch a ride out to Offutt with you if it's on the way? To the BOQ," she said.

"Bachelor Officer's Quarters?"

Donna smiled. "Yes. I'm not married any more and I don't have an apartment yet. I'll get a place pretty quick, but it's BOQ for now."

Well, who's picking up who? "I am sure as hell available. "Offutt can be on the way and so can dinner if you're not to awfully tired from the flight."

Donna swiveled toward me. "Aren't we being fed on this flight?" She seemed to answer her own question because she quickly added, "Yes! Dinner will be great but how hungry will we be if we eat an in-flight meal?"

"Flight meals aren't what they used to be," he said. "Especially the dessert." Donna's eyes perked up.

"Well, then, if we're not that hungry, then let's just do Baskin-Robbins for a hot fudge sundae," he suggested. Donna's eyes rolled up. "That's worth two hours on the rowing machine." She chuckled. "Or . . ."

Traver swallowed the last bit of Pepsi. "Or what?"

With a sheepish smile she said slowly, "Or . . ." She looked at him intently and rolled her R's. "Orrrr . . . I don't have to check in till tomorrow." Her eyes searched his for a clue. She had taken a huge risk.

"By God, hell, yes!" *I'm being picked up!* Here sat next to him the sort of gal who would not get hung up on him for not calling her the next day to reassure her that the preceding day had happened.

"I'll miss my first day of deer hunting."

Donna smiled and said, "I'll take that as a yes?"

"Yes!" he said. "We could go dancing after a nice little dinner and I could show you a little of what I know of Omaha. Heck, we just might go over the river into Iowa and gamble a bit." *You're not a motel woman.*

"Donna, would you like to stay at the Omaha Hilton downtown? Maybe we could get the top floor so you could see it all from there."

"That's awfully expensive. May I share the cost, Traver?" Donna asked seriously.

"Sure, but that's not necessary."

"It's not necessary, but I would like to."

"Fine," he said as he reached his hand over to hers palm up, and Donna took it and held it with both her hands.

She looked at him. "I'm so glad I caught this flight. I was going to stay over in L.A. and go tomorrow. Traver, are you married? Sorry I'm so direct. That's the colonel in me."

"No. Single," and he squeezed her hand.

"I've been married, but now I'm divorced," Donna admitted. "I have two daughters, college age. Their dad felt he needed to re-create his youth and he just left. We had a solid marriage I thought." A tiny tear welled at the corner of her left eye, which she wiped away quickly. "No games, Traver, just straight up. You have any kids?" she asked.

"No, I don't."

"Well, then, I'm your girl for the evening," Donna whispered.

Traver said with a smile, "I'm usually not this easy to pick up."

Donna burst out laughing. "And I'm normally not this hungry."

"Do you mind if I knock off a few more ZZZs? I promise I won't dream about anything that makes me yell."

"No, you go ahead, and I think I'll take a nap, too. You did promise me dinner and dancing."

They both woke up as the plane was landing. The rigmarole of deplaning, getting their luggage, and acquiring the rental car took just about an hour.

"Where are we going?" Donna asked.

"How does the Show Boat over in Iowa sound?"

"What? No downtown hotel?"

Traver navigated the car out of the rental parking structure, with her bags in the trunk and his on the back seat. He had placed his two rifles in the trunk, also. "Let's go to Bellview. That's right next to Offutt. There's a great steak, potato, and green beans place there," he suggested. "No dancing, but the food is good, next to home cooking."

"You're the boss," Donna said as she settled in the passenger seat. She took a deep breath. "Smells good here." He chuckled. "Wait till we get on 1-75 and pass the stockyards. You'll smell a different song."

"Oh? You think I'm a city girl? Mister, I've smelled my share of shit," she said giggling.

He patted her thigh briskly. "You said you have to report tomorrow?"

"Yes, by 1600."

"Do you have a duty station yet? I mean, besides flying the Looking Glass?"

"No," Donna said. "I'll most likely be put on T.A.D.—temporary staus—until I'm assigned to a section. I have to fly the test DC-9 a bit and requalify in the 9's, but that's a cake walk."

"What were you flying at Travis?" he asked.

"I was in the **Marine** Asset Tracker System."

As he pulled off 75 and headed toward the Toad Stool Restaurant Bellvue, he decided he was going to kiss her on the lips. He pulled into a dark parking space and turned to see Donna's sparkling eyes. He leaned over, and as their lips met, Traver's right hand instinctively came up to caress her left breast.

"Ummm." Donna murmered. "Not fair."

Her kisses became firmer and her tongue lightly touched his teeth.

She breathed, "You have a gentle touch, a caring touch."

"You," Traver sighed, "are very, very attractive and touchable."

"Why, thank you, sir." Her stomach growled. "Okay, mister, it's feed-me time."

Donna pulled on her jacket, and Traver went around to open the door for her. She encircled his waist with her arm, and they glided into the restaurant.

They sat in a corner table that was very private and ordered the stockyard special, eating slowly and enjoying a getting-to-know-you conversation.

Plates scraped clean, Donna asked, "How far away is dessert?" She grinned.

"Oh, maybe thirty minutes. When I'm in Omaha, I usually stay at my brother's."

"Is there something closer?" she asked sweetly.

"Sure."

"Is it clean?" she wanted to know.

"I suppose so."

"Okay, let's go for close and clean. I am bushed and stuffed. Do you mind, Traver?" she said coyly.

"Not a bit, let's go," he said with enthusiasm.

Just at the I-75 interchange was the motel, and Traver stepped into the office to get adjoining rooms. He came back to the car and gave Donna her key. She gave a long look at my key and her key.

"You didn't assume that I was going to sleep with you, did you."

"No, but I sure would enjoy it!"

Donna looked at her key again. "Thank you, Traver, you are a gentleman." She lowered her eyes and tucked her room key under her chin, deep in thought. Then she gazed into his eyes and said softly, "Can we get a king-size bed?" She handed her key back to him and he sprinted to the office.

In a few minutes Traver returned with only one key. "Number 7."

"Lucky 7," Donna announced, "my lucky number."

"Jackpot!" he crowed.

Traver carted in the bags, and she unlocked the door. "Brrr, it's chilly in here," she said as she walked to the wall heater and turned up the thermostat. Instantly the gas pilot light lit the main burner and the natural gas sprang to life. He stood next to her and tried to feel the warmth. "It is chilly," he agreed.

Donna turned toward him and said lightly, "Who's first for the shower?"

"You go ahead," Traver said.

"Okay." She unzipped her luggage's side pocket to take out a night shirt and a robe. "See you in a bit."

He rummaged through his bag for a clean T-shirt and boxer shorts, and in just minutes Donna came out of the bathroom, bundled up in a bathrobe with her bra and panties in her hand. "I left the water running," she murmured as she passed by him.

As he headed for the bathroom, she pulled back the covers on the bed and climbed in. She clicked off the bedside light and pulled the sheet up under her chin, eyes closed.

When Traver opened the door and flipped off the bathroom light, he noticed with disappointment that Donna was already asleep. He quietly walked over to his bag to deposit his dirty clothes when he noticed her panties and bra on the chair. He glanced at the bed to make sure she was asleep, and he reached out to touch her bra. His fingertips exploded with feeling as the soft pearl-white material came in contact with his dreams. Donna made a moaning sound as she turned in her sleep, and he slipped without a rustle under the covers. When he switched off the light on his side of the bed, the room became onyx black.

"Goodnight, Traver," she breathed gently, and her hand came across his chest and her body snuggled next to his. "Sweet dreams, marine."

He put his arm around her. "Sweet dreams."

*   *   *

The early morning came without announcement, and Traver awakened to find Donna's body pressed close, her night shirt ridden up to her waist. They both were relaxed from the earthquake of loving.

Morning had a solid foothold, the sun rousing the pair.

"Traver, this has been a beautiful date. We'll be able to see each other again?" she questioned in a soft voice.

"I live in California. It could get to be an expensive date."

"Traver, this *can't* just be a one-time thing," Donna said as she sat up.

He leaned over and kissed her. "It won't, believe me. But we have to get you aboard and checked in and I need to get out to North Platte for some deer hunting." He got out of bed, slipped on his boxers, and went to his shirt to get a pen. He wrote down his address in California and Skip's number for her in Nebraska. "Call me when you get settled, okay?"

She smiled and saluted. "Yes, sir!"

"I don't mean it that way, Donna," he sighed. "You have just as much say in this relationship as I do. I won't read anything into you calling me except that you want to talk with me, okay? I'll call you when I get in."

"I didn't take it any other way, Traver," she let him know. "I was concerned that I was a little forward on the plane, but I learned a long time ago that when I have a deep feeling, I need to explore it. If it means I get a little bold, well, that's the colonel in me." She patted the bed next to her. "Marine, get over here and kiss me! That's an order!"

He marched back to bed and kissed her passionately.

Donna just barely reported to her duty station on time, and Traver headed out to North Platte to meet up with Skip and his brother. He understood that he would be making a few extra trips out to Nebraska that didn't involve deer hunting this year. And the cost was of no consequence. He had missed opening day of deer season!

CHAPTER 3

*For an instant, yesterday became today like a whirlpool going
round and round yesterday and today whirling and touching just
momentarily—but long enough to be heard.*

THE FREEWAY OF TIME

WHILE DRIVING OUT to west Nebraska on I-80, Traver thought about
Donna. He hadn't dated much lately, just too busy with work, and then a
really great gal just falls in his lap—well, sits next to him.

The Grand Island rest stop came in to view and he needed to get rid of
all the coffee he had been drinking. He quickly scooted into the restroom
and pissed. Back at the rental car he got out his cell phone to call Skip,
and he looked west out of the windshield to see that western Nebraska
was catching hell: black clouds billowed pregnant with hail and snow. He
needed to get to North Platte quickly before that early fall storm hit. Just
then a huge lightning bolt flashed across the sky, his hair standing on end
it was so close. Boom! A clap of thunder retorted.

Traver turned on the cell phone and punched in Skip's number. The
phone beeped and flashed, and the screen went blank. The words Lost
Call flickered by. *Goddamn it, these electronic pieces of shit!* He re-input
Skip's number to be sure and hit the call button. That got him a hissing
static sound, a ring, and a connection. "Hey, Skip!"

But no human response, just the heterodyne sound of two transmitters
keyed up on the same frequency.

"Skip, goddamn it, talk to me!"

THE NEBRASKA SAND HILLS
1859
YESTERDAY

Siren's crew remained aboard except for the small group of shipboard personnel that moved down onto the planet's surface and into the town of North Platte. They were searching for evidence of the sleep ship. In 1859 no airships flew, and trains were just starting to penetrate the West. Above the Nebraska prairie town floated a star ship with unimaginable technology. "Skip, goddamn it," blared in the ship's com center.

NORTH PLATTE
1995 and 1859
TODAY

Back beyond the dawn, more than one hundred years back, in fact, the cell phone's call was received in the veterinarian's office in North Platte, Nebraska. With other crew members playing her office workers, Captain Siren posed as the town's new vet now. In 1859 that was not difficult, with her knowledge of medicine and health that was light-years ahead of the local Nebraskans. She did well.

Traver's cell phone call got tangled up in the lightning and the storm's electromagnetic anomalies and played out on the star ship's communication system. It was down-linked to the captain in the vet's office in North Platte.

One hundred plus years separated the call, but somehow time had overlapped and wrinkled in both moments—1859 and 1995—became one. Were these numbers somehow related? Did the electromagnetic gyrations of the storm scramble the radio spectrum? Or was an energy-spiraling whirlpool spinning time in a bottle?

Whatever it was, it was first contact for the star ship E-DON and a real distraction for Siren. Her senses were stunned by this voice on the communicator system

1995

"This goddamn electronic piece of shit!" Traver growled into the phone.

"Shit?" the receptionist asked Siren. "Captain, what does this person mean, shit?" Siren shrugged her shoulders.

"You on and off bundle of crap!" Traver shouted.

Again the communication device blared in the captain's office.

"Captain, who is this? Is he from our crew?"

"I don't know," Siren responded. "Who else would have a com device here but us? It does sound like his equipment treats him like ours does now and then, though." She chuckled with the rest of the crew.

"Seriously, captain, who is this?" the gal at the desk asked. "We can't plot this signal, the voice is just radiating out everywhere. No start point. Like it's not there but we hear it! None of the people here have anything like this."

A member of the crew chimed in, "It's just got to be one of us and the sun's flaring is causing problems."

"You goddamn son-of-a-bitch!" Traver threw down the cell phone and the connection with the captain's com room and 1859 ceased in a crackling flood of static and then silence.

"What was that all about, captain?" the aide asked again. Siren smiled. "That's all about what happens when equipment falters," she answered. "Now let's get back to work."

Although Siren dismissed the communication to her crew, she had been affected by the voice that radiated everywhere in the room. He wasn't a crew member. Somehow that irritated voice stirred a sensation in her soul memory, something basic and ancient, something that she needed to know more about.

"Captain, did you hear all that?"

"Yes, I did, but I don't know what it means," Siren responded. "Let's check some of our communication equipment."

1995

Traver glared at the cell phone he had just thrown onto the asphalt. He stomped on it one more time for good measure.

Both Traver's and Siren's day continued without further incident. He grumbled about electronic devices working only when they wanted to. But she daydreamed all day about that voice that lit up com central.

Off in reverie again, Siren fingered the necklace that held the Way's Orb, and into her memory fluttered a scene of her as a little girl walking with her mother at the great ocean's edge and a man meeting them.

Traver tried to shake off his frustration and headed for the pay phone at the rest stop. He dialed Skip's number, and after the fourth ring, the answering machine engaged and took the call. "Skip," he said, "I called you on my cell phone and I think your answering machine screwed with me. Hey, before I run out of time, I'll be there in an hour." Another lightning bolt flashed across the horizon as he hung up, and he was momentarily lost in the scene of the oncoming storm. He thought he saw a ship sailing in the clouds' swirling mass. *Cloud pictures.*

*   *   *

The ship's engineering officer came into Siren's office and sat down, looking at her quizzically. "Captain, how do you suppose we received that last bit of transmission?"

"Are we sure it wasn't some crew member trying to contact us?" Siren said in response.

"The sun has been flaring for a couple of days, so maybe it is distorting some of our transmissions back to us," he suggested.

"Perhaps," the captain said as she looked around her command area. "Check this out and get back to me."

"Yes, ma'm."

Siren was deeply puzzled, although she tried not to show it to her crew. *Who is Skip? That caller is somewhere out there.*

She knew there were no voice electronic communications in this time, only a wire that sparked long and short static discharges. The voice had to come from somewhere other than the world they were in orbit around. But no other worlds in this solar system are inhabited, she reminded herself. This was the first inkling of an advanced technology. No trace of her world's star ship crash of thousands of years ago, except for Indian legends about star people. *Did this first communication somehow come from the lost ship's crew? Or was this message lost in time?*

I-80 TO NORTH PLATTE, NEBRASKA
FROM THE PHONE BOOTH

Traver returned to the rental car and as he opened the door a hint of Donna's fragrance tickled his senses. He remembered their bodies short-circuiting all which-a-ways and then their quiet snuggle. He was shaken out of his dream when a flash of lightning seared the sky and a clap of thunder focused his attention to the moment.

He needed to get back on the freeway and to North Platte pretty quickly. He settled on 65 m.p.h. and turned on the heater to warm the chill. He adjusted the seat belt a bit and held the steering wheel with his left hand and with his right hand he sipped the warm coffee he had poured from the Thermos.

Traver's thoughts drifted back to Donna. He shook his head back and forth in amazement. *How could I meet such a strong, beautiful person? I've been looking for a love like this.* His emotions reeled from all the excitement of Donna.

He finished his coffee and watched the road unroll before him, thinking about deer hunting and how the weather might mess up the first day's hunt. The deer would be hunkered down and not moving around. He didn't miss anything by staying in Omaha with Donna. *I didn't miss anything and I gained everything!*

Donna again in the forefront of his thoughts. He reached instinctively into his shirt pocket for his cell phone to call her. *Ha! I crushed that piece of shit back at the rest stop.*

Traver decided he would call when he got to Skip's. A few more miles unfurled and he couldn't shake his desire to let Donna know that it was a fairy-tale experience meeting her like that on the plane, it was special and their loving wasn't just a wham-bam-thank-you-ma'm thing.

At the first gas station along the highway, he pulled over to the pay phone and called Offutt Air Force Base locator and asked for Lieutenant Colonel Donna Williams to be attached to Looking Glass. The person who answered asked if he had the unit number. "No, but she's a new transfer and most likely would be assigned to training that midnight flight."

"Yes, sir, right away."

Well, I'll be, midnight still is important. Traver had operated with D-9's Looking Glass flights in Vietnam, and they always referred to themselves as the midnight shift.

"Sir? Lieutenant Colonel Donna Williams is at BOQ and her number is 555-9893."

"Thanks, say that again slowly so I can get it down."

"Sir, I can patch you to that number if you want."

"Yes, please do."

The phone buzzed three times and then a soft voice answered, "Hello?"

"Donna, Traver here, did I wake you?"

"Traver? Oh, yes, hi, Traver. Yes, you woke me, but I'll forgive you. Can't stay away, huh?" she said with the lilting voice of a satisfied woman.

"No, I can't stay away from you!" He chuckled. "I wanted to tell you how great I feel and that last night just doesn't happen to me all that often and I'll be back."

"I know Traver, and it's been quite a while for me, too. When will you be back from hunting?"

"Ten days from now," he told her.

"Great. You're penned in. That's a ballpoint pen, not pencil, so you have to keep the date."

Another lightning flash and thunder rumble caused Traver to say, "Donna, I got to get, a storm is breaking and I don't want to be in it any longer than I have to. Bye, and miss me."

Donna smacked him a kiss over the phone and hung up.

He decided he would call her back when he got to Skip's so they could talk longer. He was so comfortable with her and all they shared so quickly. *I was ready for her and she was ready for me. How many times does that happen in a man's life?*

His thoughts shifted to the just-finished summer fruit season at his ranch in California's San Joaquin Valley. He coped with the intense pack-out chores by thinking about hunting up in the Frenchman Preserve in Sand Hills. He may have missed the first day and the Big One, but he was nicely compensated by opening day with Donna.

He pulled up at Skip's place and noticed his brother's truck but not Skip's. The note on the garage door said come in and take a nap, watch TV, or fix a snack. Skip and Raymond were in town and would be back before dark.

He went inside and fixed that snack, plopped down on the couch, and went fast asleep. He awakened to the automatic garage door opening and Skip and Raymond coming in through the basement and up the stairs into the kitchen.

They greeted each other in the kitchen, and Skip kidded him about opening day and bagging a doe on the plane. He was amazed that Traver would put off hunting for a gal. He reminded Skip that he was getting older—fewer gals were hitting on him and deer hunting was getting more like work. Everyone had a good laugh at that.

Sitting at the kitchen table, the guys talked way past midnight, when Cathy, Skip's wife, came in from work with five pounds of beer-battered, deep-fried chicken livers and rice with brown gravy. They ate like pigs, wiped their plates clean, and downed the last drop of iced tea.

Four thirty the next morning rolled around all too quickly, and with a Thermos of coffee they headed for the canyon, eager to pop a good-sized buck. Traver lifted his head to scent the morning. The air reeked of the low-lying scrub brush and cedar-tree scent. Someone had a morning fire going in their hearth. The guys were south of the Platte River, so there was no water or wetland smell, but overhead hundreds of swans and geese were honking their way to the river.

Traver noticed a grasshopper moving slowly on the ground; it was deep brown, having lost its youthful spring green. Soon the freezing days and nights would end its existence. It made him think, *God, it's good to be alive!* He wanted to just lay back and enjoy the morning and not give a shit if a deer came by or not.

He raised his rifle to use its scope to scout things out. The early-morning fog and the fast-moving clouds scudded by so fast that through the scope it looked like a changing landscape in a movie. The light was going from extreme brightness to dusky gray, only to shimmer again as the clouds whisked by. A slight frost was forming on the barrel of his rifle, and he felt the biting cold on his fingers.

All the signs indicated that the deer had not come this way this morning. The snow tracks were old. They were all small tracks, but something attracted Traver's thoughts from his daydreaming.

The winds were coming at him and keeping his scent from drifting down into the larger valley. Nothing was out of place there. He reached for his coffee, one of the pleasures of being up so early. Good strong coffee. As he sipped, he checked the safety on the rifle and wiped the frost from the gun barrel.

He got out a piece of beef jerky to chew on. Then he noticed a movement in the upper draw of one of the canyons. Putting the cup down, he slowly released the safety and turned for a full view. Sure enough, coming down almost the center without the cover of trees came a large buck. He raised the Remington to his shoulder and through the scope he could see the ol' buck was indeed a granddaddy. A head-on shot, in fact, a quick, clean kill.

The gun went off with a loud boom and a heavy thump at his shoulder that left his heart pounding. It was a good 300-yard shot. He jacked in another round and sat waiting to see if the buck would get up, but there was no movement.

When he reached the buck, he rolled it over for cleaning and there, stuck in the buck's side, was a broken arrow. A good half of the shaft was clean into his stomach, just missing his lungs. That's why this big buck was not using cover, he was almost dead from blood loss and was moving on adrenaline.

This arrow looked rather peculiar to Traver, roughly made and rather primitive, like something from a hundred years ago. The feathers were turkey, attached with tree pitch and wrapped with horse hair. He pulled out the broken arrow and, after studying it a bit, tossed it over to his pack where his rifle lay.

Getting the buck prepared wasn't too difficult, packing snow inside the animal's chest cavity to cool it down. Then he gathered his gear, with the broken arrow and the Remington, and headed off to find his brother and Skip.

Marking the spot was easy enough, all the hills here in the Frenchman can be seen from just about any hilltop. He could see the windmill, so he would know where he had left the deer.

With the windmill in sight off to the left, Traver walked northwest to where Skip was supposed to be. He took it at a slow, steady pace. After all, he was nearing forty-seven now, and the old body was taking a little longer to do the heavy stuff.

Crunching along in the snow, his breath steaming, his thoughts drifted to the article he had read in the trash magazine about Germany building a star ship. Apparently someone had found a repair manual in a UFO crash site in the Alps. *Maybe.*

What about those two children found wandering at the Stone Creek battlefield, blood still fresh on them? Apparently the boy and girl, seven and three, were being kept in Washington by the FBI and were having a hard time adjusting to present time. Well . . . How would he react popping into the future a hundred and fifty years from now?

Overhead, a jumbo jet streaked due west toward L.A. or San Francisco. Looking through his rifle scope, he recognized the United Airlines markings. That put him in mind of meeting Donna. He determined to call her tonight and tell her about the buck.

He slung his rifle across his shoulder, oriented himself in relation to the windmill, and walked toward it. Suddenly he saw a flash off to the right, and using his scope saw his brother and Skip. They were heading toward the truck, and so would he.

Trudging along, Traver thought about finding himself in future, like the two Civil War kids. That would be tough. But going back to the past, now that was something else entirely. That would be a fantasy come true. What would he take?

A .22-caliber rifle and a .22-magnum pistol, because he could carry lots of ammo and a 22 is a good round. But everything back then was black powder. Perhaps he ought to bring the pistol and pick out one of the two black-powder rifles he owned, probably the Kodiak .50-caliber twin rifle and a .45-.70 Trapdoor that used a brass casing and primer. But then why bring anything? He could buy one or two back there. What could he use for money? Buying money of the period from collectors would be expensive but easier. Hey! He could research the gold strikes in the area and mine enough to get started. That would be fun. So he wouldn't be on anyone's claim back then, he would find an area being mined today where a few hundred pounds or so wouldn't be missed. Smiling, he felt pretty smart about solving the dollar problem.

Also, he had better be pretty healthy before going back. He would have all his teeth pulled and have two sets of dentures made. He would have his appendix taken out. His tonsils had been taken out when he was four years old. Back in the past even a minor medical situation could be deathly serious. Hell, he would have to read up on natural remedies because he couldn't bring a pharmacy with him. Maybe going back in time was going to be a little more of a hassle than just staying here. *On the other hand, going back would eliminate all the bullshit taxes.* No one wanted to work in California, it was too easy to get welfare and stay on it. Working people were paying all the bills, businesses were moving out of state, and those left behind had to cough up more tax dollars to support the freeloaders. He was already putting land up for sale and looking for a new state to retire. He even looked at Tasmania, but he couldn't take his collection of rifles there, especially the older ones.

Chuckling to himself, he wondered how to bring the best of today to the best of yesterday.

The sky was a hard blue, the snow a stark white, and the windmill was outlined in shadow by the bright sun. Skip and Raymond were approaching him in the truck, and they drove over to where he had dropped the buck. They loaded it in the back of the truck, and, forgetting about the curious broken arrow, Traver white-lied his "buck" shot to 400 yards. By the time Skip and Traver had taken the buck to the ranger station for tagging and then to the processing butcher, the shot had grown to 500 yards.

Raymond was jawing about the huge buck he had seen, but following it he came upon a well-maintained fence so he didn't cross. Skip popped up, "That's most likely the north boundary of the Peterson place. The foreman's name is Roy and he's a good friend. Dr. Peterson will probably let us on to pop a big one, I'll ask her."

Skip drove the truck into in the meat locker yard in Maxwell. Darrell strode out to take a look at the buck.

"How do you want this done?" he asked Traver.

"Jerk the best and grind everything else into deer salami and smoke it, nothing fresh on this trip."

"Same as last time?" Darrell wanted to know.

"When it's all dried, ship it to California," said Traver and pulled out his wallet.

Darrell put up his hand. "I'll send you the bill when we ship the jerky and salami."

"Thanks, Darrell!" Traver saluted, and the three hunters piled in Skip's truck to head back to North Platte.

Raymond and Skip jawed about Marine Corps buddies that they both knew, and Traver dozed off.

Soon Skip was pushing on his shoulder. "Rise and shine, handsome, we're home!" Skip looked at his watch. "Plenty of time to get showered and duded up before Gary's BBQ."

Raymond and Traver stayed in the garage cleaning the rifles, and shortly Skip came back down from upstairs with a beer for Raymond and two Pepsis, one for himself and one for Traver.

"Hey, Traver, a Donna called, here's her number."

"Thanks." He took the paper and put it in his wallet.

Raymond glanced over at him. "Who's this Donna?"

Looking up from cleaning his Remington, Traver said, "She's a 9 Driver for Looking Glass at Offutt."

Raymond raised his eyebrows at that. "That's pretty secret shit, Traver. How did you meet her?"

"She picked me up on the plane ride out here!"

Raymond grinned. "Oh, sure."

Skip added, "Well, what do you think might be important enough for Traver to miss opening day—he was opening day!" That gave Skip and Raymond a good guffaw at Traver's expense.

Oiling his 7 mag, Traver said, "Go ahead, boys, enjoy yourselves. Remember me when I'm off to Omaha for a few days to get my weapon nice and slick."

With the rifles cleaned, Raymond's in his case and Traver's resting on the work bench, Skip ordered, "Showers, boys. Can't go to Gary's place stinking."

CHAPTER 4

THE SAND HILLS OF
WESTERN NEBRASKA, 1995

Surviving alone sometimes
wasn't so wonderful . . .
it could get a person
left in the world alone.

Laura remembered her husband and the heart attack he had in the
Sand Hills—how alone he was when he died

SOUTH CANYON

IN MAXWELL AND down South Canyon Road, where there was a grand
stone house with barns and outbuildings for ranch hands, Laura was
upstairs in her bedroom shedding her work clothes. Her worn boots were
yanked off and her dusty socks were tossed in the clothes hamper, and she
wiggled her now-liberated toes. She stood up, unzipped and dropped her
jeans, and stepped out of them. Wearing only her panties and bra, she
went into the bathroom. The full-length mirror on the wall opposite the
sink captured her full physique.

She stopped a moment to look at herself. No particular feature
attracted her. She basically approved, solid, for one thing, and at fifty
that's a good thing. Leaning forward, she peered at her face, noting how
the weather was drying it out. The suntanned V on her chest contrasted
sharply with the rest of her milk-white chest.

She reached in the shower and twisted on the hot water. Her hands unfastened her front-clasp bra, and she surveyed her breasts. Full, firm, and creamy with tiny rose-pink nipples.

But her satisfaction was short lived. Laura closed her eyes, which were stinging with tears. They ran down her cheeks and fell on her breasts. She squeezed her hands into tight fists, and her lips hardened into a painful frown. She remembered how her husband, Bill, would stroke and kiss her breasts, whispering how beautiful they were. Her nipples became partially erect and she raised her hands to touch them, saying in a soft crackling voice, "Bill." She shook her brownish red curls back and forth, again whispering, "Bill." She took a deep breath, dropped her hands from her breasts, and in a daze tested the water again. Adding a bit of cold to the hot, she stepped in and let the shower's water pepper her back. Then she turned, so the water could gently massage her face and chest. A shower like this after a day's work was luxurious and a shower like this could ease her heartache.

LAKE MALONEY, A FEW MILES WEST OF SOUTH CANYON

Back at Skip's house . . .

"Hey, Traver!" Raymond yelled. "You going to use all the hot water? You better shave, you never know, there might be some hot chicks at Gary's.

"Hey, Traver!" Raymond called again. "Are you still dating that lawyer?"

Traver turned off the shower and answered, "Ha! She's dating me. Why?"

"Why?" Raymond repeated. "Hell, you got to have some so you don't go crazy!" He laughed. "I'm pestering you because Ruth has a gal she wants you meet."

"Oh?" Traver answered, not enthusiastically.

Raymond grinned. "She's the UPS girl."

Traver raised an eyebrow at that.

"She is really friendly, a little more than filled out."

"Fat?"

"No," Raymond said, "she's a UPS driver and you can't be fat, you have to lift a lot of heavy packages."

"Okay, tell Ruth she's on." *I can date two chicks in Omaha.* "What's her name?" Traver wanted to know.

"Jill, and she's a cowgirl at Hemet," Raymond said.

As Raymond got into the shower, Traver dug around in his bag for socks, skivvies, T-shirt and threw them on his bed. Getting dressed, he picked up Skip's phone and called Donna at Offutt. The BOQ told him that Colonel Williams was on assignment and would be gone the next fifteen days. Disappointed, Traver left a message and hung up.

SOUTH CANYON

A few miles away at the Peterson ranch, Laura was getting out of her shower and preparing to shave under her arms. She raised her right arm, exposing her armpit, and thought, *Why am I shaving? I'm not wearing a sleeveless dress that will show my armpits.* She began shaving anyway, settling on a feeling of personal pride for good hygiene. She shaved every evening when Bill was alive. *Why am I thinking of Bill so much?* At that interior question, her tears welled up again. Bill had died on this day ten years ago. Wracked again with sorrow, Laura cried out, "Goddamn it, Bill!"

Screw it! I'm not going to Gary's.

Walking into her bedroom, she took an old robe and wrapped it around her body. Barefoot, she went downstairs to make a cup of hot chocolate. In the front room, she sat in her favorite spot on the couch. Shivering a bit, she tugged her robe close, pulling it tightly about her. Looking out the big picture window, she became lost in the vast view. Wiggling her toes, she remembered how her daughter—was she two or three?—would pounce on them and pull at them.

Laura put her head back and drifted off to sleep. Her rhythmic breathing caused her to relax, and she stretched her long, shapely legs out to rest on the coffee table. She didn't remember falling asleep, but suddenly, from a distant dream world, Laura sensed a bell ringing. She groggily reached for the phone, and said in a raspy voice, "Hello?"

It was Jane. "Oh, hi. Yes, I was asleep. But I'm awake now." A moment passed. "Well, I was thinking about just staying here at home." Another moment passed. "No. I'm really fine, not sick, just tired. I'll think about it, Jane, and thanks for calling."

Laura hung up and gazed out the big picture window to see a pair of hawks soaring in an updraft of wind. The hall clock chimed. *I might just as well go. I'm awake now.*

LAKE MALONEY, GARY'S PLACE

Raymond and Traver pulled up in front of Gary's place to a crowd of cars. "The last of the summer and early fall's barbecue and the deer hunt are big deals, Raymond said. "Let's go see what's what."

Skip and Cathy were already there, nursing their first sodas, regaling the folks with the details of Traver's 700-yard shot that felled the buck. The distance seemed to lengthen in direct proportion to Skip's enthusiasm.

The brothers walked around to Gary's back door, where the barbecue was in full progress. Traver surveyed the folks, gathered in lively conversation in small groups. He admired the view of the lake and turned to say something to Raymond, but his brother had vanished. Looking over the crowd, Traver noticed a striking woman just disappearing into Gary's back patio area. Her movement was graceful, and her snug-fitting jeans accentuated a round rear. He wondered what color her eyes were and what her voice sounded like. He wandered over to sniff the air where she had passed, hoping to absorb her fragrance. He glanced around when he realized that someone might have been watching his foolish behavior.

Standing on the patio, Traver began thinking about Linda, the lawyer, whom he dated now and then back home. Just before he had left for hunting, she had shocked him with an off-the-wall comment, something about including another woman on their next date for her to enjoy and for him to watch. Traver was more shocked than excited, but this relationship was always about Linda anyway.

He wondered what the UPS girl would be like? He dismissed that thought. Linda wasn't exactly a sexpot, and he wasn't interested in a Linda-type girlfriend. Donna was something else, with her tanned breasts and striking nipples and just good-people feelings.

As quickly as that thought filled his brain and his pants, Traver saw the long-legged beauty come into view. Again he noticed that her belt buckle spelled BILL in silver letters. *She sure as hell doesn't look like any Bill I've ever known!*

He decided that Bill must be her husband, just his luck. But he still wanted to meet her.

Laura was crossing the patio to find Jane in the downstairs portion of the house. Jane was helping her sister-in-law set the table with salads, pickles, olives, and beans. When Jane saw Laura coming into the room, she yelled, "Laura!" The women embraced, and Jane said softly, "I had forgotten what today is for you." Laura just nodded her head. "I almost didn't come."

Jane saw Laura struggling to smile. "It's ten years now." Laura took a deep breath. "I need to get my shit together and get on with living. Maybe I'll catch a man here this afternoon."

"What do you mean by 'catch a man'?" Jane asked.

"Oh you know, bag a guy who is rich, good looking, and a sex maniac," Laura declared.

"Sex maniac?" Jane exclaimed.

"Yeah. Sex at least once a month whether he needs it or not."

Jane giggled and said to her friend, "That sounds like Traver Wells, but I think he's still out hunting. I'll point him out if I see him here."

Jane put her hands out to Laura. "Thanks for coming. But I think Traver will need attention at least two or three times a day."

Laura raised her eyebrows. "I could get used to that! Just what does this Traver Wells look like?"

"He's fat and bald and he limps!" Jane teased, then she added, "Honey, he's a hunk and he's down-home people and so easy to please. I swear that man gets all of Gary's single women clients all jazzed up."

"He's a rounder?" Laura asked.

"No. Actually he's pretty conservative, and I don't think he's ever dated anyone here. He strikes me as pretty particular when it comes to women."

"Ohhhh," Laura stretched that word out.

Traver had settled in at the barbecue pit, talking to Gary's neighbor Jeff, the county sheriff. Gary came over, slapping Traver on the shoulder. "How far was that shot today?" Gary asked.

"Probably 300 yards, to be honest."

"Skip is saying 900 yards now!" They chuckled at that. "Don't laugh, Jerry." Gary said. "I've seen Traver do a thousand-yard hit. And that was with a black-powder Sharps! Even more difficult than a 7 mag Remington with a scope." Gary paused. "I'm not going to be able to get out and use my deer tag, Traver, how about you taking it and filling it for me?"

"Well, sure, no problem," Traver said. "Getting my buck this early in the season was a bit unexpected and I do like traipsing out in the hills here."

Traver's attention was lured away by the appearance of "Bill." Gary noticed and yelled out, "Laura! Laura!"

She turned to see who was calling her. She saw Gary and headed toward them. Traver could see that she was older, even though she didn't have a slack muscle anywhere.

Laura's world went into slow motion. There next to Gary was a man who stood out from everyone else, like a bright beacon in a sea of darkness. She almost stumbled and her breath caught momentarily. Her nipples instantly firmed hard, something that hadn't happened since Bill.

"Laura," Gary said as he took her hand, "let me introduce you to Traver."

Laura released Gary's hand and grasped Traver's. "Traver," she said firmly.

"Laura," he responded, taking her hand.

Gary said, "Laura runs the outfit next to my place over on the Frenchman." She was smiling. "Well, I own it, anyway, but my men run the place. Is it Traver Wells?"

"Yes, do I know you? I mean, have we met?" he asked.

Laura's emotions were roller-coasting. "I would have remembered that," she said. "Hey, I hear you took out a good-sized buck out by the saddle today, next to my place."

"Yep." He liked this gal's smile and her quickness right away.

"I'm very glad to meet you, Traver." It came out in nearly a whisper. They were still holding that handshake. Clearing her throat, Laura went on, "My range starts just a bit further past that saddle. If you ever stray onto my range, you've certainly got my permission to hunt. If anyone tries to stop you, just tell them that I said it was okay."

"Will they believe me?"

"They better!"

Traver realized they were still locked in that handshake. It was turning into "I want to get to know you" hand holding, with emotion traveling back and forth between their palms. When he felt her fingers twitch against his palm, it sent ripples of excitement up his arm. When they released the lingering handshake, her fingers lightly trailed across his palm, stirring his lifeline. He struggled to say something intelligent, but their hands had communicated far deeper than words.

Her fingertips reached into his heart, touching yesterday's soul. He was dizzy and drifting. Laura quickly looked away. "Excuse me, please," she said as she stepped away from him, and Traver was riveted by the undulating roll of her rear. *What an aura she radiated!* He wondered what touching all her exciting places would feel like. His lips burned in anticipation of that first kiss.

Laura retraced her steps and, passing closer to him, asked, "Gary wants you to fill out his deer tag?"

Traver nodded yes.

Laura turned to Gary. "Say, Gary, introduce him to Sharon. She's hunted quite a bit in that area and she could give him some pointers."

"Now, Laura, don't go making plans to marry off your daughter to my old buddy here."

Flustered, Laura said, "No, no, not Sharon." *I mean me, not Sharon! Am I blushing?*

Traver could see that Laura was nervous, and he senses something in her voice that told him she was as interested in him as he was in her.

"I'd like you to meet my daughter," Laura said speculatively. "I don't think Sharon is here yet."

"Okay, okay," Traver said, grinning.

Laura noticed that he was taking long swigs of Dr Pepper., "You don't drink, Traver?"

"No, I just don't like the taste."

Laura cocked her head slightly, as if to say, *That's a point in your favor.* "Well, see you later." She turned and scanned the crowd for Jane, who might have more information about this guy.

Laura reached the table where Jane and a few other ladies from town were talking and sat down with a plop. She was just thankful that her knees had not buckled during her conversation with Traver.

Completely unprepared to be bowled over by a man, Laura's thoughts were careening all over, among them the surprising one: *Can I still become pregnant? I haven't had a period in six months.* She was oblivious to the conversation around her, running her fingers up and down her frosty can of beer. She fanned herself absentmindedly, realizing that her breasts felt steamy and her legs were bouncing back and forth at the order of her pelvic muscles.

When Jane sat a fresh beer with a loud "clunk" in front of Laura, she jumped, startled away from her overheated reveries.

Seeing the condition her friend was in, Jane said, "Sooooo, you've met Traver."

"Yes," she whispered and dropped her head to hide the tears welling up in her eyes, "and what the heck am I going to do?"

Jane rested her hand on Laura's knee and said in a loving voice, "Girl, get your shit together and go get that man!"

Laura perked up and hugged her friend. "Thanks, Jane. I'm fine now."

"But not until you let Traver know he's in love with you!" That caused both the women to laugh, raucously enough that it caught the attention of Traver, who was across the room. Just at that moment, Sharon sat down next to her mom.

Gary noticed and said quietly to Traver, "Sharon is a knockout. Just like her mom thirty years ago." He paused a moment. "It looks like Laura is struck by you, Traver. Watch out! Don't go and get mother and daughter in a tizzy over you, it could get ugly!"

Traver raised his eyebrows.

"Well, Laura likes you, I can see that. And Sharon is a strong-minded young woman. My advice is to hunt deer—and that's all!"

Later in the evening Traver sat by the lake's edge in a wooden lawn chair, gazing across Lake Maloney at the lights of other houses ringing the lake. Mosquitoes buzzed and he was slapping at them. Crickets were singing and dogs were barking off in the distance. The dark starlit sky was so close you could reach out and touch the quivering points of light. A giant bullfrog croaked before jumping into the water, and with that splash the lake noises began all over again.

He closed his eyes in reflection. *By God, life is good.* He sensed on the gentle lakeshore breeze the scent of moist dirt, swamp water smell, barbecue smoke, and roses.

Roses? It reminded him of the so deep red nearly black roses he raised in Tampa when he was growing up. He often picked a bunch for his grandmother. She was so happy she buried her nose in the lustrous, fragrant petals.

"Mr. Wells?"

His eyes fluttered open, taking a minute to focus on the present. "Yes?"

"I hope I didn't wake you." Standing by him was the spitting image of Laura.

"Sharon?" Traver asked.

"Yes," she said brightly. "May I sit with you a while?"

"Of course."

As she positioned another chair next to his, he realized the source of the rosy aroma was Sharon.

As he fumbled for words, she pulled up another lawn chair.

"I hear you got a big one today."

"Yes," Traver tried to sound nonchalant about it.

"Skip tells me you did a 900-hundred yard shot with a 50/90 rolling block," Sharon said skeptically.

"It was a 7 mag. Remington and about 300 yards," Traver declared.

Sharon grinned. "Skip does stretch things a bit." Then she patted Traver's leg. "But I've heard Gary talk about the buck you dropped a couple years ago with a 7 mag at a thousand yards."

"That was with the Sharps," said Traver.

Traver was little taken aback by how forward this young lady was. But he kept the conversation going. "I made a few 700-yard shots, but this one was just too good to be true."

"You got him at the saddle?" Sharon queried.

"Yep."

"I'll bet that's the one I've been watching all summer. There is another one that's as big or bigger. I think he's hanging out in the little canyon a bit west of where you took this one today. That's Enchanted Canyon. Gary says you're going to fill out his tag?" She waited for my answer.

"Yep," Traver said briskly. *Goddamn it, why was I answering her in monosyllables, like a lame cowboy?*

Traver was little unnerved. Sharon was a looker, all right. Short curly dark hair, long elegant neck, high cheekbones, full lips. But way too young.

Sharon jumped up from her chair, with a youthful bounce. "I have to go. My date is picking me up, but if you go out tomorrow, go up the smaller canyon. You might jump the big one and get a good shot. If you do, call me."

And she was gone. Along with the scent of deep red roses of my childhood memories.

Traver leaned back in the chair, hands clasped behind his head. *I would like to go back to the saddle area. It had a great feel to it and it would be great to whack another big buck.* The smell of steaks sizzling on the barbecue lured him over to Skip. "Skip, you want to head back over to the saddle and go into Bill's, uh, um, I mean Laura's range tomorrow? Her daughter says there's a big buck just a bit further to the west in one of the smaller canyons."

"That must be Enchanted Canyon. I would love to go, but I'm tied up until noon."

Traver considered for a moment. "I could whack the big one and get in by noon to clean up and see if I could distract Sharon from her date enough to, ahh . . ."

Skip interrupted him, "Down, boy, she's got a boyfriend."

"I know."

"Don't you go getting everyone excited, you don't live here," Skip laughed. "And I think her mom might not like that." He paused. "Gary tells me Laura held on to your hand quite a while. Listen, take my truck in the morning and go by yourself. Don't even think about calling Sharon."

"Okay." Traver agreed. "Then I'll just to have to call her mom."

Skip froze in his tracks. "Are you serious? Jesus, Traver!"

He smiled and popped Skip on the shoulder. "Only if she calls me."

"Oh sure, go out with mother and maybe the daughter and you'll start all sorts of hell."

"Don't worry, Skip, I'm here to deer hunt." *But that doesn't mean I can't dream about Laura.*

Later, Traver did just that. He put his head on the pillow he brought from home and pulled up the flannel sheet with the old quilt made by Kathy's mom. He mused about the gal at Gary's, beautiful, striking, and handsome. A survivor, a person who worked hard and cared. That belt with "Bill" emblazoned on it—knowing that it was her late husband, Traver felt a twinge of sympathy. *Dying is big time final, never again to hold or kiss or even see your lover. Jeeze, how do you carry on when your partner dies?* Laura surely showed him her strength, raising a daughter alone.

Traver, still on his back, stretched out his legs and tried to project his thoughts to Laura, as if she could feel his presence. He wanted to make a connection with her. *What are Laura's needs? What are her wants and desires? I want to please her to no end!*

Lowering his hands from his head, he rolled on to his stomach and hugged his pillow. That felt more natural. *What does Laura need?* Traver's first thought was sex, but he knew it was more than that. *I'll get to know her true feelings—and then sex!'*

Traver slept till six the next morning. Because he quit smoking seven years ago, he needed a strong cup of coffee to begin the morning. A hint of the eastern light was peeking through the basement window, and the freezer motor rumbled as he swung his legs out of bed and placed his feet on the cold tile floor. Dressing quickly, he bounded upstairs and went to the counter to pour himself a cup of coffee, which he cradled in his hands as he reverently raised it to his lips and sipped. Closing his eyes, he let the hot, rich liquid flow down his throat, delighting all the sensitive areas that signaled his brain just how luxurious the first sip was. "Damn! That's good!" he muttered.

Opening his eyes, he set the cup down and stretched for a moment, finally acknowledging Skip.

"Going out to the saddle or Enchanted Canyon today?" Skip asked.

"Ah, I'm going to, uh, what's Laura's last name?"

"Peterson."

"Okay," Traver continued, "I'm going over there to scope out the west side of the saddle and then go over to this Enchanted Canyon place." He downed more coffee.

Skip reached up to the cupboard over the kitchen sink and pulled out a topographic map. With it spread on the table, he pointed his finger. "Here is the saddle, over here is the windmill." A couple inches over he indicated the three canyons. "Here is the Peterson place. I don't know which one is called Enchanted Canyon. Usually all three are referred to as Enchanted Canyon."

Poring over the map, Traver said, "Say, Skip, look here. The features are awfully deep in the western canyon." The topographic lines were clustered closely together, indicating steep inclines.

"Yeah," Skip agreed. "I've been up it once and it's awfully steep and very difficult to climb out. You've got to go back out the way you came in. That gets to be a real pain in getting around. Of course," Skip needled, "you being younger, it probably won't bother you!"

Traver packed two Thermoses of coffee and a couple of Spam sandwiches. He decided to take five 7 magnum rifle shells and his Remington rifle. Giving Skip a wave, he went out the back yelling, "Be back about noon!" He fired up Skip's four-by-four and headed down to Henderson and over to the Frenchman. He parked the truck at the usual place, put a note on the dashboard telling where he was going and that he would be back about noon.

Morning was just reaching the canyon floor, leaving it still in shadow, so it seemed darker there. A couple inches of snow had fallen overnight, but the snow didn't crunch as he walked over it. Everything was still and not even a hint of smoke drifted from anyone's hearth. The ash trees were yellowing, and now and then a leaf would release and float to the ground. All of the poison ivy leaves were a bright red. The rotting leaf mulch was broadcasting its earthy smell.

As he brushed through a tight place in the trail, the scent of juniper exploded. The aroma of pine, cedar, and juniper always awakened deep feelings in him, most likely a holdover from a prior life lived in the forest and around trees. This was luxury for Traver, walking along a deer trail, sniffing rich cedar and juniper, absorbing the golden hues of the ash that were so rich and heart expanding.

Coming out into a wide meadow, Traver saw three fingers of canyons. *Enchanted Canyon.* He settled down under a stunted cedar tree, opened the bolt of his rifle, put a round in the chamber, and left the bolt open. He opened a Thermos and poured his second helping of steaming black coffee. Leaning back against the tree trunk, with the low branches hiding his presence, he sipped the coffee slowly as he scanned the meadow. The smell of coffee would spook a deer, but it was a pleasure he wanted.

A few turkey buzzards circled overhead while Traver returned the Thermos to his pack. Removing the single round from his rifle, he got up, slung the pack over his shoulder, and cradled the rifle in his arms. Walking along the stunted cedar tree line, he headed toward the lush green and steep walls of the westernmost canyon. Making his way to a clump of cedar and sumac, he hid. He had noticed some tracks, and the deer that made them was fairly large. He got down to a prone, stretched-out position, drawing up his rifle so he could use the scope. With the round back in the gun and the bolt closed with the safety on, he waited.

A slight movement in the canyon caused him to peer into the twelve-power scope. A buck, and a huge one at that. He slowly let off the safety, thinking that this would be a good 600-hundred yard shot. Perhaps the buck would retrace and head back toward him, making the range even shorter, so he waited a bit longer, not wanting to take the extreme shot if it wasn't necessary.

Another movement off to the side of the canyon wall caught his attention. *God! Two bucks?*

He held his position. Suddenly he saw that the second movement was a bow hunter wearing buckskins, creeping closer to the big deer. This deer hunter is truly into it. *He's hunting with a bow and he's dressed up in buckskins to boot.*' He decided not to interfere with this hunter stalking his prey. From this distance it was like watching a ballet. When the deer stopped, the hunter would freeze. As the deer lowered its head and begin to crop at the low-lying vegetation, the bow hunter repositioned himself, seeming to know when to move and when to stop as the buck raised its head to smell the breeze. It was beautiful choreography.

After the buck stood in place for a long time, he began to move, taking quick steps. The hunter raised his bow with a notched arrow, pulled back, and coughed. The buck froze in its tracks, turning its head to look at the bowman. Twang! The bowstring sang as the arrow flew to its mark. The buck reared up on its hind legs, its front feet pawing the air. The arrow drove through its neck. It ran about eighty to a hundred feet before dropping to the ground. The hunter stood, notching another arrow. He slowly approached the deer.

Adrenaline was flowing through Traver's veins and his heart was pounding as if he had shot the deer. *Jesus! What a shot!* The buck had no idea what hit him. He ran on physical impulse.

Barely daring to breathe, Traver watched the bowman approach his kill. He took a long knife from his waist. He raised his arms to the sky, knife in the left hand and bow in the right. His face turned sunward, he seemed to be giving thanks for the kill. Then he nudged the buck with his bow a couple of times. No response. Thinking the buck dead, the bow hunter leaned over the animal's head to grab an antler and cut its throat. With the speed of a lightning strike, the buck jerked back its head, burying his antlers into the bowman's chest and stomach. Traver saw a flash of red and heard an agonizing human yell.

The hunter staggered, clutched his stomach with blood-red hands. He staggered two steps and collapsed, motionless in the snow. Traver jumped up and grabbed the cell phone he had borrowed from Skip. He frantically punched 911. He told the operator to call Skip or Gary Williams in North Platte. He was on the Peterson property at Enchanted Canyons, and a hunter had just been gored by a buck. He needs medical help and fast.

The face-down bow hunter seemed lifeless. Traver rolled him over to see a loose flap of chest skin and the hunter's guts protruding from the gash in his stomach. Traver almost vomited, but he took a couple of deep breaths and swallowed back the sour taste. He took off his coat and folded his T-shirt into a square to place over his stomach wound. Traver's long-sleeved shirt wrapped about the hunter's middle made a pressure bandage.

The 911 operator was still on the line. She said that Skip and Laura were on the way.

AT LAURA'S RANCH

Laura slept in that morning, still mooning a little over the man she had met at the barbecue. She sat on her bed and watched the morning build. Shivering a bit, she wrapped her arms around her chest, realizing that she still had a pair that could attract a man. Not just any man. "Traver," she whispered.

She walked into the bathroom and turned on the overhead heat lamp to take the chill off before she showered. She chuckled and wondered what Traver would think about her having a two-cup coffee pot in her bathroom? *That's getting a little ahead of myself. He hasn't even asked me for a date.*

After her quick shower, she felt her nipples turn hard as goose bumps rose on her arms. She looked at herself in the bathroom mirror and gave herself points for her firm body and honey-colored hair. Twisting herself sideways, she gave herself points for her firm breasts, which remained perky even though she breast-fed Sharon. Her nipples looked like beautiful pink tea roses. *Maybe Traver likes pink tea roses.*

The coffee was done, Laura noticed. She poured a cup and went back to sit down on her bed, taking her first sip with both hands holding the cup. Her eyes closed as she sipped.

Her thoughts returned to Gary's barbecue. She rehearsed all the details she had observed about Traver. His belt buckle looked like a piece of elk antler inlaid with turquoise. He carried himself with dignity but not arrogance. He smiled easily, although she wasn't too happy about him smiling at single good-looking girls there.

Laura remembered, too, her onrushing emotions that upset her usually controlled demeanor. It was a wonderment to her, something she hadn't experienced for how long? Years, she decided. Ten years at least.

With the guile of a teenager, Laura tried to think of a way to see Traver again. *I'll call Kathy, I know Traver is staying there with her and Skip.*

On the third ring, Skip answered. "Skip, this is Laura. Is Mr. Wells there?" A moment. "He's already left for Enchanted Canyon to hunt? No. That's fine, just tell him I called. Thanks. Is Kathy up yet?" Laura asked. "May I speak to her? Kathy, don't laugh. I called to talk to Mr. Wells." Laura blushed a deep pink. "Oh, so you noticed?"

She continued, "Kathy, I've got to tell someone. Traver is a hunk. I've haven't felt like dating, but he is something special. I'm not sure how to see him again."

Kathy said, "How about if you drop by for a casual dinner tonight, just us and you and Traver. That won't look too pushy."

"Oh, Kathy, would you do that for me?" Laura chatted a while longer with Kathy, then they hung up.

Feeling wonderful, Laura jumped up from the edge of the bed. She began pawing through her closet, looking for what to wear to dinner. She had a spring dress, a little too sheer for a fall evening, but it did show off her assets. With a little coat over it, she decided, it would work. She hadn't felt this excited for a long, long time.

Still on a cloud, Laura dressed for the morning in ranch work clothes and gave Roy a call. Her foreman was just getting ready to head out to the south pasture. They talked about the week's work. "Boss, I sure hate Mondays." Laura grinned, thinking about having dinner with Skip, Kathy, and Traver, and it gave her a shiver. *Mondays just might be the best days.*

When she climbed into her crew cab Chevy, getting ready to follow Roy, her cell phone buzzed. She pulled the phone from its holder. "Hello?"

"Dr. Peterson, this is the 911 operator. There's been a hunting accident on your property at Enchanted Canyon. A hunter has been gored by a buck."

Laura froze. *Traver was hunting there!* She found her voice, "Where exactly?"

"Not sure. Just Enchanted Canyon. I called Skip, too."

"Who's hurt?" Laura held her breath.

"I don't know doctor. I'm sorry."

"I'm on it!" Laura said, shutting off the call. She ran back into her house and grabbed her doctor's bag. Within seconds, her truck tires were spewing gravel.

BACK AT ENCHANTED CANYON

Having done all he could to help, Traver began to take a closer look at the hunter. His buckskins were handmade, with an old-fashioned design, and his moccasins were like boots lashed with rawhide thongs. Traver realized that was no bow hunter from town—this hunter was an Indian. Perhaps he had come off the reservation to hunt. *But why all this old-time stuff to hunt with?*

Off in the distance a horn honked. Traver stood up and waved his arms. It was Gary's 4 X 4, but Skip was driving. He headed directly for Traver, coming to a snow-throwing stop. He jumped out, shouting, "Is he dead?"

"No! Let's get him in the back of the truck!"

Skip laid a blanket on the truck bed, and we wrapped the other one around the injured man. Together they carried him to the truck, and Traver jumped in the back, too. "Skip, haul ass to the hospital!"

Laura's truck was barreling up the dirt road as Skip was bumping down toward the hard-top road that led to town. Laura was still sniffling when she saw the truck and recognized Traver in the back holding on for dear life. Laura exhaled. *Oh, God! Thank you, God! He's not hurt!* But her mind raced around. *So who is hurt?*

She pulled off to the side as Skip slowed, bellowing out his window, "We are going to the Maxwell hospital!"

She yelled back, "No! Go to the North Platte hospital. It has a better trauma center!"

"Okay!" And Skip stomped down on the accelerator.

Laura pulled in behind Skip and called the North Platte hospital, telling them a chest wound was on the way from South Canyon Road. She ordered hemoglobin and advised that a trauma team be ready. As she talked, she kept her eyes on Traver, bent over the victim. She admired his concern and his desire to help.

The brakes squealed as Skip rounded his truck in front of the hospital emergency doors. In a flash, the orderlies had the hunter on a gurney and wheeled him in.

A man approached Traver. "I'm Dr. Hodges. What happened?"

"This fellow was gored by a buck. I saw it happen."

Laura stepped up to Traver and the doctor, standing silently by, amazed at the detail that Traver provided about how the man was injured, although she was still wondering who he was. She didn't want to interrupt. She noticed that Traver's jacket was covered with blood, and his hands, too, were crusty with gore. Those were capable hands, she decided, that could build things and at the same time could gently reach out with a loving touch.

Laura continued watching him interact with the E.R. doctor. She noticed that his mustache needed trimming. His unshaven whiskers reflected gray-silver, and his short military-cut hair and eyebrows were dark brownish-black. *What did he just say—something about homemade arrows?* She took a deep breath, she was so attracted to this man that her professional interest in this medical emergency never kicked in.

Traver stripped of his faded dungaree jacket, and Laura noticed a little paunch. But he looked fit nonetheless. Good looking rear, too.

Finally, she came out of her distraction to hear Traver end his story. "His guts were hanging out of his stomach and I shoved them back in."

Hodges said, "Okay, let's get in there and fix him up. You'll be sticking around?"

Traver nodded.

After the doctor left, Laura and Skip began to quiz Traver about the injured bow hunter. Traver was sure the man had come off the reservation, he looked Indian. Skip said, "There hasn't been a reservation around here for more than sixty years," and Laura remembered that there had been one nearby in the '20s.

Traver was adamant. "Well, by God, this guy is an Indian and wearing buckskins and he's from somewhere out here."

Skip shrugged his shoulders and Laura shook her head.

"I left my rifle and your cell phone out there. Can one of you drive me back there?" Traver asked.

Skip quickly turned to Laura and said, "Can you take him back to that spot?"

She smiled, "Of course." *Hell yes*, she thought with excitement.

Traver washed the blood off his hands, although his jacket was still stained. He climbed into Laura's truck, leaned his head back on the seat, and sighed heavily.

"Take it easy, there, Traver," Laura said softly. "You've just had a pretty traumatic experience."

"Me?" Traver responded. "That guy's guts were hanging out."

"Pretty serious injury, being gored," Laura went on.

They rode along in silence until Laura decided to distract Traver by talking about Enchanted Ranch and its canyons. It had been in her family for more than a hundred and fifty years, and it was clear from her description that she loved the land, it was a source of pleasure, even with all the hard work it took to keep it going.

Laura stole glances at Traver, as she recounted the history of her family and the ranch. As she spoke, Traver became aware that her interest in him was more than friendly. She was looking into him, seeing his wants, his failures, his sorrows, and his loves. He craved that look of desire from a woman, and especially this woman, not only of his body but also of his spirit.

With the adrenaline finally draining out of his body, he could not help but stare at her, taking inventory as she drove down the highway. Her onyx pupils were like dark velvet upon pearls. Her eyebrows were a honey color. The little lines radiating out from the corners of her eyes told of her days out on the Nebraska Sand Hills. Her curly hair, just touching her shoulders, was copper-gold. Her skin was a warm tan. Her hands, holding the steering wheel, showed elegant long fingers, with clean and close-clipped fingernails. For an instant he imagined those fingers touching his lips, and he yearned for those fingers to softly scratch his back. Her breasts, with a decided upthrust, pressed against her Western short-sleeved shirt.

Laura could sense his stare. "When the emergency is settled, Traver, would you like to have the twenty-dollar tour?"

Traver was a little embarrassed, because he had been staring at her chest, and that was the only tour he was interested in. "Um, sure, why not? How much do you have here?" he said as casually as he could.

She almost said "38B," but she didn't know about Traver's sense of humor.

"Eighteen thousand acres. A bit more than Gary. He's been wanting to buy the place, but I'm hoping Sharon will want to settle here." Laura sighed. "I thought it might happen, but Sharon's been infected with 'cityitis.'"

Traver chuckled at that.

He does have a sense humor, Laura thought.

"Well, here we are," she declared. "How close can we get?"

Traver gestured toward a clump of cedars and sumac. "Over there are my rifle and pack. The buck and the cell phone are just over here." He pointed out some four hundred yards west.

Laura drove over to the trees to retrieve the rifle, and he climbed out of the truck to look for the buck. In a few minutes, he was standing by the deer and had pocketed the cell phone. When Laura navigated the truck next to him, she killed the ignition. It was wonderfully still and quiet, so different from just an hour ago. She walked over to Traver. "That's a nice one," she said admiringly. She lifted the animal's head, pulled out the arrow, and studied it closely.

"Traver, look here, that's not a store-bought arrow. It looks authentic Indian."

Traver took the arrow and rolled it in the palms of his hands. It certainly looked handmade. "Let's look for the bow and quiver, maybe we can find some more arrows."

Laura found the bow and arrows, and Traver uncovered the long knife. It seemed to be a trade knife, well cared for. Laura hefted the weapon, peering at the metal. "German steel. A very good blade."

With no logical explanation for what the implements they had at hand, Laura said, "We might as well dress out and clean this buck and not waste it." Quickly Laura opened the buck's chest and stomach, cautiously removing the windpipe and the scent glands. She packed snow in the buck's chest cavity, just like Traver did, to keep it from spoiling any further. "Probably only be meat for the dogs, but it won't go to waste," Laura observed.

While they manhandled the deer into the back of her truck, Traver's shoulder brushed solidly against her right breast. He was surprised by its firmness and by the warm feelings that were welling up in his chest. He began to wonder if Laura was having similar feelings, although she did not give him a second glance as they drove away.

If he only knew what Laura was thinking. *He touched my breast. Accidentally. But still, he touched me!* Tears stung her eyes, as she was remembering her last morning with Bill. He kissed her and caressed her breasts, saying, "You have the most exciting breasts in the county." Her response, "You better not be surveying all the breasts in the county!" And she swatted his rear.

She tried to wipe the tears away stealthily, so Traver didn't see. She became aware that the temperature in the truck was heating up, way up. She felt on fire.

Traver did see Laura rubbing away her tears, and he sensed the flames radiating off her. *Fuck! I'm feeling like a horny kid! I want to hold her, but I'm scared to make the move.*

Laura felt her nipples firming, and she was glad her jacket would hide her erotic feelings. At the same time Traver was shifting in his seat, trying to make room for his blooming erection. He needed to walk it off, but he was too embarrassed to tell her why.

"Could we pull over a minute soon so I can get rid of that coffee I drank this morning?" Traver said plaintively.

Laura blushed. "Coffee?"

She stopped at the side of the rode, and Traver got out and walked behind the truck. The chilly air helped solve the problem. He got back into the truck cab.

"You forgot to get rid of the coffee!" Laura teased, letting Traver know that she was quite clear on what was going on.

Changing the subject, which was getting too hot to handle, Laura said, "Let's drop the buck off at the butcher shop and I'll have it ground for dog food."

"You sure did a quick and efficient job gutting that buck. Have you done that a lot?" Traver wanted to know.

"Well, yes and no. I've done it quite a lot, but not necessarily on bucks. I run a cattle spread, but I'm also coroner for the county, so I do a fair number of autopsies."

"You're a coroner?" Traver asked in amazement.

"Yes, but remember, I'm a doctor first, and I was quite a good thoracic surgeon in my day. That is, before I started playing poker and drinking," she said in a deadpan voice.

Traver's mouth dropped open with dismay.

Laura broke out in a deep rolling burst of laughter. "Just kidding you! Being the coroner was my way of retiring so I could run the ranch after my husband died."

"Well, thank God you're not an alcoholic."

"Traver, do I look like a drunk?"

"Noooo. You're a fine-looking woman that any man would be proud to have on his arm."

Laura looked at him steadily and asked, "Any man?"

Traver had a falling sensation, like he was being pulled under by Laura's eyes.

She stopped the truck, put it in park, and leaned over to touch his lips with hers. "A special man," she murmured.

He grabbed Laura by the shoulders and held her close to him. It was an awkward position, but their bodies sang the ancient melody of two souls finding each other once again. They kissed harder, and he rubbed his hands up and down her back. When he reached to cup her breasts, Laura shivered with pleasure. Just then a horn blasted a couple times as it passed their truck. Laura and Traver jumped and separated, with Laura turning a bright red.

Laura looked like a kid caught with her hand in the forbidden cookie jar. She sighed. "That's my ranch foreman, Roy." Then she reasoned that Roy is a fine man, a gentleman, and he will not tell anyone about what he just saw.

Little did she suspect what was running through Roy's mind. *Okay! The boss is finally getting out! She is too good of a woman to go it alone.*

Laura straightened her hair and put the shift lever into drive. They were both silent the rest of the drive. Not a self-conscious silence, but a calm and trusting communication without words.

They stopped at the butcher shop and dropped off the buck, and then Laura drove him to the hospital. When they parked, they turned toward each other. Traver reached out his hand and placed it on her leg, saying, "Not just any man?"

She returned his smile. "No, I'm afraid that I'm awfully particular." She paused and then went on, "But in your case I could make an exception."

Traver chuckled a bit.

"I'll find you tomorrow when all this emergency stuff gets down to a low roar, and I'll take you on that twenty-dollar tour."

"Okay. It's a date," Traver said as he got out of the truck. He came around to her window. "I'd give you a big wet kiss, but the tongues would wag." He raised his eyebrows.

"Oh yes, those wagging tongues," she teased.

"See you tomorrow, Traver," Laura whispered, and he watched her drive away.

*   *   *

Skip was having a cup of coffee in the waiting room and talking with a nurse when Traver walked in.

"Hey, Traver, come here. This is Cathy's friend, Thelma. Thelma, this is Traver Wells."

She took his hand and said, "Are you related to the Wells folks in Carney?"

"No. No relation."

"Well, Traver, this situation is very weird. Get some coffee and I'll fill you in."

Traver got the coffee and sat next to Skip on the waiting room couch.

"This fellow we brought in, he ain't from around here, First of all, no ID, just a little medicine bag on the left side of his buckskins full of his personal magic. He woke up in the operating room just before the anesthesiologist was going to gas him. He freaked out and the nurses said he turned as white as the sheets over him. He was hollering something fierce, not like he was in pain but like he was a scared person. He wasn't yelling in English or Spanish, he was speaking French."

Skip took a breath. "He's in recovery now. The doc says you saved his life with that compression bandage and the first aid you did on his gut wound. Fortunately none of his organs was punctured, just deep lacerations. Shock and loss of fluids and possible infection are his worries now. The doc is going to let him come to, but he will be restrained so he won't hurt himself or anyone else. Doc thought you and he were friends because you made the 911 call. The doc wants one of us to stay with him—preferably you!" Skip took a gulp of coffee. "I have stuff to do."

"Now, who is this guy and where did he come from?" Traver questioned.

Before Skip or Traver could fashion an answer to those questions, the emergency doctor came in. "He's coming around, let's go in."

In the recovery room, they saw the fellow mumbling and rolling his head back and forth. "He's not in pain," the doctor informed them. "He's on some la-la-land fluids."

Suddenly, the bow hunter opened his eyes, looking alert. He scanned the room, looking at the ceiling, the door, and the men gathered around his bed. He tugged at his restrained hands.

The doctor asked, "How are you feeling?"

The fellow looked at him with dull eyes.

"Just for shits and grins," Skip suggested, "does anybody know French?"

"Why do you ask?" the doctor wanted to know.

"Well, doc, this was the Frenchman hunting preserve early on. There was a French trading post on the Platte River just north of Hastings, and some of the Indians spoke very good French."

"Skip," Traver said, "this guy didn't just step out of a hundred years ago! Man, that's too bizarre."

"Well, humor me," Skip challenged, "and let's find someone who speaks French."

"No problem," Traver interjected. "I do."

He placed his hand gently on the Indian's shoulder. "*Bonjour, comment t'allez vous?* How are you?"

The hunter was frightened, but clearly he responded to French. "*Où sont je? Ce qui est cet endroit?*" Where am I? What is this place? In a rather gruff tone of voice and speaking French he asked, "How have I been taken from death's throw of that buck?"

"*Bon, vous parlez le français.* Good, you speak French," Traver said in a reassuring tone. He continued in French, "This place is where when a man is hurt, he is put back together. Do you understand me?"

"*Oui.*"

"The buck you shot with your arrow ripped open your chest and stomach. I brought you here for help."

The bow hunter was quiet for a moment and then said in a worried tone, "You saw my insides? You saw my heart?"

"*Oui,*" Traver answered, "but you are healing. Do not worry."

"*Merci. Comment vous appelez-vous?*"

"My name is Traver."

He considered that briefly. "Traver, I do not understand everything, but I will call you the Man That Touches My Heart. You are a noble warrior." Exhausted by the effort to converse, the Indian's eyelids started to flutter and then dropped in sleep.

Skip and the doctor wanted a play-by-play account of what was said. Traver related in English their exchange, calling the patient "Frenchy."

The doctor said, "He'll sleep all night. You guys might as well go on home and get some rest."

Skip and Traver had quite a conversation as they drove back to his place on Lake Maloney. Skip kept repeating in awe, "This fellow is not from here, I mean not from this time. This fellow is from the past."

"This is bizarre, shit." Traver shook his head in response. "This stuff just doesn't happen. Like he just popped out of his time and into our time this morning and he didn't know it and he just kept on hunting? Skip, goddamn it, that just doesn't make sense."

"Traver, his clothing, that arrow, they're old, at least an old design. Say, where are his bow and quiver of arrows?" Skip wanted to know.

"Oh, hell! They're in Laura's truck."

Skip took out his cell phone and hit connect. "Hey, Laura, Skip here . . . Sure. He's fine, he came around and talks French . . . Nah! Not me . . . Traver speaks French . . . Oh sure, just a second. Here's Traver."

Traver took the phone and heard, "*Cheri, comment allez-vous, bon?*"

"Wow! *Merci, madam, merci beaucoup.*" I gave the phone back to Skip.

"Hey, what was all that?" Skip laughed when he took the phone back. "Any chance you coming in to town so I can look at those arrows and that knife? What? Just a minute." Skip turned to Traver. "Laura will drop off the bow and the hunter's stuff but you have to spring for dinner."

"Tell her she's on," Skip said loudly so Laura could hear.

"Okay, around 6:30, we'll see you at my place." Skip shut off the phone and tucked it away in his pocket.

*   *   *

Oh goody! Dinner tonight with Traver. What will I wear? The sundress appeared in her thoughts. Laura was a little giddy. She hurried to her closet. *Umm, not a lot of fun stuff, just work clothes.*

Looking into her closet made Laura realize, a little sadly, that all she did for the last ten years was work, work, and more work. Flipping through the hangers, she did find hiding behind the coats a sundress of bright colors, green, blue, yellow, orange, and red stripes.

Off came her work clothes and boots. Standing in white socks and pink panties and bra, she slipped the dress over her head. *Not bad.* She twirled and caught sight of the clock by her bed. There was just enough time to go to town and get her hair done.

"Normally I stay out of this stuff," Skip hemmed and hawed. "But Laura is a real good friend of mine. She's the best and I don't want you to mess with her, Traver. What I mean is, just be honest with her."

"Skip, I know she's a special person. It shows in the way she treats people."

"I'm serious because, bub, I see she's treating you real special. And I haven't seen her so lighthearted since Bill died."

"How long has her husband been gone, Skip?" Traver asked.

"Ten years."

"What happened?"

Skip heaved a big breath. "Bill and I were hunting . . ." His voice turned shaky. "He had a heart attack and I just couldn't get him out of the field fast enough and to the hospital in time. Laura doesn't blame me at all but I blame me!" Skip wiped his eyes with the cuff of his shirt.

Traver turned away so Skip could round up his emotions. In the silence that followed, Traver realized that he was thinking a lot about Laura these last few days, so much so that Donna had faded into the dim past. *What did I want from Laura? A night of passion? Sure, but many nights, not just one night! I wanted to touch her everywhere and forever.*

A cowboy song in the background broke his reverie. "Today I Started Loving You Again." The lyrics went: "What a fool I was to think I could get by . . . I'm right back where I've really always been "What a fool I was, thinking I could get by. I'm right back where I've always been." *Jeeze! How did a song like this just happen to play on the radio at the instant it spoke so strongly to me?*

"Ten years since her husband's passing," Traver mumbled. "It's just amazing how people carry on."

"Well," said Skip, "you just have to get along."

Traver looked at his friend and exclaimed, "Fuck getting along! There's more to life than that. It's a team thing. And when half of your team disappears—well, it's tough to keep going."

Skip took in that thought then pointed out the window, "Hey, Traver, let's stop here at the gas station and get a pound of deep fried chicken livers."

"Great."

Traver dug in his pocket and came out with a ten-dollar bill. "We'll get a couple Dr Peppers to wash it down with, okay?"

The fellas made their purchase and went out to sit at a picnic table under an umbrella.

"Say, Skip, what if this fellow did come from out of the past? How far back do you suppose he's from?"

Wiping crumbs from the corner of his mouth, Skip answered, "I don't know, but maybe those arrow markings will tell us something." Skip finished his share of the chicken livers before adding, "My Dad might know. He's a bit of an Indian buff. If I had one of the arrows we could show it to him."

Traver nodded, then said, "Wait a minute! I've got a piece of an arrow I found stuck in the buck I shot over on Gary's place. I put it in my pack and I'm sure it's still there." He walked over to the truck and lifted out the pack. He rummaged around and there, at the bottom, was the shaft of the arrow.

Skip rolled it around in his hands before saying, "Yep, it's a Plains Indian arrow. Probably Sioux, maybe a southern branch of the Lakota Sioux. Dad will know for sure. Let's go see him before we head for home."

Skip's father lived just past the hospital on a patch of ground that he grew popcorn on. Pulling into the long gravel drive, Skip saw his dad over at the barn working on a corn husker. The old guy came over, wiping the grease from his hands.

"Hi, Dad! This here is Traver, remember him? He's from California and hunts on Gary's place and he was at the barbecue."

"Sure do. Hi." He stuck out his hand. "Good seeing you again, done any good this season?"

Traver smiled and said, "'First day, well, first day for me. Good."

Skip burst out laughing. "Two-legged deer in Omaha, Dad."

"What you boys doing keeping an old man from fixing his corn-binder?"

"Not much, Dad, but we would like you to look at this arrow."

Skip's dad took the arrow and examined the perfect point attached with pine sap and wrapped with horse hair. "Too bad the tail feathers are broken away. It would make this easier." He handed it back to Skip. "Lakota Sioux. Where did you get it? I've never seen one in such fresh condition."

"Really?" Traver said.

Holding the arrow up, the old guy remarked, "This here arrow is new made, but it's of a style, oh, a hundred, maybe a hundred fifty years ago. Where did you get this?"

"I found it over on Gary's place at the saddle that connects to the Peterson place," Traver answered.

"Well, it's original, but I don't know how it stayed so pristine. Even the break being so fresh. Was it on the ground, in a tree or bush?"

"No, sir, it was sticking in the deer I shot the other day. It didn't seem that important, with bow season just closing and the regular deer season opening."

"Someone is bow hunting with very expensive antique arrows or they have learned to copy the Lakota arrow extremely well. I think this mark on the arrow means Twin Bears."

Skip replaced the arrow on the dash of his pickup truck. "Say, Dad, can Traver and I help you with the binder?"

"Boy, you sure could. Got a froze-up bearing and I can't seem to get it off the shaft." It took the guys a half-hour of beating and cussing, but finally the bearing gave way. They replaced it with a new sealed bearing and the corn binder was as good as new.

With a big wave to his dad, Skip and Traver grinded out of the gravel driveway on the way to Lake Maloney. When they got to Skip's, Traver got right into the downstairs shower. He took his time, enjoying the feeling of the water hitting his neck, jolting awake his body cells. As the water cascaded over his neck and shoulders, he heard the dogs fire up, barking wildly. He chuckled, it was probably Peppy teasing Kashia, such a little poodle teasing a big Keeshond.

Stepping out of the shower, Traver hovered over the sink, patting the shaving cream on his face and taking a moment to stare in the mirror. He wasn't in the habit of studying himself, but he was surprised at what he saw, time marches on, but he ended his shave with a broad grin at himself. He was put in mind of a childhood song, and he belted out "Yo-ho-ho and a bottle of rum, fifteen women on a dead man's chest, yo-ho-ho . . ." He made sure Skip and Cathy could hear his song.

All ready to go, he ascended the stairs, calling up to his friends in a booming voice, "You know, Skip, that race horse with those legs that run all the way to heaven? Hey, Kathy, do you suppose this fox is interested in me?"

Still coming up the stairs, he bellowed, "Hey, Skip, what's that fox's name again? You know—the one with the great rear end?"

"Trev, you better watch out!" Skip answered him.

As he entered the kitchen, Traver saw Kathy and Skip sitting at the breakfast table, giggling and smiling, and beside them was Laura. Traver came to a sudden stop, like pulling on an emergency brake. He had supposed all along that the dogs barking was them playing, not greeting Laura.

"OH SHIT!" he exclaimed. "You're here early." He smiled lamely.

"That fox? Legs that go all the way to heaven? My word!" Laura played along with the joke. She posed in a provocative way, flaunting her muscular calves and sexy ankles. "And just what about me reminds you of a race horse?"

Traver blurted, "FIRST PLACE, of course!"

"Do I get a ribbon, Traver?" she asked sweetly.

"Darling, you ARE the blue ribbon!" Traver loved bantering with this vivacious woman of the honey-golden hair and haunting eyes.

"Fifteen women on a pirate's chest? What's that all about?" Laura teased him again. Then she turned to Kathy and said, "Don't wait up for us, I might keep him out, well, at least until 9:30."

Skip laughed, which spiraled into a coughing jag, and Laura shot him a quick look. He finally croaked out, "Traver, you got yourself in a heap of shit!"

Laura added, "I'm a high-maintenance woman, no shit."

Skip broke out laughing and coughing again.

Traver took Laura's hand. "Let's go sing, girl."

"Come on, cowboy!" She grabbed his arm.

They waved at Skip and Kathy and walked outside. "Here, you drive," Laura said, handing the keys to Traver.

She had come in an old Mercedes convertible, black and white. Traver whistled lowly. "Great machine, let's go." He opened the door for Laura, went around, got in the driver's seat, and fired it up. "Sounds great!"

He stuck his foot on the throttle and the Mercedes came to life. "It's a V-8," Laura said. He backed off the throttle and cruised at 50 m.p.h. The car's top leaked and the chilly air whistled through the cracks.

"A V-8 diesel?" he asked.

Laura smiled. "Yup. A Jaguar engine."

"Where are we going after we see Frenchy?" Traver asked.

She thumped her forehead. "I forgot the bow and quiver and knife. I was so distracted thinking about this evening. Traver, how important is it?"

"Well, Skip wanted his Dad to look at the stuff and see if he can identify the tribe."

"Okay. Then let's head back to my ranch, pick them up, and drop it all at Skip's dad's," Laura said, scooting closer to her date. "Traver, tell me about yourself."

"I'm retired military, U.S. Navy and finished out in the Marines. I do a little tree fruit farming just to keep busy."

"Do you enjoy the farming, Traver?"

"To a point."

"Turn here, this is a faster way to the big house. Go on," Laura encouraged him.

"I hate the long twelve—to fourteen-hour days. Seven days a week during the summer. But I do love all the free time for the rest of the year."

"It must be a good life." Laura sighed.

"I catch myself whining about it all the time," Traver replied.

"It's the next gravel road. There, turn here and up about a mile." As they pulled up to the ranch house, Traver was taken aback at how massive the place was. All built with stone from all around the ranch, he guessed.

"Traver, stop here a moment." They stopped at the peak of a hill, looking down on a green valley, where an old split rail fence ran along the side of the house by the stream. He wondered where the long pole trees needed to make those fence rails came from. The buildings were constructed of stone with heavy timber beams, while the barn had a tin roof and the house had a cleaved slate gray roof.

They sat quietly and watched the clouds filter into the valley. Traver said quietly, "The clouds give this a haunted feeling."

Laura agreed. "This time of year it's fog. You know, the entire area can be clear and my valley here will be socked in with this dense fog. But even still, it is enchanting, isn't it?"

Traver pointed at the barn, raising his eyebrows in question. "Great-granddad Dahle and his wife Annie built the barn first. There were a lot of railroad workers that did the construction. It's just massive, and the engineering is amazing, with some beams held together by railroad spikes."

Traver watched Laura as she told the story of the barn, admiring the way the setting sun made glints in her gold hair.

Then Laura pointed out the big house. "It took great-granddad and his family and hands four years to build this place. Annie wanted a huge fireplace with a thirty-inch hearth opening for cooking. The stone for the house came from the Rockies. Dahle offered cattle and hog meat to the railroad in exchange for them bringing loads of stone back to North Platte for him. The timbers, all cedar, came in from way up toward Canada. The house is extremely solid and it takes quite a few days of roaring fires in the hearth to warm up all the stone mass as winter sets in."

"Laura, this is just beautiful!" Traver said appreciatively.

Her face glowed and her eyes closed slightly. She sighed, "Traver." He cupped her face in his hands and her hands came up to clasp his. "Laura, Laura . . ." he repeated.

"I'm so tired of being alone, Traver."

He pulled her forward till their lips touched and they kissed gently.

When he pulled back, Traver said with feeling, "This is what all those shit-kicking country songs are about. You're so goddamn lonely and you come in contact with another person just as lonely. I know this is just a date, but I'm saying, I don't want to leave you. Ever."

Traver wanted to skip the boy-girl game, that was for kids. Older now, he wanted honesty and he wanted to get to the point. It was clear to him that Laura was the strength and beauty of the land and the salt of the earth. Loving this woman was going to complete his life, bring to reality a dream that neither Donna nor his lawyer lady friend ever came close to fulfilling.

The only sounds they heard were the clicking tree crickets and the crooning peacocks. Laura snuggled closer to him. "Traver, I have dreamed of soft kisses and I have cried for a special one to hold. I do not take this sort of risk with just anyone. My guts are hanging out." Her eyes were misty and her breath was moist and warm.

Traver put his right hand around her shoulders and pulled her close. "Laura," he whispered, "before we get too involved, I need to tell you about a wound I received in Vietnam."

She stiffened slightly.

"Well, I was shot in the groin and cannot get an erection."

She froze.

"I'm so very sorry to hear that, Traver," she managed to say, "but I still care about you."

Traver's hard-to-disguise smile alerted her to the tease.

Her mind working at light speed and a smile curling on her lips, Laura sighed. "I guess it will just have to be oral sex with us."

Traver turned red in the face and Laura started to giggle. "Traver, I saw a bulge in your crotch. I think everything is in working order."

Traver began rubbing the inside of her left thigh with his fingertips. "You'll have to stop that or we'll never get back to town," Laura said breathlessly.

"Just a second . . ." She got out of the Mercedes, went into the barn, and came back with the bow, knife, and quiver of arrows. She put them on the back seat and slid back into the front seat, adjusting her dress. "Traver, this is awkward for me . . ." Her eyes looked away and her eyes made tears. "You are the first man I have let touch me in ten years. Hold me, just hold me. That's what I need right now."

He leaned over, putting both arms around her waist. Her hands came up and rested on his shoulders, and her head bowed into the cradle of his neck. Barely containing her sniffles, Laura rested there for a few minutes. Then, she pulled away and said, "Thanks."

She wanted to get the conversation on a different plane. "I have a picture of myself when I was seventeen sitting on my dad's souped-up Mercedes, parked right here, after I won a race." She pulled it out of her wallet. It showed her holding her racing helmet in one hand and her trophy in the other, while her skirt rode up, revealing some creamy white thigh.

Looking at it, Traver whistled. "Holy shit! You were a fox even then!" He looked at her appraisingly. "Can I have a copy of this for my wallet?"

"You want a copy when I'm offering you the real thing?" Laura tossed back.

Traver fired up the Mercedes and found his way back to Skip's dad's place fairly easy. Laura was impressed. "I'm a quick learner," he told her. "Hey, Laura, let's stop and see Frenchy."

"All right, but what are you up for after we check in with Frenchy?"

"You tell me," Traver said.

"Oh . . ." Laura thought a moment. "Let's get a bottle of champagne and some corn dogs with lots of mustard and park up at the north end of the lake."

"Corn dogs and champagne?" he repeated.

"Why sure, aren't I worth it, Traver?"

"Boy, I don't know . . . corn dogs, well, not everybody gets that treatment."

Her eyes sparkled. "You know, Marlene Dietrich's favorite meal was hot dogs and champagne."

"Well, my mouth is watering now that you mentioned mustard and corn dogs and Marlene Dietrich."

They pulled over at the hospital to find Frenchy resting quietly. The next stop was the liquor store, where Traver splurged on an $80 bottle of champagne and two plastic cups. At the Gas and Go they picked up six corn dogs.

There was a chill in the air by the time they parked at the picnic spot at the north end of Lake Maloney. "Let's stay in the car, it's too cold to sit outside on these benches," Traver suggested.

So the pair sat in the car eating corn dogs and sipping champagne until after 10 p.m. Laura scooted down and nestled on the head rest, while the radio softly floated the notes of a piano piece. "Mozart," she said.

"I play," Laura whispered.

He leaned over and touched his lips to her mustard-flavored lips. "You play?" he said suggestively.

Laura thumped him on the shoulder. "The piano, you fool."

Leaning down, he kissed her again, this time tickling her lips with the tip of his tongue. When she parted her lips, he pushed deeper.

He whispered, "You play well?" He began kissing her ears.

"Mostly classical," she breathed.

"Huh?" I asked.

"Piano, I play the piano."

He snuggled closer. "Play for me someday, okay?"

"What? Play with you?" She tried to sound disgusted, but she couldn't keep from laughing at her own joke.

He laughed, too. "Okay." Grinning, he pretended to go for his zipper. She grabbed his hands and brought them to her lips in delight.

They embraced, and Laura held Traver especially tight. "I need to share some stuff with you. I was very happily married and I had a wonderful practice. For years after my husband died I wondered, why Bill? Then I came to the realization that it was Bill's time and it was Sharon's and my time to go through that." She fell quiet.

"Why aren't you still married, Traver? I'm sorry, that just popped out."

"That's okay, Laura." He leaned his head back on the seat and exhaled. "Somehow the person I was and the person she was when we got married disappeared. We are still the best of friends."

"Are you still close?"

"No. She is in Florida where we grew up. I stayed in California when I got out of the military."

That was enough information for Laura. Something else was about to pop out. She drew his hand very deliberately to her breast. She trembled a moment as she guided his hand around her firm globe. He felt her nipple rising beneath his palm. "Traver, will you stay with me tonight? I want this very much."

He murmured took a deep breath. "Laura, if I stay with you tonight, I may not want to go in the morning."

"That would be okay," she assured him.

He lowered her dress straps and bodice. At the barest touch, Laura gasped and trembled. Her legs closed on his hand as it was drenched in a gush of warmth.

She sighed, "Traver." Then she took a deep breath and shivered. "You knock me out, Mr. Wells!"

"Laura," he said, looking directly in her eyes, "you are not the average woman. You have a spirit in you that I am so comfortable with."

She met his forthright declaration with a smile in her eyes.

He couldn't resist going on. "And you have the most sensuous breasts I have ever wanted to kiss and hold."

Laura's breathing quickened and she took a deep breath. "It seems like we have been saving ourselves for just this moment."

They were certainly a mature man and woman, but for the next thirty minutes Traver and Laura were indistinguishable from a couple of hormone-addled energetic teenagers, arms everywhere and long kisses.

Eventually the make-out session slowed to a warm but full embrace, and the couple decided to straighten their clothes in some semblance of propriety.

"To the hospital," Traver announced.

*   *   *

Laura dropped Traver off at the hospital, where he intended to wait until Frenchy woke up. He settled down in a lounge chair next to the Indian's bed, squirmed into comfy position, then dropped almost immediately to sleep. Traver's next moment of awareness was the morning nurse, briskly opening the blinds and announcing in a cheery voice, "Going to be a great day today." He rubbed his eyes, sat up, and grunted a barely intelligible, but he hoped polite, greeting. He wasn't at all ready for so much sunshine until his nose sensed the fulsome aroma of dark, black coffee. Laura was standing there with a box of donuts and two large cups of steaming caffeine.

"You're spoilin' me rotten, gal." Traver made sure she heard him.

"That's exactly what I have in mind," Laura answered, giving him a peckish kiss on his forehead. "Let me bring another chair in here so we can have our breakfast. Gut bombs and thick coffee."

Laura stepped out into the hall and dragged in another chair, placing it next to Traver's.

"How did you sleep last night, Traver?" she wanted to know.

"I went out like a light. I slept very soundly, almost as if . . . ah, well, as if something had fallen into place and I was complete." He studied Laura's face for a reaction. A small tear formed, and light pouring through the blinds made it appear to be a diamond resting just at the edge of her eyelid. "Good morning, light of my life," he said quietly as he reached over to touch her hand.

"How come we haven't met before this?" Laura asked with some emotion.

"It's strange how stuff goes, isn't it?" he responded.

"Oh, hi, Dr. Peterson!" said the nurse who came in to check on the patient. "You working today?"

Laura turned her head. "No, today I'm just the donut fairy."

A low moan came from the bed and they all turned to see Frenchy's head roll to one side and his eyes flutter. Laura stood up and went to his bedside to hold his wrist. Frenchy's eyes focused on her, as she smiled broadly Frenchy relaxed.

Traver took a spot right next to Laura. "*Bonjour, mon ami. Comment allez-vous?*" Traver was asking how he felt. The Indian looked at him with watery eyes and said he felt a heavy stone sitting on his chest and stomach.

"His pulse is strong," Laura said positively.

Frenchy's nostrils flared as he noticed the pungent aroma coming from Traver's coffee mug. He offered a sip, but the patient shook his head, asking instead for water.

Traver put down his cup and stepped to the bedside table, where a water glass and pitcher sat. He filled a glass and placed it in the Indian's hands.

"Just a sip," Laura indicated.

He made a scrunched frown. This was not water from the river. "Tastes strange," he said. "Not brown."

Traver dumped the water out of the patient's cup and added some coffee. The Indian sniffed it and smiled. "*Merci!*"

Laura asked where he came from: "*D'où viens-tu?*"

He answered, "Four days ride toward the snow wind." According to Laura, that would put him in the middle of North Dakota.

"*Non,*" he burst out. "Lakota!"

Traver and Laura laughed at his response.

He continued solemnly, "Ah, the deer had much strong spirit and I was so stupid. Thank you for helping me."

Laura left the room for the nurse's station, so she could read Frenchy's chart. He had suffered torn chest skin and muscles and a rip across his stomach. All in all, she decided he was lucky to be alive. Traver getting him medical aid so quickly had made all the difference. Laura asked the nurse to bring a pot of coffee and a glass of orange juice to Frenchy's bedside.

Laura went back into the room to see Frenchy and Traver deep in conversation. They stopped and looked at her when she entered. She studied Frenchy's face for a few seconds and then directed a question to Traver.

"He's not from here, is he?" she said solemnly.

"What do you mean—from here?"

"He's from yesterday!" Laura cocked her head in a flash of understanding. "He's from out of time. How did this happen?"

Traver answered quietly, "I do think he is from the past—it all fits, the arrows, the clothes, just like Skip's dad said."

Laura sat down in the big easy chair and sighed. "Holy shit."

Frenchy looked at her quizzically and repeated, "Holy shit."

"*Non, sacre bleu.*"

"Ah," he said, understanding lighting up in his eyes.

That amused Traver and Laura.

*　　*　　*

Laura suggested that they push the patient's bed over to the window. After a grunt and shove, they had him against the open window, where the smells of early fall came wafting in. Frenchy breathed in deeply the chilled fragrance of damp hay and moist earth, but as he looked out the window his breath stopped in mid-exhale. His eyes widened and he moaned and plopped back down on the pillow. Laura cranked up his bed slightly so he could see out the window more easily.

Looking out over I-80, Frenchy was spellbound by the huge diesel trucks flying by and the little cars and pickup trucks speeding past the larger trucks. He glanced back at Laura and then looked out the opened window and at the freeway traffic. "Holy shit!" he breathed.

"No!" Laura exclaimed. "Cars and trucks."

Frenchy repeated, "Cars and trucks."

Smiling at him with a twinkle in her eyes, in French she said, "Wagons."

"Madame?" Frenchy said as he turned to look at Laura.

"Madame Laura Peterson," she said, pointing to herself.

He responded, a finger at his chest, "*Je suis* Twin Bears."

"Yes!" Traver slapped his knee. "That's what Skip's dad thought from the mark on the broken arrow I gave him."

"Twin Bears," said Laura, getting the Indian's attention. She opened a box of doughnuts and took out three. She picked up one and tasted it, making a "yum" sound. "*Gateau*," she told the patient.

Twin Bears was intrigued and took the doughnut Laura offered him. He sampled it and his eyes lit up. "Ummmmmmm," he said, which is a common affirmation in any language.

Then Laura sipped the orange juice and passed it to Frenchy. He gulped down the whole glass, his eyes as wide as half-dollars. He sighed with pleasure.

Twin Bears asked them about what this place is. Was he in the spirit world?

"No." Laura reassured him. "You are in a great medicine lodge, called a hospital. You are our guest and you are healing so you can hunt again. But it will take at least a moon for your strength to return. Please rest now."

He smiled. "*Oui*, I will rest."

Laura touched his bandages. "And leave this shirt on. It will help you to mend."

"Twin Bears," Traver addressed him, "we have to leave for a while, but others will come and help you. We will be back at sundown."

Laura stopped at the nurses' station and checked Twin Bears' chart. She lined out Frenchy, wrote in Twin Bears, and then made a few notes about what they talked about with the patient and what food he had. She gave the chart back and asked that more orange juice be sent in. "Traver, you need to go show Twin Bears how to use the bed pan and urine bottle." She laughed when Traver opened his eyes wide at that order.

Her cell phone rang and she dismissed Traver with a wave of her hand toward Twin Bears' room. "Hello?"

After a few minutes, Laura came in. "Honey, I have to go to work. Old man Jones passed away and I have to do the autopsy. I'll be back in a bit. Are you okay with staying here?"

"Sure," Traver said. "I'll call Skip and tell him were I'm at."

In Twin Bears' room he poured himself a cup of coffee and got out his cell phone. The Indian watched with curiosity.

"Hey, Skip, Traver here."

"Where the hell are you? I've been worried about you," Skip said.

"I'm at the hospital with Frenchy, whose name is really Twin Bears."

"No shit!" Skip said. "Kathy was betting that you and Laura got crazy somewhere and stayed out all night."

"Naw, Laura dropped me off at the hospital last night and I slept in Twin Bears' room. I wanted to be here in case he came to and got scared. Hey, Skip, this guy is from yesterday." A moment passed. "What?" Traver asked. "No. I'll hang around until you get here. Hey, stop off and get Twin Bears' stuff from your dad's place and bring it. Okay, bye, Skip."

Twin Bears was still staring at Traver in wonder. He called Skip back and asked for Laura's phone number. He punched that in and hit dial.

When Laura answered he said, "Hi, it's me."

"Oh! Do you miss me already?"

"Well, yes, but Twin Bears was watching me talk to Skip on the phone and I want to give him a chance to talk with you."

Traver handed the Indian the phone, who put it to his ear. His eyes enlarged to silver dollar size and he threw the phone on the bed.

Traver reached over to pick it up. "Hey, Laura, just a minute, Twin Bears is freaking out. Hold on. Twin Bears, this is Laura. She is a long distance from here right now. Oh, maybe a day's ride or smoke signals," he said.

He looked at Traver strangely and asked, "She is not in the talking stone?"

"No. Only her voice, here, you talk with her." He held the phone out again, and Twin Bears took it very slowly and put it to his ear again. His face became very still with concentration for a moment. He took the phone from his ear and studied it. He turned it over several times, and in doing that he hit the off button. When he put the phone back to his ear, Laura wasn't there any longer.

He handed Traver the phone and he held it so the Indian could see the dial screen with the flashing numbers being input. Pushing the green button, Traver rang Laura and handed the phone back. Twin Bears heard the ringing and then smiled. "Bonjour, Song of the Canyon," he said boldly, addressing Laura. Then a beat. With a smile on his face, he gave the phone to Traver. "Song wants to sing to you."

Traver heard Laura belting out, "*Frere Jacques, frere Jacques, dormez-vous . . .*" Then, giggling, she hung up.

Twin Bears looked at me and counted off on his fingers, "Doughnuts, coffee, juice, phone, cars, trucks?" And then in French, "This place has strong medicine! What else is there?"

"There is so much, but first you need to get well. *Au revoir.*"

Traver walked down the hospital hallway to the nurses' station, where he stopped and asked, "Does anyone here speak French?" One nurse spoke up in response. "Mr. Wells, there is an aide, high school, who takes French. She will be here at nine."

"Great! Will you have her drop in and talk to Twin Bears?"

Traver went out front to wait for Skip, and when he arrived they went out for lunch at the Gas and Go for a big order of chicken livers.

About that time, at the Gas and Go, Traver's phone buzzed. "Hey, don't talk like that!"

Skip looked over at him with an expression of mock surprise. "That sounded bizarre, who was that?"

"Laura, she was talking dirty to me."

Skip roared with laughter. "You'd better watch out, Traver, I swear she's going to capture and abuse you."

"Oh, boy!" Traver clapped his hands together. Between bursts of laughter he managed to say, "She's coming over here, so we'd better save her some livers."

In just a few minutes Laura pulled in, driving her crew-cab Chevy. When she got out Traver did a once over and thought, "Holy shit! This gal's legs go on forever!" She had on blue jeans, an off-white Western short-sleeved shirt, scuffed boots and a belt buckle as big as a salad plate. She had gone home after the autopsy, showered, and changed into knockabout duds.

"Just a minute, boys, I've got to get an order of gizzards and a big gulp." She walked into the store, her rear rolling provocatively in her snug faded jeans. Traver felt sweat forming on his brow.

Skip whistled under his breath. "She's got a new walk, Traver. You're in trouble!"

When Laura emerged from the store, she was bearing a big soda in one hand and a greasy white bag in the other. "Can I join you boys?" And without waiting for an answer she sat down.

Skip said, "I heard that old man Jones died yesterday."

"Yes. Heart failure," Laura said.

Skip paused and then said, "Damn! I told him to knock off all that bacon and greasy pork."

"That didn't kill him, Skip," Laura mumbled between popping deep-fried gizzards in her mouth. "He had a massive heart attack because of an overactive sex life."

Skip turned bright red in the face as Laura smiled a devious grin. "Naw!" he managed to get out in disbelief.

Laura continued with a dead-pan face, "Well, who do you think called the doctor? It sure wasn't old man Jones! I heard it was a widow from over in Corning."

"You're shitting me! Goddamn it, Laura, don't mess with me like this!"

Laura turned to Traver. "See how he likes that spicy gossip?" She laughed. "Skip, it was just a heart attack."

"You see what I have to put up with, Traver?" Skip groaned.

"Well, I have to get these supplies to the boys. Traver, I'll be by Skip's later and we can go visit Twin Bears. After that, dinner is on me." Laura strolled provocatively back to her truck.

"Well, buddy," Skip said. "Sounds like she's taking command."

"Not really," Traver came back.

"Well, she's persistent when she finds what she wants. To my knowledge she hasn't dated since Bill died."

"Skip, how old is Laura?"

"Older than you by probably five or ten years. You're what? Forty-three?"

"No. I'm forty-seven."

"Well, Laura is at least fifty."

"Is that a problem, Traver?"

"Naw."

Skip observed, "It's obviously not a problem with Laura. I can see a difference in her already and it's you she's all a tizzy over." Skip looked at him. "You're good for her, Traver, just don't fuck with her, please?"

"I won't, buddy, I'm really getting attached to her."

Laura was right on time in coming back, just as she said. Traver went out to her car, got in, and they drove off.

CHAPTER 5

MILE MARKER 287
PAN BREAD, STEAK, AND COWBOY BEANS

WHEN LAURA AND Traver entered Twin Bears's hospital room they saw a girl dressed in a candy-stripe uniform sitting next to him. She had dark hair and eyes that were sparkling with interest in the Indian. She was showing him some books and speaking in French and some Indian dialect.

Twin Bears looked up and smiled broadly as Traver and Laura came into the room.

"Hello, Laura. Hello, Traver," he pronounced in a good approximation of English. "My friend helps me to learn." Then in French he said, "This is Ray of Sun."

He spotted his weapons in Traver's arms and he took them greedily. "*Bon.* I have missed my knife."

The visitors approached the bed to see four books scattered about. "Look," Twin Bears said as he opened one of the books. It was a history of the Plains Indians. He turned to a page and pointed to a photo of an old man on a horse and a woman with children beside her. Pointing to the old Indian, Twin Bears said, "Two Horses. I know this man, but he is not that old. He is as I am, still a hunter and brave. How can this be Two Horses?"

Laura said, "This is a picture taken in . . ." She studied the caption at the bottom of the page. "In 1869."

"What is 1869?" Twin Bears asked.

"It is what we count for years," Laura answered.

"How the sun has run through the sky, yes?"

One hundred and twenty-nine years have passed since this picture was taken." Laura held up her fingers. "Twin Bears, see my fingers? It would take twelve fingers to represent each sky journey of the sun from when this picture of Two Horses was taken."

Twin Bears processed that concept. Finally he said, "One hand . . ." He held up five fingers. "This would be five suns' full journeys?"

"Yes," Laura answered.

"Then I am six hands that I have seen the sun's journey." He crossed his arms over his chest with the satisfaction of understanding this concept.

"You are thirty years old," said Laura, smiling at him.

"You are fifty full suns, yes?" He looked her questioningly.

"Yes."

Traver avoided Laura's glance. "How many suns, mister?" He flashed his fingers in quick succession.

"You're forty-seven?" Laura asked, with surprise in her voice.

"Did you think I was older?"

"Yes, I did." Then she murmured, "I'm three years older."

"I'm okay with that," Traver told her. He saw some doubt clouding her eyes. "Truly I am, but I'll age faster than you."

"Hey! One day at a time, okay?" Her smile returned and her eyes cleared. "One day at a time and every night in my arms." She looked radiant.

Twin Bears kept rolling these numbers around in his mind. Finally he said, "I am not one hundred and twenty-nine suns but only thirty, but how can this be?"

"You journeyed from yesterday into today. Do you remember any strange things on the day you hunted and killed the buck?"

Twin Bears knit together his eyebrows in thought. "*Non*, I do not remember any strange things. I was just walking in the canyon. There had been a storm, with great tongues of fire in the night sky. When I woke up in the morning, I was amazed to see snow all about."

Laura looked at Traver before saying, "Lightning storm, but our weather was calm the other night."

"Are you thinking that there might be some sort of electromagnetic anomaly around Enchanted Canyon that could link the past to the future?"

"I'm no scientist." Laura shrugged her shoulders.

Twin Bears's voice was subdued as he asked, "Can I go back home?"

"I really don't know, Twin Bears. When you get better we'll go out to the ranch and see what we can find out," Laura assured him, soothingly. "When you leave the hospital you can stay with me, and that will be in just a few days."

"Can't I just go back to my village?" he asked plaintively.

"We'll work on it." She patted his shoulder.

Traver tried to be jolly. "We are leaving now, but we'll be back tomorrow."

The Indian brightened up. "Juice, coffee, and doughnuts?"

"You're a quick learner," Laura said with a giggle. "Yes! We'll bring them!"

Traver and Laura linked arms as they walked out of the hospital.

"He's a pretty intelligent person, Traver. You saw how quickly he absorbed the concept of counting years."

"Yes, I did, and I think he'll catch up with English real quick. Say, where are we off to now?" he asked.

"How about cowboy beans, steak, and pan bread? Just up Interstate 80 a bit. It's a hole in the wall, but the chow is the best in the West, mile marker 287."

Laura got into the car and throttled down the highway. "This old Mercedes sounds good," he told her and scooted close to kiss her neck.

"Oh! Don't do that or we'll have to pull over at the next rest stop and dance."

"Okay," Traver agreed. "Pull over!"

"But I'm hungry!"

He reached over and cupped her breast in his hand.

Gripping the steering wheel hard, she crowed, "To hell with supper!"

"Oh, all right, I'll be a good boy."

The meal was scrumptious, and the drive back to North Platte was quiet. Traver drove as Laura snuggled up next to him.

"Will you stay with me tonight?" Laura asked.

"No, Laura, I'll stay with you forever."

"But how do you know that our sex life is going to be satisfying?"

"Oh, I know how to take care of myself."

"You're terrible, Traver!" she said, eyes flashing like lightning. She reached between his legs and put her hand over his crotch. "Oh! Traver, I do believe your arthritis is acting up. I can feel a joint getting stiff."

"Oh, you can, doctor? Well, what can we do to help that out?"

"My prescription is to pull over and get crazy."

"Don't you want to go home and be comfortable?"

In a husky voice Laura said, "No one comes down this road this time of night."

Traver stopped. He turned and welded his lips to Laura's and their hands caressed each other. He slid his hand under her shirt and stroked her silky bra until Laura's breathing became ragged. He slid the fabric away and kissed each tiny pink nipple. "Oh God, Traver!"

Laura moaned quietly. "Yes!" she screamed. Then she shuddered and her head fell back on the seat. "Traver," Laura whispered. "I . . . I . . . had forgotten . . ." Her voice trailed off.

"What about you, Traver?" She moved her hand to his crotch. "Oh, you do like me!"

"I wanted you to be first," Traver said softly.

Looking at him lovingly, Laura whispered, "Are you sure this is where you want to be?"

"This is where I want to be," he said firmly, holding her close.

Laura breathed heavily, "That is just what the doctor needed. Where did you get your training?"

Traver chuckled. "The U.S. Navy. Saisabol, Japan." She punched him playfully. "Come on, I love you, no matter what."

She was tearful as she put her disheveled clothes back in order, wiggling and readjusting her bra.

"I'm your girl, Traver."

He said proudly, "Well, I think I'll keep you!"

"You better! I've given you my all."

"Hell, I just might sell all my stuff in California and move in with you."

"You would do that for me. Traver?"

"Let's see, you've got land and a good job and a great body."

"Oh yeah? And what do you have?"

Grinning at her, he said, "It's hot and heavy."

Laura yelled, "You're bad and I'm taking you home right now."

When they pulled into her ranch house area, the dashboard clock read 10:15. Laura got out of the car to turn on the porch light and unlock the door.

"Hey, Laura, you'll still be wanting me in the morning? I mean, this ain't a one-night stand?"

"Get in here, cowboy, this instant!" she ordered,

"You know that if I don't show up at Skip's the tongues will really begin to wag."

"Don't worry, I'm sure they're already wagging." Laura smiled and came over to kiss him. "You better want to stay around because you like me, not because the tongues are wagging."

"Wagging tongues," he leered, raising her blouse and unfastening her bra. "Wagging tongues," he whispered.

Off in the distance coyotes began howling. That broke the erotic spell and the two lovers embraced tightly.

"Come on, Traver, my bedroom is upstairs. Follow me."

The big bedroom windows reflected enough starlight into the room so they could undress and climb into bed. Laura nestled into his shoulder and said softly, "Traver, welcome home."

Home echoed in his thoughts, how wonderful that felt to hear.

*   *   *

They awoke the next morning in each other's arms. Eyes wide open, Laura breathed into his ear, "I love you, Traver."

She went to the shower and he rolled over to sleep again. In just a moment he felt a soft kiss on his cheek. "Hey, sleepyhead, are you going to sleep your life away?"

He stretched and yawned. "Come sit beside me a bit. I want you to know how much I like you."

She perched on the bed next to him. "Like me?"

He ran his hand up under her blouse, lightly rubbing her bra over her nipples.

"That's wonderful, but you need to get up and get a shower. It snowed last night. Let's go over to the canyon and see what we can find out about our visitor from the past."

Traver took a hot shower and came down into the kitchen for some coffee and a bowl of oatmeal.

Laura loaded the remaining coffee into the Thermos, and both left by the back door, hand in hand, en route to Laura's crew cab. The frosting of snow made everything look new and fresh.

"It's sort of like us," Laura murmured, breaking the silence.

"How?" Traver asked.

"New snow. A fresh page. We can make all the marks we want to on it together."

Traver smiled.

Laura kept barreling down the road, rolling down her window halfway and breathing in deeply. "Traver," Laura's voice choked in a sob. "This is harder than I thought."

She pulled the truck to a stop and put it in neutral to let it idle. She turned to look at him, not even attempting to wipe away her tears. She nodded toward a clump of low cedars. "Bill died over there. This was the last place that Bill saw the world. I still have warm feelings for Bill, but I know that I must move on."

"What can I do to help?" Traver responded.

Laura smiled at his sincerity. "Just give me your support and I'll get through this."

She reached for the cup of coffee he had poured for her and took a long sip. "Now, let's investigate Enchanted Canyon," and she ground the truck into gear.

She halted the truck before a striking panoramic view, and they stepped out to drink it in. The cold, crisp morning air felt good on Traver's face, and he glanced at Laura, her skin glowing rich and pink.

"What are you thinking?" she finally asked him.

"Oh, I was just considering how lucky I am and how much you are a part of this land, how you *are* the land. Laura, I want to move out here and be with you. This is just right for us!"

She was flustered with emotion and intently watched as Traver reached into his pocket and got out his key ring. Slowly he removed each key, sliding it through the circle. When the ring was free of keys, he took Laura's left hand and, kissing her palm, he slipped the key ring on her fourth finger, a perfect fit.

Holding her hand and gazing into her eyes, he said, "The fourth finger has a nerve direct to the heart. My heart to your heart. Laura, will you be my life?"

She looked at the chrome key ring shining on her finger. "Will I be your life? Yes!"

They hugged and then started to walk, hands clasped. Every now and then Laura lifted her hand to look at the key ring on her finger. As they approached the opening of the canyon, Laura pointed. "There's a deer trail that winds upward along the canyon. I've walked it before. It just goes up to the end of the canyon."

They mounted the trail, which was not used much. In about twenty minutes they were at the end of the canyon. It was cozy, with the walls rising on both sides. When they got back out into the meadow, the north wind picked up.

"Smell the snow coming?" Laura asked him. Before he could answer, a snowflake landed in her hair. Traver reached for it, but it melted as soon as he touched it. Another flake fell, and soon the sky was filled with white puffy dots. They leaned together against the truck a long time, watching the storm coming in. She now and then raised her ring finger and just stared at it.

Soon the hood of the truck was blanketed with snow. Traver suggested, "Hey, let's head home and get a big fire going in the fireplace and make some hot chocolate and get crazy."

"Boy, that sounds great!" she agreed. "You drive, Traver."

They got in the truck and lazily headed back to the ranch house. The north winds were driving the snow hard now and drifts were beginning to form. When they arrived, Laura and Traver climbed up the stairs to the porch and warmed up their lips with a kiss.

Laura cocked her head to one side. "You've never really seen the house."

"No," he said, "it went by in blur on the way to the bedroom last night, remember?"

"Stomp your feet, honey, and let's go inside." She opened the heavy hardwood front door, and they entered. A thick rag rug graced the entryway. On the left were rifle racks, now holding umbrellas, a shotgun, an old cane, and a rather beat-up bag of golf clubs. Laura kept a tight hold on his hand. "The cane and clubs were Poppa Joe's, my granddad."

Laura pulled the rug back with her foot to expose what looked like the butt of a forty-four-caliber brass shell casing pounded into the plank flooring. Pointing at it, she chuckled. "I've been told lots about this. Here is where Poppa Joe just about shot off his wee-wee. Dad told me that Poppa Joe bought a new double-action 44/40. When he stuck it into his belt, he somehow activated the trigger. It blew out the end of his pants zipper and the bullet ripped out the inside of his pantsleg and ended up punching a hole in the floor here. It pretty well shook him up. When he calmed down, he took out the spent shell casing and drove it into the hole, stomping it down with the heel of his boot and cussing"

On the right of the entry was a rough but nicely fabricated heavy wooden bench with coat pegs above it. Laura reached down and raised the hinged bench top. She had a faraway smile. "I used to hide in here, but mom always pretended she could never find me."

Then they stepped into a huge front room with an open beamed ceiling clear to the roof. The second floor had two bedrooms and a bath off a balcony overlooking the front room. Massive wood and stone stairs led to the balcony. The great fireplace was directly in the center of the house. On the stone-wall chimney, about two feet above the gray granite stone mantel, hung a huge painting of an Indian woman throwing what looked like stars into the sky. It was a rich and vibrant work of art, and Traver paused, trying to think where he knew this Indian woman from. Something deep was stirring. He was hearing a sound.

Laura came up behind him for a hug, asking, "Is she gathering stars or throwing stars?"

He did not hesitate. "Star Thrower."

Laura squeezed him. "Yes, the painting is called *Star Thrower*. It's by Remington."

"Frederic Remington?" he asked.

Laura pointed to the signature. Sure enough, there it was, Remington.

"It makes me think of the beginning of mankind and the stars in the universal sky. She looks so lifelike, but her face is distant. I know her, or I'm going to meet her someday," he whispered.

Laura patted his stomach. "She *is* beautiful and I am jealous that she excites you."

He turned to answer her hug face to face.

"Like I'm going to hang this painting in your bedroom."

Laura blushed. "You better not!"

He patted her rear and kissed her. But he thought as he glanced back at the painting, *I know this woman. Was she in my dreams?*

"Who is she?" Traver wanted to know. "That's not a Plains Indian face, it's different. I know this face, but from where?"

Laura felt his emotions and tried to distract him by gesteruing toward the rest of the room.

Three big stuffed chairs were covered with Indian rugs, and desks and assorted tables in various sizes finished out the rest of the big room's décor. A huge bearskin rug on the floor accentuated the couch and chair and the fireplace area.

Laura pointed out how that bear's nose was chewed off. "I had a pet coyote a long time ago. I raised her from a pup. Sissie just loved growling at this rug and chewing on the nose."

Laura began laughing at a memory. "Poppa Joe! Gosh! He must have been about ninety at the time. Well, he got down on the floor when he saw Sissie and me coming toward the house. He got under that bear rug and pulled it around him. Sissie and I burst through the front door and I yelled for mom. Sissie went to the bear rug and started yapping. Poppa Joe rose up with the rug around him and roared. Sissie peed on the floor and her leg slipped in the piss on the slate floor. The poor thing couldn't leave fast enough. Every hair on her back stood straight up. It scared me, too, and I screamed and pissed in my pants, also.

"Out the front door came Poppa Joe growling, with the bear rug still wrapped around him. Sissie must have gotten up some gumption because she made a run at what she thought was a black bear. Well, the end of the story is that Poppa Joe got himself bitten two or three times, twice on his ankles and once on the cheek of his ass. After that Sissie kept a wide path around the 'ol bearskin rug and Poppa Joe."

Traver started laughing about midway in the story, enjoying Laura's vivid development of the scene. "That must have been rich to see!"

"Yeah." Laura patted his arm.

She pointed to the right, just past the fireplace. "The kitchen is behind the great fireplace. What you see is, oh, I guess, a dining room. There is a neat breakfast nook just off the kitchen with a beautiful wood cook stove. Years ago we had an electric stove put in. There is also a huge bathroom off the breakfast nook, where now there is a washer and dryer. Over the bathroom is a ten thousand-gallon water tank. Remember, water freezes during the winter. The chimney goes up through the tank in a hollow pipe, so during the cold weather, the residual heat keeps the water in the tank from freezing."

"That's damn good thinking," Traver said, amazed. "When was that built, Laura?"

"Oh, 1861 or 1862, I think. I replaced the tank in 1968 with one made from stainless-steel. Boy! Was that expensive. I also redid all the water pipes in copper nickel.

"The other side of the fireplace is a hallway with two bedrooms and a bath." Laura opened two sliding doors just past the entryway. "This is the study, the library. Go on in," she coaxed. "I want to change and get a quick shower. You make yourself comfortable." She gave him a quick peck on his cheek and was off upstairs.

Inside the library he could hear the heater's fans starting to shuttle the warmed air throughout the house. He reached over to the wall and pushed the light switch. It was a beautiful room, dating to the 1920s, he guessed. A couple floor lamps came to life, their curved ornate stained-glass shades glowing ruby red.

The wood cases were filled with books, and anchoring the furnishings was a huge carved desk. There was a baby grand piano sitting off in one corner, a bronze statue of a buffalo resting atop it. As he was taking all this in, Laura, barefoot, came in, her footsteps hushed by the thick turn-of-the-century carpet. He sensed Laura standing there, her fragrance was early prairie grass kissed with dew.

"You like this room, Traver, I can tell."

"Yes. I like this room very much, Laura. In fact, I love it!"

"It's special for me, too."

She came closer and her hands came around his waist. "As I grew up, I spent many hours here with dad and Poppa Joe. I've read most of these books." She snuggled into his shoulder and kissed his neck softly. "You would have liked both men, Traver."

Then, off in thought, she mentioned, "Mother was the catalyst that kept dad and Poppa Joe focused on work. Both men would rather have been hunting, fishing, or camping, out in nature all the time. I was an only child, and dad said Poppa Joe wanted a boy terribly bad. I was spoiled rotten by them both, but you would never guess that, right?" Laura smiled. "Mother would complain when we came in from town shopping and I had pants instead of a new dress, or a shotgun instead of a new purse or pair of shoes."

Laura choked back tears. "You know, she was a strong pioneer woman, Traver, and yet she was as fragile as a wisp of campfire smoke. She was God's angel on Earth. What I most remember about my mother was that, by God, I was going to play the piano and go to church on Sundays."

"You play?"

"I do."

"Will you play for me?" She nodded, walking across the room, still barefoot. Her jeans were held up by a woven rawhide belt that cinched in her white western shirt. She removed the buffalo statue from the top of the piano, raised the lid, and pulled out the seat just slightly. When she sat down, her jeans stretched tightly over her rear, and she wiggled as she caught his eye.

Her hands gracefully poised over the keyboard, and with a downbeat, the room became the center of his universe, vibrating in harmony with the piano strings. She played with feeling, one that he shared instantly. When the haunting melody ceased, Traver said, "Laura, you are the melody of my soul. Let's sing it all of our lives." She sighed and he continued, "What is it that you're playing? It's stirred my soul from somewhere before."

"It's from the movie *Somewhere in Time*, based on a melody by Paganini."

That was a lightning strike to his memory. He remembered the woman in that film. He fell in love with her character, and the concept of the film had always intrigued him.

Laura picked up the song again. "I was taken aback when the actress spoke on stage to the fellow who went back in time to meet the actress woman. You remember, Traver?"

"It's when the actress realized the fellow following her and trying to meet her was exactly who she had been fantasizing about as a lover. She had not recognized him at first and then the realization of who he was struck her. She was shaken that what she had longed for had shown up and she had apparently not recognized him."

Laura's hands floated in mid-air. "I, too, have just realized who you are," she said, as her hands again touched the keyboard to bring the haunting melody into being. He was the person she had longed for these past ten years since Bill had passed away.

Laura's finger caressed the last lingering note, and he slid next to her on the piano bench. She turned toward him. "I love you, Traver, and you are just in time!" They embraced.

Still in the clutch, they saw lights playing across the wall. Headlights.

Sharon stomped her feet free from snow on the porch and came inside. Sharon yelled, "Mom!" She caught sight of us both. "Oh, Traver, there you are. Everyone is wondering where you are. Mom, I wasn't sure you were here."

He smiled at her. "Your mom captured me and won't let me leave."

Sharon looked at her mother and then back at him. "Mom?" Sharon said slowly, dragging out the syllable. Laura held up her left hand and Sharon looked at it. Laura said, "Sharon, Traver talked me into this, this ring."

"Mom, you are kidding, aren't you?"

"Well, honey, Traver and I are going to be married."

Sharon blushed. "Mom!" She came over to her mother, kissing her cheek, and then came over to Traver. "Treat her real good or I'll kick your ass"

His mouth dropped open, and Laura burst out laughing. "That's my girl!"

Sharon popped his shoulder with her hand. "Just kidding. Mom can take care of herself, Traver." Then she grinned. "Congratulations, you guys!"

Sharon addressed her mother. "How wild is this. Mom, I came out here to tell you that John and I are getting married. Let's have a double wedding."

"Honey, that's wonderful. But Traver and I will have just a little ceremony over in Maxwell. Are you staying tonight?"

"I could, but I told John I would be right back, but I could call him."

"Do it, honey. I want to visit with you."

They went into the front room where Sharon called her fiance and told him she was staying with her mother. The snow storm was barreling into town, and John said he was glad she was staying at the ranch. He also mentioned that it was great that Laura was getting married, but he thought it was too soon. "Just meeting Traver and all that."

Traver yelled to Laura that he would bring some firewood up on the porch so that it would be dry for later use to get through the night. He found a wheelbarrow and brought at least ten loads of wood up to the porch and dumped them at the steps. Laura came out with a cup of hot chocolate. She looked toward the north. "Traver, look out toward Enchanted Canyon." There was an eerie bluish glow. "What's causing that? Sunlight being reflected by the snow flakes?" she guessed.

Traver continued to stack the wood when Laura said, "Oh, Skip called. When you're done with this call him back." He sipped the last of the hot chocolate and told her thanks.

Task accomplished, he lit a fire in the living room fireplace and called Skip. When he answered, they talked about the snow and how deer hunting would be great tomorrow. Traver told him he was staying at Laura's for a few more days.

There was a moment of silence, then Skip exhaled. "Traver," he said in a firm fatherly voice, "don't embarrass Dr. Laura. You're staying out there with her is going to get around town."

"Skip," he interrupted, "on Sunday Laura and I are going to Maxwell and get married at her church."

Again the phone became silent. "Married?"

Grinning, Traver said cheerfully, "You and Kathy be there bright and early."

"And don't tell anybody," Laura said.

"You and Dr. Laura are getting married Sunday?"

"Yep." He signaled Laura to come over and handed her the phone. "It's Skip. I just told him we are hooking up Sunday."

Laura cuddled the phone. "Hi, Skip." A long silence followed. Traver could see tears sliding down Laura's cheeks. She wiped at her tears and looked over at him.

"You bet, Skip, this one is a keeper." She grinned widely. Chuckling, she said, "You know we'll get Traver down to the creek." She grinned and so did Sharon. He thought, *Trout fishing, great!*

Laura handed the phone back with that cute cut of a smile at the corners of her pink lips.

Traver took the phone. "Yeah, Skip?" The rest of the conversation concerned Twin Bears and his English lessons with the candy striper. When the hospital brought a television into his room, Twin Bears made them turn it around to see how everyone got into the box. When he understood the television was similar to the phone, he just shook his head and went back to bed.

Skip mentioned that the doctor said Twin Bears will be discharged Monday.

"Great!" Traver responded.

He got off the phone with Skip and found Laura and Sharon in the kitchen. Both had a glass of wine.

"Wine?" Sharon asked him.

"No, thanks. Say, you-all want me to make supper tonight?"

Laura looked at him with raised eyebrows. "You cook?"

"Yeah. You don't know what a lucky woman you are to have trapped me."

"Come here, I'll show you lucky!" Laura smiled enticingly.

"Mom!" Sharon said, laughing. "What's got into you?"

Laura turned and looked at her daughter. Grinning, she did a thumb hitchhike gesture, "Him!"

"You gals go in by the fire and visit and let me get supper." They both moved into the front room.

He yanked open the refrigerator door. Not much in the way of fresh vegetables, but the freezer sported a huge bag of pork chops. He pulled them out and found some rice in the dry stores and spinach in the canned-goods section. He also snagged some frozen zucchini squash out of the freezer.

He thawed the squash and pork chops and began grilling them while the rice boiled. He heard Laura and Sharon sharing laughter. "Oh, Mom, Dad would be so happy for you. I think he would like Traver."

He heard Laura saying, "Honey, I am so happy."

"Mom, I'm just so glad you're not going to be alone."

"Not anymore," Laura told her daughter delightedly.

Traver stood at the stove grilling the pork chops, his thoughts drifting everywhere. Glancing around the kitchen, he realized that Laura's husband, Bill, had once been there, standing in the same spot, most likely. And now he was warming Laura's bed, and a quick thought passed over him of being the other man. Hearing Sharon say that Dad would have liked him really made him feel funny, almost like he expected Bill to come in at any moment and catch him and Laura in flagrante.

Suddenly the smell of burning meat brought him back to the moment. He flipped the chops and listened to the sizzle as the pork hit the grill again.

I never thought about being a second man in a woman's life. Even though her first man was gone, he was not completely at ease with the new situation. He went to the kitchen door that opened onto a short hallway into the great room and watched Sharon and Laura.

His heart ached for Laura and all that she had lost. *I love her but am I the best man for her?*

Turning back to the stove, Traver tried to analyze his emotions. *Am I just reaching for Laura out of loneliness? Is this a case of lust that will burn out shortly? Jesus. When I first saw her at Gary's, that was raw sex smacking me in the head, but I also felt a deep sense of longing in my heart. Making love to Laura is so, so . . . what? Right up there with a good cup of coffee first thing in the morning.*

He piled the cooked pork chops onto a plate and shut off the grill on the huge kitchen stove. He had planned to make some barbecue sauce, but all his soul searching left him distracted. All he had time to do was put on the squash, warm the spinach, and make brown gravy for the rice.

Laura came into the kitchen to give me a big hug and a pat on the rear. "Something in here sure smells good."

During supper Traver told Laura that Twin Bears was being released Monday.

"Do you think he'll like one of the bunk houses?" Laura asked.

Traver thought a second. "Yep."

"Good, then tomorrow morning we can straighten it up."

Sharon said, "Mom, you've got a great cook here. Just taste this burnt chop! You'd better not lose him."

Laura held up her hand. "I have his ring and he's mine!"

"Yep," he said. "I'm hers."

They left the table, put up the leftovers, and went back into the front room. Traver loaded the fireplace with more wood until the flames roared and the warm red and orange reflections danced around the room. He ran his hand along the large piece of granite that formed the mantelpiece. It wasn't polished but it wasn't rough either.

Laura saw him and said, "Poppa Joe told me Christmas stories when we used to hang our stockings there for Christmas." She mentioned that she put a big round rock on the mantel to hold her big stocking. "I always got an orange, a tangerine, walnuts, Brazil nuts, almonds, and hazelnuts. And I wanted more, so I hung up a big stocking. All I got that year was stones."

Laura pointed out to him a small name carved in the side of the stone. He peered at it to see "McNeal." She said, "McNeal was the Scot stone mason that built this fireplace and advised Great-Granddad Peterson about this house's construction." She reached for a box of old photos. "Here, this is a picture of him in his uniform." She handed Traver a sepia studio shot. A handsome man stared back at him. He had a big handlebar mustache, hair full and ruffled, and pants held up with suspenders. He was holding a trapdoor rifle. She handed him another picture. "That's Annie, my great-grandmother." Traver was stunned by her resemblance to Laura.

Laura sifted through more pictures and picked up one she clasped to her chest. Looking at Traver, she said wistfully, "I remember this picture," and she handed it to him. Laura looked about five or six years old. Her hair was short and curly, framing her smiling face. "Poppa Joe had just given me my first pony. He told me that if the pony didn't work out, we could eat it!" She smiled warmly at the remembrance.

Traver chuckled. "Sounds like Poppa Joe was a fun person."

Sipping her wine Laura added, "He was the one who put the big windows in this room. The danger of Indians and bandits was pretty much diminished by this time."

"When was that?" he asked.

Laura looked away in thought before speaking again. "I suspect around 1890 to 1895. The plate glass came from Pittsburgh I think."

"What sort of work did they do?" he asked.

"They raised food, well, meat. Great-granddad ran cattle, but he felt other forms of meat would sell better. He raised pigs and chickens along with the cows. He hunted buffalo and all that meat went to the railroad. Of course, as the railroad moved west, he shipped the meat east. A lot of the engineers and workers building the road beds and drilling the tunnels and constructing the trestles and bridges out in the Rockies helped build this place at one time or another."

Laura dug into her picture box again and handed Traver a bundle of old photos. It contained a pictorial history of the raising of the house. In every picture there must have been at least ten to twenty men working at various tasks. Laura said, "He had trained in Sweden to be an engineer and studied mathematics also. I think he came to America in 1855 at the age of twenty. The house is designed to withstand an attack by Indians or bandits and any geological events. The railroad hauled back granite from the construction of the railroad bed and tunnels in the Rockies so Peterson could have it as building materials and he traded meat for the stone. He was familiar with cement, concrete, and mortar mixtures. The doorways and window openings are framed with red brick from Ohio. The roof is cleaved slate tiles so that no flaming arrows can set the place on fire.

All the doors and windows are shielded with half-inch boiler plate over three-inch hardwood doors and window shutters."

"Jesus!" Traver whistled. "This really is a fort!"

"The fireplace radiates heat in three-hundred-sixty degrees all around the home and a water tank, which was a converted old locomotive boiler, which sat above the kitchen. A windmill pumps the water over the back cook area into the house. To select this site, wells were witched to identify good water sources.

"Annie met Corporal Peterson not long after he got out of the army, around 1861 or 1862. She was from England and touring out West. She was stranded here due to Jayhawk activity on the Kansas and Nebraska border. That's how they met."

Traver tossed on a few more logs and Laura continued talking about her ancestors and their home. "You know, I feel like Poppa Joe as I'm telling you about this place. Come here." She took his hand and led him out to the back porch just off the kitchen. She kicked at the mounting snow drifts, unlatched the heavy wooden shutters, and swung them closed over the window. "Those are the original shutters. See all the dents in the boiler plate over the wood? Those are bullet strikes."

He reached out and touched some of the dimples. "You mean there were battles here?"

"No, just stray Indians trying to steal stuff and a few bold Jayhawker bands. Great-granddad ordered a Sharps 50/110 rifle. He could pick off a rustler or a raiding Indian at a thousand yards. Finally the Indian stuff stopped. They were afraid of his big gun. He also bought punt guns, four of them."

"A what gun?"

"Punt guns, two-gauge, single-barrel shotguns. Come here, I'll show you what they were used for." She took him to a corner of the house and removed an eight-by-eight wooden plug so he could see outside. "The parts of the house that weren't able to be covered were the four corners. So these holes were drilled so you could load the punt gun with buckshot, stick it through the hole, and, BOOM, everything coming up to the house gets mowed down. I have three of the punt guns, want to see one?"

"Sure."

Laura led him to the entryway, opened the bench, took out an oilcloth wrap that held the gun.

"Holy shit!" he exclaimed. The hole in the barrel was half-dollar size.

"It's got one hell of a thump."

"I would guess so."

She returned the punt gun to the bench box, and they walked back to the sofa in front of the fireplace. Sharon joined them.

"Traver," Sharon announced, "you feel so right." She looked at her mother a moment. "Mom, I haven't forgotten Dad, but you are glowing and radiating warmth that I haven't seen since he died."

"Thank you, Sharon," Traver said gratefully.

It was quiet a long time before anyone said anything else.

When the clock in the entryway chimed ten times to break the stillness, Laura exclaimed, "God, where does the time go? Let's hit the hay."

She took his hand and they went upstairs together. Laura yelled back at Sharon, "Your room is all fixed up, honey."

"Okay, Mom, night-night."

Traver whispered to Laura, "You and I are going to bed and your daughter is here?"

"She knows that we're going to be a team. She's fine with us being together. In her eyes we're as good as married now."

The bedroom was a bit chilly so Laura went over to the wall heater and turned it up a little. "I wish the fireplace gave off more warmth, I just love the wood heat." They shucked out of their clothes and snuggled in the bed's flannel sheets.

In the morning there was a good nine inches of snow on the ground, and it looked silently beautiful. Traver slid out of bed and kissed Laura. "You stay under the covers and let me do the coffee and get a fire roaring in the hearth."

All that was peeking out from the blankets were her nose and eyes. "Okay," Laura whispered.

He started the pot in the kitchen and poured two cups of coffee, setting the pot back in its holder. He settled in at the breakfast table, his steaming cup of coffee before him. The house was hushed, but outside a gusting wind was moving the ash tree branches. He heard the wind whistling and looked back at the cup of coffee he had poured for Laura. It remained there, steam rising from its hot liquid surface. The cup, which held his attention, had a tiny chip on its rim, although everything else in the kitchen was fuzzy. He was wrapped up in the moment, an inexplicably deep sensation that swallowed his consciousness.

NORTH PLATTE, NEBRASKA, 1860
THE VETERINARIAN

It had snowed just lightly during the night. Siren noticed it through the window as she made coffee in her kitchen. She had spent a restless night, sleep escaping her as she drifted on a sea of thoughts. She often returned to that mysterious experience a few weeks past when that voice, like an ethereal transmission, was heard by her and her crew. That voice had stirred deep waves of emotion in her.

That morning, at the sink in her small home in North Platte, she let her hands rest on the sink's cold porcelain. The small wood fire she had lit in the wood-burning stove smelled so fragrant that she moved to stand beside it, where her blue-and-white speckled pot was beginning to boil her coffee.

Standing there in her robe, she felt the wood-fire warmth to be similar to the warmth she had felt when she listened to that voice calling Skip. They had never determined where the call had originated.

The bubbling coffee attracted Siren's attention. She slid the pot off the stove and went to the cupboard to fetch a cup and saucer. She noticed a small chip on the cup's rim. For some reason she liked this cup. As she poured the steaming black liquid her kitchen seemed to become an isolated place. The coffee cup and saucer and table were in sharp focus, all else was in a fuzzy contrast.

Siren reached for her cup and everything outside of her immediate surroundings seemed to disappear. It was just her, the coffee cup with a chip on the rim, the hot steam curling up, and the warm kitchen.

NORTH PLATTE, NEBRASKA, 1992

THE PETERSON RANCH KITCHEN

The coffee smelled so good. The warm kitchen had that cozy, distinct feeling to it. Traver stirred the steaming cup of coffee. Everything except the table faded.

Slowly a hand came toward the other cup. A beautiful hand, with a pinkish white glow and fingernails ever so clean and pink. He wondered how Laura kept her nails so clean and pretty out here on the ranch and then he thought, *It's her doctor's training, clean hands.* The long fingers grasped the cup of coffee and her fingers reminded him of when she played that haunting melody on the piano in the library room and her wonderful kisses, her warm breast, and her soft melody of loving. He watched her fingers caressing the cup of coffee.

No key ring on her finger, he noticed. *Had she taken it off?* He began to cast his gaze along her left arm and up to her chest. The image looking back at him was not Laura in a blue robe. This image had dark hair and gray eyes and large breasts, a wonderful smile showing pearl white teeth through soft pink-rose lips. He was stunned as the image faded into the rising steam from her coffee cup. Her eyes held his gaze with a ghost-gray and a hint of almond shape. It was not Laura. And then it was just swirling coffee steam and the kitchen.

NORTH PLATTE, NEBRASKA, 1860

Siren reached for her cup of coffee, anticipating its warmth on her lips. Her fingers gently touched the cup's rim, feeling the chipped spot. The steaming coffee was the center of her focus that instant, and she heard that voice echoing in her mind. How could a voice haunt her so? And why so strongly at this moment?

Siren looked up expecting to see her kitchen, but the room she saw was not hers. It was larger and filled with objects she didn't recognize. In fact, in front of her sat a man, deep in thought, his hands cupping his coffee. Then slowly he looked up at her and their eyes welded. In a breath's beat, Siren was back in her kitchen, touching her cup of coffee. Completely alone and looking into nothing.

Siren hesitated briefly in lifting her coffee to her lips. The liquid was hot and rich and quickly her emotions centered on her first sip. Her heart was racing as she sipped again. Her entire body was awakening as she saw again in her thoughts the image of that man.

Siren shook off the puzzling experience, feeling the warmth from the stove. She was feeling the aching loneliness that so often plagued her, yet the vision she had just seen somehow comforted her, easing her gnawing emptiness. This was such a beautiful morning. She felt strongly that she had had a glance at her future.

THE PETERSON RANCH, 1992

NORTH PLATTE, NEBRASKA

What is today without tomorrow and both building on yesterday?

"Traver," Laura said, dissolving the image before him. "The coffee smells out of this world." She came into the kitchen snug in her blue housecoat and reached for the hot cup with her left hand, a replay of what he had just seen.

"You still have your ring on," he muttered.

"Why, yes, I'll never take it off." Sitting down, she added, "Traver, you look a million miles away, are you okay?"

That image came to him again. *Who did I just see?*

"Oh, sure, fine," he mumbled and sipped his coffee. *What an instant! A moment of beauty, what a haunting gaze from those gray eyes.*

Looking over at Laura, he thought, *Just as beautiful.* "I love you, Laura." But again the vision of the woman reaching for the coffee just a moment ago in his daydream appeared.

Sharon came into the kitchen and poured herself a cup of coffee and sat with them at the table.

"Honey, take the crew-cab in case you need the four-wheel drive going into town," Laura said as she took another whiff of her coffee.

"What about you guys?"

"Oh, we don't need to be in town until Monday. The honeymoon comes first and then the marriage!"

They all laughed at that.

Laura said, "We'll fly over to Maxwell."

The three settled down at the breakfast table, savoring their coffee. It was so quiet the wind could be heard blowing in the ash tree outside.

"Mom, as I went to sleep I was thinking . . ." Sharon cut a slight smile, "Traver doesn't have a stone to hold down his Christmas stocking for the mantel."

"Let's go get one!" Laura jumped up but sat right back down again. "Wow! The room is spinning!"

Sharon considered her mom a second before saying, "Mom, I am so happy to see how much fun you're having from last night."

Laura grinned real big. "I think I'm a little hungover." She was quiet and then she got up slowly while looking at Sharon. "Hon, get the sticks." Laura had that little curl at the edges of her lips. Now it was pretty clear someone was going to get teased, and Traver was sure it would be the newest member of this group.

"Put on your coat, Traver," Laura said in a demanding tone.

Sharon came back into the kitchen holding two sticks about five feet long. The sticks looked like whittled-down one by fours, with a handle fashioned approximately a foot up from the bottom.

"What're those for?" Traver wanted to know.

"To help us dislodge the stone you might want," Laura answered.

"Where is my stick?"

Laura again. "There are only two sticks, one for me and one for Sharon." Her slight grin returned. She was still a bit woozy as she glided over to her coat. "Come on, Traver." She waved her hand toward the back door and almost stumbled, which made her giggle.

The snow was still coming down lightly as they went out. "Hey, Laura, is this necessary? Can't we do this when the weather is better?" he asked.

"Sure, we can, but right now is better."

Sharon and Laura weaved as they headed toward the creek. The sticks helped them to keep upright as they walked. He followed them down to the little stream behind the barn. He was taking in the beauty of it all: the white snow blanketing the land, the little stream, not frozen and cutting through the white surface of the snow, and Sharon and Laura tromping along through the drifts. Every now and then they would giggle. They reached the stream first.

"How big of a stocking will you hang up, honey?"

He thought about that for a second. "Oh, about the size of one of my hunting socks, about this big." He gestured with his hands about the size.

"Well, then, come here to the stream's edge and lets look for a pretty smooth one about grapefruit size."

He said to himself, *This really is not necessary right now,* but both Sharon and Laura were prying stones from the sand, discussing each one's good and bad qualities. They used the sticks to push the stones loose and that seemed like a reasonable activity to Traver.

"Hey, honey," Laura yelled, "come see this one!"

He walked over to mother and daughter to see Sharon had pried loose a gray granite one.

Sharon asked if he would pick it up. He bent down and picked it up. Laura asked him to wash the mud from the bottom and he did. Sharon took the stone and hefted it. "Mom, it's too heavy." She handed it to Laura, who commented, "Yes. It weighs too much and, besides, it's too flat." She tossed it back into the stream.

He glanced at Laura, who looked stunning, with snowflakes in her hair and red in her cheeks. Sharon yelled, "Over here! This one is perfect."

Laura and Traver moved over to where Sharon was and saw she had pried loose another stone. Laura asked him to pick up the stone.

"Sure." He bent down with his rear in the air.

WHAP! Sharon landed a swat. Traver's rear stung like it was on fire. Then he heard a rush of air and a big splash. Laura was ready to take her swing at him when she lost her balance and fell into the stream. She screamed when her body hit the icy water. Sharon was doubled over with laughter.

Traver realized what had just happened. The entire rock hunt was a ruse to get him to bend over so both gals could whup him. However, the tables turned for Laura, whose equilibrium was apparently still compromised by last night's wine. Traver started to guffaw in chorus with Sharon.

"This water is freezing!" Laura gasped. Traver gallantly reached out his arm to help her out, and she yanked hard.

"Holy shit!" he yelled and tumbled face down into the stream.

"My God! This water is cold!" Traver yelled. Shivering, they helped each other up and out of the stream. Sharon came over and kissed him. "Welcome to the family, Traver!"

They all three ran for the house and went in through the back door and on into the kitchen. Laura was stripping off her wet clothes as she ran upstairs. "Traver, get a hot shower downstairs before you take a chill!"

In about thirty minutes they were back in the kitchen. Traver was swaddled in a heavy Indian blanket, and Laura appeared in wool socks and thermal drawers.

Sharon chuckled. "Boy! You two are a pair."

Traver got up, holding the blanket around him, and refilled his cup with coffee. He poured Laura another cup, her bright, clear, and sparkly eyes watching him. She laughed again. "I have never missed before!" she exclaimed. "But I'm glad that when I did miss, it was with you."

"Hey," he said, "how often do you pull that stunt?"

"As often as we get green-horns here," Laura retorted.

"Green-horn, huh? Thanks, guys,: Traver said, rubbing his sore bottom.

Laura took her coffee upstairs and in a few minutes she was back dressed in her ranch work clothes. She also carried a rifle with a beaded doeskin sheath. The beadwork was mostly hues of blue along with black and white beads. She put the rifle in the beaded doeskin sheath on the breakfast table. He was looking at the beadwork as she said, "Go ahead, Traver, heft it." He took the sheath off the gun and saw it had an octagon barrel with a beautiful brown patina.

Looking at Laura, he asked, "Is this the 50/110 your great-granddad had?"

"Uh-huh."

He cocked down the lever that lowered the block and peeked down the barrel. "Jeeze, these groves are deep, just like new."

Laura took two shells from her pocket. "Want to smoke it cowboy?" She grabbed the gun and out the back door she went, with him following. Standing on the back step, Laura looked out toward the back road entrance to her home site and shaded her eyes. "See that fifty-gallon drum?" She chambered the 50/110 shell and pulled the lever up, closing the block. She hefted the gun to her shoulder and almost immediately BOOM! WHAP! The drum jumped, and the recoil knocked Laura back slightly. She pulled the lever down and the empty shell ejected. She slid another round in the chamber, turned, and handed him the gun. "Lean into it Traver."

He took the rifle and pulled the lever up to cock the block shut, adjusting his blanket so it wouldn't fall off. He held the gun with his left hand where it balanced nicely. He raised it to his shoulder and, taking a deep breath, exhaled slowly again. The gun went off with a BOOM! WHAP! The barrel jumped, his shoulder lurched back, and his blanket dropped. There he stood, buck assed naked, smoking gun in his hands.

Well, of course, he felt like a goddamn fool. As he handed the gun back to Laura, she said between giggles, "Good shot, cowboy."

He bent down, careful not to expose his bottom for another whacking, grabbed the blanket, and draped it around himself again. Laura leaned up close, "Don't worry, only one spanking." And she laughed deeply.

When they were sitting in the kitchen again and he was looking over the big 50/110, a buzzer sounded and Sharon got up. "Your clothes are dry, Traver." She went to get them.

"You're a good shot, Traver," Laura said. "That barrel you hit is a good fifteen hundred yards away. How did you sight it?"

"Dead on," he said as he wiped the barrel and chamber to remove the oil from their hands. "We need to swab the barrel. I'm using triple X black powder." Laura went to the sink to wash the gun's barrel and oil it. Later in the day, Laura and Traver went to the barrel they'd shot at and both rounds were about a foot apart.

Sharon stayed for lunch and then took the white four-wheel-drive truck back to town. Sharon came over and hugged him. "Good to know you're part of the family, Traver."

He hugged her back. "Thanks, I'll keep my ass out of the way from now on."

"Ah shucks" Laura said, "I was hoping for another shot at it!"

"Mom," Sharon kissed Laura and held her. "I'm happy for you!" Sharon turned and went out the door.

CHAPTER 6

THE HONEYMOON AND THE WEDDING

THE NEXT THREE days they stayed at the ranch visiting, sharing their love, and taking an occasional phone call. It was like they had dropped out of society and the world was theirs alone.

Sunday morning, lying in bed and looking out the window that faced toward the sand hills, Traver put his arm across Laura's stomach. She turned toward him, the sheet falling from her chest and exposing her perky breasts.

"It's going to be warmer today," she said as she sat up.

"You have beautiful breasts, Laura," he whispered as he lightly touched them.

She glowed. "They are in your hands."

About thirty minutes later, as they let their spirits settle back after lovemaking, he said, "We're getting married today."

"Yes, but this has been awfully quick, Traver, are you sure?"

"For me this is just right," he declared.

I held her closely to me and said, "Woman, today is a good day to get married. I don't have any marrying duds with me though." He rubbed her back in a soothing motion. Her face was radiant.

"Your clean boots and jeans and a flannel shirt will do."

Rubbing her rear, he said, "Then let's shake our asses and get married."

"Oh, Traver, you say the most romantic things!"

He chuckled at her. "Only when you're shaking it."

"Traver, you need to stop that or we'll never get to the church on time."

"We have forever, honey."

"Get dressed!" she ordered playfully.

We made coffee and got around. He headed toward the Cadillac out front that Sharon had left when she took her mom's truck.

"No, honey," Laura said as she headed over to the quonset building with the huge front door at least thirty feet across. She unlocked the sliding doors, and as she rolled one door aside Traver saw a Stearman biplane with yellow wings and a black fuselage. He rolled the other door aside.

"You fly, too?" he asked.

"Yep!" She turned and looked at the plane. "This was Bill's baby. But I don't mean anything by that statement, Traver, it was just his greatest toy. This damned old plane." She kissed him and went over to the prop, pulling it through about eight times.

"Get in, cowboy. Front seat and step where the footprints are painted or you'll fall through the cloth wing. Buckle in and don't touch anything!" She climbed into the back cockpit and fooled around with the switches. He saw the stick rotate and the rudder pedals go in and out. "Clear!" she yelled. The big radial engine coughed and spit fire and smoke and exploded into action as it caught and began to spin the prop. Laura ran the R.P.M.s up a bit and the engine smoothed out and the plane began rolling slowly out of the building.

Out in the open, Laura let the engine idle down a bit. She yelled at him over the noise, "Got to warm up, we'll be in the air ten minutes or thereabouts. Going over the saddle and then northeast to Maxwell. Hang on!" She punched the engine and they began to roll.

Laura ran down the driveway to take off.

"Whee!" Traver called out as the biplane lifted in less than five hundred feet.

"She's low on fuel and light. I'll fly over to North Platte and fill up before we return. We're going to go at only five hundred feet so you can see the country."

The plane banked and they headed over to the saddle. "Hey!" Laura yelled. "Let's take a 360 over the canyon that Twin Bears came down."

Traver scanned the ground below. It looked like the other canyons to him.

Laura headed northeast over to Maxwell. There in a wide valley nestled a church, its lonely spire pointing skyward. About twenty to thirty vehicles lined up out front and there was an old Piper Cub plane parked there, too.

She lined up and buzzed the gravel road. A truck coming down pulled to a stop. Laura did a wing-over and realigned, letting it down on the road and then taxiing into the church parking lot. She killed the radial engine and as it windmilled to a stop, they stood up and stretched, got out, and jumped to the ground.

"Goddamn that was fun—but cold!" Traver crowed.

"Best ride I've had in years," she said as she kissed him. She put her arms in his and they walked toward church.

Folks were filing in, and Laura and Traver joined the crowd.

"Just a moment, honey," Laura whispered. She went over to the pastor and hugged him. They talked several moments, and he looked over at Traver and smiled and then hugged Laura again. She took off the key ring Traver had given her and gave it to the pastor. She was beaming as she returned. Taking his arm, she said, "I'm getting married today!"

After the service the pastor stepped away from the lectern, smiling and looking at the congregation. "Folks, Dr. Laura is getting married today."

There was a slight murmur of surprise expressed by the congregation and then clapping. "Also, folks, I have an unusual ring here. It looks like a key ring and Laura tells me that it's the most valuable thing she has. Please, Dr. Laura and Traver, step forward. Laura, you'll need to get me a license tomorrow for this to be legal as far as the state is concerned."

Laura smiled back at him. "I have to come to town tomorrow anyway, no problem."

Within no time they were introduced as husband and wife.

Traver and Laura spied Skip and Kathy and quickly went over to them. Kathy and Laura hugged. Skip patted Laura on the shoulder. "You kids take good care of each other," and he sniffled.

Traver shook Skip's hand and said warmly, "Thanks, man, you and Kathy are the best."

Skip added, "You all come over when you get settled and let's have some steak, green beans and some of my best goulash."

After about an hour of visiting with the churchgoers and accepting congratulations, they got in the Stearman and flew over to the landing field at North Platte, fueled up, and headed home. Traver helped Laura swing the plane around, with him on one wing and her on the other, and they pushed the plane back into its hangar. Making sure that everything was off and secured, Laura put metal plugs in the exhaust. She said that a ground squirrel had gotten into a pipe years ago, and when she cranked the engine its guts blew everywhere. "Yuck!" Traver scrunched his face at that bit of news.

They walked arm in arm back to the ranch house. "Mrs. Traver Wells," Laura said wistfully as she squeezed his arm fondly. "I'm sure glad you showed up in my life, Traver."

They got into the house, and he put a fire in the hearth. Laura called the hospital and made sure that Twin Bears was still being released tomorrow. "Everything is still a go for Twin Bears," she told Traver as she hung up the phone.

Their Sunday was one of talking and visiting together. Before they knew it, midnight was chiming on the hall clock, "Bedtime?" Laura questioned. The groom sighed, got up, chunked a few logs on the fire, and closed the spark screen.

Laura took his hand. "I love you." Her dark eyes sparkled.

The next morning they went to into Maxwell, changed vehicles, and drove over to North Platte Hospital. Twin Bears was ready to leave. *Poor fellow,* Traver thought, *a bundle of buckskins, a bow and arrow, a knife and nothing else.* Someone had dressed Twin Bears in a jogging suit and new tennis shoes. He looked like he belonged to today.

"Twin Bears," Traver said as he extended his hand to shake. The Indian grasped it warmly, saying, "Traver." His English was improving rapidly.

Laura said, "Hi, Twin Bears." He smiled and shook her hand. She continued, "We're going to have you as a guest, as long as you like, out to our place. You can stay in the big house with Traver and me or you can stay in the bunk house. You choose when we get there."

Laura drove the crew cab toward the ranch, with Twin Bears in the front seat and Traver in the back. Twin Bears began to express how he understood where he was at the moment. He was confused because he recognized natural features around him, and yet he knew things were different. He sounded like he wanted to go back.

As they passed the Enchanted Canyon, Twin Bears said, "My mother was born over there." He pointed toward the north. "A gentle spirit came from a giant silver moon and loved his grandmother, and when his mother was born a golden moon shone.

His grandmother had a girl, Two Moons, his mother. That is why Twin Bears hunted in that area so often. It made him feel close to his mother, since she was gone now. "What do you call this place today?" Twin Bears asked.

Laura said, "This is the Frenchman, but we call it Enchanted Canyon, too."

Twin Bears said, "The spirits are very strong here." After a long silence he added, "I knew this Frenchman. He taught me to speak French, and he was a good man."

Twin Bears turned to look at Traver. "Skip's father knows so very much about my people. I like talking with him, but it makes me homesick. I saw pictures in a book of some of the people of my camp. Skip's dad said all in the pictures were now spirits. That makes me sad." Twin Bears wiped his cheeks, dotted with tears, but he said slowly, "But I have new friends."

When they drove into the Enchanted Canyon area, Laura asked if he wanted to stop.

"Can we?" Twin Bears asked.

"No problem," Laura answered. She took the north fork of the road and headed over to the canyon. The western sun was streaming into their eyes, almost blinding them. Twin Bears stared at the canyon. He pointed. "Over there, we would spend the fall. Maybe ten or twelve of us. We hunted and dried berries and deer meat."

Laura smiled at the Indian and said, "Yes, there's still evidence around there of some occupation." She addressed him again, "Were you married? Did you have a family?"

He looked at her. "A long time ago. But my woman died giving me a brave. No, I did not take another."

Laura covered his hand with hers. "I know how you feel. I lost my husband, but look what showed up in my life." And she jerked a thumb over her shoulder toward Traver.

Twin Bears perked up. "You two are still moonstruck." They all laughed.

When they left Enchanted Canyon and pulled into the ranch, Twin Bears said the main house was too big, and he took up in the bunkhouse. They left him there. He had a TV, which he turned on right away. As Laura and Traver walked to the house, Laura said, "Traver, help me with Bill's closets. I think Twin Bears can wear Bill's things."

"Bill's things?"

Laura looked at Traver." It was so very hard to get rid of them. I had lost Bill, so I held on to his stuff. It helped my day-to-day existence. But I'm stronger now, with your love and how you make me feel."

They took a load of Bill's things to Twin Bears. The late afternoon and early evening was a sort of fashion show. Twin Bears tried on every piece of clothing. The boots were too tight, but everything else fit well. Twin Bears said, "I am a very wealthy man with all this. Thank you, Dr. Laura."

As the weeks rolled by, Skip's dad came over to talk to Twin Bears and go fishing with him. There was a large cache of walleye fish in the freezer and cottontail rabbits, too. Laura went over now and then to visit with Twin Bears, finding that her guest settled in quite well.

After Twin Bears got settled in, Roy agreed to look in on him while Laura and Traver went to California for a honeymoon. Traver needed to tend to things at his ranch and put it up for sale.

Laura loved his place, and it was so beautiful with all the fruit trees around. She loved the house and especially the bedroom.

They stayed right at three weeks. During their stay in California they were called by Laura's foreman. It seemed that Twin Bears had gone missing. The foreman had seen Twin Bears the morning before, heading out toward Enchanted Canyon. He was walking and had waved at the foreman.

Laura had the sheriff go out to the ranch and take a missing person's report from her foreman. After she got the news, Laura said, "Traver, my God, I hope Twin Bears hasn't gotten hurt somewhere out there. You think there's a possibility that he found his way home?"

He shrugged his shoulders. "Hard to say, he sure went out there a lot. I suspect he was still homesick."

Laura came into the front room at the California ranch and sat next to Traver on the couch. She leaned over to him and with her bare foot pushed on the coffee table. "You know, honey, I did not realize what an operation you have out here."

"It's been good to me," he replied. "Lots of money came through here. I'm awfully glad that I invested most of it."

"Traver," she said slowly, "while you were at the real estate office this afternoon, the phone rang. I thought it was you so I answered it. It was a Mary Lou calling for you."

"Oh? Did she tell you what she wanted?"

"She said for you to call Dr. Hickman." Laura was quietly waiting so he put his arms around her.

"Mary Lou and I dated now and then, mostly when she wanted to," he sighed.

"She is a doctor?" Laura asked.

"Yes. A general practitioner, actually she is my doctor."

"No. Nooooo, she isn't. I'm your doctor. Were you guys serious?"

"No, she wanted a man around when she went out."

Laura added to that, "And sex all the time?"

"I would have liked that, but she wasn't horney like you are."

"Horney!" Laura whooped and whopped him on the head.

"Traver, invite her for lunch, and tell her you're married and that I will be along. I am curious to see if she comes to lunch."

"Honey, she's a fox. She looks like a Playboy centerfold."

"A fox?" Laura mumbled. Then she looked up and grinned. "And how many tarts will get their hearts broken now that you and I are hooked up?"

"Oh, probably ten or twenty at least."

Laura stood up and flashed a grin that showed her perfect teeth. "I'll just have to get you back to Nebraska pretty quick before all your tarts come around!"

He reached for his cell phone on the coffee table and navigated to Mary Lou's number. There were several rings before she answered. "Hey, Mary Lou, Traver here . . . Yes, I got your message. Dr. Laura Peterson gave it to me. I know you don't recognize her name, she's not from here. She is from Nebraska. She is the county coroner there. Douglas County, Nebraska . . . No, no, she and I are married." It was quite a few minutes before he could say anything else. "This happened on the hunting trip a few months back . . . No . . . This is the first time I've been back here. Say, Laura wants to know if you are free for lunch tomorrow with us? If you are, meet us at the Smuggler's Fashion Fair bar at one o'clock . . . Okay, it will be great to see you too." He hung up and looked over at Laura. "Now, don't be getting catty tomorrow."

"Who me?" she answered innocently.

He rubbed her rear and then said, "Yes, you. Jeeze, Laura, how does your ass keep getting better and better looking?"

It wasn't long before their bodies were coupled in passion and they both exploded. Afterward, they kissed gently and longingly.

"Mr. Wells," Laura moaned, "what are you doing to me?"

"Why, Dr. Peterson, I am stealing your heart."

"It's Dr. Wells now, sir, and how can you steal that which I give you freely?"

She put her head against his chest, and he cradled her in his arms and became her shelter, her island of safety, and her deepest love. He, too, fell asleep. At around two or three o'clock in the morning, they stirred about on the couch, got up, and went to bed.

They awoke around eight-thirty in the morning. They just lazed around, deciding what to take back to Nebraska and what to sell at the yard sale. He felt that since Laura's place was furnished, he should sell all his furniture. Laura was in the bathroom fixing up while he was rummaging around his dresser, packing his clothing.

"Laura!" he called. "Do you think Roy would appreciate some of the kitchen stuff like the freezer and refrigerator and the washed and dryer?"

"Probably," she said. "But if not, I'd bet that Sharon could use them. Honey, how should I dress for lunch? I want Dr. . . . ah, what's her name . . ." She giggled. "To see what a fox you caught."

He smiled to himself, stopped what he was doing, and went into the bathroom where Laura was facing the full-length mirror. She was wearing a bluish-pink bra and panties, and from behind he could see her front and rear. Stepping closer, he reached out and tickled her ass. Laura swallowed and placed both hands on the bathroom sink, closed her eyes, and took a deep breath. "You stir my very depths of existence." She turned to face him, her chest heaving, nipples erect and skin flushed. He stepped into her opened arms and they held each other.

"Oh, Dr. Wells, you have great bathroom manners," he whispered.

The ringing of the phone interrupted them, and he picked it up. "Hello? . . . Good morning Mary Lou. No, we are just waking up. Thanks for calling." He was quiet as Mary Lou talked. "Okay. We can be there at two-thirty instead of one o'clock. Yes, Laura is looking forward to meeting you also."

Laura rolled over in bed and said, "Damn! I feel like I'm meeting your former wife. This is such a strange feeling, Traver."

He kissed her. "Whatever happens, you will be enchanting."

That word echoed in Laura's thoughts. Enchanting was a word that said it all regarding her feelings for him.

As Laura got out of bed she turned and looking back over her shoulder, her hair fluffed all about, she whispered, "Yes, and you're the wizard I love." Her back was so smooth, with the vertebrae showing the muscles in her back. "Let's get around, Big Boy, you take a shower and shave."

"Yes, ma'am."

They pulled into Smugglers a little after two in the afternoon and didn't see Mary Lou's Vet in the parking lot.

"She's not here yet?" Laura asked.

"No."

"I'm a bit nervous, Traver." They got out of his crew-cab truck. Laura had chosen a full white skirt that didn't even begin to show off her ass, although her blouse did give a wonderful view of her firm upcurved breasts. She wore three-inch heels, which put her right at his height of six-three.

"Mrs. Wells, you look stunning."

"Why, bless you, you say the nicest things. Just what a girl needs to hear."

They went into Smugglers, were seated and ordered plain tomato juice.

Laura said to him, "She's here, Traver."

His back was to the door and he didn't turn to look.

Laura gasped. "She stunning!"

Almost immediately he heard Mary Lou's Southern drawl. "Traver, it's good to see you."

He stood up and turned. Holy shit! Mary Lou did look breathtaking. They hugged and he turned to Laura as she stood up. "Dr., Dr.—ummm," he stumbled. Laura smiled broadly and reached out her hand. "I'm Laura."

Mary Lou smiled. "Mary Lou." And they shook hands.

Awfully damned nice of them, Traver thought.

They sat down and ordered, although he was not as relaxed as he had hoped to be. As he and Laura drove home, she sat next to him. "Traver, Mary Lou is gorgeous."

He patted her leg. "I have never seen her looking like that before. It's apparent that she really got fixed up today. But it is you I got, babe."

She looked at him in the rear view mirror. "Yep! I got you babe!" She placed her hands on his right leg and stared out the front window of the truck. "Traver, she's beautiful and she's young."

He took his right hand from the steering wheel and covered her hands that were resting on his thigh and squeezed. "Laura, that relationship was on her terms, and I was okay with that, but you're another situation. Besides, you got the best ass in the world."

The next morning they hooked up the U-Haul trailer and headed west. They picked up I-80 out of Sacramento and decided to do some sightseeing and visited a few state and national parks on their way back to Laura's ranch. They took two weeks going back to Nebraska. It took them most of the afternoon to tote in all his stuff from California. Laura wanted everything in its place.

"Honey, I'll get supper started," Traver volunteered.

"Good."

He dug out the last of the walleye fish from the freezer, which put him in mind of Twin Bears. He had been gone almost six weeks. He started the rice, defrosted the fish, then put the asparagus on.

Laura came in and sat down. "What are we having tonight, cowboy?"

"Walleye, rice, and asparagus, with a sauce for the rice."

"Ummm! I'm going up and shower, be back in a few minutes."

When dinner was finished, they sat in the kitchen and watched the sun disappear through the back door window. Laura cleaned her plate twice. "That's damn good fixin's, mister, I'll keep you around a bit longer." Laura sighed. "That fish got me thinking about Twin Bears. I hope he somehow got back home again in his own time. He used to go out there a lot, maybe he was there just in time when the door opened, so to speak, and he walked right through it again."

CHAPTER 7

TWIN BEARS RETURNS

SPRING HAD COME and gone and early summer was upon them. Some wonderful lightning and thunderstorms came in from the north. Skip and his dad had begun to dig deeper into researching the history of the Frenchman and Enchanted Canyon area. They discovered an interesting account of "Crazy Frenchy," a young man who trapped in the Platte River around the 1840s or so. While on one of the trips running his trap lines, he came upon a beautiful maiden who he thought was an Indian, and they became friends. She accompanied him on his trap lines.

She was interested in Frenchy's friends and where they lived. On the following trip, in checking his trap lines, she came with him again. Frenchy awoke the next morning to find that she had gone. A storm had come through the area and her tracks were easy to follow. They ended in the westernmost part of the canyon and her tracks just stopped in mid-stride, and she was nowhere to be found. Frenchy camped in the meadow the rest of the season, but she didn't reappear. Is that when Remington met Frenchy? Yes. The old man spent the rest of his life waiting for her return but he died never seeing her again. But Remington painted Star Thrower from Frenchy's descriptions.

"It sounds like our experience with Twin Bears," Laura said to Traver.

"Similar, but in reverse," he said. "If this is true, then how many others have gone back and forth? It would be interesting to know how many folks have been missing from here."

"I've never even considered that aspect," Laura said. "Folks disappearing from here and showing up in the past?"

"And folks showing up that seem to be out of place," he added.

Laura thought briefly. "We have owned this place since 1861, so there are not a lot of people that have been out on this private land." She got up. "It's late, Traver. Come to bed and let's dream together."

"Dream?"

"Wouldn't it be wonderful if I could get pregnant and we could have a couple of babies?"

"No, honey, we are too old to chase after children."

She frowned at him. "Okay, then we can borrow Sharon's child when she gets pregnant."

"Great!" He rubbed Laura's tummy. "Let's go practice making a baby!"

*　　*　　*

The next morning as they were having breakfast, they heard the dogs barking. There was a knock at the back porch screen door and Laura went to answer it. Within seconds she shouted, "It's Twin Bears!"

Traver jumped to his feet and ran to the back door, and there stood Twin Bears wearing his buckskins and all of his hunting gear. He had a grin on his face. "Did you miss me?"

Laura grabbed him. "Where have you been?"

"Any coffee and doughnuts?" he asked, sniffing the air.

They laughed as Laura grabbed his hand and pulled him inside. "Come in, come in!" She put her arm around his shoulders and steered him into the kitchen.

It was suspenseful as Traver and Laura waited for Twin Bears to tell them what happened.

"I have been home. It is still there and I was missed. The canyon opens and closes during lightning storms," he explained. "Sometimes it stays open perhaps one or two days. I will stay here for now and maybe go back home during the next storm." He studied them for a long moment and then in a strange voice asked, "Would you come with me the next time the canyon opens to my camp and be in my day? You can still come back here."

Laura closed her eyes to mere slits as she considered the idea. Her look conveyed thousands of words. Finally in a quiet and subdued voice she said, "Well, we'll think on it, but for now, tell us about home."

"Is it a very long journey?" Traver asked in wonderment.

"There is not much to tell. Everyone thought I had gone on a long hunt." He took a sip of coffee and looking at us over the rim of his coffee cup he grinned. "It was a long journey, I suppose, more than a hundred years. My dog was happy to see me," he added.

Laura smiled her lovely smile. "Our dogs sure do fuss when we don't come home, even for just one day."

"I sure have missed you and the TV, and I've really missed Pepsi!" He said it as a joke, but in fact he really meant it. He asked again, "Come to my camp with me, for just a bit?"

It was stone quiet for a few seconds and then it was Traver who spoke first. "You mean that the canyon is still open?"

Twin Bears paused. "Traver, I am not sure, but while I have been gone, I have been able to pass twice. I just didn't come right back here. I wanted to see how long of a time the pass would stay open. Most times it's been at least a day. Each time I have gone back and forth I think I have come back always to the running time. It's always as if I have just left my camp in regular time. I had been gone one and a half moons, six or seven weeks by your figuring, right?"

"Correct," Laura said.

Traver tapped his finger on the table in thought as he considered this. "So it seems as though the pass is connected to a specific run of time, and as you go back and forth there is no chance of overtaking yourself?"

Laura said, "That makes sense, Traver."

He continued, "I was thinking that time is just man's way of ordering his activity from day to year, and we really don't have any idea of existence without time as a reference point."

"How about those creation stories, like those of the Hopi, for example, where they came from the third world to this world, the fourth world, via a cave? Doesn't that sound awfully close to Twin Bears coming from his world to ours? But ours is already peopled. What if a hunting band that was also moving their camp came through Enchanted Canyon and no one was there? Do you think the story of creation would go like 'The people were wandering and settled in a new land'? Perhaps passing through a gate, a door, or whatever that momentarily connected the places. Those doors, or gateways, or caves could even be planet to planet or star system to star system," Laura said.

Traver could tell Laura's quick mind had caught his meaning. "Time travel," she mused. "The universe's way of dealing with distance and populating the star's worlds. Just a moment." Laura got up from the table and went into the front of the house to the library. After about three minutes she returned with a very old book, red leather bound with gold-edged pages. Traver reasoned it was a Bible of some sort. "Here, Traver, read this."

He looked at the title, "Cloak of the Dawn."

"Laura," he sounded surprised, "what are you doing with this book?"

"Oh, it's great-granddad's book. He brought it and a few engineering books with him when he came to America." She thought a moment. "I think that was 1856. I got interested in it when I became a doctor. I always wondered about the entwined snakes forming the caduceus, a badge of being a doctor. This interprets snakes as representing worm holes, you know, space's stellar freeways. Read it. I think you'll see the connection with the Canyon and Twin Bears going back and forth between his time and our time. And just maybe some Masonic stuff."

When Traver read it, he was impressed with how the text described events that were similar to what had just happened with Twin Bears. He always believed that what people did not understand was attributed to God or the angels.

"I haven't read this book in a long time. Time, ha!" Laura exhaled abruptly. "Boy, it takes on a new meaning now with all that has occurred. What interested me in this book was the description of magical cures. According to this text, there is a goddess related to serpents, and the serpents are considered a worm hole that connects to universal bodies. I was interested in this because at times these worms were called Tura or Dura. Guess what? The outermost layer of the membrane system protecting the spinal cord is called 'dura matter.' This must go back to Egyptian times. I think there's a relationship here."

Later Laura and Traver were deep in thought about time travel and the universe when Twin Bears interrupted them, saying, "Come with me."

This broke into Traver's daydream. "What?"

"Come with me," Twin Bears repeated. "Let's go look at my time. I think the pass will stay open to at least tonight and probably tomorrow morning."

Laura said, "That might be risky. If we go, we better take some extra stuff in case we get shut out of getting back home for a couple of weeks."

She got up to call Sharon and her ranch foreman. He and his crew were up north fixing fences. Traver heard her saying into her cell phone, "Traver and I might be gone for a few weeks, not sure yet. Okay. Thanks."

She shut down the cell phone and looked at Twin Bears. "You fix the Thermos and I'll get my day pack."

Traver got his day pack and strapped on his .45 caliber pistol. He tossed in a box of shells and a few boxes of MREs, so they wouldn't starve. They drove the crew cab out to the canyon. Laura put the keys in the ashtray, and they started walking.

"Hey, Twin Bears, what does it feel like when you're going through?" Traver wanted to know.

"It feels something like this." He spread his arms and turned around.

"Boy, that's weird." I said. "You feel nothing."

As we entered the middle canyon Laura piped up, "This is the most gentle of the three canyons. It's like an unpaved freeway roadbed. Look at how wide it is and how it gently slopes upward." A pause. "A highway to heaven."

When they got to the top, Twin Bears stopped and pointed west and a bit south. Traver's mouth dropped open and so did Laura's. Off in the distance, at probably three miles, was a small camp of about thirty teepees. Twin Bears said, "My camp is in that direction." He pointed nearly due west but they could not see anything. "We are now in my day."

Laura turned and looked behind them; the truck was nowhere to be seen. "Look, honey!" she exclaimed. "Behind us!"

Traver turned and whispered, "Jesus, we are actually here!" His voice had a catch.

Laura turned to Twin Bears. "Can we walk back down the canyon from the top here and be back into my day?"

"Yes, but just a minute." He put two fingers between his lips and made a noise that sounded like a turkey. Off in the distance a dog began barking wildly. Off to the left, out of a clump of dwarf cedar trees, came a scroungy, skinny dog, almost wolf-looking. Twin Bears was smiling. "There's my dog, Lunch." He laughed loudly. "I tell him the only reason I keep him is if I fail to capture a deer for food, I shall eat him. I think he understands that, too!" Traver could have sworn that Lunch was smiling at him. The dog ran around the group several times, sniffing at their strangeness and stirring up a cloud of dust. Twin Bears grunted and Lunch stopped and hunched flat down on the ground, watching them.

"Let's go back," Twin Bears said. He slapped his leg and Lunch came to him and stayed. They picked their way back down the middle canyon, and after about a hundred yards Laura spoke up, "Look, Traver."

She pointed at where the truck could be seen. Laura started backing up and all of a sudden she disappeared. Within seconds she reappeared. "That was spooky! All of a sudden you are there and then you are not. I've never had a sensation like that before. You are either here or there." She looked at Traver rather funny and then stepped back away from him and faded out again.

She phased back as she walked back into their day and time.

"Traver, there's some vision distortion, like trees and shrubs shifting places. But it's so quick you don't notice it at first. Then I watched and very slowly stepped back into yesterday and then into today again."

Traver asked Twin Bears, "How long has this been this way?"

Looking up at the sun, the Indian said, "Since before sun-up."

"Do you think it will hold for a while?" Traver inquired.

"No, the storm was a little one last night."

Laura came over to Traver and embraced him. "Honey, let's go home, I'm really not ready to go any farther yet."

He held her close, patted her rear, and turned to their companion. "Twin Bears, are you coming with us?" Traver looked at Lunch. "Him, too?"

Twin Bears answered, "You bet, TV, coffee and doughnuts and Pepsis."

"Damn, Twin Bears," Traver shook his head, "you're starting to sound like you'd rather be in our time than back there."

The Indian was silent a moment. "Yes. A difficult decision. Old friends there and new friends here. A tough choice," he said seriously. "I walk and love two lands."

Laura said, "No, you walk one land but love two times."

Twin Bears mulled that over. "Yes. Like two beautiful squaws."

They got back to the truck and Twin Bears opened the door. Lunch was not going to get in. They began to drive off slowly. Lunch ran alongside about twenty yards, as Laura drove toward the fence line. She stopped and Twin Bears made that turkey noise again. Lunch ran up to them but stopped short of getting in the truck. Laura drove farther, and Lunch followed. After about a mile, Lunch jumped into the back seat with Twin Bears. The dog was still uneasy and wide-eyed, but he tried to take his cue from his master.

As they pulled into the front of the ranch house, all the dogs came up barking and Lunch barked right back. It took a few minutes for them to get used to each other, but they did. Twin Bears headed over to his bunkhouse, yelling over his shoulder that he would see them tomorrow.

Once Laura and Traver were back in the house, Laura turned to him, running her hands over the front of her jeans. "I was back and forth a couple of times today, and I was afraid I would lose you." Her dark eyes showed a longing for him to understand. "When I was back in time I had completely lost you. What if I had gotten stuck there without you or Twin Bears?" She put her head on his chest and her arms around his waist. "I cannot live without you, Traver."

He bent his head down and kissed her. "I felt the same loss when you disappeared. You were a hundred years in the past and I couldn't do anything to help you." They hugged tightly. "From now on, we only go in and out together."

"Okay! That's a deal! Together," Laura said emphatically.

"Are we going to go back again?" she asked.

"Let's think about it," Traver said quietly.

Exhilarated and exhausted by their time travel, Laura and Traver went to bed. In the morning, he awakened to stare at his lover, tangled in the sheets, with a luscious leg and foot hanging off the mattress. One arm arched across the top of her pillow, just above her golden hair, and her hand rested on her stomach, holding the sheet in place. She breathed lightly, her lips parted only enough to allow in the summer-morning breeze. Traver rose to one elbow, to look at her more closely.

A few strands of hair had fallen across her forehead. He reached over and gently brushed them aside. Her face glowed, as though a sunrise was blooming in her skin. He looked at the muscles in her neck and remembered how sensuous it was kissing her neck and tickling her ears with his tongue.

She rolled over and placed her head on his chest, her honey-gold hair tickling his nose. Their naked bodies seemed to lose boundaries, Traver couldn't tell where he began and where Laura began, they felt like one body. She raised her head and kissed him. "Let's get around. I've been thinking about a trip back to 1860."

"How can you think about getting around at a time like this?" Traver whispered.

WESTWARD HO!

The morning presented a hard freeze. It was tough for the lovers to get out from under the warm sheets.

They showered together, put on their work jeans, and went downstairs. At breakfast Laura said that they should go to the library and see what was happening in 1860 around here.

"What I remember from school is that the Pony Express had a route through here about then. Abraham Lincoln was President, or had just been elected," Laura declared. "Fort McPherson was established in 1863 or 1864. Fort Cottonwood was an older name for McPherson. I seem to remember an Indian war in 1864. Let's do the research. We don't want to drop in and be clueless."

She continued, "I was also thinking about transportation. No cars or trucks then. We'll want to ride in. I have some excellent stock, good horses. For example, Fort McPherson is only six miles from the canyon, south by east. Riding, that is only a few hours, but walking, that's a day at least."

Traver gazed at her. "You are really getting into this, aren't you?"

"I sure as hell am!" she said, grinning. "Twin Bears can guide us, and if we study up on the history, we can avoid making mistakes. We don't want to become a part of history."

They finished breakfast and went out to the bunkhouse to see if Twin Bears wanted to go into town. He said sure, but he wanted to stop off at Skip's dad's place and visit. He didn't want to go all the way into town. He said he'd like some doughnuts. He gave me a Liberty sitting half-dollar coin dated 1860 that was in mint condition.

Traver glanced at the coin and told Twin Bears, "A half-dollar in this condition is worth at least eight hundred dollars."

The Indian's eyes widened.

As they pulled away from Skip's dad's place, Laura said, "The library in North Platte will have the information we need. Take the second exit and go to Fourth Street and turn left. The library will be on the left side."

They spent the entire day there, unearthing 1860 to 1865. Laura brought him a Xeroxed copy of a picture from a book. "Look here, honey. The McDonald place in 1860 at Cottonwood Springs. That's below the south channel of the Platte River, near my place but closer to Bradley. Look at how the women are dressed, those long dresses and bonnets."

He smiled at her, "You would create a scene, showing up in your jeans like a man."

"But look at the men all dressed up. This photo was probably taken on a Sunday, they're so dressed up."

"Well, you had better wear some sort of skirt instead of pants," he advised.

She laughed. "I'm wearing that old split skirt, and no big fluffy sort of clothes. We will make friends with McDonald. We probably should ride over and introduce ourselves if we go."

Laura showed Traver her research.

"There were two forts in Nebraska before 1860: Fort Kearney in 1848 at Grand Island and Fort Laramie in 1849. Stationed at Fort Cottonwood were Seventh Iowa Cavalry, Company G, First Nebraska Veteran Volunteer Cavalry, First Nebraska Mounted Militia, Company A, Company B. Four twelve-pound cannon, two three-inch Parrot guns, one hundred mule wagons and equipment.

"Look here, Traver, here's a sketch of Fort Cottonwood. Look at how close the artist put the river. I don't think the river ever flooded this far south.

She pointed at the two pictures, Fort Cottonwood and Fort McPherson. "I didn't know that Cottonwood and McPherson were the same forts. That's interesting. See here, on the plat map? This is Ben's place, you hunted there. Right here is Frankie's father's place. Over here, where Cottonwood turns into State Farm Road, that's the road you took to hunt off South Canyon Road on Gary's place."

Laura pondered the two sketches. "Great-Granddad Peterson bought Sections 5, 9, 3, and 11 from Union Pacific. It was four sections. Later on he bought Sections 15 and 17. Section 13 was up for sale, but he was superstitious and wouldn't buy it."

She leaned back in the library chair and looked up. "There was an old family legend about how great-granddad befriended one of the Oregon Trail travelers who died and left the contents of his wagon to him. I remember grandmother saying that there was a small chest of gold coins. He used all the gold to purchase the land."

She looked over at Traver. "We still own all that plus three more sections that I bought. The old Ferris place and the Adolph land and E.O. land were picked up around 1908. That part is just six thousand acres. After World War II, dad picked up another ten thousand acres toward

Bradley, across the river. Both ranches operated as one but the Bradley place is leased out. Maybe someday Sharon will run it and I'll sign it over to her."

"Just how far back does your family go in this area?" Traver asked.

Laura thought a moment. "In 1858 great-granddad was stationed at Fort Cottonwood. He was a corporal when he mustered out in 1860, just before the Civil War. He probably would have left if he hadn't been helped by that man in the wagon train."

"What was that man's name?"

"I really don't know. I never heard anyone say what his name was."

Traver tapped his finger on the table in thought. "You know, if we go back, it's possible you may run into your Great-Granddad Peterson."

"To tell the truth," Laura looked serious, "I've thought about running into James Peterson. Would he recognize me? Mom used to tell me I looked just like great-grandmother when she was young. In 1860 and 1861, James wasn't married. He met great-grandmother in late 1861 or 1862, I believe. She was from Swindon, England, and her name was Annie. We never did know what she was doing out here in the middle of nowhere. I always thought she was exploring the West. I heard that she was tough as nails and gentle as a sparrow."

"Well," Traver said, "you could run into him. Do you think you'd recognize him?"

"Yes," Laura said matter of factly. "I'll know him. I have seen his picture."

Traver speculated about what identities they should assume, maybe land speculators from the East.

"Oh, sure, that will get us into trouble right off the bat! Everyone hated land dealers. How about being railroad right-of-way purchasing agents? I think the railroad began showing up about the time we'll be there." She thought a moment. "The gold spike was driven at Ogden, Utah, in 1869, so I feel sure that by 1863 or 1864, the rail service was a daily occurrence, at least to North Platte anyway."

"We'll need some form of money if we stay any length of time in the past," Traver was thinking of practical matters.

"Gold," Laura suggested. "The problem is that we'll have to pay three hundred dollars now and back then it was worth only twenty dollars an ounce or less. We'll purchase bars and melt them down into little nuggets," Laura was full of ideas. "We'll also take some good firearms. You pack some exotic pistols and I'll bring a couple AK-47s, full automatic with the hundred-round drum and ten or twenty round clips. We can pack most of that in the saddlebags. We'll pack in some MREs and set up camp with Twin Bears. This could be quite an outing."

They Xeroxed copies of the research, picked up their stuff, and headed over to Skip's dad place. Twin Bears was having a Pepsi, and he waved "hi" at them.

Laura said, "Are you ready to leave?"

Skip's dad, Mitch, said, "He's going to stay here with us a few days so we can visit more."

Twin Bears looked at Laura, as if to ask if that was okay.

Laura said, "No problem, at least you won't burn out the TV."

They laughed.

"Twin Bears, have you talked about the trails you know from your day to Mitch?" Traver wondered.

"No."

"Just a minute." Traver went out to the truck and brought back a state map and copies of state maps from the Pony Express years. "You transfer the routes today onto the copied maps. It will help us orient ourselves while we're back there."

Mitch looked up. "Are you going back soon?"

Traver glanced over to Laura before saying, "No. Laura and I want to get to know 1860 a bit better at this end, and I need to get a lot more time in the saddle before we leave."

Mitch offered, "Take a wagon so you can carry enough supplies." He looked at Twin Bears. "Can you drive a wagon?"

"I can learn," the Indian replied. "I'll stay here a couple more days and learn to drive a wagon, okay?"

"Sure, no problem."

*   *   *

Laura and Traver got into the crew cab and headed out South Canyon Road to Laura's place. It was silent except for some gravel hitting the underside of the truck. Laura broke the silence. "Would you like to wine and dine me this evening?"

He reached over and rubbed her faded blue jeans. "You've got an E ticket tonight."

"What's an E ticket?" she asked playfully.

"At Disneyland each ride had a lettered ticket, from A to E. The E tickets were for the best rides."

"The best ride? I'll take it," Laura said, grinning. "You know, we're about to embark on a ride to the past, and I'm pretty excited. After every storm we'll need to go up the canyon all prepared to see if we can get through. I'm a little afraid about getting stuck back there, but if you are with me, I can accept that."

He patted her leg again. "We'll get back, and, boy, will it be the trip of a lifetime!"

Laura rubbed his leg. "I love you so much. Thanks for being here."

They drove on in silence until Traver pulled the truck in front of the ranch house. Laura got out and unlocked the door. All the dogs and even Lunch were piled up at the front door. They scratched the dogs' ears. Laura said, "Let's take Buster with us when we go back. He's a good dog, and he and Lunch seem to be good buddies."

"That's fine with me. I think a dog with us in 1860 will be good protection."

Traver went into the bathroom upstairs and began shaving. You know how you get that feeling when you're being watched? Well, he had that feeling. Traver turned to see what might be causing the feeling and there was Laura standing just a few feet back from the door. She had on a sleek black strapless grown, her breasts overflowing the ruffled top. Her toes peeked from under the hem of the gown.

Laura's head tilted slightly to one side, waiting for his response.

He made a drawn-out wolf whistle. "Holy shit! You fix up beautifully!"

"So you like it?" she asked softly, slowly raising her gown to show her calves and then her knees. "Look, honey, no panties!"

With a lascivious smile, she dropped her hem and turned to leave.

Traver tried to finish shaving, but his hands were shaking with excitement. When he jumped into the shower, within seconds Laura was right there with him. They embraced full bodied while the hot water splashed over them.

She kissed him hard and hopped out of the shower, toweling dry and disappearing. Traver tried to focus on the moment as he dried off.

Laura was humming in the other bedroom, as he pulled on a pair of black slacks, a long-sleeved white shirt with French cuffs, and black polished Western boots. As he slipped on the second boot, Laura drifted into the room. She was poured into her sleek black gown and was wearing high heels. Around her neck was a gold chain with a three-carat diamond pendant, and she was wearing diamond post earrings of at least a carat.

A beautiful diamond bracelet adorned her right wrist and on her finger was his key chain ring, out of place. Needless to say, she sparkled.

"What's next?" he asked, almost out of breath.

"Champagne and corn dogs and dancing till dawn." Her smile said it all.

Laura tottered out into the long hallway in her heels, Traver bringing up the rear in order to watch her rear. The car was parked close to the porch.

After he gallantly opened the door to the crew cab and bowed slightly, she daintily stepped up into the passenger seat. There was the sweet, scent of fresh-mown alfalfa on the breeze. "You smell great," he told her.

As they drove out to the highway, Laura broke the silence. "Traver, I've been thinking about going back to 1860 with Twin Bears. I'm not so sure why I would want to do this, except to see my great-granddad. I mean, is it even scientifically possible? I have no idea what I would say to him, and I'm not sure I would tell him who I was. It wouldn't be fair to him." She looked at Traver pensively. "I would like to go, though."

Traver put his hand over hers. "I'll go with you. This is an adventure."

"Okay," she sighed, relieved. "Let's go before winter sets in. We can get started tomorrow." She looked out the side window, musing, "Corporal James Peterson. How will I approach him? I'll ask around the fort to find out where he is. I'll just watch him for a while, just to get me used to seeing him. Traver, you'll come with me for this, won't you?"

"Hell, I wouldn't miss this for anything."

"I plan to take a few pictures of him and me together. Do you think they will come out? Past and future together?" She paused. "What if there is no such thing as past and future? What if it is all now and there are ways to shift up and down?"

"That's an interesting thought, Laura, shifting up and down!"

Traver turned into the driveway of the Depot Restaurant. "Here we are," he called out.

Laura pulled out her lipstick, touched up her pink lips, and fluffed her hair. He opened the door for her, and arm in arm they entered restaurant.

Off to their left someone said, "Hi, Doctor Laura, haven't seen you in a while."

Laura looked over and smiled. "Dorothy, how's your dad?"

"Very well," she replied.

Laura leaned over and whispered to Traver, "Her dad hears about an illness on TV and the next day he has it. When he came to me with those imaginary illnesses, I would get the biggest and baddest-looking needle and shoot him up with saline water. He finally got tired of the big-needle treatment. He swears that I cured him, but then he started going to a different doctor."

"Laura, how long have you been out of your practice?" he asked.

That distant look came over her. "Oh, after Bill died. I just couldn't work."

The waitress asked, "Table for two?"

"Yes, please."

Traver seated Laura and then he sat down.

"The last time I ate here, Bill and I were celebrating our wedding anniversary." Tears welled up in Laura's eyes.

"Oh, wow! I didn't know, honey. Would you rather leave?"

"No," she said, making a face. "This is another day and I am so in love with you, Traver. I couldn't do this with just anyone. It's your strength that I'm hanging on to."

"Hi, Dr. Laura!" She glanced up at a man who was about her age standing by their table. "I heard you remarried. Is this the lucky man?"

Laura said in a low tone of voice, "No. I'm the lucky woman!" She introduced them.

When the man walked away, Laura leaned closer to Traver and said, "He tried to date me right after Bill died." She shivered slightly. "What a creep. Look at his beady eyes."

"What does he do here?"

"He is a funeral director." Laura shivered again.

After looking over the menu, the pair ordered the house specialty, steaks.

When the waitress walked away, Laura said, "Let's begin training for 1860 tomorrow." She got out her cell phone and called Twin Bears, explaining that they were ready to start the trip to the past. "What?" she asked. "Oh, okay."

Laura addressed Traver. "Twin Bears wants to take Skip's dad, Mitch, with us since he is such a history buff."

"Shit! This is turning into a full-blown tour," Traver said with fake exasperation.

"Mitch knows a lot about that time in history. He can drive the wagon, and you and I and Twin Bears can ride horses. What?" she said into the phone. "Okay then, tell him to get his shit together!" She laughed. "He will know what shit is." She hung up. "Traver, can you believe that Twin Bears wanted to know why we wanted to take shit with us on this trip?"

A little later, Laura pushed her totally empty plate away. They were so stuffed that they did not even look at the dessert menu the waitress offered. Traver took out his credit card and slipped it into the holder with the bill. When the waitress stepped away, Traver crooked his finger and Laura moved closer to him.

"The only dessert you're getting, young lady," he said, "is a spanking." She started giggling. "Promise?"

"You can take that to the bank!" he folded his arms and grinned. After he collected his credit card and pocketed the receipt, he said, "Honey, let's go for a walk down this way for a bit. I haven't been in old town in quite awhile." He clasped her hand in his and they intertwined fingers. Walking along slowly, they swung their arms.

After their little tour, they drove over to Skip's place to get Twin Bears and Mitch. They wanted to spend the night at the ranch and make preparations for the trip.

The next morning Laura told Roy, her foreman, what they were planning to do. He was going to show them how to hitch up a wagon team and drive it. Traver picked up a pair of jacks that were smart and easy to work with. Laura's line foreman cut out four horses that had some maturity to them and they took long rides. After a couple of weeks, Roy asked if he could go back with us. He could manage the stock. Traver agreed because he believed an experienced wrangler would be valuable to them.

The next bit of business was armament. They all had the standard 9mm Browning, semiautomatic pistols with the fifteen-round clips. The Browning was their only hideout gun. They had 44-40 double-action Rugers for sidearms at their hips and 44-40 saddle rifles. All of the men had AK-47s and two drums of a hundred rounds, plus thirty-round clips. The AK-47s were full switch-over automatics, but they could select semiautomatic, too.

Traver's biggest concern about the journey to 1860 was running into Red Legs. They were guerrilla bands who wore red leggings from their boots up to their knees. If they suspected you were smuggling free slaves, they asked no questions, they would just shoot to kill. Mitch said if you run into Red Legs, just mow 'em down with the AKs.

Mitch gave them a quick history lesson concerning the period of time they were heading into. The 1854 Kansas-Nebraska Act ruled that both states could choose whether or not they wanted to allow slavery, and that was what precipitated the "Red Leg" issue.

In 1859, John Brown had been hanged for treason and there seemed to be quite a lot of that in the North Platte newspapers. Since they would be showing up in 1860, Skip's dad said, all he knew was for sure they needed to be ready to defend themselves.

Mitch went on in a bit in more detail about the John Brown issue and was quite specific about things. Brown was a radical abolitionist whose attempts to free the slaves cost a number of lives and helped indirectly to bring about the Civil War. In 1855, he followed five of his sons to Kansas. Brown led an expedition to Pottawatomie Creek, where his men brutally murdered five pro-slavery settlers. A number of small battles broke out between Free State men and those who wanted slavery.

After that they checked out their weaponry, Traver was dismayed to find that Mitch damn near shot up the crew cab the first time he used an AK-47. Traver gave Mitch instead a thirty-caliber carbine, which he had used during World War II. This meant carrying extra thirty-caliber ammunition, but what else could they do?

Laura suggested packing Bill's 30-caliber single-action Ruger. That made sense to Traver. He also included his 270 Winchester bolt-action deer gun. Roy brought his seven mag Remington and Mitch brought his 270 also. Traver speculated that with the firepower they had, they could hold off Fort McPherson if necessary.

Mitch chuckled and said, "Maybe until the canon starts up?"

Traver thought a bit and then, scratching his whiskered cheek, said, "I think they had four or six twelve-pound field canons, a couple Gatling guns, and four three-inch punt guns. The Iowa Cavalry, Company G, had one hundred wagons and teams of mules for them. There was also the First Nebraska Volunteer Mounted Cavalry with the First Nebraska

Mounted Militia, Company A and Company B. I think there were also a hundred-eighty men and officers at the time we'll be back there. The fort was originally Cottonwood Springs, between Fort Kearney at Guard Island and Fort Laramie, Wyoming. It was situated on the Oregon Trail, and McDonald's Trading Post was the first structure built in that area. Fort Cottonwood was renamed Fort McPherson in 1861."

Traver figured they would carry ten cases of MREs and five cases of beans, along with coffee and Spam. They could get other supplies at North Platte.

Twin Bears said, "Some Pepsi, too?"

Everybody laughed at that.

"It wasn't invented then, but okay with the Pepsi," Traver said.

Sharon and Laura worked on getting together their clothing, in a style as close to that period as possible. They collected old boots and dungarees, worn hats without labels, thick leather belts with no huge buckles. They each carried a knife that was of that period and a pocket knife.

They spent quite a bundle of money buying gold bars to melt down and pour into water to make it look like gold nuggets. They went into Omaha and Lincoln to buy a mess of coins dated 1858 to 1860. Each had a thousand dollars in silver coins and five hundred in gold nuggets.

They purchased VHF radios that had a range of fifty miles, just in case they got separated. They all had period watches and compasses. They also picked up a barometer, because they needed to know if a low-pressure cell was coming, which meant a storm brewing and their ticket home. Laura brought three toss-away thirty-five-millimeter cameras. They had surveying equipment, since Roy and Mitch were posing as surveyors.

Laura and Traver were the railroad representatives, and Twin Bears was the guide. It all seemed to be well thought out, but would they be believable? The piles of stuff they were going to take back to Twin Bears's time were growing. They divided the items into "nice to have," such as Pepsi, candy bars, and junk food. Other piles were "need to have," such as clothing, food and MREs, and "equipment," including AK-47s and ammunition, a shotgun, 44-40 holsters, sidearms, nine millimeter semiautomatic pistols, and a new 45-70 lever Remington rifle. A 45-70 was a good round in case they ran out of ammunition and had to buy extra while they were back in the past. Traver had let Twin Bears target practice with the Remington behind the barn, and he had rapidly become a good shot. Traver explained to the Indian that the bullets of today shot smokeless powder. His 45-70 shells were black powder, and when he used the old shells he needed to clean the gun every time he finished shooting. The last pile was books. Skip's dad had spent quite a bit of time with those old books, and he had gone to the library to read a microfilm of newspapers from Omaha. That was the best source of information. Mitch had deduced that Twin Bears's time was 1859 or early 1860 and in turmoil over slavery.

All those heading back in time got together for supper on the day before the Fourth of July celebration at Gary's on Lake Maloney. Roy's wife Thelma was there, but she was not going. They wanted at least a couple of people in on what was going to happen, just in case they didn't get back. Sharon was there and would stay behind.

They were eating and chatting when Mitch put his fork down and spoke a little loudly to get the diners' attention. Everyone glanced up at him. He looked around the table slowly and said, "Something has been bothering me. You all know that we are going back to around 1859 or 1860. From what I've been reading, that's quite a troubled time in this area. You may recall that while the American Civil War kicked off in 1861, Nebraska, Kansas, and Missouri were already in border wars. This was the period when Kansas was called Bloody Kansas. The abolitionists had to stop going to Kansas through Missouri because they were being attacked and killed in Missouri. So in 1860, they rerouted themselves by going through Nebraska and then back into Kansas from the west. However, the Jayhawkers of Kansas discovered this new route and began going north into Nebraska, raiding the wagon trains, which were worse than Indian attacks. In the year 1860, Nebraska was on the verge of becoming a free state in the Union and it was full of turmoil about freed blacks. I guess what I am getting at is our canyon, and this area in general, is in a borderline situation. We're going into a situation where within just a matter of months there is going to be all-out war between the States. What I do know is that during the 1859-1861 period, Nebraska was a pretty messed-up place to be, especially on the Kansas border."

Mitch continued grimly, "What if we get attacked by these Jay Hawker bands? We might have to kill them. Of course, it goes without saying, better them than us! What is bothering me is what if we kill someone that will become important in the future and our time changes because of that?"

Nobody answered that right off.

Traver spoke up first. "I've thought about that. I think that since we are all here at this moment and going back in time, what happens there back in 1860 is already reflected in today."

Laura looked him with raised eyebrows. "Since when are you a time expert?"

He winked back slyly and said, "Since I've been reading Einstein's book on theoretical time and time travel and the book you gave me. Einstein developed theories and mathematical formulas to prove time travel. What I found most interesting is his work needed an observer to prove time travel. He also needed to accelerate the traveler to light speed. There are two flaws in his work. He needs speed and he needs an observer." Traver gestured toward Twin Bears. "Did you see the rocket ship that he came in on? All the observations are us seeing him interact with us." He raised both hands. "I don't understand any of this, but I see Twin Bears and I have seen 1860, as you have, Laura. There is more to time than acceleration and the speed of light, but I am no scientist. I still want to go back." He paused. "If I have to whack some sons a' bitches that want to kill me, better them than me!" He picked up his coffee and drank a big swallow. Everyone agreed as they finished and decided it was time to go.

CHAPTER 8

IN TIME YESTERDAY

TOWARD THE END of July everyone begin staying at the ranch.

Sharon was going to drive over to the canyon every day to see if they had come home early. Laura wanted her truck to be left at the canyon. She would lock the truck and bury the key a foot's pace from the driver's rear tire so anyone could use it if he or she came back early.

They had just about finished lunch and had the weather channel on the TV, which was predicting a late summer storm with lots of thunder showers to come to the area tomorrow. Laura told everyone that would be good conditions for the trip. They loaded the wagon, packed the saddle bags, got everything into the barn, and locked it. Sure enough, the next morning, August 1, it began looking stormy. Dark clouds were gadding about and strong north winds were blowing. Twin Bears sniffed the breeze and declared that it was raining about fifty miles to the northwest.

Their wagon was tarped down with well-used canvas. They donned old-looking rain slickers and rode away for the canyon. Laura drove her pickup to the clump of trees where Traver had watched Twin Bears get gored by the deer. He had trailed her horse behind him on the way, and she came over. "The barometer looks good and falling fast."

There was a silver streak across the dark sky and then a big BOOM! They remained in saddle and Mitch held the mules. Traver glanced around. At nine o'clock in the morning, it was as black as night. Laura was next to him and she reached out her hand to take his. A huge arc of lightning exploded and Laura jumped. The rain began. The lightning and its follow-up thunder came as regular as belching after a cucumber salad.

Twin Bears spoke up, "Feel your skin sort of crawl and your hair stand up? It's open, let's go!"

They slowly headed up the canyon from 1995 to 1860 while the rain pelted down.

We knew we were there! The big storm had suddenly disappeared and clear skies were all about us. Laura said, "Strange how either end opens with a storm. I'll bet the lightning is like a static capacitor being charged. The energy dissipates as the door is kept open."

Twin Bears rode up and said, "Let's camp over there, where I do. We can defend our position very well there." The two dogs, Lunch and Buster, came loping up to the group and moseyed around, eyeing their every move. Twin Bears smiled and spurred his horse and called over his shoulder, "Camp is about two miles to the river." They began following along behind him.

They set up camp by late afternoon. Twin Bears placed the campfire thirty feet or so away from where they were going to sleep. He explained that bad men always go to the camp fire and never think the campers may not be there. He laughed.

They didn't set up the tent, just stretched the wagon tarp out and slept under that.

Before dark they sat alongside the wagon, eating the sandwiches they had brought along for their first meal in 1860. The chicken, lettuce, and tomato with mayo was tasty and, with the corn chips, went down quickly. Laura got up, went to her backpack, pulled out a greasy white bag, and produced four corn dogs. She smiled and Traver's mouth watered.

"Can't be in 1860 without corn dogs!" she said teasingly.

Laura and Traver ate them slowly, savoring each bite.

"Hey! Where is the champagne?" he asked.

Laura smacked her head. "I forgot!" Smiling, she said that she must be losing brain cells and he knew what she meant by that.

Laura spread out the map of the area and pointed to the McDonald place. "Tomorrow we call on them. It's Thursday, everyone should be home. How long will the ride take, Twin Bears?"

He looked at the map, frowning. "We leave early and we will get there about noon." He smiled. "Just in time for coffee and doughnuts."

"Well, tomorrow is show time for us," Laura replied. "Let's get some rest."

As dawn was breaking on this early August day in 1860 along the south fork of the Platte River, five people from 1995, Laura, Traver, Roy,

Skip's dad, Mitch, and Twin Bears were stirring for the day. They got a fire going for coffee and shortly afterward they were off.

For the second time in Laura's and Traver's life they were back in time.

They discovered the year to be 1860 when they stopped at Fort Cottonwood. Laura reined up her horse alongside Traver, as the group took a northwesterly direction.

"What ya thinking, Traver?" She sounded surprisingly sensuous. He turned slightly, laid the reins on old Stamp's saddle horn, and let him walk as he pleased. "I was thinking that I'm not the first one to do this. I'll bet all the others were scoffed at and looked at as quacks or mad men. I am pretty much relaxed about this after Twin Bears's trips back and forth. I'm not worried about the door disappearing." He smiled reassuringly. "I'm more worried about being mistaken for free borders by the Jayhawkers. I'm worried about bandits and raiding Indians, but Mr. AK should educate those groups."

Laura was looking proudly at him. "Honey, I feel so protected by your presence, I could go anywhere and I know you will keep me safe. I'm a little nervous, I know I'm close to home but, what? Some hundred and twenty-five years earlier?" Her eyes held his. "But as long as you are with me I am home."

Traver moved old Stamp next to Laura's horse, and on contact her horse swung its head and sniffed at Stamp. "Quit that, Sissie, you're fooling with my man." Laura smiled real big as her horse shook its head and whinnied.

"Traver," she sad breathlessly, "we're really back here. It blows my mind. I expect any minute to see a contrail up in the sky from one of those East Coast jets." They both looked up and saw nothing of the sort.

"Strange, isn't it?" Mitch called out. "No jet trails!"

Laura and Traver both nodded their heads in agreement.

"Traver, I expect to see the freeway when we top that hill. If I don't see it, I will really know we're back in time," Laura said determinedly.

Sure enough, as they topped the hill Laura was talking about, not only was the freeway not there but also the diverting channel from the Platte River to Lake Malone was missing, too.

They came to a halt, taking a few moments to look around. Riding wasn't any different in 1995 than in 1860, but when they saw the absence of landmarks they knew, it really sunk in that truly they were in the past.

Laura mumbled, "This is what Twin Bears must have experienced when he found himself a hundred twenty five years or so forward, but for us it's reversed."

They took a few minutes to have a drink of water. Roy got out his topographic map and set the compass on it to orientate the map to the north. "The fort's that way." He pointed to a familiar hill. "About a two-hour ride. The McDonald place is this way." He pointed almost due north. "About ten minutes just over the next hill." Before they got started Laura suggested that they not volunteer much information. "Let's don't spill our guts. That will raise suspicions. Just answer the questions asked."

All of a sudden Laura got an expression on her face that Traver interpreted as if something unexpected had popped into her thoughts.

"What is it, honey?" Traver asked.

"I just remembered that women do all the cooking here." She got that devilish smile. "If you think I'm cooking all the time, you're crazy!" They laughed at her expression.

Leaning close next to her and in a low voice, he said, "Baby, you're cooking all the time!"

Laura pinked up and showed her radiant smile. She slapped her horse with the reins and the horse went into a trot and off she rode. The rest followed suit.

Traver looked around in wonderment: Although he was back in time, so much still looked the same. He figured the settlements would finally put things into perspective, and that was about to occur.

The McDonald place came into view around eleven o'clock, and they rode straight up to the barn that had a house attached to it. There was a wagon already hitched standing out front. Skip's dad yelled, "Hello, in the house!"

Shortly afterward a woman's head appeared at the crack of the doorway. Her hand shaded her eyes to see them better. "Hello!" she called back. "Come in, we have fresh coffee!"

They rode over to the hitching rail and tied up their horses.

Twin Bears was driving the mule team with Mitch sitting beside him; their horses were tethered to the rear of the wagon.

Mitch told Twin Bears, "You stay here with the wagon. Sorry, but that's expected in this time."

"I know. I have lived with this all my life."

"I'm sorry," Mitch repeated again.

Twin Bears smiled at him rather sadly. "That's fine, but today I have something extra. I know how to dance with time!"

Mitch looked at him. "Dance with time? That's exactly what this trip is about."

The lady greeted us with tin cups of coffee and introductions were made all around. Mrs. McDonald asked if our guide would like some coffee, and Twin Bears's ears perked up. "Yes, ma'am!"

She took a closer look at him. "You speak very good English."

He smiled and began speaking to her in French and in his own tongue of Lakota Sioux.

Mrs. McDonald turned to Mitch. "What do you-all do?"

He answered, "We work for the Union Pacific railroad, ma'am. Those two are Laura and Traver, and they are the representatives. Roy, Twin Bears, and I are the surveyors."

"Is the railroad coming through here? The Pony Express has only just now begun here. What will happen next?" Mrs. McDonald exclaimed. "Now, Mr. McDonald will not be home until late this evening. He is in Maxwell selling cattle. Can you stay a bit until he returns?"

"No. We will not be able to wait, we are on our way to the fort and then to North Platte."

Mrs. McDonald turned to him. "Traver, I see that you are wearing a Masonic ring."

Traver had forgotten to remove it before the trip. He gulped and said "Yes, ma'am, I am."

"Oh, good. Mr. McDonald will be pleased to visit with a fellow brother. Will you be in the area long? Mr. McDonald wants to start a Blue Lodge, but there are so few Masons out here. Perhaps Mr. McDonald can call on you while you are in North Platte, or perhaps later this week or next? Where will you be staying, Laura?"

"Mrs. McDonald, I am Traver's fiancee. But I have been trying to convince him that not setting a date to marry does have some drawbacks." She smiled sweetly, as she was enjoying this.

"I shall speak with Mr. McDonald concerning this matter," said Mrs. McDonald seriously. "Traver, you must think about Laura's reputation out here. You-all should marry right away."

Traver spoke with mock seriousness. "Now, Laura, I have told you a hundred times that I just cannot think along those lines right now. I have a job to do and so do you. Just stop thinking those thoughts or I shall dismiss you. "

"Why, Traver, you will do no such a thing to her!" Mrs. McDonald huffed. "No such thing at all!" She stomped her foot.

"As you say, ma'am. The coffee is wonderful, but we must be off. Thank you for your hospitality. I hope we shall see each other again. Laura, we are leaving for the fort, please mount up!"

"Yes, sir," Laura said obediently as she jumped into her saddle.

Traver tipped his hat and said, "Ma'am," as they departed.

Mrs. McDonald called after him, "Thank you for the visit and I'll tell Mr. McDonald to look you up. Bye, Laura, you keep talking to Traver."

As Traver caught up with Laura, she turned and laughingly said, "It's not every girl that can get married in 1860 and 1995, too." She smiled and began to whistle.

They sighted Fort Cottonwood a little after three o'clock. Seeing the fort pretty much convinced them that they were actually in 1860. From where they came upon the fort, they could see a dozen Indians or so camped outside. Traver chuckled to himself, "No mad scientist, no whizzing and clanging machines, just a walk up a canyon and time simply loses its boundaries."

A flash of sunlight from one of the watchtowers indicated that someone was glassing them to see who they were. Traver wished that he had brought along a pair of binoculars.

Mitch had mounted his horse at the McDonalds' farm, and Roy and Twin Bears rode in the wagon. Mitch came up to Laura and Traver. "You see that glass on us a moment ago?"

"Sure did. Do you think we're okay?" Traver wondered.

"One woman, three men, and one Indian is a weird combination. We could have a problem," Mitch conjectured.

They spurred on the horses. Twin Bears slapped the backs of the jacks with the reins. They took their time riding in.

No one from the fort rode out to meet them. "I guess we passed the glass test." Traver yelled back to Mitch.

"Yup!"

They rode in the gate, waved at the guard, and then rode over to the Administration Headquarters. Traver got off his horse and went up onto the porch. The sergeant standing there looked him over thoroughly. Before he could say anything, Traver barked, "Sergeant! Snap to! Please tell the major that Warrant Traver Wells, U.S. Marines, retired, is here to pay him a visit."

"Yes, sir!" The sergeant disappeared inside.

Looking around at the group, Traver said, "Well, he doesn't have to know that I was a Marine from 1959 to 1978."

In a few minutes a major wearing uniform pants and suspenders and a scuffed pair of boots appeared. He had an undershirt on top and he needed a shave. He stuck out his hand. "Warrant Wells? I am Major McPherson. I've been in the field for the last two days and only now got in. What may I do for you?"

Traver smiled back at him and said, "I just stopped in. We are surveying rights of way for the Union Pacific and thought I could talk with some of your men about how they feel about the proposed routes and to let you know we are in the area. My assistant, Miss Peterson, works with me. Mr. Roy Becket and Mr. Mitchell Williams are surveyors. Twin Bears, over there, is our guide."

The major cast his eyes over at Twin Bears. "Lakota Sioux?" the major asked.

Twin Bears perked up and responded in French how pleased he was that the major could recognize his tribal ancestry and speak French and Sioux.

The major looked at Traver's right hand and then met his eyes. "I see you have traveled."

Traver raised his hand enough to show his ring and answered, "Yes, Ohio." The major shook Traver's hand again, giving him the grip of a Master Mason. Traver responded with the pass grip and the major smiled. "Brother, can you be here Saturday evening? All us Master Masons are gathering to consider forming a lodge here at the fort."

"I will certainly try," he replied. "It just depends on where I am. Anyway, I just wanted to stop in and let you know we're in the area. We stopped at the McDonald place and he was out."

The major responded, "He's over at Bradie trying to round up a few brothers for Saturday's meeting."

"Well, I will try to be here, major."

They shook hands again. "I'll be camped just outside North Platte, south side of the river," Traver informed him.

"Warrant Wells, keep an eye out for Jayhawkers," he advised.

"Thanks. You think they may get that close to North Platte?" Traver asked.

The major shook his head no.

Laura got off her horse and walked around a bit. "Major," she said, "is there a pastor and a church around here? Warrant Wells and I want to get married Sunday." She wanted to open a conversation with the major. Laura was thinking about her great-granddad, James Peterson. "And, major, are there any troopers that have an engineering background that could possibly help us with a route selection?" The major immediately responded, "Why, yes. That would be Corporal Peterson." Laura's heart skipped a beat. It was the first time she had heard her great-granddad's name spoken by a person who worked with him and knew about him.

"Corporal Peterson," Laura repeated. "Is he here?"

"No, ma'am, Corporal Peterson is on border patrol. Jayhawkers, you know."

Laura was cool. "Perhaps this weekend Warrant Wells and I can return to the fort to meet Corporal Peterson?"

"Yes, ma'am. In fact he returns tomorrow. There is a sick friend here that Corporal Peterson has been helping. I'll tell him that you railroad people wish to talk with him."

Laura smiled at that. "Thank you, Major McPherson." She wondered if the fort had been renamed after him after the Civil War.

My God, he's here! Laura thought. She went off into a daydream about her great-granddad.

The major turned to Traver with a questioning look.

"Mrs. McDonald put the idea of getting married in her head," Traver informed him.

The major cast his eyes skyward in a show of pity. "Ah, yes! Mrs. McDonald has a way of getting things going." He chuckled.

Turning to the group, Traver told them, "Mount up!"

They waved good-bye as they left Fort Cottonwood. Laura rode up close to him. "Here, take my ring, and you can give it back to me Sunday. You do want to marry me again, don't you?"

"Every day, yes! I will love you!"

"Mrs. McDonald with be glad to hear that you are taking me as your wife and keeping me from being talked about." She smiled and nearly laughed. "You know how tongues will wag." She wiggled her tongue and seductively licked her lips.

They pitched their camp by late afternoon, just by the Platte River.

They put up two Army surplus tents, one for Laura and Traver and one for Roy, Mitch, and Twin Bears. They were drab-green six-person tents. The cooking fire was a good fifty feet from the tents. They used a little green brush after dinner to make enough smoke to run off the mosquitoes and smoked out the tents, too. The dogs slept close to the tents, and we slept without putting up a guard.

Breakfast was best-smelling and succulent smoked bacon and eggs from Mitch's Rhode Island Red hens and pancakes with maple syrup and boiled camp coffee. They ate like pigs and gulped down the coffee. The cool breeze brought scents of cedar and pickle weed.

Sipping his coffee and looking up at the hill behind them, Roy lazily commented that from what he could tell, it looked like they had camped right smack in the middle of Route 83. Traver looked around but nothing struck him as remarkable. Laura agreed with Roy, judging from the hill just south of their camp. "No traffic this morning," she said, chuckling. "By the way, Roy, remind me to give you a raise in salary. You make a damned good breakfast!"

"Yes, ma'am, I certainly will." Roy grinned at the dying embers of the camp fire. He looked over at Traver and grinned. Then Roy addressed Laura. "Ma'am, you got to remember that this food is what we brought. I understand that in this day and age, the available foodstuffs were terrible."

"That's fine," she shot back, "you still deserve that increase in salary."

After breakfast they went into the town of North Platte to open a bank account. Roy, Laura, and Traver were the account holders. They deposited just under a hundred eighty ounces of gold and close to two thousand dollars' worth of silver. The bank teller seemed nosy about the metal, but Traver told him to just take the deposit and give him a receipt for it. This teller seemed awfully young to be handling money in a bank.

"Twin Bears, you want to hang around with us and see the town?"

"You bet!" he said.

They got on their horses and rode around the town, passing where the depot would be a hundred and sixty years later.

Twin Bears pointed out the Stockman's Hotel. "I hear it's very fancy."

Laura looked at him. "Have you ever been in there?"

"No! I'm not crazy! An Indian who goes in there gets scalped!" He was smiling. "Lose hair, and what's worse is he loses all his money!"

They all had a deep belly-roll laugh about that.

"You both go," Twin Bears urged them, "and I'll go over to the livery stable and visit with other Indians."

"Laura," Traver suggested, "why don't you check into the hotel and stay here and the men will stay out at the camp? At least you can have a bath every day."

"And leave you alone at night? No, sir. I stay with you."

"Well, tongues will wag about it."

"Just what do you want to bet the good ladies of North Platte already know about you and me?"

"Well," she thought a moment. "We will just have to find a pastor and get married today." She put her hand to her mouth. "Oh, my God!"

"What's the matter, honey?"

Her eyes were as wide as silver dollars. Crestfallen, Laura said, "I never went to get the license for our marriage at home. I can't believe that I forgot that!"

Traver poked her playfully with his finger.

"Let's go get married right this minute!" Laura begged.

"Okay," Traver said. "You go check us in as Mr. and Mrs. Wells and I'll go find us a preacher."

He was back in a matter of ten minutes or so.

"Well, darling, where's the parson?"

"Right up there on the hotel steps!" he said excitedly.

Laura and Traver were promptly married again. As he put Laura's key ring back on her finger, he thought back to the moment he had decided to give her this just to hold her till he could get her a rock. However, it was very apparent that she would have nothing else. It was the key ring or nothing.

He heard Laura saying, "You thinking about that afternoon in my truck?"

His smile told her yes. Laura looked at her left hand and then kissed the ring. He kissed her lips. "Mrs. Wells, I sure do love you!"

"Mr. Wells . . ." she sighed. "You spoil me rotten." He got another wonderful kiss.

"Yep!"

This time the pastor filled out the papers and copied a second form and gave it to me. "This is your license. I'll record this one at the county court house. Congratulations!" he said.

Laura eyed Traver closely. "You sure must love me to marry me twice!" She whispered so the preacher couldn't hear.

"I told you any day and any time. I just didn't realize that 1860 would be that time. You are the only one!" He kissed her. "Let's go back 'in the hotel!"

"Not so fast, Mr. Wells. A girl has to have a bath!"

"Okay, I'll hold my horses," the groom said reluctantly.

"You'd better not!" she squealed. "You have a wild cowgirl who wants to ride hard!"

They had tied up their horses at the hotel when a boy came over to them. "Take your horses to the livery for fifty cents, folks?" he offered.

"Fifty cents!" Traver exclaimed. "Son, that's a good amount of money for a two-block walk."

"Yes, sir. It is a rightly sum, but I will unsaddle them and brush and feed them also. I'll look after them for you."

Traver asked, "Then every time the missus and I come in, will you take care of our horses?"

"Yes, sir."

"Well, son, where I come from, a man is as good as his word."

The boy smiled up at him. "My paw said the same thing, but now it's just me and my maw and my sister." "Also, where I come from, the mark of a businessman is that he has at least two coins in his pocket to jingle."

"Sir?" The boy looked intensely at Traver.

He continued, "So since you and I are entering into a business deal, let me give you fifty cents for my horse and fifty cents for Mrs. Wells's horse." He thought for a moment. "And a dollar for tomorrow. Mrs. Wells and I will be leaving around noon today." He dug in his pocket and pulled out some of those worn coins they had brought with them. "Here you go, son, two half dollars and one dollar."

The boy took the coins and felt them and held them tightly in his hand.

He stood there, looking at Laura and Traver, and Traver put his hand in his pocket and jingled the rest of his coins. The boy followed suit and jingled his. Taking his hand out of his pocket, he stuck it out for another handshake. "Thank you, Mr. Wells, ma'am."

Traver could tell the kid was awestruck with Laura's beauty.

He gave the boy the reins of their horses. "'Son, now that you have some jingle money in your pocket, you be sure that some of the older boys don't hear your money and take it."

He grinned at Traver and said, "I know when to jingle and when not to. I jingle coins when I get home so mom can hear I've had a good day."

Traver's heart was swelling. Here was a, what, thirteen—or fourteen-year-old, thinking about his mother first and not about going to buy candy for himself.

"Oh, son, what's your name?"

"Will Lasater, sir."

"Well, Will," Traver dug into his pocket again and got out a quarter and flipped it to him. "Get yourself a piece of candy and a couple of apples for the horses. If there's enough change, take your mom and sister an apple, too."

Will caught the quarter and his face split into a grand smile. "Thank you, sir!"

"Oh, Will, one more thing. You know down by the river, south side?" Traver pointed just about due south.

"Yes?"

"My men are camped there. Will you go and tell them that the Mrs. and I are staying in town tonight?"

"Yes, sir!"

"You can ride my horse. His name is Stamp. The men's names are Roy and Mitch. Tell them we will see them tomorrow night and that Twin Bears will be back by nightfall."

"Yes, sir!"

Laura watched as Will took the two horses and began walking them to the livery stable. "Hey, Will, do you ride?"

The boy turned, his feet kicking up the dust. "Yes, sir!"

"Well, then, climb up on ol' Stamp and ride him to the livery."

"Yes, sir!" Will was up on Stamp in a heartbeat. He sucked his lips and nudged Stamp's sides with both feet and the horse jumped into a trot off toward the stable.

Laura moved over to Traver and put her arms around his waist. He could see she was emotional. Her eyes were misty and her breath was deep. "I loved watching you interact with Will. Traver, I felt like you were talking to our son." The tears broke over her eyelid's dams and traced their silvery path down her dusty cheeks. "Oh Traver, I wish we could have a son like Will!"

He held her in his arms and asked, "Honey, why do you keep saying that you can't have children?" He looked deeply into her eyes.

"I'm too old, you old fool," she said.

"That's bullshit. You're not too old. You've got the body of a thirty-year-old. You've the heart of a grandmother, but you've got the sexual urges of a teenager!"

She wiped her cheeks. "There you go again, talking dirty to me." She couldn't help but smile.

She pressed herself more tightly against me and kissed me on the lips. A couple of older women were passing by and looked askance at Laura and me. As they got out of earshot, Laura whispered, "I guess people don't kiss out in public here." She smiled and swatted him on the butt. "Go tell Twin Bears that we are staying in town tonight while I go and get a bath. And don't you go jingling around any dance hall hussies, either."

"Hussies? What happened to tarts?"

"This is 1860, sir."

Traver put his hand in his pocket and jingled his remaining coins.

"You'd better watch that! You just might get something going," Laura scolded him playfully.

"I know," he said, as he patted her rear. "Hmm. Dust is puffing out of your clothes, you had better get your clothes washed, too."

"Can't do that. My other clothes are back at camp."

"Well, then, Mrs. Wells, let's go and buy you some new duds before you bathe. Nothing fancy, maybe some cowboy clothing?"

"Yippie! Cowboy clothing!"

"I'll go find Twin Bears, and when I get back, I'll get me a bath, and you and I will go do the town tonight!" Traver headed off to where Twin Bears said he would be, just outside of town and a bit north. Traver walked perhaps an eighth of a mile before he saw a huge cottonwood tree and a group of ten or twelve men and a few women and children playing. He smelled food cooking.

Twin Bears spotted him and came up. They shook hands and Traver told him what had been going on. Twin Bears looked him over from head to toe and then said, "You got married again!"

"Yep."

"Well, I'll head back to camp and tell Roy and Mitch that you and Laura will be in town for the night."

"Oh, before I forget it, Traver interrupted, "there's a kid coming over to tell you the same thing. He's a good kid. Will is his name. Invite him to eat with you-all. Okay?" he asked Twin Bears.

"Yes, sir."

"Open one of the MREs and take out the chocolate bar and give it to him."

As Traver headed back to town he was struck by how it looked just like the scenery from an old cowboy movie. Then he suddenly had a prickly feeling on the back of his neck, and he touched his hip where his pistol was. He was fairly far out of town and the pistol would come in handy, but he turned abruptly and no one was there.

As he continued on, he thought about how he had never considered the smells and the weather in those movies. It was getting hot and sticky, and the flies were beginning to land on him and everything else.

Yep, it's going to rain. That's what got my hackles up.

He looked up and over toward the northwest. The clouds were puffing, and it looked as though a storm might come along at any time. He heard a voice say, "Rain by tonight."

Traver turned and saw an old man behind him. He hadn't even heard a footfall. *Was it he that I had felt?* He was scruffy-looking, sporting a ten-day beard, and he smelled of whisky breath and sweat.

"Yes, sir, the rains a-comin'. You can smell it and nearly feel it," he observed. "You new in town feller?"

"Yep."

The old fellow cocked his head to see Traver better. "You don't talk much, do you?"

"Nope." Traver looked the disheveled guy over closely. "Sometimes a person spills out his guts and then everyone knows his business."

The old gent had begun looking at Traver's belt, where his 44-40 showed and his hide-out pistol peeked out from the front of his jacket. "That there sure do look like a fine piece of machinery." He motioned and Traver looked down at the Ruger and then back to him.

"Machinery? Strange description of a pistol."

The guy smiled a near toothless grin. "Used to be a gunsmith back east. Came out here and just lost everything."

Traver took out the pistol and let him feel it. "It's got teeth."

"I never heard that saying about being loaded before, some bite!" the old man said.

As Traver released his grip on the gun and the old man hefted the pistol, he rolled back the loading lever and took out a shell. After inspecting the Ruger, he put the shell back and released the hammer back to its lowered position.

"This here gun ain't like any I ever seen before. It don't have any milling marks on it." He looked at the pattern marks and then looked up. "The eyes ain't what they used to be years ago. No, sir! But this here ain't no regular pistol. You had this here one made special for you?" He handed the gun back to Traver.

"Yep! It's special all right," Traver agreed.

"You gots any iron that needs working on?"

"No. All my smokers are in excellent condition."

The old man said, "Good description. Ha! Smokers!"

CHAPTER 9

THE SAWTOOTH SALOON AND A PAPER AIRPLANE

"Say, old timer, what's your name?" Traver wanted to know.

"Bill."

"Say, Bill, have you had lunch yet?" Traver asked the gent.

"No."

"Want to join me? No whisky, just a good lunch."

Bill looked at him and answered, "Sure, I would like that. The Sawtooth has the best eats in town."

As they walked over to the Sawtooth Saloon, Traver stopped midway in the dirt street. The sun was blazing down and flies were buzzing. The Sawtooth Saloon had its double swinging doors framed with huge crosscut saws.

Bill was watching Traver take in the sight, and Bill said, "Them saws likely cut all the timber for North Platte and some for Fort Cottonwood, I suspect."

Traver was thinking of the vast amount of energy it took just to make a two by four. He shook his head. The hitching rails out front were full of horses and one mule. Bill walked up and patted its rear. He spoke to it. "Good girl."

Traver said, "Girl? I thought mules were not sexual."

Bill grinned. "Who knows? But this here mule is like a hellfire woman. Name is Swift Kick. Watch yourself, mister . . . ah . . . Whadja say your name was?"

"Wells. Traver Wells." And he stuck out his hand to the gent and they shook.

"Bill Thompson," he said. "Watch that mule, she's got one hell of a kick." He headed up onto the raised wooden sidewalk.

As Traver heard his boots echo on the boardwalk, he thought, *Goddamn, 1860!*

Traver noticed two buzz-saw blades made into signs. One read "Beer 5¢" The other read "Whiskie, two bits." *Cheap booze.* He remembered that the whisky was probably poor quality with no ice. *Jesus, there's nothing to enjoy about drinking in this time.*

As he stepped across the boardwalk, he stopped in the shade, as the smell of cigarette smoke begin tickling his nose. It stank worse than any other cigs he had ever smelled. He caught the smell of stale beer and a trace of sour puke that was at least a day old. It all was drifting out the doorway of the Sawtooth, and he hesitated as he walked into the dark room. As Traver's eyes adjusted to the dim light he made out the figure of a man behind the bar and a few sitting at a round table near the back, talking. A half full fifth bottle of amber liquid sat in the middle of their table. Two cigarettes, smoke curling up, were in a bowl. Shot glasses, all empty, sat on the table in disarray. A few men were standing at the bar, having beers, and two men at a table near the bar and in the back of the room were having food. The stink was overpowering, and Traver almost didn't go in any farther. But Bill had already barged in and taken a seat at a table near the door. Traver sat down next to him.

The only light peeking in the room came from a few windows high up on the side wall and the swinging front doors and the two large plate-glass windows. The kerosene lamps scattered about the place were unlit.

Traver sat down in a well-worn and scuffed chair at a table that had stains and gouges where a knife had been stuck into its surface. This was the real West. Not a movie set. Traver had never realized how primitive it was. He sat there in amazement, on his second day back in time. This certainly was not the good ol' days as some writers referred to it nostalgically. This was rough and comfort was spars as hen's teeth. Traver was brought out of his thoughts by Bill, who told him, "Order the meat and potatoes!"

"What else?" Traver said, grinning.

They walked over to the bar and the bartender gave them the once-over. "Bill! Goddamn it, no drinks for you. Get out of here!"

Traver spoke up quickly, "Excuse me, Bill and I are having lunch here. Steak and potatoes and milk, please?"

Someone in the back of the saloon snorted, "Milk!"

Traver heard the echoing comment and turned.

"No milk," the fellow added, "it usually sours by now." It seemed to be said in an apologetic sort of way. Turning back to the bartender Traver said, "Okay, then we'll have soda water."

The bartender chuckled. "Sasparilla!"

Traver leaned back and roared, "Hell, no. Pepsi, please."

"What?" the bartender exclaimed.

"It's a private joke," Traver said loudly right in the bartender's face.

Bill and Traver settled in as comfortable as possible at a round table next to the front door.

"Alice!" the bartender yelled. "Two lunches!" And he poured two big mugs of Sasparilla and brought them over to their table.

As he sat the mugs down on the table, just for the hell of it Traver asked, "No ice?"

The bartender's face scrunched up. "What a joker! Ice is in the winter." He walked away, laughing.

"Now don't you go getting sick on us, Bill." From out of a door toward the back of the saloon came a woman bearing huge plates of steak and potatoes. She didn't even look at them as she sat the plates down. "I've got string beans from my garden, fresh today."

She left and in just seconds returned with a plate of biscuits and a bowl of butter and the string beans. She looked at Bill and asked, "How you doing, Bill?" He was poking in his potatoes and cutting his steak. He rocked his head back and swallowed. "Fine."

She turned to Traver. "If you need more, just yell." She continued, New in town?" she asked.

"Yes, thank you for asking." He gave her a dime tip. She looked at it as if she had never seen one before. "It's a tip for your service," he said.

"Thank you, sir." She went back into the kitchen.

Bill swallowed a hunk of meat. "Alice is a good person. Her husband died a while back and she's having a tough time of making it with her daughter and a teenage boy. The boy is a help to her, he helps travelers with their horses."

Between bites of meat, Traver asked, "A kid with no shoes and a torn pair of coveralls?"

"Yep, that's Will. You know him?"

"Yes, he's caring for our horses."

"Oh?"

"Yes, my wife's and mine."

"He'll do good," Bill assured Traver.

Traver thought about how nice it was to meet Will's mom. He popped another piece of steak in my mouth. *God, this was great!*

"Man, Bill, this is great food!" Bill motioned with his hand, yes. Traver managed to eat only half of his plate of food. Bill asked Traver if he was going to finish it, and Traver handed Bill his plate.

"What's your name again?"

"Traver Wells, call me Traver."

"Well, Mr. Wells, I notice you have a hideout pistol under your vest that looks real different."

"Boy, Bill, your eyes seem to be pretty good right now." The old gent grinned.

Somewhere in the saloon a catchy tune began on a banjo.

"Well, can I look at it?"

"Not here, Bill, I don't pull guns in a saloon—unless I intend to shoot, that is."

Bill looked at Traver seriously and intently. "A wise thing."

Right then Alice came out to see if they needed anything else, and Traver said, "No, but that was some fine cooking." She smiled her appreciation.

"It's nice to hear from folks that appreciate good cooking."

Traver quickly said, "You ought to open a regular cafe here in town."

"Oh, sure," she answered. "Mister, it's all I can do to feed my family and keep the payments on the farm, much less start something else and worry about how to pay for that, too."

"I met your son this morning." She became all smiles again.

"He is a good boy, but he needs to be getting along with his future."

"The future is the best goal to work toward," Traver agreed.

"Again, thanks for the tip, mister."

"You're welcome."

Traver leaned back against the wall and pulled off a handbill. It was a notice of a bank sale of two storefronts in North Platte. He looked it over and put it down. "Bill, what is your expertise with firearms?"

He rubbed his stomach. "Long guns mostly. I sporterized the 45-70 and the 50-70 government guns into custom walnut stocks and carved the stocks with hunting scenes. Why do you ask?"

"Oh, I was just thinking. I'm a businessman, you know? I see here that there are two shops, store fronts for sale." Traver showed Bill the handbill. "You think a custom rifle and pistol repair and a lunch room could make a go of it in the same place?" He asked.

"Maybe."

"I was thinking that cowboys and men coming in for lunch would see your work and would nose it about to folks looking for a new hunting rifle or such. I can even show you how to keep milk fresh for lunch. You think Alice would be interested in setting up a restaurant?"

Bill looked at him with dismay. "We don't have any money, mister. No sense in even talking about something like this."

"Bill, I said I am a businessman. We can work out a partnership, you, Alice, and me and my wife." As I was getting ready to say something else, Alice came back for the plates. Before Bill would let Alice take his plate, he begin cleaning it up with a biscuit, until there was not a speck of food or gravy left. "There, now you don't have to wash this plate!"

Traver was folding that handbill into a paper airplane, so it would fly. As a kid, he could make one of the planes fly a good fifty feet. On the back wings he tore the paper strips to make flaps to point downward, so the nose would stay up.

"Mr. Wells, what the hell are you making there?" Bill looked closely at the airplane.

"Bill, this is called a plane where I come from." Traver felt okay with telling Bill that much. Traver had already decided he was going to let the old guy burn off a clip of 45s from the 1911 semiautomatic pistol he carried under his shoulder.

"A plane? What does it do?"

"Lookey here, Bill, watch this!"

Traver took aim at the top of the saloon doors that were about twenty feet away and that opened onto the street. He raised his hand and thrust it forward, releasing the paper airplane. It shot silently straight above the swinging doors, just as Traver had aimed, and out into the afternoon's heat.

"Well, I'll be damned!" Bill exclaimed. "An airplane, you say, but what does it do?"

Traver smiled at the thought of what people might think about seeing a paper airplane come sailing out of the saloon and into the warm afternoon on Main Street.

Out in front of the saloon and across the street, the town veterinarian, Siren, was walking to the hardware store when the plane caught her eye as it flew on the afternoon air toward her. She watched, stunned, as it settled at her feet.

Her thoughts raced back to her early days at flight training back home. She was immediately in the control pod of the wing soaring on the thermals of her home world, Edon. She re-experienced the turns and banking maneuvers, the diving to search for thermals and updrafts so she could soar longer. She thought immediately about the model she had constructed for the annual contest at school to see what unmanned wing could stay afloat the longest. Her wing had won. Her mind was racing with thoughts, based on this tiny paper plane she held in her hand. She smiled with pleasure and then her expression turned to surprise when she realized where she was: in a cow town in a time of very little technological development.

She looked down and thought, *This is not possible. The aura of its maker is still phosphoresing in it.* Looking at the few folks on the street and a cowboy riding, she knew at once that none of them had made it. In this time a horse was transportation and a gun was the only machine. There were wagons on the street and trains belching steam and smoke in the East. These folks were only in the primitive fire period in terms of utilizing the energy of the air, this lifting body was far too advanced. She noticed how the flaps had been folded into the plane. *Whoever made this knows something about aerodynamics.*

Siren, a star ship commander posing as a town veterinarian, raised her head to take in the dusty main street. Nothing seemed out of place. Apparently she was the only one on the sparsely occupied street who had seen the plane glide. She was drawn to the saloon, but she dismissed it as the origin of the plan. None of the men in there had ever impressed her as thinkers; they knew about running cows and drinking bad booze.

There was a shimmering, huge violet and red-purple color to this wing, as it was known to her. She surmised by its trajectory that the mini-plane had flown out of the saloon. *Holy Edon! What if one of my crew was doing this? Flying this out of the Sawtooth? No one was supposed to display any technology not already developed at this time. No one was supposed to go into the saloon.* She would put a stop to this right now.

As she looked at the wing again and sensed its residual aura, she had the feeling that no crew member had made it. *But who else could it be? It had to be a crew member.* She started toward the Sawtooth to get her crew member out of there and impress on him that displaying this sort of technology simply would not be in anyone's best interest.

The aural charge of the person who had folded this paper into a delta-winged airplane had filled the molecular gaps. Like a capacitor charging up, his aura's electrical charge was accumulating between the macrocosms in the paper. Siren, super-sensitive to this signature of human energy, had noticed a vibrant violet-red, purple glow to the aura. *Aura stigmata doesn't occur at every touch, there is a trigger. An emotional peak or spike, a super charge, a harmonic that affects cosmic space of matter. It wasn't fear that triggered this energy, it was excitement of being in the past and of interaction with everyone.*

Siren realized the cosmic coincidence, that she was passing the front doors of the Sawtooth Saloon the moment that someone tossed the plane out the doors. Every experienced star ship captain knew the feeling of auric sight. *There is a direct, unbroken link between me and the person who made this. I know this aura! I would know him anywhere!* Siren saw the shimmering colors that caused her to gasp for air. It was not a crew member but a stranger.

Siren stood fixed to the spot, her mind racing back to when she was a little girl back on Edon and Monk was with her at a beautiful pool of water. She had been looking at her reflection in the water and all of a sudden a rainbow of color swirled about her that was reflected in the still waters. It so surprised her that she had looked up into the sky, expecting to see a rainbow. But there was none.

"What have you seen, Siren?" Monk asked her. Quickly looking back at the pool of water, but seeing only her reflection, she said, "I thought a rainbow had fallen upon this pool of water and on me." She looked to Monk for further explanation.

"Siren," he spoke softly and slowly, "you have heard older folk speak of how you look one to another. You know of the colors of health, joy, illness, and emotions that are ever so strong."

"Yes." Siren rocked her head and quickly stole a glance at the pool for further inspiration. "Yes, Monk, I know about our energy field, the aura. But have never seen such."

"Siren, you have just now glimpsed yours," Monk declared. "We have a life force, an aura. Each of us differs, even though we are human." He smiled. "And, Siren, what is human?"

Siren smiled and responded, "Not animal or mineral, but in all of us, we differ because we are a collection of our all, of what we see and feel." She reached out to pinch Monk and giggled. Then very seriously she said, "There is a conductivity of our spirit and an energy that we radiate and that few of us see."

Off in thought, Siren looked back into the little pool of water, watching her reflection as if it were her twin sister, knowing every thought and emotion they shared. Was her reflected twin looking out from the water at her?

Monk broke the moment of wonder. "Siren, this life-force energy can be boosted by emotion. And many times it becomes visible by those who are not so sensitive. Just now you have glimpsed your own aura, I suspect because you quieted your thoughts so you could become sensitive to your spirit's reflection and not just your physical reflection. Now your thoughts are rumbling around in your head and you are distracted and cannot see them again. Cast your gaze upon your hands, palms up, and bring your attention away from your reflection."

Siren pulled her gaze away from the pool's surface and her eyes moved to her hands.

"Siren, be quiet, be still. Look into your palms and let your life force shine. Your energy will guide your thoughts as you see color again."

Siren began to see her hand shimmering and the edges of her fingers glowed a beautiful violet. Her attention was drawn there and she heard Monk's words no more, for the moment of color took her breath and froze her attention.

"As a star ship captain, you will need this skill, that of a Way Walker, so you may understand other lives and what they have held and touched. Under certain circumstances, usually because of a tremendous concentration of feeling, or love, some of this energy can be left in an object, much like a cell stores static energy for later use. You can many times transfer your aura knowingly, or unknowingly, by proximity. Just touching the object allows the energy to transfer. That object becomes marked, with an emotional signature. Only another human can discharge this stored signature and many times just by holding it."[1]

That comment of Monk echoing in her thoughts, she looked down at the glowing piece of paper folded into a lifting body. The maker of that plane had filled the paper with his life force. Smiling, she stooped down and gracefully and gently picked up the glowing little paper airplane. A spark jumped between Siren and the plane's color. She twitched. Inside the saloon Traver jerked, too, as if he had experienced a static charge. He clasped both hands and rubbed them together. "Boy, that felt weird." He looked around with the feeling that someone was watching him. Still sitting in the saloon with Bill, Traver felt everything seemed distant, and yet a fullness shaped every cell of his attention.

Outside, in the summer's hot afternoon, the vet, Siren stood there with the folded paper plane in her hand, feeling another person's energy. She wondered who in 1860 would know about lifting bodies. After looking closely up and down the street, she decided that the saloon was the only possible place from which the wing could have originated. It operated on kinetic energy, a push or a throw and that speed, or energy, launched it as it passed through the air. Very primitive but highly advanced in conception. She knew it would require a tremendous amount of power, because of its long, sharp construction and minimal wing displacement, to accomplish extended flight.

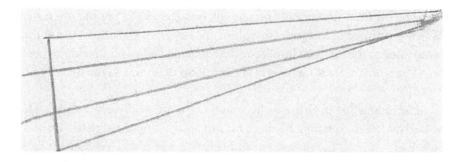

She thought back to her flight training days at home again in that atmosphere. Now she was a stellar flash ship captain, with little need for atmospheric flight. With magnetic generators, there was no need for chemical power plants.

She returned to the moment. As she stood in the Sawtooth Saloon's doorway, she unfolded the paper airplane and saw it was a handbill concerning two buildings for sale by the bank of North Platte. She refolded the plane and held it at her side.

Her entire body began to sense a newness, a tingling sensation. Her sensitivities became heightened. The Way began to enter into her thinking. Something different was radiating this energy. At the doorway, she let her eyes adjust to the dull light.

"Hi, doctor," the bartender called out in greeting. "Want a beer?"

She shook her head, "No, thank you," and looked around the room, recognizing nearly everyone present. Then she saw that Bill was sitting with a stranger. He glowed with the colors of the wing. She saw a handbill on the wall next to the stranger, a twin to the one of which the plane had been made. She could not take her eyes off the stranger, even as she slightly turned her head. What was keeping her attention to this man? He seemed to be a part of the surroundings, but something was out of place. His aura had faded. He had a different presence, certainly, he was not one of the cowboys.

His boots were worn, his pants and shirt were typical. He wore no hat. His face was turned, so she could not see it plainly, but, still, this man was out of place. *What was it? What was it?*

Finally the stranger's face turned to her, and for Traver the barroom seemed to disappear. There was only the woman standing at the door and him sitting at the table. It was like a dream he had had many times. He was in a library where lots of people were gathered, and he noticed a woman standing off from the crowd. She was tall, goddess-like in her silent stature. When she turned to look directly at him, his emotions exploded. And at the same instant, they clicked into a comfort zone he had never known before.

The woman standing quietly at the saloon door now made that dream a reality.

He caught his breath and his thoughts went wildly everywhere. He sensed his hands touching her hair, his fingers slipping through her image's softness. His nose caught a scent of freshness. He fantasized that his face was burrowing into her lustrous dark hair.

There stood his dream come true, but what about Laura. *I belong to Laura, but, my God. the lady at the door!*

These were some difficult feelings.

The bartender had called her doctor and she was holding his paper airplane. As she began to step forward, Roy showed up at the doorway. "Excuse me, ma'am," Roy said politely.

"Roy, over here!" The woman's face snapped back to look at Traver, knowing that she had heard that voice before, saying nearly the same thing. "Hello, Skip, are you there?" *Was this the person she had heard on the speaker at communications central during that storm last year?*

She needed to think about all this, and standing in a bar's doorway was not the place to think! And being distracted by this stranger would certainly not produce clear evaluations.

She became momentarily flustered. Liquid fire had just flowed into her veins. Even her breasts seemed to smolder and yearn to be touched. That was a feeling she had never experienced. Well, at least not this fever.

Her breathing quickened as she absorbed this man's full image. No man had ever pulled at the depths of her soul like this. She stood quivering with fear that he knew how she was feeling. She felt stripped, standing there naked. She wanted to flee but her feet were stuck to the ground. Her soul wanted this man to see her nakedness.

Her lips struggled to form words. "Who . . . who . . ." Finally, she managed to sputter, "Who made this?" She waved the plane in her hand. Bill was just about ready to tell her, and Traver kicked the old guy's leg under the table to shut up. Bill jolted, but he got the message and said nothing.

Traver was totally distracted by the woman who had just stepped in with the paper airplane, but something made him hold his peace.

With no response to her question, Siren turned to leave. Traver caught her silhouette in the sunlight. Her breasts were ample, her waist nicely cinched, and her rear end was comfortably curvy. He was so captivated he was speechless.

Siren was still holding the crude paper airplane in her right hand as she left.

*   *   *

She wanted to raise the paper plane to her cheek to feel the vibrations still alive in it. She wasn't thinking logically at the moment.

Just then Bill commented on how beautiful the doctor looked. It caused the vision to fade from Traver's thoughts. And the same comment brought Siren back to the cow town of North Platte in 1860, where she was standing in the doorway of the Sawtooth Saloon.

She closed her eyes momentarily and gathered all the light of the universe and combined it with her energy. Opening her eyes a second later, she projected an image of herself to the compelling stranger before her.

As captain of a luminal star ship, she could choose a man to be her partner. She would choose this stranger. By him she would be held, be comforted, be loved. *Oh, Moons of Edon, cool this blaze that consumes my heart.*

"Doctor," the bartender interrupted, "is something the matter?"

Siren looked at him but did not speak. *Everything is the matter!*

Traver was thunderstruck. He saw an image of stars behind her. She raised her hands to the back of her head and she removed her helmet and placed it down. She unfastened her braids and her dark hair fell to her shoulders. She lowered her hands to waist level, then turned them palms up. Her lips parted and Traver knew that he was to touch her hands with his and press his lips to hers.

His eyes riveted to the vision, he observed her gown, open clear to her navel and fitted snugly to her full hips that tapered to shapely legs. The gown was transparent, and he could see her luxuriant privates. She crooked her head, as if she knew Traver's yearning for her breasts and the love between her legs. He felt invited to rest his head upon her breast and to be consumed by the fire at the apex of her legs.

This was the image Siren had shared with the stranger. And now she struggled with what to do next as she took tentative steps to leave the saloon, her eyes focused on the stranger a moment longer.

Traver felt as if he were floating toward her, her eyes drawing him. He watched as she took a deep breath that revealed breasts and nipples hardening with excitement.

Traver knew he would never be the same. There was something different about her and he felt sure she sensed a difference in him. He continued staring at the swinging saloon doors, through which she had just departed. *She knew what she had in her hand. She wasn't from 1860.*

He just then began to realize that she knew what an airplane was. He thought, *She is not from here. I know it.*

CHAPTER 10

TWO BIZARRE EVENTS

TRAVER KNEW THERE was something different about her. He stared at the swinging saloon doors, where she had just stood. Her image was still there, an aura she left behind. He felt drawn to her and a little afraid. She was out of time, too, she knew about airplanes. *Who is she? Time*, he thought, *forward maybe.*

Looking at Traver, Bill said, "Why didn't you tell her you made that thing?"

"Bill, you won't understand, but it's best that this is forgotten. Who is she?" Traver wanted to know.

"She's the animal doctor here. The vectren."

Traver laughed. "You mean a veterinarian?"

"Yep! That's it."

"Well, Bill, I've got to get. I'll be seeing you around. Please don't mention any of this to anyone, Bill, Okay?"

"Any of what?" the old gent said, grinning. They got up and left the table.

Outside of the Sawtooth Saloon in the fresh air, Roy and Traver watched as the doctor headed back to her office.

As she stepped through her office doorway, the receptionist looked up. "Oh, hi, captain!"

Siren said nothing in return. She was still wrapped up in thought about what had just taken place.

"Captain?" the receptionist asked again. "Captain?"

"Huh? Oh yes?" Siren finally acknowledged, returning to the moment.

"Is something the matter?"

Siren gave her a blank look, and then she said, "I've just experienced two bizarre events: one for me and one for here, 1860!"

"What?" The secretary put down her pencil.

Siren stepped over to one of the large leather chairs in her office and sank down into it. She was still rattled by the stranger at the saloon.

"Captain, go on." The secretary looked directly at her.

Siren looked up at her aide. "I have just met who I would choose first, whom I saw as a child at my first viewing. But I am not sure that he is even from here." Siren glanced away for a second. "He is not from here," Siren said emphatically as she looked back at the receptionist.

"Not from here?" the aide responded, shocked. "What do you mean? Not from this town?"

"I don't know what to think. He is just different." Siren had a distant look in her eyes. "His lips felt as though they kissed my soul." She heaved a huge sigh.

"He kissed you?" The aide expressed surprise.

"No, he didn't kiss me, but it felt like he did."

"Where were you?"

Siren turned to her. "That's the second soul-shaking thing!" She took out the small paper airplane, spread its wings, lifted it up, and launched it across the room. The plane glided to a stop against the opposite wall.

The aide watched in astonishment. "Holy Edon!" she whispered as she placed her hand over her mouth.

"Holy Tri-Moons, exactly!" Siren added.

"What is that doing here?" the aide asked. "Captain, we are in a period where only kites and hot-air balloons are available. That flew as a wing flies! Where did this wing come from, captain?"

"It flew out the door of the Sawtooth Saloon." Siren got up. "When I went in and asked who it belonged to, no one would tell me. But I know it was the stranger."

The aide picked up the wing, unfolded the paper, and then refolded it. "Captain, this is not possible. Not for here and for this time."

In a distant voice Siren said, "I know." She ran her hands over the top of the desk, just to feel something solid. "I know. I know. He is not one of us. But I briefly saw his aura!"

"Oh, captain!"

Siren smiled. "Yes, but he doesn't realize his aura is so ancient that he is a Warrior Maji."

"A Maji?" her aide exclaimed.

"He is a Maji. Bright purple-violet and tri-moon spectrum of color across his face," Siren added.

The aide put her hand to her chest. "Captain, is he a survivor?"

Siren looked away. "No. That is more than 100,000 years ago?"

"Captain, maybe he is a learned man here?"

"That's possible," Siren answered.

"What will you do, captain?"

"What we will not do is react too quickly. We will wait with patience and watch and see what he does."

"If he is different, how will we know?"

"What he does is different. He checked his wrist. He had a round device strapped on his wrist, much like my Comm." Siren raised her wrist to expose a tiny bracelet-like gadget.

The aide gasped. "Captain, he had a Comm?"

"No. Not like ours, but he looked at it and seemed to be satisfied with what he saw. There is nothing like that in this town."

"Captain, is he truly like us?"

Siren smiled. "I sure hope so!" She blushed and her aide did, too. Siren breathed deeply. "I would choose this man first!" she said aloud.

"But, captain, if he is not from our system and not even from here . . ."

Siren interrupted, "He is from here, but years in this day's future I would guess."

"From the future!" her aide gasped again. "Captain, we can't do that!"

"I know, I know. I was not prepared to encounter anything such as this!"

"Captain, may I speak out frankly?"

"Yes, of course."

"Captain, regardless of the time or place, become the woman that he makes you feel you are."

The two hugged each other.

It was obvious that Siren was becoming aware of the woman in her. This was a smoldering fire that she had never before experienced.

Siren walked out of her office to cool off, and, looking toward the saloon, she saw Traver step out with Roy.

As Traver left the Sawtooth he noticed the doctor standing out on the boardwalk, in front of her office. He almost raised his hand in hello, but he hesitated because they had not been introduced. Also, she simply was not what she presented herself to be, if she knew what a plane was. He didn't want to stare too long, but he also didn't really want to take his eyes off this woman. He had to look away because his excitement was giving him all sorts of intense feelings.

As Traver and Roy headed back over to the hotel, they had to pass the bank again. Traver looked back and saw that the doctor was gone. He told Roy to go on ahead, and Traver walked into the bank to see a few cowboys cashing pay vouchers. The bank teller saw him and said, "Mr. Wells, I'll be right with you."

Looking around at the building, Traver noticed the red brick structure, the big plate glass window, and what he considered to be a flagstone floor. The chair he sat in was heavy, with a comfortable leather cushion and back rest.

"Mr. Wells?" the teller called out.

"Yes?" He got up.

"And what may we do for you today?"

"We?" I asked, looking around in astonishment.

"Yes, we. The bank and myself."

Traver looked at him a bit. "Well, you can tell me what the minimum bids are on the two stores being auctioned next Monday will be."

"Are you going to be starting a business?"

"No. I am just interested in an investment."

"One moment, please."

When the bank teller came back, he said, "The old bakery will need to bring in fifteen hundred dollars."

Traver answered testily, "I asked for the minimum bid, not what the bank feels the value is."

"Excuse me? Mr. Wells?" an elderly gentleman interrupted. "I overheard you, and I can help you. I am the bank president. Thank you, Mr. Wilbar." The banker dismissed the teller.

"Mr. Wells, please come into my office." He turned toward his office, and Traver followed him in and sat down in front of his desk.

"Will you be paying in gold or paper?" the banker asked in a friendly tone.

Traver studied the banker's round continence a few seconds before answering. "If the price is acceptable, it will be paid in gold nuggets."

The banker leaned back in his chair and tapped his teeth with a pencil several times before saying, "I would need seven hundred dollars to clear the deal."

"Thank you." Then Traver added, "And the other building?"

"It's a run-down shack at the north end, a storage barn that a freight company used. I don't believe you would be interested."

"Okay. Does the old bakery have a fireplace?"

"No, it doesn't," the bank president answered as he moved closer to his desk. "It has a wood-fired stone oven just out back, and that is in great shape. I suppose, though, a fireplace could be added."

"Just how large is the building?"

"It has two rooms. One room is sixteen feet by twelve feet. The other room is twenty feet by sixteen feet. The rooms are connected. The floor is stone, like the one here in the bank. As a matter of fact, I think that the bank and the bakery were built at the same time."

"I will pay a thousand dollars for it if you put on a new roof and add a stone fireplace with a good foundation and a proper porch and floor."

The president pondered the offer. "You said gold nuggets?"

"Yes. You understand though that your teller must not advertise how I pay for things?"

"That's not a problem. Yes. Mr. Wells, I think we could arrange all of that."

"You think? That's not a contractual statement!"

The banker looked sharply at Traver. "You're quite specific and clear, Mr. Wells. Yes, I can do that. For a thousand dollars in gold, you will have a clear title."

"Good. I shall discuss this with my wife and I will let you know by Friday noon." Traver stood up and they shook hands. "So good to chat with you. And thank Mr. Wilbar for his help."

Traver got outside quickly and headed up the main road to the hotel.

Walking into the hotel lobby, he saw Laura was sitting in the guest lounge. She was stunning in a white silk blouse. Her collar was fastened around her neck and her puffy sleeves came just past her elbows, She had on a black skirt that came down to her boot tops when she stood up. Her breasts showed off the blouse nicely.

Traver walked over to her, and she extended her hand. "Mr. Wells, the pastor will be here at sundown to marry us. Go get cleaned up, a bath and a shave. I'll stay here and wait for you. Now you hurry up, honey!"

"But didn't we get married in Maxwell?" he asked.

"Yep! But this is McDonald's pastor. Marry me again and I get the ring back. I'm enjoying all this marrying stuff."

In less than an hour Traver was back, all shaved and clean. The barber didn't have a customer so he got a hair trim right away. The bath came next, and afterward he put back on the clothes he had come into town wearing.

Laura was still in the lounge but with a man in a black suit. As Traver came over, she stood up. "Pastor, this is my husband to be, Mr. Wells." The ceremony was quick.

"Mrs. McDonald will be pleased to hear of your marriage," the pastor told us.

The following morning came with thundering raindrops banging on the windows of the newlyweds' room.

Laura and Traver lay there in the sagging bed, enjoying the noisy downpour and squeaking springs.

She chuckled. "This is undoubtedly the worst bed I have ever slept on."

He laughed at her. "Me, too! I expect that this ol' bed has had a lot of workouts!"

She blushed and said, "Not like our loving!" She snuggled up closer to him. "What are we going to do today while it rains? There's no shopping and no coffee shop."

"No what?" he exclaimed. "No shopping, no movies, no coffee shop . . . Wait, that's it—a coffee shop with cinnamon rolls and a lunch only!"

"What?" Laura asked.

Traver put his arm around her and scratched her through the sheet. He told her what had happened the day before, how he had met Bill and Alice, Will's mom, and how he threw a paper airplane out of the Sawtooth.

Laura sat up in bed, holding the sheet close to her chest, covering her wonderful breasts. "You made a paper airplane and tossed it out the door and the veterinarian brought it into the bar and asked who made it? That's interesting. Did she seem to know what she was holding?"

"I'm sure she knew it was an airplane. Why pick it up and try to find who made it?" Traver suggested.

"She has to know something," Laura declared. "How could she possibly know?"

"From what little contact I had with her, I would say she is not from around here. There's an 'intelligence' about her. You can sense it."

"What do you mean, intelligence? Something like from the future?" Laura asked, as she twisted her hair up. "Do you think someone has developed time travel, like a foreign government? Is she Russian or something?" Laura stopped and looked out the window. "Maybe someone not in our time, maybe further in our future, got it right with Einstein's stuff or some other theory." Laura returned her gaze to him. "Honey, we are in the middle of something weird. Let's go slow with this and try to find out who we're dealing with. I do want to get back home again."

"Red Legs and now this," Laura sighed.

A huge flash of lightning brightened the room, followed by a thunderous boom. "Whee! That was close," squealed Laura. "Let's go to the camp and get Buster and have that vet take a look at him, you know, like a professional call."

"Okay," said Traver, "if the rain stops."

Laura snuggled up to him. "You know, Mr. Wells, the only thing to do in 1860 when it rains is to stay in bed and give the mattress a workout." The lightning flashed in Laura's eyes and slowly her hand found what she was seeking. "Goddamn, Traver, I do love you!" She pulled the sheets back, and side by side they fell asleep.

When they awakened, the sunlight was strong and flowing through the window. It was quiet, no thunder or pounding rain. Traver whispered, "Mrs. Wells, are we going to stay in bed all day?"

She stretched and yawned. "Not a problem, cowboy. Boy, a cup coffee would be great right now!"

He hugged her. "Sure would! I'll get dressed and go see if I can round up a cup for you."

By the time Traver got back, Laura was dressed in her split riding skirt and Western-style white blouse. The coffee was in a white china cup and was far too strong, but she licked her lips. "Only a few sips of this stuff is all a person needs. Let's go out and see how the boys are doing and get some better coffee." She put the cup down, strapped on her 44-40, slipped the shoulder holster on, and put on her deerskin vest to cover the shoulder pistol.

"There's no better coffee," Traver grumbled.

"You think we'll be back tonight?"

Traver said, "I was thinking about Mitch and Roy coming into town for the night. I'll tell the clerk so he doesn't freak out when two men show up to use the room and we don't."

Laura and Traver stopped at the desk and handed in the key, and he told the clerk that two of his men were coming in this evening to use their room. Laura had her new dress and blouse folded up and retied in the paper the dress shop had wrapped it in.

As they left the hotel, they found Will was sitting on the raised wooden walkway.

"Good morning, Mr. Wells, Mrs. Wells. Are you leaving?"

"No. Not right now, son. Got to go to the bank first," Traver told him. "Say, where can a fellow get a good cup of coffee?"

Will thought a moment before saying, "No coffee except at the hotel here and they boil it too much. Mom makes good coffee down at the saloon, though. Can I get you some?"

"Thanks, Will. Maybe when we get back."

"You sure look pretty today, Mrs. Wells," Will complimented Laura, but his bravado caused him to turn red in the face. He put his hands in his pockets and dropped his head. Then he looked up, smiling.

Laura returned his smile, saying, "Why, thank you, Will. That makes my day."

Traver scruffled Will's hair. "We'll be back in a bit, son."

Laura held Traver's arm with both hands as they walked over to the bank.

Stomping their boots on the wooden-plank walk just outside the bank, so as not to be tracking in any dirt, Traver held the door open for Laura, making a mock bow ushering her in and then following her.

The teller loudly said, "Good morning, Mr. Wells!"

The bank president came out of his office door in a rush. "Mr. Wells!" He looked at Laura. "The bride?"

Laura said, "Boy, good news sure travels fast around here."

Mr. Sanders laughed. "Bad news is even faster. Come in and sit down. Is the bakery a wedding gift for Mrs. Wells?"

"No, like I said yesterday, it's a business deal," Traver answered him in measured tones.

Mr. Sanders looked slightly puzzled.

"Yes. We want the property," Laura spoke up, "but I would like to see it. Will you please show it to me?"

"Yes, let me get the key."

The trio walked out of the bank and headed south toward the stockyards and freight companies. Laura leaned over to Traver, "This will develop into a good property." She winked.

Traver responded, "I know. In a few decades this will be all the train switching yards for the Union Pacific railroad."

"Here we are," Mr. Sanders declared.

Laura looked at the building and then at Traver.

"It's brick."

"Yes, and very well built, too." Mr. Sanders unlocked the door and they went in. Laura was pointing as she said, "That wall there, the south wall, is where the fireplace goes. I want a large one that can hold two racks that swing out so coffee can be kept warm during the winters. Now show me the ovens."

"They are just outside, out back."

They went out the back door and Laura looked around. "This needs to be enclosed so the winter won't keep us from baking." Laura looked at the bank president. "What will it cost to enclose this area and put in a good stone floor, brick walls, windows on the south and west sides, and a good roof?"

"I imagine that two hundred to three hundred dollars extra will do that."

"That's included the thousand dollars that Mr. Wells offered," Laura said decisively. "Can this be started right away?"

"If there's brick and glass, I'm sure it can be done right away," Mr. Sanders assured her.

"We will take it." She shook his hand. "Deal!"

Mr. Sanders replied, "Deal."

"We'll be back tomorrow to sign the papers or maybe on Saturday. You're open on Saturday, aren't you?"

"Yes, until four in the afternoon."

"Good! We will see you then."

"Before you and Mr. Wells leave, let's go back to my office so I can pencil together the contract."

They walked back to the bank, and when they crossed the threshold, Mr. Sanders said politely, "Can I get you something to drink? Water?"

Laura answered, "A good cup of coffee?"

"Best cup of coffee in town is Alice's, down at the saloon. Just a minute." Mr. Sanders got up, went to the front door, and yelled, "Will! Boy, come here."

Traver could see through the big plate glass window that Will jumped up and ran over to the bank.

"Here, son, go down to your mom's and bring us back three cups of coffee." He gave Will a quarter.

"Yes, sir!"

"There now, Mrs. Wells, it's just a bit of a wait. Mr. Wells, let me sketch out a contract and deed."

As Mr. Sanders picked up his pencil to make the draft copy, Traver said, "Okay, here is how it needs to start out: One-third ownership to Mr. and Mrs. T. K. Wells. One-third ownership to . . . just leave that blank for now. The other third ownership . . . leave that blank, too. I'll fill in the other partners' names when we are ready, and then we'll record the deed."

"Just who are the other partners?" Mr. Sanders asked.

"All you need to know at present is when the gold nuggets are going to arrive. It will be tomorrow. Roy Thompson or an Indian named Twin Bears will bring the payment to you."

"An Indian!" Mr. Sanders looked shocked.

"Yes, an Indian. I trust him with my life. You would do well to have a friend like him."

"Of course," said Mr. Sanders.

Will came back into the office with the three white ceramic mugs of coffee, and he gave the quarter back to Sanders. "Mom said thank you. I told her that the coffee was for Mr. and Mrs. Wells."

"Thanks, Will," Laura said. "This coffee is very good."

After Will left, Sanders handed the first-draft copy of the contract to Traver. He read it, gave it to Laura, and then she read it as she sipped her coffee. "Mr. Sanders, this looks fine, but there is no performance statement."

"What it that?" he asked.

Laura put the document down on his desk. "Well, if you don't get done what we have agreed to and paid for, on time you forfeit a percentage of the sales amount daily until the work is done."

Sanders considered this. "By God, that's an excellent idea. It will solve a lot of procrastination. What if the work can't be done because of foul weather or material shortages?"

"That's a good point," Laura said. "We can discuss that at the final draft. But I believe that is not a problem. Reasonable delays can be listed and even accidents that may slow the work should be considered, also."

They heard stomping feet outside on the plank sidewalk and then the thuds of heavy boots on the slate stone floor. They heard the teller saying, "Hello, corporal, how can we help you today?"

A rich voice said, "I wish to open a savings account. What interest do you pay?"

"Half a percent, sir, compounded, of course."

"Good. That's acceptable. I have some gold coins left to me by an old gentleman who died at the fort. He didn't have anyone, and he left me his wagon and contents. I took it because I am getting out of the Army next month."

Laura perked up and looked over at Traver.

"How much will you be depositing, corporal?"

He replied, "One hundred fifty-dollar silver coins and five hundred twenty double eagles."

"That's seven thousand dollars total!"

Hearing this, Sanders jumped up from behind his desk, nearly upsetting his chair. "Excuse me. folks!" He rushed out the office door and into the front of the bank. He introduced himself and asked the corporal's name.

"Peterson. James Peterson.Corporal, 5th Calvary, mounted."

Laura dropped her coffee cup and it crashed to the floor, shattering into pieces on the stone floor. Frozen in time, she wasn't even breathing.

Sanders came back into his office just as quickly as he had left. "Is everything okay in here?"

"Yes." Traver said.

Laura looked apologetic. "I'm dreadfully sorry. My cup slipped from my hands. Let me clean this up."

"No, no, that's not necessary, Mrs. Wells. I can get Will to do it."

Sanders went to the bank's front door and yelled again for Will.

Then Traver and Laura heard Sanders saying, "Corporal, my bank will be proud to hold your money. You realize that the money will be sent to Omaha to the cash vault there. You can ask for gold or silver when you make withdrawals, but paper is easier to work with. Just let me know at least two weeks in advance if you want a large amount of gold. Again, thank you!"

Sanders came back to his office, and Laura, in a daze, stood up. She held on to the chair for support.

The soldier out at the teller's station was her great-granddad. It was silent out front, but Laura knew he was still there. She turned and faced the door. Looking back at Traver, she said, "Honey, I'm going to see him."

Traver nodded at her.

She stepped out of the office and into the front part of the bank, to meet her past.

"Corporal Peterson?" she said softly.

And then it was quiet.

Standing just outside the doorway, she watched a tall, well-built soldier turn toward her. He had a rich black handlebar mustache. His hair, also black, was a bit long. He was tan and wrinkled from being out in the sun and wind for days on end. His uniform was dusty and sweat stained. He was wearing suspenders and had a Colt 45 peacemaker at his hip, slung down low.

His eyes were dark coal, and they locked onto Laura's eyes, and for a moment she felt a charge of energy shooting through her.

"Ma'am?" he said.

Laura stood there, stunned, looking at him, her insides quaking. *This is not possible*, she thought.

Within James Peterson's space, something was stirring in him also. This woman was strikingly good looking. He saw the gun she wore, and it looked to be a Colt 44-40. He continued inspecting her closely. He was drawn to her, a feeling he had never before experience in all his twenty-six years.

"Corporal Peterson," Laura finally managed to say again, with a dry throat, "it's good to meet you. I am Mrs. Wells. My husband and I stopped at the fort Wednesday of this week. We met Major McPherson, and I asked if there were any troopers who knew the land around here. My husband and I represent the Union Pacific railroad and we are surveying for a possible route from Fort Cottonwood over into Utah. Major McPherson mentioned that you were an engineer and knew the lay of the land." She stepped closer to him and extended her hand. "It's good to meet you."

As they shook hands, Laura shivered at his touch. She felt like crying with joy and hugging him close. James also felt the energy flowing. He looked confused for a moment.

Their hands were still clasped when Laura, her voice breaking, said, "I hope that we can get together and look over some maps soon. We have to leave next week."

They were still holding hands as Corporal Peterson said, "Saturday and Sunday I'll be at the fort. I will be on patrol Wednesday through Friday this week. Perhaps those days will be acceptable?"

"Do you attend church, corporal?"

"Yes, ma'am."

"Well, then, how about Sunday afternoon?" Their hands slowly loosened and slipped to their sides.

He was smiling now. "How about you and your husband attend church with me and my men Sunday?"

Laura nodded her head in agreement. "We would treasure the time together, corporal."

"Fine, then Sunday or sooner at the fort."

"Yes, it's so good to meet you, corporal." Laura slowly turned away and came back into the bank president's office.

"Oh, ma'am . . ."

She turned back again.

"What did you say your name was?"

"Mrs. Wells, Laura Wells."

Peterson gave a tilt of his chin. "I'll see you soon, Mrs. Wells."

Laura came into the president's office and sat down. She looked at Traver with wide eyes. "Holy shit! I just met my great-granddad!" Laura was silent as she re-examined her feelings.

The teller said to Corporal Peterson, "Here is your pass book. Seven thousand dollars total deposited, and we thank you for choosing our bank to do business with."

Sanders excused himself and left the office for a few moments.

Laura's tears were streaming down both cheeks and dropping on her deerskin vest. "Traver, that is my great-granddad out there! My God! I met him and I touched him. I saw him and I heard his voice. Traver, I wish I could tell him who I am."

Her tears were becoming a flood now. Traver went over, stood behind her, and rubbed her shoulders. She raised her hands and rested them on his. "I love you," she whispered. She dropped her hands, took out a hanky, and wiped her eyes and cheeks. "Let's go. I need to walk a bit. I met my great-grandad," she gasped.

Laura and Traver stood outside at the bank's door and watched as Corporal Peterson rode away. As they started walking, Traver heard Roy whistle and yell. He and Mitch were on the wagon, and Buster was riding in the back.

"Hey!" Laura yelled. "What are you guys doing in town so early?"

Roy called, "We got tired of eating those MRE's. Any good cafes here?"

Traver pointed up the street. "That saloon has some good fixin's. Let's go. It's early yet, but we'll join you for lunch." He reached over and scratched Buster's ears. "You miss me, boy?

The dog began to whine and let out a howl.

Laura laughed. "I swear he wants to talk."

"Watch this," Traver said. "Buster, let's go to the doctor!"

Buster dropped his head and got under the wagon's bench seat.

"He's been scared of the doctor ever since I took him to be neutered years ago. The vet!" Traver said, looking at Laura. "We need to pay a visit to her and take old Buster with us. Let's eat first though." He pointed out the Sawtooth Saloon.

"We'll walk, and you—all go ahead and drive the wagon up."

Sitting at a table in the saloon, they told the bartender they wanted four lunches.

He yelled, "Alice, four lunches!"

After a bit Alice emerged, carrying two plates of steak and potatoes and tomatoes. She recognized Traver at the first glance and perked up. "Oh, Mr. Wells, good day to you. I'll be right back with the other two plates." She was right back, and she said. "Say, I want to thank you so much for giving Will all that candy. He shared it with his sister and me."

"Alice, I want you to meet my wife, Laura," Traver said, gesturing to her.

Alice wiped her hands on her apron and then shook Laura's hand. "Good to meet you."

Laura responded, "This is Roy, our foreman, and this is Mitch."

"Hi, fellas, you enjoy your food. The tomatoes are from my garden," Alice said proudly.

"Do you bake, Alice?" Laura asked.

"Oh yes! The best bread and pies you'll ever eat."

"Have you ever baked cinnamon rolls?"

"Cinnamon rolls? What's that?"

"Come," Laura said, "I'll show you. Can I go back in the kitchen?"

"Ah, sure, come on."

Laura turned back to her tablemates, saying, "You guys go ahead and eat, and I'll be baking for a while."

Roy took about half of Laura's plate of food, and Skip's dad took the rest. In about forty-five minutes, the smell of cinnamon rolls filled the air.

Roy sniffed. "Damn! Miss Laura hasn't baked like this since Bill died." He glanced over at Traver real quick. "Sorry, Traver. That just popped out."

Two cowboys stepped in the saloon door and looked at the bartender. "What smells so good?" one asked.

The bartender shrugged his shoulders and hollered for Alice. She came bustling out of the kitchen.

"These cowboys want to know what smells so good.

"Cinnamon rolls!" she said in a happy voice.

"We'll have some, please."

As Alice passed by Traver, he leaned over and said, "Fifteen cents per roll. They'll pay it."

She strode to the back smiling.

Presently Laura came out with two plates, a roll crowning each, and coffee. She sat them down at an empty table in front of the two cowboys. "Thats twenty-five cents each. boys."

One feller took a roll, had a bite, and started a grin a mile wide. He picked up his coffee and took a swig. "Gladly!" He gave Laura fifty cents.

"Thank you, boys." And Laura returned to the kitchen.

Before long a few more cowboys, seduced by the aroma of the cinnamon rolls reaching out into the street, stomped in.

When Laura came back to the table, she said, "Alice made four and a half dollars in a little over an hour. She's amazed."

Laura smiled at Traver. "Your idea will work."

"Yep, I thought it would," he agreed.

"Say, Roy, you two stay in town tonight and we'll stay out at the camp," Laura told her foreman. "Let's go visit the vet Traver. I told Alice not to make any more rolls till we talk with her."

They went outside and Traver put a leash made out of an old piece of rope from the wagon around Buster's neck. The dog didn't like it much, being tethered. Laura, Traver, and Buster walked over to the vet's office and went in.

A young woman, perhaps twenty-five or so, well dressed and very shapely, looked up from her desk. "Yes? How can I help you?"

"I brought in old Buster for a check-up. He's not acting too well nowadays. Can the doc see him today?"

"The doctor is out back with Mr. McDonald. His horse is down. I think she can see the dog."

"We can wait," Traver said.

"I'll go tell the doctor that you're here. Just a moment."

After the woman left the reception area, Laura said, "Everything looks in place here." She got up and began looking closely at things. What she missed was the pin-sized camera that was recording their conversation and their pictures.

"What are you looking for, honey?"

"Oh, nothing in particular, just something that might not fit. After all, she seemed to know what an airplane was."

Traver sat there, scratching Buster's ears. "What do you want, boy?" Buster began his whining talk and barking. "Good boy! You'll be okay with the doc, she seems to be competent."

Laura was over by the secretary's desk. It seemed to be orderly, but maybe just for show.

When the woman returned, she said, "The doctor will be right in."

No more had she announced this than the doctor walked in.

As she stepped into her office from being out back, she saw Traver immediately and their eyes made contact. Her gray eyes were like a stormy, foggy day with an occasional spark of sunlight that danced in the sky. Traver froze, and for him time stopped. Every sound echoed as if it came from a good distance. He could hear himself breathe in and out, and with each intake the woman filled his senses. When he breathed out, he felt empty, even though Laura was standing beside him.

"Mr. Wells?" A man's voice. He had come in behind the doctor, and he extended his hand to Traver. "I am McDonald. I heard that you had stopped by."

Traver shook the man's hand.

The doctor was smiling, but her face could not even express the rapture she felt. No one in the room existed but the stranger. *I'm a woman, and this is how a woman feels about her man.* Tears began to form as she thought about all that she had missed. She had had other rewards: She was a Knower of the Way, a Luminal Star Flash Ship Captain. She took a deep breath. She realized she had missed a lot. This new feeling of being a woman was so different, so basic, and so strong.

She quickly wiped away that tear and tried to come back to the moment.

Siren noticed the woman with the stranger. Her heart collapsed. *He has chosen her!* This woman, tall and beautiful, radiated an energy, just like that of the stranger. Siren, the woman, was crushed. But Siren the star ship captain remembered her duty on this expedition. She had to act to find out who these two people were and not allow her heart to sway her from her responsibility to her ship and to her crew and to her home world.

Buster whined, and the stranger looked over at the dog. Traver said, "I know, boy, it will be just a little bit yet."

The captain tried to cover her amazement. *They can speak with the dog!* She immediately looked back at the stranger, baffled. The captain caught Laura looking at her. Siren felt like a woman again.

Always before, when situations arose, she was the captain, the final recourse and decision maker, concerning all things and events. Right now, she was the town vet, the star ship captain, and, as never before, a woman. Siren understood that Laura considered her a threat. Siren was unsure how to act.

Laura was getting vibrations from this woman, but she couldn't quite interpret them. Laura thought the vet was beautiful, with her shoulder-length dark hair, her arching eyebrows, her smooth complexion, her tea-rose pink cheeks and lips. Laura's intuition told her that the vet was a threat to her, but why was she feeling that way? Laura slipped her arm through Traver's, to show this woman that he was taken. But Laura felt embarrassed. She had never had that territorial feeling. Other new and strange emotions welled up in Laura's chest. Nevertheless, in spite of her emotional upheaval, Laura realized she didn't dislike the vet. She just sensed the vet was out of place.

"How can I help you?" the doctor addressed Traver after McDonald left.

Traver pulled on Buster's rope. "Buster seems a bit sluggish."

The doctor reached over and scratched Buster's ear. "Not feeling well, boy?" Buster whined.

Astounded that this dog understood her, what had the dog said?

Laura became part of the conversation. "Not only not feeling well, he's wanting more canned dog food." She was testing the vet, to see if she would understand the words canned dog food or at least the concept of processed food.

Laura kept her arm firmly attached to Traver's in a possessive manner. That made Siren ache inside, another woman so close to the stranger. In Siren's home world, Edon, Laura's behavior would not be appropriate at all. The women in her world were the ruling sex; men expressed all the emotions.

The doctor ran her hand down Buster's back and then his legs. Looking at Traver, she said, "He's neutered."

"Yep. Too many problems with him pissing on everything."

"You want to leave him overnight so I can watch him? That would cost you a dollar. You can pick him up tomorrow." "Come on, boy." Traver gave the woman at the desk a silver dollar and his name. As he and Laura left, Laura turned. "Better be a good boy," and the dog whined and barked.

When they were out the door, the young woman said to the doctor, "Captain, look at the replay." On a small hand-held device, the last few minutes of Laura and Traver were being played back. Laura was saying, "Everything looks in place," and she was· inspecting the room.

"Captain, no one has ever looked for something before. This is not present-time behavior."

"Did you see how Mr. Wells talked with his dog?" Siren asked.

"Yes, captain, and that's not possible here in this time. What do you think?"

The vet declared, "What I think is, we sit still and see what occurs. At least two of the crew can watch them," the captain directed her aide.

When Laura and Traver got back to the saloon, Alice was done with lunches. She, Laura, and Traver sat at a table and Laura went over with Alice what they had been thinking for her to get into: a coffee and cinnamon roll restaurant.

Traver was listening to Laura as she and Alice were talking and looking out the saloon's large front window. Two men standing across the street were looking toward the saloon. For some reason, they stood out like sore thumbs, dressed as they were in city duds.

Bingo! It struck Traver as a cowboy passed them. The two men were just too clean. *Strange. If I didn't know better, I would have thought them from back East.*

He interrupted the two gals. "Alice, have you ever seen those two men before?" He pointed across the street.

"Oh, sure. They work for the doc."

"The people doc or the animal doc?" he asked without taking his eyes off the men.

"For the animal doctor. Why do you ask?"

Laura had spotted the two fellows by now. "They look out of place," she said. "It strange the way they're just standing there."

"Why they do look awfully clean, don't they? They aren't cow hands," Alice said emphatically.

"I think they're watching us," Traver mused.

Laura turned to him. "You're being too sensitive."

"I would admit to that," he said, smiling. He did not want to mess with or distort history or their future. So far, it seemed that they had operated according to plan. Their stuff came through okay. Twin Bears came through and killed a deer that might have jumped in front of a truck, causing the driver to die. Now the deer is dead, and the accident with the truck won't happen. This sort of thinking could snowball into a kazillion what-ifs.

He touched Laura's hand and rubbed the key-ring wedding band. "I just don't want to change anything, now that you're in my life."

She smiled at him.

"Now, Alice, you want to go see the building we're talking about?" Laura asked her.

"I do, but I have no money."

"Give it time. You'll soon have too much money. What you always want to do is listen to your customers and serve a quality product at a price just a little bit higher than your competition," Laura advised.

"For more than the other places charge?" Alice was skeptical.

"Sure, you will be amazed at how people will come to you. You'll be hearing folks saying that they know a good place for coffee or lunch. That the food is excellent—a little pricy but quality is worth it. It's the price that makes folks think they are being treated extra special."

It was exciting to see all of this register in Alice's thoughts. "How long do I have to pay you off for the initial investment?" Laura looked at Traver. "Oh, I'd say about two years after the Union Pacific comes through town here."

Alice thought a moment. "Okay, you would know, being railroad employees and such. Okay!" She stuck out her hand. "Partners!"

Laura shook her hand and so did Traver.

"Let's go, partners, and check out the premises," Traver said.

After the three left the proposed café site, they walked over to the bank. Traver told Sanders he had a deal and introduced him to Alice. "She's one of the partners," Traver explained to him. Sanders was all smiles because he knew Alice from the Saloon.

"Well, Alice, you're going to open a bakery?"

She started to say something, but Traver interrupted. "Boy, Mr. Sanders, you can sure make a good guess."

"Well, now, that's why I'm the president and Junior is a teller." He smiled broadly, thinking he was smart as a tack.

"Mr. Sanders, go ahead and transfer the funds. Here's my signature."

Sanders looked at the deed and then back at Traver. "Traver T. K. Wells. What does the T. K. stand for, Mr. Wells?"

"T. K. is what I use on all my legal documents. A forger would normally write Traver Wells. See what I mean?"

He nodded his head. "Boy, you're sharp! Now, I'll get a crew out there right away for the fireplace and some brick masons to start closing in the baking ovens."

Alice came over and quietly said, "Those two fellas across the street are watching us. I'm sure they're following us." She had a serious look on her face.

At that moment Bill, the old gent, passed by the bank, and he jumped when Traver called out, "Hey, Bill! Come in here right now!" He turned in a sort of dazed way and stopped. "Do us a favor? Go over to the hotel and see if you can find my men, Roy and Mitch, and tell them to follow those two men over there. I want to overtake them down at the old bakery. You got that?"

"Yes, sir!"

Bill turned and headed for the hotel. In a few seconds he disappeared inside and later appeared with Roy and Mitch. Bill pointed out the two fellows, and Roy nodded his head at Traver. Bill stood there at the hotel and watched as the men moved toward the two clean-cut fellows. It was time for Traver and company to make their move.

Two women customers walked out of the bank, and Traver followed closely behind them. The bank president handed Traver the key to the bakery, and for a moment he, Laura, and Alice stood on the boardwalk.

Laura was telling Alice how she could get set up first with just coffee and hot cinnamon rolls, while the remodeling work was in progress for the new coffee shop. "No lunches yet, just coffee," Laura advised.

Traver glanced in the shop windows they were passing and could see the reflections from across the street of the men following them. Roy and Mitch were about twenty feet behind, shadowing the shadowers. They seemed oblivious that they were being followed.

At the bakery, Traver and his companions stopped, and he raised his hands, pretending to point something out to the women. The men following them stopped, just as they did.

To the women Traver said, "Let's go around the building where they can see us heading toward the river."

They rounded the corner, and Traver was in hopes the men would cross the street, too. When they had gone far enough to allow the men to reach the corner of the bakery, Traver turned abruptly to face them. Sure enough, they were right where he expected them to be, with Mitch and Roy only ten feet behind them.

As Traver turned, he quickly snatched his .45 caliber pistol from his shoulder holster and leveled it at the men. Roy and Mitch followed suit, and the men were covered front and rear. They froze in their tracks, and Roy barked, "Boys, just keep walking!" Mitch added, "Right now!" To that Traver added, "Come over to me and don't make any quick moves with your hands!" Roy stepped up behind them, chambered a round, and poked one of the fellows in the back. "Move!" he commanded. Both of the men walked slowly toward Traver.

As they got closer, Traver stepped back so he could not be viewed from the street. When he figured they were out of sight, he ordered one of the men to stand facing the bakery and to put his hands on the brick wall, feet outstretched. Traver told him in no uncertain terms, "Don't move!" The other man was placed in the same position. Roy put his sidearm to the man's head and Mitch did the same with the other man. Laura drew her .45 pistol and said, "Boys, I've got you covered, too, so don't you move! Traver, you frisk them."

Traver replaced his .45 and begin patting them down. What he found looked like a cell phone or a radio and a tiny TV camera, which he placed in his pocket. The other man had a device that appeared to be a cell phone and nothing else. Taking out his .45 again, Traver told Laura. "Go get the wagon and be real quick. Boys, you just stay as you are. Alice, you go back to the saloon. Don't say anything about this. We'll get back to you." She nodded her head yes.

Laura scooted around the corner and up the street to the wagon.

Within minutes she was back and wheeled the wagon around the corner, to where the group was.

"Get in!" Traver barked to the two men. They got into the rear and Traver instructed them to sit down, back to back. He used the old rope to tie them together. "Let's go to the camp!"

As they began to roll away, Traver yelled at Alice, "Go tell Will to go to the animal doctor and bring her to the camp. Will knows where the camp is. Roy, let's get out of here!"

Laura got in the back with Traver. As he tossed the two cell phones and the TV camera out the rear of the wagon, Traver said to Laura, "Tracking devices, most likely."

One of the fellows asked, "What are you going to do with us?"

Traver let him stew a moment, as he sat there staring at him. "We will do nothing to cause you any harm. Will you also agree to that about us?"

The other man said, "It is not our intention to harm anyone."

Traver studied that one. "Okay, then. Laura, put your gun back in its holster. I trust you," Traver told the man.

Traver put his gun away, too. "What we intend to do with you is just to get the doctor out here with us. She is not what she pretends to be nor are you boys." It took them a good thirty minutes to reach the riverside camp.

"Who do you think we are?" the older of the two asked as they pulled into camp.

"I'm not sure," Traver said. "But we'll just wait and see. Are you boys hungry? We're going to have some snacks."

"No, thanks. That's fine," the older of the two said. Traver dug out a couple MREs for Laura and himself.

"Hey, Roy? You hungry?" Traver asked.

"Nope, I had breakfast at the hotel with Mitch."

The two men watched Traver open his dark-brown plastic bag that held the food. He purposefully spread out the contents, beans and franks in tomato sauce, a pack of crackers and peanut butter and cheese. A packet of coffee and hot chocolate, wiping paper, gum, matches, and a plastic spoon. Traver opened the pack of beans and franks, got a spoonful, and popped it in his mouth. "Damn! That's good!" he exclaimed as he smacked his lips.

The men watched him closely. "You know? Maybe we will have some of your food," one said. "We have never seen food like this."

"Oh?" Traver said.

Laura got two more bags. "Chicken and barbecue sauce." She tossed it to one of the men.

"Beans and franks." She tossed that one to the other man. In no time they were smacking their lips.

"This certainly is excellent food!" the younger of them said.

The older man asked, "Where did you get all of this?"

"We brought it with us," Traver answered.

"You brought it with you from where?" He spooned another heap of barbecued chicken into his mouth.

"Where?" Traver asked quietly.

Laura came up with an answer. "From a long way away."

"Well, it is sure not from here," he said. And then he quickly shut up. Just a small slip of the tongue could give away so much.

"Hey, Twin Bears!" Traver shouted. "Go out about a hundred yards and take the AK-47 with you and a drum of ammo. And take the walkie-talkie and cover the camp. Oh yeah," he cautioned, "make sure you stay on channel nine!"

Twin Bears went into the bigger tent and came out with the AK, drum clip attached, and a hand-held walkie-talkie for himself and one for Traver. They turned them on and the electronic switch beeped. The captured men looked at the radios and then at the rifle and immediately they knew that their captors were more than what they appeared to be also.

"The captain will not be bringing any weapons!" the older man shouted.

"Captain?" Traver looked quickly at them. "Is it doctor or captain?" he asked.

Neither man answered. Traver believed that they had slipped up big-time by calling her captain and they knew it. *Captain of what? A captain of an army of the future? But how was that possible? Hell, we're from the future! It could happen!*

Laura leaned over closer to Traver and in a low voice said, "Captain of what?"

He shrugged his shoulders. "Hey, Twin Bears, go ahead. Don't do anything unless I give you the signal. Full automatic, about twenty rounds just short of the left of us should do it."

Twin Bears was smiling broadly as he left and mumbled, "Big thunder!"

"You boys want something to drink?"

"That would be fine," the older one answered. "What does he mean 'big thunder'?"

Traver ignored the question.

Traver nudged Laura. "Watch this."

He reached into the box sitting just outside the larger tent and pulled out four Pepsis in aluminum cans. He gave Laura one and she turned so the men could watch her. She popped open the can, it fizzed, and overflowed the Pepsi can. She quickly put it to her mouth and drank. "This is so good!" she sighed.

Traver got two more cans and gave them to the prisoners. "Drink up, boys!"

Popping their cans, they sipped their Pepsis and lit up like Christmas trees with pleasure as they tasted the drink. They began examining the cans. "Pepsi," the older man said. "This is better than sasparilla."

Laura and Traver laughed.

"What?" the older man asked.

Laura managed to say, "That would be one great commercial."

"Commercial? What's that?" the younger man asked.

Laura said, "It's an annoying way of trying to get people to buy stuff."

"Buy stuff?"

"Yeah, like buying a lunch at the saloon."

"Oh, I see." Both men answered at once. They downed their Pepsis and said, "Thank you."

One asked, "What sort of container is this?"

"It's aluminum, a metal can." He grabbed his empty can and squeezed it nearly flat.

Both men's eyes opened wide.

"Go ahead and squeeze your can," Traver said. The older man did and he was fascinated that he could collapse the can so easily.

"Hello the camp!" a child's voice yelled.

"Hello!" Roy yelled back.

Out of the brush came old Buster, running into camp. He came over to Traver, talking all the way.

"How you doing, old boy?" Traver addressed the dog. Buster did his woo-woo-woo sounds again. "It's great they took good care of you." He scratched Buster's ears. "Go say hello to Laura."

Buster turned and went directly to her, making his wooing sounds.

The older man watched in astonishment. "You can talk with your dog?"

"Sure," Traver said, chuckling, "but I don't understand him talking to me."

The older man laughed. "For a minute I thought you could really understand him. That would really make me wonder who you are." The older man's eyes reflected friendship rather than hostility.

They were still sitting considering each other when the wagon broke through the brush, with Will driving it. The doctor or captain, whichever, was sitting next to him. She looked even more attractive to Traver than in town earlier today. He felt a surge of feelings in his chest. *What a stunning woman!* But those feelings in his chest confused him. He was so satisfied with Laura, and yet he yearned for this woman who was called captain. *How is it that two women could strike my soul with such a hammer?*

Will stopped the wagon and the horse stomped its feet and whinnied. The boy quieted her with, "Easy girl." And that settled the horse down.

CHAPTER 11

HEART'S FIRST CONTACT

The past, the future, and light-years' distance,
But a heart is a heart is a heart in any time

THE DOCTOR, THE captain, whoever she was, remained seated when the wagon came to a halt. She still had on the clothing Traver had seen her wearing at her office. He took in her presence as a gentle spring breeze brings a promise of rain and wildflowers. Her radiance struck in him the promise of wonderment. He turned and saw Laura watching the doctor, too. Traver believed that Laura was sensing something also. *Does Laura sense what this captain is doing to me?*

Traver knew Laura was a sensitive person, and she would have to deal with the feelings Traver had for the captain. Laura glanced over at Traver with a wonderful smile on her face. She stepped closer to him, as if letting the doctor know that Traver was hers.

Traver's thoughts were rumbling all over, trying to figure who the captain was and who her underlings were. Captain sounded like a military title, but no one in that time had hand-held devices. Traver remembered a lot of talk about advances in the 1940's, involving Einstein and Tesla's unified field theory, and about a destroyer that was outfitted to become invisible when a magnetic field was activated. That ship disappeared while it was tied up at dockside and reappeared at another Navy yard. The buzz in all the articles was that the ship moved in time when it became invisible. Traver had always believed that the ship didn't move in time but just moved from one place to another on the same day. But if the story was true, had the government actually perfected time travel and these people were from Traver's own future?

Then Traver realized that they had also traveled in time. Maybe Enchanted Canyon had been the site of a time-travel facility, deep in Earth's past, built way back in earth's history. Maybe Enchanted Canyon still had the field coils buried deep in the ground, and so when lightning storms occurred, the coils charged and created the arcing of the gravity-well, so both times could touch and overlap. Or maybe the canyon was where two fields touched and a storm could electrify an effect on time.

It was a tense moment for Traver, waiting to see what would happen next, but not a fearful moment. Time would soften the newness and clarity would produce a general comfort. Knowledge always won out.

As Will pulled to a halt, he jumped down, tethered the horse to a bush, and put a feed bag over its nose. The doctor jumped down and walked over to the fire ring. She had nodded to the two men and briefly looked them over. "You okay?" she asked them.

"Yes, we are," they said in a businesslike manner.

She turned and said to Traver, "I'm here as Will said you asked. Why do you have my men like this?"

"Well, doctor, why did you have your men following my wife and me? It's very strange behavior for a veterinarian. What was I to think when Alice said these two here worked for you?"

"Yes, I see the strangeness of the situation." She studied Traver for a long time. "I suspect that you sense something different about me and my two men here."

"Yes, I do."

"I sense something about you and your party, also." The vet paused long enough for Traver to consider that.

Traver answered with a question. "Are we at a standstill?"

"A what?"

"A standstill," he repeated. "What to do next?"

"Ah! I see. I can do a couple of things and let's see what happens," she said.

Traver reached in his pants pocket and pulled out his walkie-talkie and pressed the send button. It made a tone. "Twin Bears, come into camp. There's no need for surveillance." Traver unkeyed.

Twin Bears responded with, "Coming in."

The doctor watched Traver but said nothing. She seemed skeptical until she saw Twin Bears coming in with the AK-47. She turned and asked, "What is that he is holding?"

"It's a rifle," Traver informed her.

Twin Bears approached them and Traver took the rifle. Slipping off the safety and making sure it was set on automatic, he pointed it away from everyone and burned off twenty or so rounds. Both men jumped. The doctor stepped back. She saw the bullets hitting the ground about three hundred yards out, kicking up the dust.

"Now," he said. "How about yourself?" He looked intently into her eyes, expecting something military to happen.

She looked around at all of us. "You are not from here! No one now has rifles like you have."

She looked over at Twin Bears. "I'm from here!" he said gruffly.

Laura spoke up, "Doctor, we are from tomorrow."

"You mean today's tomorrow?" the doctor wanted to know.

Traver called to Will. "Take the wagon back to town, but come here first."

"Mr. Wells, we are from far away also, but in distance, not in time manner." Traver held up his hand to stop her from saying any more. Will came over to Traver. "Will, do you like the doctor?"

"Yes, sir." He put his head down and kicked his bare foot at a clump of dirt.

"Will, do you trust her?"

He looked back at her again. "Yes, sir."

"You can head back into town, son."

The doctor watched as Will drove away. Turning from watching Will, she looked back at Traver. He commented, "Children don't have the clouds of distrust that adults seem to be surrounded with."

The doctor smiled at that. "Then I see that you are a child in a grown-up body. I like that!" Traver shook her hand again. "Please, let's discuss our lives. I am sorry that I had to get you out here like I did."

The doctor, the captain, suddenly went quiet and raised her hand in a motion to stop what was being said. "I am so very sorry, I have been awfully impolite. Here we are and we don't know each other's names." She looked directly at Traver. "I call you the stranger, even though I have heard that you call yourself Mr. Wells. You don't know who I am, as far as my name goes. I am Siren." She bowed her head as she spoke her name, which sounded like a lilting melody. I noticed that both her men bowed their heads, too. "My two crew members are," she pointed to the older man, "Monk, my teacher. And Pawlls is one of my engineers."

Returning her gaze to Laura, Siren said, "I have met you, but I don't know your name." Laura smiled. "I am Mrs. Wells, but call me Laura."

Siren's heart nearly stopped beating for a second. *His wife! He has chosen!* She wanted to cry and to turn and run, but the captain in her kept her steadfast and holding her ground. Quickly, Siren looked away to recover. "He is Twin Bears. I recognize him from town on lots of days. I do not know the other two men of your party, Mr. Wells."

Traver said, "That man is Roy, our foreman, and the older man is Mitchell, Mitch for short."

"Thank you for the introductions. But I need to tell you that I am a luminal star flash vessel captain."

Laura's eyes widened and Siren noticed. "Is something wrong?" she asked.

Laura stammered, "No, no, I just wasn't expecting to hear star ship!"

"Do you know what a star ship is?" Siren asked, astonished.

"Why, yes, I do. And that's what is so amazing, that you say such a thing here in 1860."

"I was very interested in where you came from, and I apologize for not introducing us sooner," Siren said sincerely.

"No, no. It's me that's sorry," Traver said. "I was very curious when your men called you captain and I was wondering what you're captain of." He looked at her closely. "Are you Miss or Mrs. Siren?"

"I am Siren, no other name, well, except for what my crew might call me when I'm not around." Her men chuckled at her disclosure. That broke the tension and warmed up the introductions a bit.

Traver simply repeated, "Star-ship captain Siren. Yes—no, no, I was just repeating your name."

"Yes." She extended her hand once again, and he clasped it. Traver's thoughts were flashing. *My God! This is a person from the stars touching me!* Goosebumps raised all over his body. *She doesn't look or feel like an alien.*

"This is good. I had not figured out how to talk with you discreetly. So, how many tomorrows are we talking about?" Siren asked quietly.

"One hundred and sixty-eight," Traver answered. "We live in 1995??. And how about you?" "We are very far from home. Tonight, I can show you the portion of the sky that we came from. It is visible from this place on your planet." Traver glanced up at the sky. "In our year we have gone to the moon. We have robotic machines that survey the planets, but no stars."

Traver interrupted, "We are just babies in this space-travel business. But then you are not from Earth?"

The doctor sensed his amazement. "You are," Traver struggled with the term he wanted to use, "aliens? Extraterrestrials?"

The captain broke in. "We are just as you, a long way from home. We are different and yet the same. So much the same. We are human also." The captain's words trailed off. Her emotions were reflecting the newness of the woman in her. Her chest was burning, and she fought to regain her composure. She spoke again, but her voice was no longer matter of fact. Her tones were softer and her two men noticed the change. They had never heard the captain speak in these tones, soft with feeling instead of brusque with commands. The captain was having problems staying on topic, finding it almost impossible to wrest her thoughts away from Mr. Wells. Monk immediately knew what Siren was going through, and he smiled at the knowledge and was pleased that his captain was feeling like a woman.

"You're . . ." Siren's voice cracked. She looked over at Laura, dismayed that this woman would sleep with this man, and not herself. Looking at Mr. Wells and falling to pieces inside, Siren finished, "Traver . . ." She tried to speak again, but couldn't until she gathered herself. "Yes, your civilization at this day in time is very young."

Helping the captain regain her composure, the older of the two men said. "Captain, you must taste a Pepsi, that is, if any more exists."

Traver laughed and pointed to him. "And what is the commercial?"

"Oh!" He laughed, too. "It's better than sasparilla!"

Everyone laughed, except the captain, who looked blank.

Twin Bears went to get her a can. She looked at it and hefted it. The younger man said, "Here, captain, let me show you how to open it." It fizzed as the can popped open, spewing Pepsi.

Stopping it quickly, she put her lips to the opening in the can and drank. "Ummmm!" She smiled and took another long drink of it. "This is excellent!"

She held the can as she looked at Twin Bears. "You're from today?"

He smiled and said, "Yes."

"How did you get involved with these people?"

"Sit down, doctor, and I will tell you the story." Twin Bears gestured to a log by the fire pit. When the Indian finished his story, Traver could see that the captain was captivated by it. "Twin Bears, what an adventure," Siren said softly. She looked around at the rest of them. "Let me tell you of my ship's journey."

Roy got up and put a couple of logs on the fire. Night had already come, and sparks flew up into the starlit sky. Siren pointed toward Pleiades, low in the northwest horizon of the night sky. "My home world sent out ships to search for others like us. For hundreds of years our ships searched our closest space and found nothing but evidence of prior civilizations and a great many planets with great ruins. Nothing of the people. Just what was left. As our knowledge became deeper, we realized that the spiritual aspects of our lives was as important as the physical things in our world." She stopped. "It is not enough to be. One must always be on the path of discovering one's spirit. We perfected and enhanced our physical bodies, improving the healing of our infirmities and our wounds. We live longer, to about a hundred eighty or two hundred years." She sat smiling at Traver's surprised expression. "In this time here, I am a young person of only ninety-six years of age."

Laura exclaimed in a joking manner, "Boy, can you put me through that youth time machine?"

"Yes, we can. In fact, Buster has been enhanced. He will go another ten to fourteen years, barring an accident."

"You hear that, Buster?" The dog raised his head and woo-wooed.

Siren looked at Traver in astonishment. "You can talk with your dog?" she asked, shocked. Everyone laughed at her serious question.

Traver had to say, "I think he understands me, but I can't understand woof-woof."

"Gosh, for a minute there I was truly impressed." Then Siren laughed, too. It was evident that she had a good sense of humor and enjoyed a good laugh.

"Anyway, my ship is a deep-probe ship. It's more advanced than the older light-star ships. All of those ships left with crews that went into deep-space hibernation for the trips. Everyone planned a return trip, but most of the older ships were one way with a data ship remote and were flown back to the mother world.

"My ship is here because of the data one of the ships returned. That deep-probe ship had problems landing, and its original objective was canceled. It became a survival trip. The planet was young but had human forms of life. The ship had mapped the planet and had done the initial scientific study before the crew was marooned. That was in this solar system but not on this planet. It was a twin world that they had landed on. This world was not yet developed in any great manner.

"The crew realized that the only way to survive was to assimilate into the population, which was the human species. The survivors of the ship did well, but eventually overpopulated the original population. This, I believe, was at a time when your planet was covered with ice. We think this is when the twins were destroyed—but how, it is not known."

Laura gasped, "Cro-Magnon!"

Siren looked startled. "What?"

Laura began telling a story of how Cro-Magnon man just showed up and out of nowhere canceled out Neanderthal man. "My God, Cro-Magnon man could be the survivors of the earlier ship's stranded crew or from the twins."

"That's rather hard to believe," Roy scoffed.

Siren smiled at that. "It's no harder than my believing all of you except for Twin Bears are from the future."

"Okay," Roy agreed. "I reckon so."

"When we arrived here, we could find no trace of the earlier ship since the twin worlds were a rubble. In fact, we were just preparing to leave and return to our mother world when that lifting body came sailing out of the saloon doorway."

Traver smiled at the thought. "An airplane in 1860 . . . I guess that made you take an extra breath or two."

"It sure did, Mr. Wells."

"Please, call me Traver," he insisted.

Siren's eyes were intent and he felt pierced by them. "Traver," she spoke. *An extra breath or two! More like tons of breaths, when I saw you sitting there!* Siren shook her head to shake out these wild thoughts. Her hair fluttered with her movement, and Traver held his breath as her hair caught the glimmers of the campfire's light. His fingers tingled in anticipation of touching her hair.

Siren was anticipating the touch of this man, even though he had already chosen Laura. It was a custom in her world for a man to have two or three women. But Siren had a problem being not the first chosen. She had to be first.

Siren returned to her story for the group gathered at the campfire. "We were happy just to have found people here, but to have a lifting paper body come floating out of the saloon? Well, I just did not know what to think. This knowledge in this time? Maybe they were survivors."

Roy got up and tossed more wood on the fire. The sparks flew into the air again, and the flames swelled.

"The warmth of the fire sure feels good!" Siren said as she held out both hands to catch it with her palms toward the flames.

"Where do you suppose humanity came from?" Laura asked her.

"We have never found a beginning race."

"Siren, are you hungry?" Laura asked.

"A little bit."

The younger man of her crew said, "Try the chicken, captain. It's barbecued. MREs."

"What was that?" she responded.

Traver explained, "They are called Meals Ready to Eat, MREs. They are cooked and prepackaged, and you can eat them cold or you can heat them." He went over to the food box and got the flashlight to search for a packet of beans and franks. "Here we are!" He tossed the packet to her.

She examined the box and then looked at him questioningly. "Perhaps another Pepsi?" she asked him with such a sweet smile.

Twin Bears got up to get her a Pepsi. "They are very good and I am going to miss them when I stay here for good," he said sadly.

"Here, Traver." Twin Bears handed him the Pepsi can to open for Siren. As she took it, her fingers touched his hand and her fingers slid gracefully along his fingers. She smiled richly. "Thank you, Traver." She knew exactly what she had just done—the woman in her was gaining confidence.

Laura caught that exchange and frowned at him. Traver knew what she was thinking and feeling. He sensed some deep shit in the near future from both women.

Siren tasted a spoonful of the MRE and pronounced it "Quite delicious!"

Twin Bears opened the pack of crackers, which she ruled as being "Sort of like some of the cooking in town." The Indian gave her the pack of peanut butter. "Here, this helps the crackers." Siren tasted it, saying, "Oh my! It does, doesn't it! What is it?"

"Ground-up peanuts," Laura said abruptly.

Siren wanted to know what Laura and Traver did in their time.

Laura told her, "I'm a coroner for the county and I do autopsies on deceased people. Before I did this, I was a thoracic surgeon. I got fed up with the system and moved home again and ranched until I met this fool here." She giggled.

"You're a doctor?" Siren asked.

"Yes, I am."

Siren smiled and said, "I have had to read and learn really fast about animals."

"You're a quack!" Laura said, laughing.

"A what?"

"A quack. It's slang for someone who does things without being educated in the field." "Oh, please don't tell anyone in town, they all think I'm a pretty good doctor." Siren finished her MRE crackers and peanut butter and drained the last of her Pepsi. "Will you come out to my ship and allow me to return your hospitality of a meal?" Siren was directly addressing Traver.

Roy said, "Out to your ship? Is it close to North Platte?"

"Oh, heavens no." Siren gestured with her hands. "It's not built for planet fall, it's way too big for that. We'll take a smaller ship out to her."

Traver caught her description and he liked hearing that.

"Just where is it?" Roy asked.

Siren looked up into the sky. "She is there!" Siren pointed to a really bright star. "It's parked just overhead and is in a polar orbit slot."

"A what?" Laura asked.

"That's our term for just hanging in a steady orbit."

Roy was still looking at that point of light. "No. I don't want to go that far up. I'll stay here if you don't mind."

Twin Bears said, "I can go to that light in the sky?"

"Yes," Siren said softly. "Would you like to go there, Twin Bears?"

"I shall think about that, but not today."

It fell quiet around the campfire. All that could be heard was the crackling of the fire and a coyote howling down by the river somewhere. Traver almost expected to hear an outburst of *Kumbayah*.

"What is this?" Siren asked. She lifted up a clear sealed package.

"It has gum, salt and pepper, wipe towels, and matches." Traver opened it for her. "Here, chew this but don't swallow it."

Siren put the gum in her mouth and began chewing. "Oh, this is very refreshing. Will it disappear like the food?"

"No," Laura said. "It just stays pliable and the flavor disappears after a bit."

"What happens to it then?"

"You spit it out," Laura said, smiling.

"I shall have to be getting back to town soon," Siren murmured. "People there might be getting worried about me." She stood up and her two crew members got up with her. They all shook hands with us and Siren apologized for having her men follow them. "But if I hadn't we would not be here now."

"Rightly so," Laura said.

"When will you be back in town?" Siren asked.

"Roy and I will be in tomorrow. We are setting up a business with Alice there," Traver told her.

Laura broke in. "I want to ride to Fort Cottonwood. Mitch can come with me. I want to spend as much time with my great-granddad as I can. But I will be back to help Alice set up her new business."

"Roy and Twin Bears will come with me," Traver said.

Laura reminded him, "Great-granddad invited us to church Sunday, Traver, can you be there?"

"Sure. Today is Friday, right?"

"Yep!" Roy said.

Siren said. "Maybe on Monday evening we can go to the ship. Just stop by the office around five-thirty or six. Until then, goodbye."

Roy took Siren's hand and helped her into the wagon's front boxed seat. Her two crew members got in the back. Roy took the reins.

Siren did not want to leave the camp. Twice she had come in contact with this man. She now knew his name and whence he came. She knew she was very strongly attracted to him and that he was attracted to her. His eyes told her that. When she shook his hand, she felt it, but when her fingers had touched his hand, when he gave her that first Pepsi, she tingled with an electrical excitement. She shivered with anticipation. She didn't want to leave, but what could she do? He had chosen and she was crushed. For the first time in her life she did not know what to do. It was time to go, and as captain of her crew she acted. Just because she knew how to leave, she did not know how to leave this man.

Siren looked distracted, her face turned due south.

Traver followed her look. "What is it?" he asked.

"I thought I saw a flash of light over there." She pointed south, rubbing her arms. "Feel that?" she asked.

"Feel what?" I did have a sense of something and goosebumps popped on my arms. "There!" she said again. "There, see that?"

"Yes," he answered. "I did see a flash, maybe the last of the sun's rays catching on something shiny."

Siren rubbed her arms again, as if she were cold. Traver felt odd also, not knowing what to do. He yelled over to Twin Bears. "Go South!" He pointed to where they had seen the last flash. "Go south, maybe a half mile and just west of that hill. See if anyone is camped over there or watching us." He put his hand on Twin Bears's arm. "Go quietly, my friend."

"How else?" Twin Bears gave Traver a smile and made the turkey gobble call, and Lunch showed up at his side. Slapping his leg at the dog, both disappeared into the darkness.

Traver looked back at Siren, who was still looking in that direction.

"Could it be any of your folks?" he asked.

"No," she replied, "they are on the ship. We three and the one at the office are all that are here."

"Well," Traver said. "Better get back to town and let us deal with whatever this is. Just a moment." He went over to the supplies and got a six pack of Pepsis and took it over to her. "Should you get thirsty before you get back to your office."

"Thank you, Traver, I shall enjoy these!" She looked deep into his eyes. "Thank you," she said in a low voice.

The captain settled down on the wagon seat, but an odd sensation still rippled in her awareness. She rubbed her thighs and then her arms, trying to instill a feeling of security and comfort. Then she turned to look where she had seen the flash of light, but there was nothing now. Something was happening to her that was out of her control. As a luminal star ship captain, she was supposed to be always in control. She knew the "Way" was strong this moment. Something important in her future was occurring this moment.

As the wagon made its turn to head back toward town she looked back over her shoulder, just past Roy's head, to catch a final glimpse of Mr. Wells. He was still looking toward the flashes of light. *What is it about him that's shaking my very foundation?*

Siren directed a thought toward Traver. *Don't forget my touch.*

Laura turned from watching the night sky and smiled at Siren. Still full of tumultuous feelings, Siren in turn raised her hand in a slight wave.

As the wagon rumbled away, Siren turned to Roy. "How long have you known Mr. Wells, Roy?"

Roy lightly flipped the reins across the mules' backs, just to let them know he was watching. "Oh, I'd say about eight months now."

"Have Laura and he known each other longer?" she wanted to know.

Roy smiled and glanced at her. "They just met and knew they were for each other. Laura's husband died ten years ago, and she was just existing until Traver, ah, Mr. Wells, showed up in her life."

"Roy, who is the scientist or engineer of your group?"

"What?"

"Well, if you've come from 1995??, the future, you must have an operator to run the equipment."

"Oh, we're all cowpunchers and Mr. Wells farmed in California."

Siren responded in surprise, "Well, how did you and Laura, Traver, Mitch, and Twin Bears get here?"

Roy laughed. "Why, we just waited for a storm and lightning and rode up Enchanted Canyon into 1860."

Siren turned to him in amazement. "Then there's no machinery?"

"Nope," Roy said.

Siren considered this a joke. "So, can you return?"

"Yes, Twin Bears has crossed several times."

Hearing this, Siren felt her captain demeanor cut in, and she could hardly wait to get to her star ship. She turned to her crew member, Monk. "Did you hear all that?"

"Yes"

"Roy, could you show Monk the canyon tomorrow?" Siren asked.

"Well, I reckon so, if it's okay with Mr. Wells."

The rest of the ride to town was silent. Siren was trying to settle her emotions. The more she tried, the more she couldn't. Her thinking just stopped and she behaved not as a captain, not as a future leader of her home world, but as a woman beginning to sweat just thinking of what this man's touch would create within her. After this evening, she felt that she would never be the person she had been yesterday. She sighed and looked away in thought.

Meanwhile, back at the camp, the fire died down as the light in the west diminished. Laura stayed next to Traver. The fire's rich oranges and reds reflected on Laura's face and hands. She looked beautiful in the reddish glow. "Traver, this sure feels strange," she whispered in a low voice.

"Is it possible the canyon is opening?" he suggested.

"No. Something else is causing our goosebumps. Traver, I don't feel afraid. I don't feel threatened, either. I feel so very loved." She looked south again and rubbed her arms. "I am feeling the most loved I have ever felt." Laura folded her arms about her and closed her eyes. "Life's twists and turns are like an old wire fence on the open range. Like a old wire fence, your life strings along. Then comes a storm and maybe the fence breaks." She looked back at Traver and for an instant thought about death. "I've got goosebumps all over my body. "Whats happening?" Her dark eyes moved from the fire to his face, awaiting a response.

Traver reached over and touched her shoulder. "Whatever it is, Twin Bears will be back and tell us. Don't worry, we have more firepower than five companies of soldiers. Don't you worry, honey." He tried to comfort her, but he, too, had a body full of goosebumps. In a quiet voice he asked Skip's dad if he felt anything. "Nope," he said, "not a thing!"

The only other thing Traver thought was that maybe it could be Indians. But why did just Laura and Traver feel it? If it were an Army patrol, they would have ridden into camp. The tense minutes continued to flow into an hour or more, and then Traver heard Twin Bears making his turkey call. Traver whistled in response, and the Indian came into camp.

"Hey, Twin Bears, what was it?" Lunch came up to Laura and she scratched his ears. "What's out there boy?" she whispered to him. But the old dog just nuzzled her.

Twin Bears finally said, "There were a few Indians up there, and I saw some other folks. They saw our fire and were just looking at us. When I got there, they were focused on the campfire with field glasses."

Traver looked at Laura and said, "That must have been the reflection that Siren saw." "Yes," Twin Bears said.

"Are they coming in?" Traver wanted to know.

Twin Bears shook his head no. "No, they have a long journey home."

Laura started rubbing her arms again. She felt the sensation of being watched from afar. She turned and looked southward again. "Twin Bears, are you all right? You look different."

"Yes, and I feel different. I have just met a long-distant relative up there. I had thought about him often and now I have met him." He sighed. "This was a very good night. A night to remember."

"That's good," said Traver, and they put their guns away. Twin Bears had a sad look as he gazed on Traver. The Indian came up to him and rubbed his shoulder. Twin Bears knew. But what did he know?

"Traver," Laura whispered, "hold me close and don't ever leave me."

"How can I leave the brightest star in the sky? How can I leave the best looking ass I ever saw?" He gave her a quick pat on her bottom. "And how could I ever leave those hot tits of yours?"

Laura blushed. "Quit that. Let's go to our tent."

They shared their love for each other all night, camped near the Platte River, accompanied by a chorus of frogs and coyotes.

CHAPTER 12

FUNNY HOW WORLDS CHANGE
AT A GLANCE

IN TOWN, ROY stopped the wagon at the doctor's office and helped Siren out. Monk and the younger crew member piled out of the back. A kerosene lamp was burning in the doctor's office, and Siren's aide came out to see what was happening. She saw it was the captain and just stood there. All four standing on the boardwalk waved as Roy turned the team around. Loud piano music and voices were coming from the saloon's doorway down the street.

Siren settled in the big comfortable leather chair.

Her aide returned to her desk, and Monk and the other crew member sat on the couch. Siren sighed, "Well, this is certainly unexpected." She looked around at her crew members. "Monk, call the ship and have a research team ready to come in and survey the canyon."

"Yes, ma'am."

Siren turned to her aide and asked, "Have the other teams returned yet?"

"Yes, we will be ready to leave Thursday next."

The word "next" was all that Siren heard. She wanted to cry. Why had this awakening to love occurred at the end of their trip? She had only a few days longer. She had no experience at being a woman in love. Her culture had impressed on her not to actively pursue a man, because it was his right to choose.

"Captain?" Monk broke her train of thought. "We need to get up to the ship to prepare the survey team."

"Yes, go," she waved her hand at him. Siren stood up and stretched. "Let's get some sleep."

Her aide said, "Captain, do you want me to talk with you?"

"No, I'm fine, thank you."

The aide paused and then said, "I know you're captain, but . . ." Her aide touched her arm slightly. "Captain, get to know the woman you are. Don't lose him."

"Thank you," Siren sighed.

The aide took the lamp and retired to her room in the doctor's office. Monk and the other crew member went to the outskirts of North Platte and lifted up to the ship. Siren walked to her tiny home down the street and sat on the couch in her parlor. She stared, off in a daydream, about Traver.

Back at the camp outside of town and in the tent, Laura was holding Traver's hand. "Are you thinking what I am?" she asked.

Traver smiled at her and gently squeezed her hand. "Sex?"

"No, silly. I was trying to remember if I had ever felt like this ever in my life."

"You mean the lights up on the hill? Twin Bears and his relative?"

"Yes, it felt to me like I was being watched, no, not watched. It was like someone was crying over me. Traver . . ." Her voice broke, and at first he thought it was because of Bill. Laura said, "But then I felt it was you looking at me. But how could that have been? You are here." And she touched his chest.

"You are here with me and not out there looking at me."

"Honey, go ask Twin Bears just who it was up there."

Laura shook her head. "No, this is fine, here and now, you and me. I do love you, Wells." Her eyes became misty with tears. "What's up there is beyond our control."

Looking at her playfully, he leaned close to her ear. "Then let's pull down your panties and get out of control."

Laura let out a screech. "You crazy fool!"

Traver cooed, "Come on, let's get some sleep. I love you so much."

At daybreak neither Twin Bears nor the wagon was in sight.

Roy was up and making coffee. Traver went over to the fire and held out his hands. "Goddamn, Roy, why do coffee and bacon smell so good when you're out camping?"

"Beats me, Traver, but to me, it smells good any ol' time and anywhere."

Traver tucked in his shirt, pulled up his pants, went to the box that held the utensils, and got out a tin cup. Roy poured.

At first sip Traver said, "Goddamn, Roy, this is pretty sharp."

"Yes, sir, that's a part of my job with Miss Laura. To see to things and to make the best camp coffee possible." He grinned and added. "If I don't, she'll fire me!"

Laura flopped back the tent flap and came out, wiping her eyes in the daylight. "I heard that, Roy." She looked smart in a sky-blue blouse, tan canvas pants skirt, and brown riding boots. She had her 44-40 pistol slung at her side, no shoulder holster. She wore her wide-brimmed El Paso gaucho hat. She looked like a Spanish woman of means. "Goddamn, woman, you look good. Don't you go and pick up any charros!"

"Oh, be quiet! No, on second thought, tell me how good I look again." She smiled big and rolled her eyes and licked her lips. Traver went over to her and hugged her close in his arms and pressed his lips hard against hers. "That much!" he said as they parted.

"Are you going to miss me while I'm gone?"

"Nope," he said, "Skip's dad and I are going to the dance hall and terrorize some of the floozies there."

Laura's eyes flashed. "You'd better not, or I'll floozie you." She looked at Roy and added, "You, too!"

He and Traver looked at each other and squealed, "Oh boy! Promise?"

"That's a promise," Laura said, grinning.

"Oh, momma!" Traver whistled.

"I love you, too. See you Sunday, bye!" Laura breezed off. Traver got a quick kiss, and she and Roy rode off for Fort Cottonwood.

As Traver sipped his coffee, Skip's dad came stumbling out of the bigger tent, still sleepy eyed. He wanted a cup of coffee pretty bad. He dug around in the box and came up with another tin cup and trudged over to the fire, getting himself a steaming cup of brew. He sat, scratching his scalp, as he sipped his coffee. "Damn! That makes all the sense in the world. The first cup is always the best." He stretched and looked around. "Where's Twin Bears?"

Staring into his coffee, Traver said, "He left late last night."

Skip's dad cradled the hot tin cup in both hands as he blew the steam away with pursed lips. "Well, well, well," he murmured. "We're actually back in time and we've met people from a faraway star. Ain't that something? Did she say what star they're from?"

"Nope," Traver answered. "I actually don't feel so alone anymore, knowing there are others like us."

Shaking his head in disbelief, he said, "But people from a different star? Man! That captain is one hell of a woman," Mitch exclaimed. "I wonder if all the star women are like the captain?"

Traver sipped at his coffee as Skip's dad scratched his chest.

"What did I hear about dance-hall girls and Laura whipping both our asses if we get involved?" He laughed and took another drink of coffee. "Traver, I've known Laura for nigh onto forty years, and I have never seen her so confident, so solid on herself. As a doctor, she's the best, and when she married Bill, she matured even more. But you have done something miraculous for her. Did I tell you that if I had been younger, I would have waltzed her." He took another sip of coffee, watching Traver over the rim with a devious smile.

Traver's heart swelled and a picture of Laura and Roy riding west toward Fort Cottonwood this morning filled his mind's eye. Laura sure sat a horse good, no question about that. That ass of hers plopped down in a saddle sure stretched her skirt and just yearned for him to grab it, or give it a Benny Hill pat or two.

Skip's dad poured himself another coffee and lifted the pot in Traver's direction, and he held out his cup for a refill.

Mitch put the soot-covered blue and white pot back on the coals and went over to a log and sat down. "What was all that stuff about last night?" he asked.

Traver responded, "You heard Twin Bears and you know as much as I do. Didn't you feel anything last night?" They were silent for a moment. The tweeter birds were waking up, greeting the morning, and geese were flying overhead. Skip's dad looked up. "Humph," he snorted. "It doesn't feel like 1860 right now, does it? And, nope, I didn't feel nothing."

Traver sank into a reverie. *A day is a day. These days must have been the same for thousands of years. What made the difference was man being there.* He thought about how well Laura was dealing with meeting her great-granddad. A flash streaked across his thoughts. *How would we deal with meeting ourselves? But that couldn't happen—we weren't born yet.*

Suddenly he had the same feeling from last night. He just didn't feel comfortable. But Twin Bears said it was an old relative and his friends. Twin Bears knew them! Traver shrugged off the feelings. He trusted Twin Bears.

Finishing his coffee, Skip's dad asked, "Where's Laura and Roy got to?"

"They headed over to Fort Cottonwood. She wants to hang around her great-granddad as much as possible."

"A chance of a lifetime," Skip's dad said. "Just think, being able to meet and visit with a relative from the past. You could see what sorts of traits that he exhibits and the ones that you have. I wish my folks were from here, it would be nice to meet them."

Old Buster strayed over to Mitch. As he scratched the dog's ears, he asked, "You been out chasing rabbits, old boy?"

"Where are your folks from, Mitch?" Traver asked.

"Ohio. It would be one hell of a ride in this day and time."

"We had better stick around till Twin Bears shows up," Traver said as he finished his coffee.

It wasn't thirty minutes later that Buster began barking and Twin Bears popped through the thickets, coming toward our camp in the wagon. The older man of the doctor's crew was riding on the seat beside him. Twin Bears tied the wagon team to a scrub brush, and both men came over to the campfire. Lunch, Twin Bears's dog, stayed at the wagon.

The crew member Monk said, "The captain thought that I could help with watching the camp and maybe take a look at Enchanted Canyon."

"That's great!" I said. "The coffee is ready."

They sat around the campfire until the coffee was gone. Twin Bears never said a thing about his not coming back to camp.

Monk stayed with Twin Bears, and Mitch and Traver rode into North Platte. As they rode past the old bakery they saw a crew there, digging a foundation for the fireplace. "Hi, boys!" Traver shouted to the workers. He dismounted, walked over to them, and said, "I am Mr. Wells, the new owner. Where's the stonemason?"

A middle-aged man with a pipe in his mouth said, "I am."

In just those two words Traver recognized a Scottish brogue. "Good. Did Mr. Sanders tell you what I want here?"

"Weel, lad, he tried to." He chuckled as he took the pipe stem from between his teeth and knocked it on a stone, dumping its ashes. "Just now, laddie, what is it you want me to know?"

"I would like the hearth wide enough to hold four big pots of coffee. Two swung over the flames and two on the side racks inside the hearth."

"And what do you want for the mantel?" he asked.

"Can we get a large enough slate or perma-stone for it?" Traver wondered.

"Probably. I'll see what I can do. Do you want stone or red brick for the fireplace?"

"What's available?"

"Both. I think. But the red brick will be easier to get. Especially since we are going to wall in the ovens. More brick, less money per brick."

"That sounds good," Traver agreed. He started to leave, but the Scotsman gestured at me with his pipe hand. "Mr. Wells, are you Scottish Wells or Irish?"

He turned in his saddle. "Why, Scottish, of course. County Aire of the Highlands."

The stonemason grinned and went back to digging the foundation for the fireplace with an approving look on his face.

"Say!" Traver yelled. "What's your name?"

Leaning on his shovel, he said. "Why, it's McNeal. Do we know each other, sir?"

Immediately Traver recognized the name, which was engraved on Laura's great-granddad's fireplace mantel."

"No, sir, we have not met. But I know of your work and I am truly pleased to meet you."

The Scottish brick mason waved and Traver gestured. Peterson and McNeal would hook up in a few years.

Riding along, Traver thought. *I have met a man today who builds a fireplace in a few years that I touched more than a hundred years later. So our meeting today didn't change time. So far.*

Skip's dad was going to ride on down to the courthouse to read records that had burned in 1918. It was during the Spanish flu epidemic when all the firemen were sick. He was writing down as much, so he could save it. As they rode toward the hotel, he casually said, "The other day Twin Bears was telling me that a group of Sioux braves slipped into town by the big tree, got supplies, and left quickly. Two of them knew him. Apparently he was quite the warrior when he was younger. Anyway, they told him they had ambushed a military wagon train that had five wagons in it. They had heard there was a wagon train carrying rifles and ammunition. They were the new lever-type repeating Henrys. They caught the wagon train late in the day and killed about half of the troopers. The next morning the Indians finished the job. There were no rifles or ammunition, but one wagon was empty. The others just had supplies. The troopers who survived the attack had apparently buried the guns and ammunition during the night, probably deep, and then put the dead troopers on top. I told Twin Bears I had heard the same story but that I had heard it all took place further west from here, in the sand hills. Well, Twin Bears described the area where they had taken the wagon train and it sounded like it was out on Laura's place, more south, down toward turkey run. I know the place well. Let's go look for those buried guns and ammo when we get home."

"No shit!" Traver marveled.

Mitch nodded yes. "Well, I've heard all my life about the wagonload of repeaters and the Indians bushwhacking it."

"You think that after a hundred-sixty years the rifles and ammunition will be any good?"

He looked at the bank as they passed. "I don't know. That depends on where they were buried. If the road was on the west side of the canyon and they were buried there, then probably some might be good. If they were buried out in the meadow? No way. Too much moisture there for sure. It would be a fun outing anyway, wouldn't it?" Mitch conjectured.

"It sure would. But I think the archaeological value is important if there's any old Henrys still out there in any sort of condition. I think we should work with the university somehow. If there are soldiers' remains, we shouldn't just dig to find guns and ammo. We should involve the Veterans Administration and the cemetery at the McPherson V.A."

Traver pulled off at the hotel. Will came around and caught the reins of Stamp.

"Hi, Mr. Wells!"

"Hi, young man!" Traver flipped him a half-dollar. Will caught it and put it in his pocket and then jingled it with the other coins. "Ah! Business is good today?" Traver asked.

"Yes, sir, very good. Oh, Mr. Wells?" He came closer to Traver. "I haven't said anything to nobody about that rifle you shot yesterday. Boy, that is some rifle! Shooting all those bullets."

"Thanks, Will. I appreciate your trust and I'll let you shoot it the next time you come out to our camp. But you cannot tell anyone, okay?"

"Yes, sir."

He went off with ol' Stamp down to the livery stable, and Traver sauntered over to the saloon.

Alice asked him to come into the kitchen. "Mr. Wells, did you see that they're working on the chimney?"

"I sure did. It will be finished soon. I'm going to purchase all of the cinnamon here and have them order a hundred more pounds to be shipped to us here. Sugar is no problem nor is flour. How's the butter supply?" he asked.

"There's more than is needed." Alice wiped her hands on her apron as she talked. "That won't be a problem."

As Traver got up from the stool in the kitchen, he asked if she knew of at least two big cook stoves.

"I can find them," she said with a smile.

"Good! Here's fifty dollars in silver. Purchase them and have them brought to the bakery."

"Why so early?"

"We have to keep the pressure on the banker and if we are there and operating, hell, he'll have to stay with it." He grinned at her.

"Good thinking, Mr. Wells!"

"Hey, Alice, call me Traver."

"No, sir, that's not right. You're a married man!" Well, that took him back a bit. "We'll set up tomorrow and do a test run with a batch of cinnamon rolls. And let's be ready for Monday's coffee and cinnamon rolls. We'll bake and make coffee outside the building, but everyone will sit inside. Say, where's ol' Bill?"

"You know, I haven't seen him yet today. Poor man, he's most likely passed out somewhere." She shook her head. "Whisky is the ruin of a lot of good men."

"Yes, ma'am, it sure is."

"God bless you, Mr. Wells, God bless you!"

Traver went over to the dry-goods store and purchased all the cinnamon, only ten pounds. A shipment of twenty-five pounds was due next week. He purchased that and ordered another two hundred pounds. "I need two hundred pounds of flour and twenty-five pounds of salt and a hundred pounds of sugar. Will you have it delivered to the bakery? Get the key from Mr. Sanders at the bank."

He went back to the saloon and told Alice she would need butter and milk early Monday morning. "I mean before sun-up. Get your milkman to do this for you. We will start cooking Monday morning and watch the quarters and dimes start flowing in!"

She put her hand to her mouth. "I hope so, Mr. Wells. You're taking a huge risk and I have invested nothing."

"Oh yes, you have! You're the catalyst for all this."

"I'm the what?"

He smiled at her. "You are who is going to make all this happen. There's something else, Alice. I'll be down there stoking the fires for the wood stoves."

Right then Will came in to speak with his mother and Traver said, "Will, can you get, say, a cord of wood down to the old bakery? We're cooking Monday morning."

"Yes, sir, I can arrange that."

"What do you think it will cost?"

Will thought a moment. "I would say probably two dollars for the wood and seventy-five cents to move it."

Traver gave him five silver dollars and told Will to save the change for more wood next week.

Traver started to turn away but then paused to ask, "Say, Will, you want to help with the fires Monday morning?"

"Yes, sir."

"Oh, and, Will, we need coffee mugs and china plates. Where do I get those?"

Will said that up the street, two doors above the doctor's place, was Bert's hardware store.

Traver stopped in to get everything ordered and delivered, but he was sure he would forget something. *Oh, yeah, tables!* Picnic tables and benches—but they would have to be built. They would have to use the smaller wooden barrels and one-by-twelve boards. *Oh, table linens! Damn! There's a lot to getting a coffee shop going!*

After he had finished his business at Bert's hardware, he stopped in at the doctor's office. That same young woman was there, and she gave him a big smile.

"Good morning, Mr. Wells. The doctor is not here. She had to go out to the Johnson place and help deliver a horse or cow, I don't know which."

He smiled and told her, "Tell her that I'll be in town until evening. See if she would like to have dinner with me and one of my men."

"Yes, sir, I'll tell her."

"Oh, and tell her that maybe Tuesday will be better to visit the ship."

The young woman's mouth dropped open. "The ship?"

He stuck his hands in his pockets and rocked back and forth on his heels, enjoying her confusion. "Why, of course, are you coming with us?"

"Well, I usually do. I'm pilot of the wing. But how do you know about this?"

"Captain Siren will tell you, I'm sure."

The woman's mouth dropped open again "You know her name, too?"

"I get around," he said. "See you Tuesday."

Traver was musing that Friday was ending nice and gentle for him. Then he heard his name being called and turned to see an older man, who smiled and opened his arms.

"Bill! Holy shit! You clean up real good! I didn't hardly recognize you."

Bill laughed and said, "I've been thinking about what you said about going into business with Alice and it made a lot of sense. It's a natural. Men having coffee and feeling good. Men like coffee and rifles, and I would like to try the business you suggested. The thing is, I don't have any stock or tools or any cash."

"Well, Bill, you start slow and set your shop up with quality first. Let's see what happens on Monday and go from there. Laura and I will have to leave soon and I can't help you all that much. I do know that guns take a lot of overhead in cash. The best way to get started is to take Laura's and my third interest in the coffee shop for the equipment and supplies and rifles. While you're getting this thing going, you can work for Alice. That would help her get started, too. You also should think about starting a hunting tour. Folks from back East or out in San Francisco will be out here soon, and some just have too much money. I rather expect you could help them spend some of it in your shop. You could start the guided hunts on Alice's place and Twin Bears and Will can be guides. You know, this is going to take off and you'll have to figure out what to do with all your money, Bill."

Bill looked a little stunned at the business opportunities being thrown at him.

Traver kept after him. "Bill, have you got some work clothes?"

"Sure, I do. Lots of old work clothes, as a matter of fact."

"Good. Go down to the bakery and organize the barrel tables and benches. Here's fifty dollars for supplies."

Bill looked at Traver in dismay. "You're sure the trusting sort!"

"Yep, Bill, and I think I can tell a winner. Focus on the topic and the job, not the income." Traver slapped him on the shoulder. "Get along, and let's have a great opening on Monday morning!"

Traver went down to the hotel and into the lounge, picking up a three-week-old San Francisco newspaper. He also looked at the Omaha paper that had just come in by Pony Express. There were lots of articles on Abraham Lincoln and the Republic. He had forgotten that the Civil War popped up in mid-1860 and really got going in 1861. Looking at some of the news items, he had to chuckle. "Old man Richards's pet pig got out and it is feared that it's now ham and bacon. The pig being missing now for eight days." And here was an item advertising Virginia cigars at two cents. Cuban cigars at five cents. Traver hadn't thought about Cuban cigars in 1860 America. Sometimes history got awfully focused.

"Hi, Traver!" Skip's dad exclaimed and sat down next to his friend. "Man, what a day! There's so much history up there in the courthouse, I just can't absorb it all!"

"Hey," Traver asked, "how are you going to put all that information out and not tell how you got it?"

"You think I'm dumb? I'm having two ladies copy the stuff I need, and I'm wrapping the journals in oil skin and will dip everything in hot wax. Then I'll bury them next to the other stuff I'm going to take back. I'll leave it so it will be old when I discover it. Then I'll say that I found it all, which will be true, but where I found it will be stretching it a bit."

"You're a pretty smart hombre."

Just then they heard a woman behind them clear her throat.

"Gentlemen, I was invited for supper."

Traver looked around and there stood Siren, wonderfully outfitted. The gown was period styled, but it had a flair of the future. Her top was not completely modest, and a little of her neck showed. Although not tight-fitting in the bodice, her blouse revealed her prominent breasts. He wanted to kiss her, but he took her hand and said, simply, "Come, let's eat."

He couldn't take his eyes off her, dressed in a blouse of rich antique ivory with a long copper-brown skirt and a wide black belt. She wore a brooch with jewels that flashed as if a hundred suns were going super nova.

His eyes were fixated on that brooch when Siren spoke. "Do you see something you recognize, Mr. Wells?"

"Ah, yes. I recognize the pattern of those jewels."

"You do?" She formed her words carefully.

"The Pleiades star cluster. From here and at this time of the year it's just up a bit from the horizon, just after the sun sets. It's a bit different but still recognizable."

Siren reached up and fingered the pin. "I do not know it by that name, to me this is the seven cracks in the sky."

He reached over and touched the brooch. "This is beautiful."

Siren placed her hands at her sides, her left hand clasping a tiny handbag. "Thank you for the dinner invitation."

She could see that Traver was totally attracted to her. The feeling, as they say, was mutual. She looked down at her breasts to see her nipples hardening. After a seductive glance at Traver, she lifted her shawl to her shoulders and gathered it about her so no one could observe her excitement.

All of this happened in the flash of a lightning strike, but to Traver it seemed to be in slow motion. "Siren?" he addressed her.

"Yes?"

"It's just Siren?"

"Yes. Just Siren. But I am the only one in the universe. Isn't that wonderful to know?" She reached out her hand and took his arm. "Dinner?" She looked at him. "I'm starved!"

The waitress came over and took their order. Steak, sliced onions and potatoes fried in butter, and boiled carrots. As they were eating the fresh bread smeared with butter, the pastor that had married Laura and Traver a few days before came over to the table. "Excuse me, Mr. Wells, it's good to see you again." And loudly he added, "And where is Mrs. Wells?"

Siren turned red in the face.

"Why, she's at Fort Cottonwood going over some maps. After all, I am the boss of the crew and just because she is married to me now, she still has to do her job."

Traver caught Siren smiling a bit at this exchange. He was laying it on the pastor thick. "I believe that Mrs. Wells and I will see you Sunday at Fort Cottonwood." Looking at Siren, he added, "Say, doctor, would you enjoy accompanying Laura and me to Sunday services at the fort?"

The pastor realized that all was fine and he wanted to leave and quit his meddling.

"Why, Mr. Wells, that would be very nice, thank you for asking." Siren turned to face the pastor. "I have not attended Pastor Stanley's services, and I will be very interested to hear his thoughts on the divine order and presence of the universe."

The pastor couldn't get out of there fast enough.

The diners were relieved to see him walk away.

Siren worked up her courage to ask a question that had been nagging at her. "Traver, how did you and Laura meet?"

"I saw her from the rear as she went into a friend's home. We were at a barbecue, and I just knew she was the one."

Siren remained silent and waiting in thought. *I feel that way about you, Traver. I feel a completeness around you I have never felt with any other person. In my culture women run most things, but in pairing it's the man who decides.*

Traver looked back at her again. "Laura is older than me. In our culture the man is supposed to be older. Listen to your heart and spirit." He addressed Siren again. "How big is your ship?"

"It's just at a quarter of a mile in circumference. It's a sphere." Traver looked surprised. "Is that big in your world?"

"Yes. We have nothing that huge except for the ocean ships that float on the water. How large is your crew?"

"We are a little more than three hundred strong."

"That few for such a large ship?"

"Yes. We have a lot of automated systems. Actually, the ship itself is not that large. It's outer skin is molecular active. It's a dynamic skin, eight hundred feet thick. If we are impacted by debris in steady speed, the skin can absorb that energy and material, and that energy transfers to our power drives. Its molecular structure is hyperactive. The impact's energy is channeled into propulsion. At flash speed, these debris strikes become particleized and ionized and simply burn off as an energy field and disappear into space. We can take a huge hit, up to six or seven feet in diameter."

"Damn! That's fission energy."

Siren smiled. "It is quite a light show."

As they finished dinner, she said, "Traver, thank you for dinner and talking with me." She stood up, so Traver did, too. Skip's dad had gone to the bar for a drink.

"May I walk you home?" Traver asked her.

She took his arm. "Yes, you may walk me home."

They walked past her office and turned west at the last street and went up two streets.

"Well, it's been a nice evening, and I feel like a very special person," Siren said softly. She looked up at the sky. "There's the ship!"

Traver looked at where she was pointing. "Where?"

She stepped behind him and over his shoulder pointed to a bright light nearly overhead. He bent back his head, to see where her finger was directed, and Siren leaned closer, pressing her breasts against his back, sending shivers through both of their bodies.

"Are you cold, Traver?" she asked innocently.

"No, not cold," he stammered.

Siren remained with her breasts firmly planted against his back. "Traver, look at the starlit sky. See how the stars twinkle? Each twinkle of a star is a breath taken by the universe."

He breathed in and out, and her breasts pressed harder against him.

"My presence is stronger because of you," she murmured.

He was frozen to the spot.

Siren was thinking how much she needed to be next to him this night. She needed all the relief she could get from the frustration she felt. Only this man could release her.

"Traver, what do you feel as you look at the starlit sky?" Siren wanted to know.

"My eyes see all the lights, but at the same time my soul senses your warm body pressing against mine. I feel your excitement. Do you sense mine, too?" Traver spoke boldly.

Siren was quiet for several moments. Her breasts were burning a brand into his back. "Yes, I feel you. Our two universes becoming one."

She started unfastening the top buttons of her blouse and undid the buttons on each cuff at her wrists. Her blouse came off. She wasn't wearing a bra. It looked more like a bathing suit top, with a silver-grayish shine to it. Siren said nothing as she reached behind her and pulled down the covering. As Traver turned to her, her breasts flowed into his chest. Her eyes reflected starlight.

A small necklace, with a beautiful jeweled orb pendant, lay between her breasts. Her eyes took on the color of the sky, with millions of sparkling flecks of light.

Traver noticed Siren's naked breasts were illuminated by the starlight. The reflected light showed a smooth skin that shimmered like silk. Then he saw a tattoo, and that jarred the moment. From her navel, a tail of what looked like a snake wound across the left side to the right and then back across her stomach. Then it went up between her breasts, with the head of the snake, jaws open, holding Siren's left nipple. That nipple looked like a ruby. Traver found this very arousing.

Siren picked up on this and smiled. She cocked her head, and her long luxurious hair fell over her left shoulder. He kept staring at the tattoo, which was indescribably beautiful, and Traver hated snakes with a passion.

He touched her stomach with his left hand and traced the path of the snake up to where it was holding her left nipple in its mouth. Siren's eyes closed and she swallowed big a few times before opening her eyes again. She took a deep breath and let it out slowly.

"Siren . . ." Traver whispered. He was still touching her nipple. "Siren, what reason . . ."

She replied before he could enunciate the question. "That is the Way. This is my family's gift."

"But this is a tattoo of a snake!"

"Traver, from my navel, the center of it all, the universe, the time, the Mother, the Way, is a passage, a tunnel, a Way from one world to another. The opening holds the egg. The breasts suckle the babe."

"Does this have, ah, is this . . . I don't know what I'm trying to ask, Siren," Traver began to fall into her eyes.

"It's also called Eve, the path the Star Woman took to leave the universe and come to Edon." That bit of knowledge passed unaware to Traver, because he was already leaning toward Siren's breasts and her necklace's jeweled orb on a chain that was flashing radiant colors. It led the way like a beacon in a dark sky to her breast.

"Traver, see how the jewels reflect the starlight?"

He leaned back away from her to better see the necklace's center jewel again, and he fixed his eyes on the orb. Her breathing was rapid, tripping off flashes of light from the jewels.

"May I be Laura for tonight?"

"Be Laura tonight?" Traver repeated, trancelike. He bent his head to kiss her nipples, and she moaned. Her breath made a sharp intake when he cupped his hands under her breasts. He was suckling one nipple and massaging the other.

"Let's go inside," Siren murmured. He pulled back and put his arms around her and kissed her on her mouth.

"Yes! Let's go inside," Traver breathed.

She stopped and locked her ghost eyes on his. "You know it's me you're loving and not Laura, don't you?"

"Yes, I am loving you both!"

She leaned to him as they closed the door to her house and stood there kissing passionately. "Traver, you are so very special."

He began kissing both her breasts again. She took her skirt, hitched it around, and dropped it to the floor. She was naked except for her blouse and the silver undergarment. She kicked her skirt away and took off her underclothing. He slid his hand down from her breasts and found her soft brush of hair. Slowly she backed to her couch and sat down and then leaned back.

Traver knelt in front of her and began tenderly kissing her stomach. She started breathing heavier, gasping for air, and tossing her head back and forth. "Oh, Eve! Traver, I've never felt this way before. You are the first."

Every part of Siren's existence was racing to the highest level. Then, as if struck by lightning, she arched her back and yelled loudly. It seemed to go on forever, as her entire body shook. She exploded again and again.

She gasped, as her hands pulled him tightly to her. She was blushing red and her tongue was flitting over her lips. Siren whispered, "I want all your seed."

He then drove fully into her and she gasped, "Again, Traver!"

The time passed quickly, and Traver awakened to Siren kissing him, her lips like the sunrise. "Thank you for letting me be Laura," she said in a low voice.

He put his arm around her and began stroking her thighs. "You were not Laura. It was Siren touching my spirit."

Tears streaming down her face. "Thank you for loving me."

He continued kissing her lips, as she focused her eyes on his face. "I love you. I tingle with your seed. I will love no other. You are my first and my last."

They kissed again, sealing her pledge.

"What do you mean, your last?" Traver wanted to know.

"You are taken. You have shared with me and I must be the first chosen. Not the second." She cast her eyes downward. "I will love no other than you."

As they sat up, Siren said, "You had better be going."

He laughed quietly. "What? No breakfast?"

She looked at him in disbelief. "You have time?"

"I have time!"

"Eggs and bacon and good coffee?" Siren asked.

"That's great!"

"But, seriously," Siren said, "you are my first chosen. Now let me put myself together. It's Saturday and I don't go to the office. But there may be an emergency."

She got out of bed, walking away naked, her breasts jiggling and getting Traver excited.

"I don't want you to go," she informed Traver.

"I'll be back later this afternoon," he promised.

"Not that. I don't want you to go back to 1995. I don't know how I could be without you. You have bloomed in my heart and have brought forth this melody of my love." She studied his face closely and asked, "What about Laura?" There was a searching in her eyes.

He put his arms around her. "You know I love her deeply."

"Do you love me?" Siren asked in a timid voice.

After a moment he said, "Yes."

Her eyes brightened. "Then what we have shared is based on love and not just lust? Laura and I are sisters in love with you. In my world, the man can have three chosens."

"Oh, there's lust all right," Traver exclaimed. "You're hot!"

"Tell me again that I'm hot and that you love me."

He kissed her, saying, "We'll never get out of here at this rate." He kissed her breasts softly and caressed them. "Now, get dressed and have breakfast. Then I can head on down to the bakery and help getting it set up. You'll come down and help, won't you?"

"If you want me to, Traver."

Yes, if you can make it."

"I can make it, I'll be there," said Siren, still a little giddy.

Traver was fascinated by the tattoo that clasped Siren's nipple. He was thinking about the Serpent Mound in southern Ohio. Still holding her breasts, he told her about the long snake carved into rolling hills that still baffles archeologists, who are not sure what Indians built it.

"Do you know how to find it, Traver?"

He thought a second before saying, "I think I can find it from the air, but it may take a while."

"I would like to see this. You say that your time thinks the Indians built it, but it could be a signal from our space ship."

"Yes," he agreed.

"We can take a flyer and be there in minutes, day or night, Traver."

"Okay, let's go then. Let's see how today goes."

Siren said, "Aboard my ship we can scan the terrain first and see what it looks like now. Maybe we'll need to visit it." She thought a moment. "It could be something the distressed star ship built as a visual beacon from the air."

He paused before asking, "Siren, why did you pick here and now to look for traces of the stranded ship's survivors?"

"This is where the robot return ship said they assimilated."

"But Cro-Magnon man showed up in Africa, not in North America."

"Do you suppose that perhaps the crew discovered the time canyon and they went through it?" she asked. "Has the time separation always been a hundred and eighty years?"

Traver shook his head. "Who knows? Have you found any traces that suggest your ancestors were here?"

"No," she said, disappointed.

"Well, let's eat and solve that problem later," Traver declared.

*   *   *

Breakfast was excellent. As he headed out the door, he said, "You know we're going to church Sunday. How much time does it take to get to Fort Cottonwood from here?"

Siren thought. "We will have to leave here at five in the morning. You're welcome to stay here Saturday night, Traver. I can have a wagon and horse ready for you."

"Siren, you know that Laura will be there?"

"I can accept that. Do you love me?" Siren asked again.

"Yes, I love you."

She smiled. "I can accept a twin love. Not first but not last, but true."

He kissed her and opened her blouse and kissed each nipple and patted her rear. "Keep those warm for me until tonight, and we'll heat it up again."

She blushed and promised, "I will!"

"I'll see you a bit later at the bakery." He started to leave again, but she called him back. "Come here a minute." He did, and she opened her blouse, showing her bare breasts. She took off the necklace with the jeweled orb and placed it over his head. "I want you to have this to remind you of me. No one else has ever seen this necklace. My mother gave it to me. This is just you and me." He looked at the orb.

Siren continued. "This represents my home world, and inside the silver and jeweled ball is soil from my home world. I want you to have it." She leaned forward and kissed him. "I love you, Traver."

She left her blouse open as she walked to the door with him. Before he opened the door, she kissed him again. "See you in a bit. I'll bring some lunch."

She stopped. "Oh, what would you like for supper tonight?"

"Surprise me!" He kissed her again.

As the sun grew stronger over the eastern sand hills, Traver thought about Laura and then of sharing his love with Siren and how it was so exotic. He was anticipating seeing Laura and hearing about her great-grandfather. And the same time he was anticipating having sex with Siren this evening. He thought about Laura's and Siren's sexual needs. Both women seemed similar. One was from here and one was from a distant star. Both were akin to goddesses in body. He had never considered cheating on Laura, and he had seen beautiful women, but none had affected him like Siren. He shook his head in wonderment. *What do I do? I love you both!*

Traver began wondering about cultures where marriage could involve more than one woman. Mormons, certainly, in his time, and in Siren's world, a first one chosen and then two or three other women.

CHAPTER 13

MONDAY'S COFFEE

TRAVER SPENT ALL morning Saturday getting things ready for Monday's opening. Skip's dad rode back to the camp and brought everything with him. The two tents went up out back. They tethered the horses there, too. Will brought down some hay and oats and helped Bill by constructing the tables and benches. Bill set up a little sleeping space in the corner of his "gun shop to be." Around two in the afternoon, Siren arrived and asked what she could do to help.

"Are you any good at making signs?" Traver asked her. "Here's the copy."

"I can do this," she promised. "I've got a steady hand now that I've gotten all that excitement out of my system." She winked at him.

The brick mason contacted a fellow who brought over two wood cook stoves. They were set up in the brick oven area.

"You'll be needing some stove pipe," the fellow said.

"I'll go down to the hardware store and fetch what's needed. You can pay me when I get back."

Traver and Bill set the cook stoves side by side and leveled them. Will brought in wood and stacked it out back. "Hey, Will, when that fellow gets back with the stove pipe, let's fire up the stoves and wire brush them and get them clean," Traver suggested.

Will smiled broadly and said, "Yes, sir, boss!"

They got the stove pipe attached to both stoves and Will fired them up. They stoked up real good. They set pots of water on them, just to see how long it took to boil and how long it would take to make the coffee.

Siren yelled, "Hey, Traver, what do you think of this?" She held up a sign that said, "Coffee 5¢. Cinnamon Rolls 30¢"

"Great sign. We also need a big OPEN sign and one that says CLOSED."

"You bet, boss," Siren answered. She was experiencing a new and different feeling. Working with Will made her think about children. Her children. She patted her stomach.

Alice was busy arranging her kitchen with the flour, sugar, and cinnamon that had been delivered. She pointed out, "The butter and milk will arrive at five o'clock in the morning on Monday."

Traver went over to the brick mason and showed him some hand-drawings of what Traver called a cool box for milk. The mason said he could build one without any problem. As Traver walked by the foundation, he noticed that Siren had carved a heart in the hearth cement, marked with Siren + T.W. She covered it with sand so no one would see it. Traver touched her shoulder and smiled.

Will yelled, "Water is boiling!"

Traver looked at his watch: eighteen minutes. "Okay, Will, dump the hot water and let the fires die out. Let's see how the ovens fire up."

Will stoked the brick ovens according to Traver's instructions, and both ovens heated up real good. He told Will that he was to fire up the ovens on Monday at one in the morning so his mother could bake the cinnamon rolls by five o'clock and no later.

Bill wanted to know if Traver would like to camp out in Bill's room so that he could wake Traver up at one o'clock. Traver told him, "Sure, Bill. Sounds like a good idea to me." Alice was putting sheets over the boards that made the tables. Siren passed by her and Alice said, "I sure hope Mr. Wells knows what he's doing."

"He does!" Siren assured her. "Believe me, just be patient and stay on target. It will take time for customers to come, but they will come!"

A couple cowboys rode by and one yelled, "What's going on here?"

Alice yelled back, "A coffee and cinnamon roll cafe!"

The other cowboy yelled, "Trail coffee?"

Siren yelled back, "Much better! Stop by Monday, we open at five! Up with the cows!"

He called out, "See ya!"

Siren made a last shout, "First customer, free coffee for life!"

Traver looked at her in amazement. "What the hell made you say that?" he asked.

"I don't know," Siren giggled. "But it's good advertising. After all, I'm the sign maker!"

Traver laughed. "Why not? Your first cup of coffee is free and it's your honor to let us know."

Siren replied, "Hey, that's even better!"

Alice chirped in, "You-all sure have a funny way of making money!"

Traver grinned. "Nope, that's just good business. Give the customer something extra and special and he'll feel pretty good about it."

The cups and saucers arrived around noon. The old boy said that they had purchased every cup and saucer he had. Forty cups and thirty-five plates. Traver smacked his head. The water! They needed water barrels and a wash tub or two for washing the cups and plates. He put Will in charge of rounding up a couple barrels for the water. The boy showed up later with an old water wagon, leaking like a sieve. He stopped and said that a fellow would give him the wagon if he could have a free cup of coffee and a roll every day for the rest of the year. Siren rolled her eyes and looked up at a passing cloud overhead. Traver tousled Will's head. "You see? You're becoming a businessman already."

"The man said that if I take it to the river and fill it up with water, it will stop leaking pretty soon." Will drove off toward the river.

Siren, as the official sign maker, said, "The wagon should have a sign on both sides and on the back."

"You are absolutely right," Traver agreed. "And the wagon out back, too."

"I'll get busy," she said.

Near lunchtime, Siren brought some one inch-by-twelve inch-by-one and a half-inch boards to the bakery and was painting them white. "How does 'Coffee and a Roll' sound to you?"

"Damned good!" he said with a big smile on his face and a wink.

"I mean a cinnamon roll, sir," she answered.

Alice kept a fire going in one of the ovens and was cooking a pinto bean and deer meat stew for lunch. It sure smelled good.

They had all stopped for lunch when a cowboy came by. "How much is a bowl of that? It sure smells good!"

Alice said, "Come and have a bowl with us, no charge today."

He jumped off his horse and tethered it quickly. It was like a big family get-together. The cowboy said that he would be back. Alice reminded him about coffee and rolls on Monday.

"I'll be sure to stop by," he said as he rode off.

Siren got up and took the bowls out back to wash.

It was getting close to three in the afternoon, and Traver sat down and closed his eyes. He was thinking about how good it would be to have a cold Pepsi or a root beer about now. There wasn't anything of the sort in 1860 that could get cold with ice on a hot fall day. He heard, "Would you like something cold to drink, Traver?" He opened his eyes and Siren was standing there, smiling at him. "Boy, would I ever."

"Come over to my office in thirty minutes." Siren turned and left abruptly. As she walked away, Traver watched her. She had a rear-end roll that matched Laura's.

When Siren moved out of sight, Traver saw Bill pull up a chair next to him.

"Have you ever had San Francisco coffee?" Bill asked him.

"I have, why?" Traver wanted to know.

"Well, there's some excellent coffee there. Before I became a drunk, I spent some time in San Francisco. I was thinking that maybe we should purchase our coffee beans directly from there."

Traver said, "You're right, Bill. We want French Roast and Colombian."

"What?"

"They'll know, I'm sure."

"It's the Roasted and Blended Farmer's Brothers," Bill informed him.

"Why, yes, it is," Traver said, who remembered that Farmer's was still in business in his time. "Bill, why don't you send them a letter about bulk purchases of roasted beans? In fact, sometime next year, you go and visit them. By that time the coffee shop should be going real good and you should have a few guns available and the train should be here by then. Your trip to San Francisco could promote your custom rifle-building business and your hunting-guide business as well. Take Will with you. That trip would give him some good business experience."

Traver leaned his head back, and as he shut his eyes again, he said, "I sure wish I could be around as you-all make advances in your businesses."

At that, Bill turned to look at him in surprise. "You ain't going to be here?"

"Nope, I'm sure not!"

Bill asked how Traver was going to collect his share of the business if he wasn't here. He leaned close and in a low voice said, "I want my share in fifty—and twenty-dollar gold pieces and in silver dollars and halves. And I want you to bury them out near a place that's called Three Canyons. Bury it every year in the center of the southernmost canyon, just as you go in. It's a box canyon. Bury it at least two feet down. I'll come along someday when I need money and dig it up."

"If that's what you want." Bill shook his head. "It's strange, but it's okay with me."

"Remember, gold coins or silver, no paper!"

Traver thought to himself that when he got home, he would dig them up and, a hundred and sixty-eight years later, the coins would be worth a mint.

Traver glanced at the clock on the bank's, front wall. About thirty minutes had gone by. "Got to go, Bill." He got up and slapped the dust off his pants. "See ya!"

Traver didn't go straight to the doctor's office. He went over to the hardware store and walked around, lookng at the merchandise. When he got to the cash register, the clerk asked, "Yes, sir?"

"Have you got a bathroom I can use?"

"No baths, sir."

"No? I gotta piss real bad!"

"Oh. Out back, you can use the back door."

Traver went out back and walked up the alley and crossed the street over to the doctor's office. As he walked in, the young lady at the desk said, "Good afternoon, Mr. Wells. The captain asked me to give you this." She reached under her desk and brought up a pitcher of a golden liquid with lots of ice floating in it.

"Oh, my God! Iced tea!" he whistled. He poured a cupful and downed it quickly. He stopped dead as he was swallowing. It wasn't iced tea after all, it tasted like some wildflowers he had smelled a long time ago as a child. It had a soft and gentle scent and flavor.

The young lady smiled. "No, it's not tea. It's from our home. It's called Shaaah."

He poured another cup and drank more slowly to sense its wonders. He swore he could hear music and he cocked his head to listen.

"Is there something wrong, Mr. Wells?"

He cocked his head to the other side. "I hear wonderful, soft sounds. It's like a song I know," he explained.

"You are hearing the captain's spirit. This drink, Shaaah, is a drink of the soul who prepares it."

He poured another cup and the song filled his ears and swelled his heart. "Is the captain here?" he asked.

"No, she is on board the ship." She paused briefly. "The captain left instructions that if you want to go up, she would like that very much."

"I can go to the ship?" he asked quietly.

"If you desire. The captain was very clear about that."

"How would I do that?"

"I can arrange it."

"Do I have to do anything?"

"No, sir. Would you like to join the captain now?"

"Yes, I would. Very much!"

"Just a moment," said the receptionist, smiling.

She picked up the cell phone-looking device and punched a button. Her voice, as she was speaking, was a melodious tone of sounds. She looked over at me. "It will be just a moment or two, Mr. Wells. Would you like for me to pour you another cup of Shaaah?"

"Yes. please. Another cup, thank you."

As Traver finished his fourth cup, a young man dressed as a cowboy, but too clean and too pale to be one, came in the back door. He motioned to Traver and said, "Mr. Wells, the captain is expecting you. Please come with me."

Traver followed him out the back door and asked, "How do we get to the ship?"

"We fly, of course. It's quite a lifting wing. We modulate the magnetic field that it generates and we fly very fast and very quietly."

They walked another eight hundred feet to a gully where two men were on guard. They waved and everyone on board of the craft, which looked like an old-fashioned Cadillac with huge wings, waved back. It had lots of windows and at the rear was what looked like a huge fifty-five-gallon drum of tubing wire. As Traver observed it, the young man said, "That's a field coil. We switch it from North Pole to South Pole, hit it with a super-cold envelope that blows a hole in the planet's gravity pull, and we shoot off the planet like a bullet from one of your pistols. It's all very fast. I'll have you ride next to me, so you can see."

They strapped in, and the young man pushed two buttons which illuminated an aura of lights in front of Traver.

The young man said, "Both lights will fall to the center point" He pointed to that place. "When the two lights phase together, we go. Hang on!" The yellow lights merged in the center and, in a flash, they were in space. They were falling toward a light that swelled from just a speck to filling the windows in the wink of an eye.

They bumped. "We're here, Mr. Wells."

As the car, which was Traver's name for the vehicle, doors opened with a hiss, he smelled fragrance that reminded him of spring rain showers.

"Come with me, sir. The captain is waiting in the steering area."

A woman dressed in a body suit took charge of Traver. They walked down a passageway and into a room where he had to undress and hang his clothing in a chamber that closed. "Your clothing will be sonically cleaned. This way, sir, we must shower."

All of them were nude in the shower as they scrubbed and then dried off in a wind-tunnel contraption.

In the next space were grayish coveralls hanging on the walls. Each of them selected a pair that fit and slipped into soft boots. The three men were smiling at me. "See you later, sir."

An older woman wearing light-blue coveralls introduced herself. They went toward the steering area. "I am glad to finally meet you, Mr. Wells. The captain has talked about you quite a lot."

"She has?"

"Yes, she has. The captain has been . . ." she paused, searching for words, "distracted." She smiled. "Well, here we are!"

A doorway slid open, showing a darkened space with a million twinkling lights.

Traver could see eight or ten human-like forms moving around inside, silouhetted against the flashing lights.

Wearing form-fitting light blue coveralls, Siren stepped over to Traver and in a low voice said, "There you are, Mr. Wells, please come in. Thank you, Swang, for bringing Mr. Wells to Steering."

"Certainly." The lady left, and Traver stepped into the space, the door shutting behind him. As his eyes adjusted to the low lighting, he realized that those glittering lights were stars he was seeing through a huge window. Siren was quiet as he adjusted to the surroundings.

"Space, the universe, welcomes you to her breast," she said proudly. He turned to look at her and she leaned in closer to say, "And so do I!" She was looking deeply into his eyes, searching for something. "I trust that my breasts will always bring the gentlest rest and the greatest excitement to you." She looked away and then back again. "As captain, I am last. My position as captain demands that I be vigilant. I do not have the pleasure of love or the comfort of sharing my bed." She cleared her throat slightly. "I must apologize for the other night. I began to lead you rather than letting you choose me. I have observed on your planet how you seek and stay with a mate. I am impressed. Our world has nine females to one male. The females cannot ask the man, and in return the male may have up to three females. I've told you this before." She watched Traver for any reaction. "As captain, I have been awfully lonely. Partly because of my pride, partly because of my job. When I saw you, well, I felt a difference in my attitude. But enough about that for now."

Traver stood spellbound, absorbing what she had just said, and then he became lost in the view of the stars. "My God, how do you keep all of this straight?"

"What do you mean, straight?"

Looking at the magnificent universal picture, he mumbled, "I mean how do you know where you are and which direction is home?"

A wonderful smile broke over her face. She reached up to a panel and touched a button. Some stars diminished in intensity and others became brilliant and were flashing or pulsing. Siren pointed to the window. "The brightest stars are guide beacon stars. We choose three, and as we travel we are continually measuring the shift of light. Slower is red and faster is blue is a simple way to explain it," Siren said.

"The Doppler effect," Traver added.

"Is that what you call this behavior?" she asked.

"Yes, it is," he answered. "Is there something special about those stars?" he asked, pointing to the screen.

Siren nodded yes. "Those," and she pointed out two bright ones, "have a constant frequency that we have measured and on which can fix our position, knowing all these stars' frequencies."

"In my time these stars are called pulsar stars," he said. "It always struck me that they could be used for space navigation."

Siren called to a woman who was at another panel.

"Yes, captain?" the woman addressed Siren.

"My friend here understands the beacon stars, he calls them pulsars. Please explain to him briefly how we use them."

"Yes, captain."

The woman turned to the view window and pointed. "Being easily distinguished from one another, these beacon stars, or pulsars, provide a means whereby a craft such as ours may accurately determine its position and location through triangulation. They also allow accurate determination of velocity from the Doppler shift of the pulsars' periods and of time retardation from the change in the beacon stars', or pulsars', derivatives. In addition their broad spectrum makes these beacons ideally suited for high-speed interstellar flight."

"High speed?" Traver was curious.

"Yes, even at luminal flight."

The woman looked at Siren, who turned and continued to explain to Traver, "Sub-light speed, we use what you see before you. Super-luminal speed, the point of light you see and call a star, becomes a line of light, and the line patterns are just as accurate as sub-light observations. But they have a different separation. Not only is the light emitting from the pulsar, but it is also creating a frequency, and with this signal we can identify where we are.

"How long did it take your civilization to set up the pulsars?" Traver asked.

Siren looked at him and so did the aide pictured on the monitor in Siren's cabin. Siren answered, "We didn't put that in place. We discovered them, as it seems your scientists have. Someone else put them in place, we are just learning about them." She continued, "We believe the Star Throwers set up the beacons. Our star travel has not been long for us."

Traver's thoughts immediately went to the painting above Laura's fireplace, called "Star Throwers."

Siren's aide said, "We reference the Galactic Center as our constant. Not where we are from. For some reason navigating is more accurate refocusing the G.C."

"The what?" Traver queried.

Siren said, "Galactic Center."

"Oh, of course."

Siren went on, "While we have been here, we have discovered an interesting thing. Your zodiac constellations lore possesses an advanced knowledge of the science of navigation in the stars. What I mean is, consider the trajectory of the archer's arrow toward the heart of the Scorpion." Siren took a breath. "The location of the Sagitta arrow at its position close to the Northern Galactic Radian point and the location of your Southern Cross marker, which accurately points out the Southern Galactic point, are accurate to one-one-thousandth of a degree. That's not a chance occurrence. Someone with G.C. knowledge has left a marker. Perhaps to where they went or came from. Or it may be a reference to the Universal Center."

Siren dismissed her aide from the Steering room. Traver and she were alone for the time being. She said to him, "Come, let's go to my quarters." She squeezed his hand gently, and they left the Steering room. As they progressed down the passageway, she said, "We're leaving for home next week. I don't want to lose what I have just found."

She stopped at a doorway, touched a pad, and the door slid open. The room sprang to life with light, sound, and fragrance. Siren pressed a button marked Private and then stepped into his arms. She laid her head on his chest and held him closely. Slowly she raised her head so her ghost-gray eyes caught his. "May I be with you until we leave?" Her voice was pleading.

Traver had visions of Laura, how hurt she would be and how embarrassed he would be if she knew. He held Siren, his thoughts ragged, "You'll be gone by next week? Why are you and your ship leaving again?"

Siren ran her fingers over his back in a loving manner. "We have not found the ship we were seeking that crashed here. Probably it was destroyed long ago. And there are no survivors. They all assimilated into the culture. We go back to the mother world with that knowledge. We need to let this world develop on its own. I expect that we will drop in here now and then to see how things are developing, and one of these days we'll make ourselves known." For a moment she was silent. "I suspect that will be when your space program reaches the fourth planet, Mars, as you call it. There is a tremendous amount of evidence there of occupation in the distant past of your time."

"Do you know, or have any idea, what the orbit of rubble is?" she asked.

"Yes, it's the asteroid belt."

"Yes," she said, "the leftover mass of the twin worlds."

"I've always felt it was a planet that blew up, not two of them," Traver said.

Siren's voice became pedantic. "No, planets don't blow up. They collide or are destroyed in battle, but they don't just explode. Here, Traver, take a look at this." Siren played the images of the twin world where the rubble was.

Watching, riveted, Traver said, "My God! They're beautiful! What happened?"

"We don't know. My hunch is that there was some sort of outside intervention. Maybe that's why our sleep ship disappeared. If that's so, then there is something out there to fear." She gazed out the large port window that displayed the universe.

"Will you come back some day, Siren?"

"Probably not." She cocked her head to see him better. "We cannot fly beyond time and surely I will have passed away by your time."

He leaned down and kissed her forehead. "For the moment, Siren, you're the center of the universe. You are the beginning with no end." He kissed her on the lips. "Siren, I choose you. You are equally chosen."

Later they lay on the bed, staring out her window into the universe. Siren was curled up and nesting in the protection of his arms. He kissed the back of her neck at her hairline as she hummed quietly. Her heart was pounding still from the moments they had shared just a short time ago.

"I am going to miss the hell out of you," Traver said.

"Stay here!" she exclaimed.

"Here? You mean in 1860 or 1995?"

"Would you stay in 1860 if I were here?" she asked.

"I should go back to 1995," he said.

She rolled over to face him. "And I should fulfill my duty as captain." Her gray eyes searched his face. "Oh! To be just a crew member right now. I would jump ship. I love you, Mr. Wells, and I would go anywhere with you, but I am captain and many depend on me."

Her tears began again. "Hold me a little longer." They drifted off to sleep in each other's arms again.

When they awoke, Traver whispered, "You know, Siren, it's not every day that I run into a Star Traveler. What I first experienced with you is your spirit and your beauty. I don't think of you as from another star system. It really did not hit me until I came aboard your ship and here I am out in space. I am so wowed!" He grinned.

Siren smiled and whispered, "Wow!" Then she lightly traced her fingertips across his chest. "You are not the first people like us we have ever come across in all our time of star travel. Your world is the only one so far whose inhabitants share elements of our DNA. I was disappointed that development is as slow as it is. I would have thought the sleep ship might have influenced this world. Traver, tell me about the time you are from."

"Out here in Nebraska, where we are now, it's still a lot like now. The only things different are big roads and motorized vehicles. We've done some space exploration, but it's mostly robotic and I'm sure if something is found, it will never be known to the public."

Siren raised up and kissed his chest and laid her head on him.

He chuckled.

"What?" she asked.

"I just realized I am the first earth man to make love in space."

Siren laughed, too. "Traver, I am so honored that you are my first, and you will be my only." Tears formed in her eyes. "My only love! But I feel like I have invaded your love with Laura. I understand your world's way of pairing. Please understand my world's way. I suspect I can handle this a little easier than you can."

"Siren," he whispered, "I will never feel guilty about our sharing of love. I do feel bad that I have broken my promise to Laura, and I'll have to deal with that!"

He drifted in thought back and forth between scenes of Siren from when she first poked her head into the Sawtooth Saloon with the paper airplane he had tossed through the swinging doors and the image of Laura riding her horse. He envisioned Siren as she stood in the parlor of the hotel, letting him absorb all that she was. He flashed on her stepping up to the wagon's bench and then pictured Laura screaming as she fell into the cold water of the stream. He shivered as his body re-experienced Siren's breasts touching his back when she was pointing out the star clusters from her home world. He took a deep breath and let it out slowly.

And Siren's twining snake tattoo. From the navel of time to the center of the universe. The serpent clasped her nipple, the jewel of humanity, the nourishment of the universe.

"Siren . . ." he breathed her name as his fingertips touched her tiny navel and slowly traced the outline of the serpent. Her stomach muscles were tight, not an ounce of fat. She lay still, her breasts lit by the starlight with a bluish blaze. As his fingertips touched her skin, goose bumps rose. "Oh, Traver, your touch travels the Way as though you remember." She closed her eyes. "Now I remember you when I was just a little child, walking with my mother."

"How is that possible, Siren?"

"Somewhere in your future, you travel the Way." She looked at him a long time in silence. She was trying to understand what she had just said.

"I travel the Way in my future?" he asked. "How?"

Siren knew the only way this could occur would be if someone like her would take him upon the Way. She was deep in thought about his future. Coming back to the moment, she said to Traver, "I want to show you my home world and the stars that form our heritage." She touched a small box and turned to look at him. "I keep this by my bed because it helps me to fall asleep." The entire overhead space of her quarters was flooded with projected stars. She brought both her hands up to where he was gently cuddling her left breast. His eyes fixed on her breast, he suddenly saw it become a beautiful flower of dazzling white with a rich golden-orange center. The petals of the flower were shiny, liked the sun's rays as they filter through holes in a roof. The center of the unfolding flower flowed as though molten gold. Its fragrance was as sweet as every flower he had ever smelled. Slowly that vision faded to starlight reflecting on Siren's breasts.

Her lips parted with an intake of breath. "Traver, the flower of life, as you sensed, blooms with love. That flower is now a part of both of us."

He raised up to her lips, touching them lightly. Siren touched a button on her bedside table and a huge screen came to life. The cluster of stars shown like blue-white diamonds ablaze. Siren said, "The Pleiades, as you call them, described as the seven stars in your world's history, were recorded by many cultures as the stars from where people came. Jilleng, the brightest star—I think your name for that one is Alcuin—has seven worlds that orbit it. Four of those worlds are as Edon and your planet here. However, there is no more life upon them. They are ruins of a once large civilization that populated the four planets. Here, let me show you . . ."

One by one the planets of the star Alcuin came into view. The ruins took Traver's breath away.

"Siren, they look so much like my world's ruins."

"Yes, Traver. All the ruins we have discovered are similar. There is no great difference in humanity. There are no monsters. There is simply evidence of people." The overhead returned to a wonderful view of the Pleiades, and it was evident that there were at least twelve to nineteen brilliant stars that made up that little area of the sky. "My home star is just to the right and up two stars." She pointed and it came into an enlarged view. "Edon." Her lips pronounced it lovingly. "Your word for this star is Maia. As you can see, Maia has three lesser stars clustered close. It is those worlds my ancestors explored first. It was a ship such as the ones we used then that were re-outfitted and sent out to look for the Star Throwers. They were sleep ships and only one, the star ship TLK, found its way home. Perhaps others sent orbs home and they simply lost their way or were destroyed in transit. The lesser stars, Souul, De, and Cala, were each between one-half and one light year from Maia. All of the other stars—in your terms, Steppe, Tagete, Celaeno, Alcyone, Electra, Atlas, Pleione—encircle Maia. To reach those systems required that our culture research our psychology and enhance our genetics so we could realistically make the trips of seven to fifteen light-years asleep."

Traver was fascinated by her story, as she continued, "It is evident that human life was as abundant as the universe is full of stars. So many worlds have had solar system travel, but all have forgotten the voyage of the stars." She paused. "All but my world." Siren turned to Traver. "No one but Edon travels the stars nowadays. All of the other worlds remember the star people, but they seem to have forgotten, or they just aren't interested in, their star history. As long as I have looked at the starlight, Traver, I have needed to be out there."

"Who were the Star Throwers, Siren?"

The scene of close-up stars zoomed back to show how that star cluster looked from earth. "Traver, that star cluster contains more than three thousand stars, but only the ones I pointed out here have worlds close by. From our star to your star is seventy light-years. We do that distance quite well now. Only a couple months and we're home. That is why I was so interested in this Enchanted Canyon of yours. Just think, if our scientists could couple the natural magnetic anomaly there to our concept of flight, we just might be able to get around much quicker. The Star Throwers, Traver, are the ones that seeded the stars we see today from the primal basket and tossed them up into the darkness to light the Way. The Way is that which I travel upon as I mature in my life's experience. The Way is a path or a road one takes to go from one place to another."

Siren stood up and put her hands on her chest between her breasts. "The Way begins here first." Her hands began glowing a violet-magenta color. Her whole body was radiating a violet light. "It was our ships from

Edon that went out among the stars. We spent as much time around our own neighborhood as we did heading out to other stars. It seemed that we were more attracted to finding the Star Throwers' tracks.

"We would stop by a system that we had visited fifty to sixty years past. Some of the inhabitants remembered our last visit, but most did not." As Siren was speaking, stars were flashing on the ceiling with their planetary bodies and the inhabited worlds and their people. Traver was fascinated that how similar people looked, just minor differences in facial features and height ratios.

They all had two legs and feet, two arms and hands and five fingers, or earth hands, one head with two eyes, one nose and a mouth. Siren reached over to the cube and touched it. The starlight disappeared and Siren's quarters went back to reflected starlight showing at her window.

"Siren?"

"Yes, Traver?"

"Being next to you at this moment, I am so taken at how small the universe has become. I hold you this moment, and I know the vast distance between our two worlds, but now I feel that there is no distance at all. I think about all that you have seen and touched in your travels, and I am overcome with awe. And I am so humbled and honored that you have chosen me."

"Chosen?" Siren whispered. "Traver, you have let me experience being the woman I am. I have seen, worked with, and directed many men. But not one ever attracted me like you do. I don't think about the distance between us. I only think about how you make me feel safe, secure, and complete." She cuddled up to him.

After a few moments, he whispered, "Siren, have you ever gone to the library in town?"

"Library? No."

"Well, there is a library in North Platte and I hope to find some books on Egypt in there. There are some images that I think you will find interesting. I'm thinking that your Star Throwers did influence the earth's ancient peoples. Some in my time think that the Egyptians had some kind of contact with a star we call Sirius. It could have been the Star Throwers."

Siren sat up again. "Show me that star, Traver."

He laughed. "Hell, I'm no astrophysicist."

"Astro . . . what?"

"A person who knows where stars are in relation to my world. But I really want you to look at some of the serpents that the Egyptian statues and writings show." He could tell Siren was interested in what he was talking about. She got out of bed and reached out her hand. "Come, let's shower and dress and return to earth."

As she was dressing, she smiled and said, "You know, Traver, we can go to Egypt and look at this firsthand."

"Fly to Egypt! In 1860! I don't know where to take you or if what I'm talking about is available in 1860! Let's just go to the library."

"All right, Traver, but it would be a big trip."

"Are you ready for some home cooking down on the planet? We're off to church tomorrow over at Fort Cottonwood, so we had better return anyway. What's for dinner?" he wanted to know.

"Ham, potatoes, carrots, and string beans. I am dessert!" Siren giggled.

"You are!"

"Completely yours!" Siren smiles.

Back down on the planet, Siren was true to her culinary word. As Traver wiped his mouth, he said, satisfied, "Good fix'n's, woman."

Siren liked that, and the sides of her mouth cracked into a smile.

"Are you going to stay here tonight?" she asked plaintively.

"I've thought about it, but I should sleep at camp. I'll be down to pick you up at five tomorrow morning."

Siren slid her plate aside and looked up. "I won't sleep a wink till I see you again in the morning."

"Yes, you will!" And with that Traver left for the camp.

*　　*　　*

Four-thirty rolled around way too soon for Traver. He had slept like a boulder in a slow road. Will helped him hitch up the wagon, and Traver climbed aboard, saying, "I'll see you tonight."

"Are you bringing back Mrs. Laura?"

"Yes, I am, Will, the doctor is going with me and coming back, too."

"She sure is pretty," Will said shyly.

"Someday a looker will come your way, don't you worry," Traver assured him. Traver tapped the reins and shortly he pulled up at Siren's little house. A coal-oil light was burning in her kitchen.

He tapped on her door and she answered, "Come in, I'll be a moment yet."

He let himself in and followed the aroma of fresh coffee into the kitchen. She had poured two cups, and beside one was a beautiful pink tea-rose bud. When she entered the kitchen, Siren said, "The cup with the tea-rose is yours."

Siren picked up her coffee.

He glanced at her, holding her cup of coffee with both hands, with its steam flowing upward and a chip off the cup's rim.

"My God!" he gasped, as he remembered the exact vision.

"What is it, Traver?" Siren asked as she lowered the cup

It was like he experienced in Laura's kitchen the previous fall, only this time Siren didn't disappear.

"What?" she asked again.

"We have been together before. I have seen you before," Traver sputtered. "Here!"

Siren, solemn, set down her coffee cup.

"I, too, know that I have met you before this time."

"Really?" he gasped.

"Well, I didn't actually meet you, but I heard you. You sounded very agitated."

"Agitated?" Traver was still aghast.

"Last year in our Com Center room we heard a voice. Your voice, now that I have encountered you. You were quite vocal concerning the 'piece-of-shit cell phone.'"

Traver broke out laughing. "No kidding? Piece of shit? How did you hear that?"

Siren smiled. "Now that we know about the time distortion out at Enchanted Canyon, probably some sort of electronic anomaly occurred. I was very intrigued by your voice, and when I heard you yell to Roy in the Sawtooth, I knew it was you. That's why I had my men follow you." She paused. "The universe works in strange ways. You had a vision of me and today it is real. I heard your voice and today you speak to me. Strange and wonderful ways."

At that Siren stood and encouraged Traver to finish. "Let's go." She lowered the coal-oil lamp's wick, and it went out.

As they left Siren's house, dawn was just beginning to glow. Flickering lights could be seen in the windows and the smell of bacon and coffee began filtering into the streets. They sat side by side in the seat, and Traver directed the wagon south, straight through town. If anyone was looking, they were in plain sight—not trying to hide anything.

After they crossed the Platte River, about a mile east of town, Siren moved closer to Traver, saying, "We are going to be gone by Thursday. This may be the last time I can be with you alone." The horse was at a gait—just above walking and just below prancing. He held the reins in one hand and circled her waist with the other. She lightly ran her fingers over the bulge in his pants and he swallowed hard. The bumping and jiggling of the springed wagon seat intensified their physical closeness. The vibrating wagon shook and bounced them into another world of feelings. As they topped a six-hundred-foot hill, Traver could see Fort Cottonwood in the distance. He looked at his watch. They were a little early, so he drove the wagon over to a clump of brush and tethered the horse out of sight of the fort.

"I shall always remember you, and I will always love you. I would give up everything for you if it were not for Laura," Traver said earnestly.

Siren blushed.

"Is it good for you with her?" she asked.

"Yes," he said. "You and Laura are the most delicious women I have ever known."

And time stood still yet again as Siren's world emptied with Traver's loving.

"Then let's get put together and go down to the fort."

They drove into Fort Cottonwood, relaxed and ready for the next step in their lives. He tied the horse to the rail outside and helped Siren down from the seat. "You have the nice scent of love," he whispered in her ear.

"They will know!"

He smiled. "Well, it's that or horseshit in our pockets to mask the scent."

"This will help." She took a small bottle from her handbag and opened it, touching a finger to it and then moistening a spot behind each ear. "Toilet water," she giggled.

"Don't put any of that on me," he flapped his hands in front of her.

He looked around.

"Are you looking for Laura?" Siren asked. "I understand, but I'm still jealous, Traver. Second is not normal for me. I must be first, I am captain."

"Don't ever say that again, Siren. You are not second—but equal."

She looked hurt.

"I love you deeply. Please forgive me."

"Nothing to forgive," she said.

"Siren, you're beautiful, but you need . . ."

"What do I need, Traver?"

Before he could answer, the major came up. "Major, let me introduce Siren. She is a vet in North Platte."

The major saluted. "I've heard of you, ma'am."

Siren smiled and offered her hand. Then she saw the pastor and, excusing herself, went over to shake his hand.

The Major said to Traver, "Mrs. Wells said that she would be back in North Platte this Saturday late."

"Oh, she's not here yet?"

"She and Corporal Peterson's platoon are out west of the Platte River. He's showing her possible railroad routes. Mrs. Wells sure is a fine example of pioneer woman. She rides like a trooper."

CHAPTER 14

OUT ON PATROL

SOMETHING TO SPOT AND JAW ABOUT

THE COLUMN OF horsemen came at a steady, unhurried pace and crossed the border near the junction of Kansas and Nebraska, close to the town of Squaw Creek, and headed toward Falls City, Nebraska, as it was growing dusk. By late afternoon the two outriders flanking both sides of the horsemen had begun to pull in closer to the main group and were maintaining their posts about five hundred yards out—one to the east and the other to the west. As the main body of horsemen crossed into Nebraska from Kansas, the point scout backtracked to inform Commander Lewis that there was a good campsite ahead, next to a small creek that would be hidden from view in a small grove of cottonwood trees—only a half-hour's ride away.

Lewis allowed three small fires to be dug in and lit for cooking once the horses had been picketed and grain fed and a proper guard stationed. He put out three lookouts, at the far points of a triangle that stretched out five hundred yards from the main encampment.

There was no loud talking or joking among the men as they hunkered down around the fire-pits. They spoke in low monotones while waiting on the brewing coffee and the bison meat to finish cooking on old musket ram-rods. They were dressed in the styles of their preference except for one item—they each wore soft deerskin leggings that covered their lower legs from ankle to just below their knees, where they were tied with rawhide laces. The leggings were stained the same color—a dark russet red.

They were members of the notorious Kansas Jayhawkers.

As a unit, these Red Legs were a tight-knit killing machine under the command of Lewis.

Nearly all were equipped with five or six pistols on their bodies and an additional two attached to the pommels of their saddles. Their rifles were all repeating lever-action Winchesters, and each man possessed two horses—both saddled and ready to ride. The two main Colt revolvers were attached on belts resting high up at hip level and slanted for cross-draw with either hand. Most had two cartridge belts slung crisscross over their chests in addition to a waist cartridge belt with the loops full of shells. In armament alone they easily carried thirty-five to forty pounds of weight.

When the buffalo meat had simmered long enough and nearly had quit spitting its juice into the fire, they began to eat and a few bottles of whisky were circulated.

For a group numbering thirty-two men, their voices remained amazingly hushed and circumspect. Presently pipes began to appear and were tamped with tobacco. Others dug out their papers and tobacco pouches to twist up cigarettes. Then started the preparations for turning in for the night. It was a mild evening with a soft breeze that barely fanned the fires, and by the time the guard outposts were being changed, most of the assassins were snoring.

Just four days earlier these men had ridden down on a four-wagon, horse-drawn train, just west of Leavenworth, Kansas, and gunned down every living person and animal except one—him, they tortured for information and then burned him alive.

In all, they had slaughtered six women, nine children, seven men, the horses, and two milk cows before they burned the wagons. The people could have been abolitionists come to lend their support in voting Kansas into the Union as a freeman state, or they could have been innocent settlers seeking a new life.

Whatever they were, they were in the wrong place at the wrong time in the history of Bloody Kansas.

Just before dawn, Lewis kicked a few boots and within minutes his men were up—splashing water from the small creek on their faces, filling their canteens and water pouches, and building up the breakfast fires.

Shortly after breakfast the men were mounted and on the move again in a northwesterly direction, away from the Iowa border and out into the open plains country.

The unfortunate man in Kansas they had tortured had revealed that the new route to be taken by abolitionists was involved bypassing Missouri and swinging further northward through Iowa and into Nebraska before entering Kansas from a northwestern direction. Lewis felt it was his duty to halt the influx of Freeman State promoters at any and all costs. Best to do it by killing them before they could arrive and settle in Kansas.

It was just before noon when the point scout reported that there were three wagons of families headed westward an easy ride away. Lewis took fifteen men, who left their spare mounts to be brought up later, and told the rear group to follow along at the regular, steady pace. They left at a trot, led by the scout, and after a half-hour's ride, the wagons came into view. At a short distance behind the wagons, they pulled their horses into a single-file column and, galloping past, they split into two columns on either side of the wagons, shooting everything that moved. The horses pulling the wagons dropped in their tracks and the families walking alongside fell to the ground dead. Two women tried to run across the prairie but were quickly overtaken and shot. No one was left alive.

By the time the rear group arrived, the men had rummaged around in the wagons for eatable supplies, and they had them ready to divide up with the others. In no time the supplies were packed up and the wagons were burning.

Moving at a good pace, by evening they had swung slightly south and bypassed Fort Kearny on the Platte River and then turned northward to camp by the river. Lewis wanted nothing to do with the Union soldiers stationed at Fort Kearny.

He was pleased with his band's progress through Nebraska. Two and a half days from Falls City, staying not far from the Kansas border, passing through Fairbury and then a little north just up to Hastings. Heading west, he was hoping to keep south of the Platte River and Fort Kearny. He passed just south of Minden.

Looking at his maps, he observed that the last three wagons had been a bit below Holdrege. He surmised that they were now halfway between Fort Cottonwood and Fort Kearny. Lewis was planning to operate with patrols of fifteen or sixteen men—each one going west as far as McCook or thereabouts—and he and the rest of the men would go east toward Fairbury. At worst, each group would be only two days apart at their farmost east-west points. Lewis especially wanted to stay away from the Platte River. He had heard that the Union Pacific

Railroad was surveying a route from Omaha to Chicago, west at least over to Denver.

Lewis was off in thought, thinking that he was more south and not as far west. He thought he was close to McCook, way south of Fort Cottonwood and North Platte. Actually, he was only about ten miles east of Farnam—which, by way of the flying crow, was only thirty-eight miles from Fort Cottonwood.

Lewis knew that the east-west wagon trail followed the Platte River and also that the railroad surveyors and army patrols would be there. He also figured from what the dead man in Kansas had said, the abolitionists, wanting to sneak back into Kansas, would at some point between Kearny and Cottonwood veer straight south or slightly southeast. His plan was to follow south of the river until he found sign of a south caravan track.

Strangely enough, by midday the next day, they had not found the sort of southern track he had expected. It was a bit dangerous for him to get much closer to the town of North Platte and Fort Cottonwood, but Lewis figured that a few more miles wouldn't hurt—he was wrong! At this exact moment, Lewis was fifteen miles due south of Maxwell, Nebraska.

The Union army patrol scout had been dawdling along, humming to himself, when he came up over a rise in the ground—his mouth dropped open and his humming abruptly stopped in his throat. There before him, at about a thousand yards, was a column of dismounted cavalry-looking men, walking their horses nearly parallel to where he sat. He promptly got out his small telescope to get a better look. They had military bearing but were wearing civilian clothing, and they seemed to be a big bunch of ruffians. As he studied the column more closely, he saw that they all had one thing in common—these men were Red Legs. "Jayhawkers," he exclaimed under his breath.

In the act of wheeling his horse around, he was practically knocked from his saddle by a fifty-caliber slug from a Sharp's rifle from nearly five hundred yards away—the Jayhawkers' scout had seen him. If he hadn't been in the act of turning his horse to ride back to Corporal Peterson's patrol, he would have been dead. The slug had caught him high up and passed through his right shoulder blade and blew out a large hole in his upper right chest.

Slumping forward and holding his saddle horn with his left hand, the reins fell from his hands, and the horse, feeling the release of the bit in its mouth, took off at a full-out run back to the patrol unit.

Peterson's patrol, with Laura and Roy accompanying them, had stopped for an afternoon rest. Roy was shooting the breeze with a few of the troopers. A couple of troopers had crawled under the supply wagon and were taking a nap in its shade. Laura and Corporal Peterson were looking at the maps he had brought along. Laura was talking with her great-granddad. He was pointing out that if the railroad track followed the river, water and fuel wood were available, but that route would flood in the spring and freeze in the winter.

He was pointing out a route north of the Platte River—about six miles north. He commented that the elevation of the land was at least six feet higher. That ground could make a big difference to the railroad in spring and winter. Laura was listening but actually paying no attention to the map. She was enjoying watching her great-granddad working his wad of tobacco around in his mouth and seeing the bulge in one cheek then being switched to the other side. Somehow he still managed to keep the conversation going without losing his wad of chew.

Corporal Peterson looked at a fly next to his map, puckered his lips, and spat a wad of juice out from under his big handlebar mustache. The wad flew straight and whacked the fly. "There, you son of a bitch!" Then the corporal realized that Laura was with him.

"Excuse me, Mrs. Wells. I forgot you were here." Looking at her an extra moment, he smiled. "The first thing I hate in this world is . . ."

Laura spoke quickly, "Flies!"

Corporal Peterson looked surprised. "Why, yes, ma'am, but . . ."

Laura chuckled. "My great-granddad and granddad hated flies. But, Corporal, I have never seen such a great shot."

He nodded shyly. "Get lots of practice out here."

Laura was grinning.

"Mrs. Wells, what's so funny?"

Laura looked at him intently. "You reckon you could teach me to spit like that?"

"Ma'am!"

"Well, corporal, it runs in my family and I never learned to spit. My mother said that was just unladylike." She paused. "Besides, mom's not here right now."

Corporal Peterson kept his left hand on the map while considering Laura's request.

"Well, what will Mr. Wells say?"

"Well, Corporal Peterson, the mister is not here right now, either. But if I can learn to whack a fly like you can, I think Mr. Wells will be rightly impressed." She grinned real big.

Corporal Peterson began to fold the map they had been looking at, and he tucked it into his leather pouch. He reached his left hand into his pocket and pulled out a pocket knife about a quarter inch wide and three inches long. It had silver sides. Laura saw the knife and she gasped. She recognized that knife. Papa Joe used it to cut pieces of chewing tobacco, like his dad did. There in front of her, Peterson cut his twist of chaw with the knife she had in her drawer.

"Well, ma'am, if you're going to learn to spit, you got to spit tobacco juice. Just spit won't kill the fly. Also, tobacco spit is a bit heavier and more sticky. Flies get all stuck up and can't fly and after a bit can't walk either.

Laura smiled. "They probably die of suffocation and nicotine. Flies breathe with every cell—flies don't have lungs."

"What? You sound like a bug doctor."

Laura laughed.

"And you want to learn to spit?" he asked in amazement.

"Yep!"

"Okay." He cut off a chunk and offered it to her.

Laura gulped. *Just pretend it's Bazooka bubble gum.* She popped it in her mouth and began chewing her chunk.

"No! No!" he admonished her. "Don't chew. Let it sit in your cheek and suck on it. Work the juice around in your cheek. Chewing is what you do to tough old buffalo meat. Tobacco you don't chew. You get it moist and suck out the juices." He spit. "Put both lips together and pucker up. Pretend you're kissing your best beau. Now, with both cheeks and your tongue, push up spit and make a pffttt sound at the end. Like this." He spit.

Laura put her lips together, thought of Traver, and spit. A good amount of juice flew out, but a hefty amount of juice was running out both side of her lips. The tobacco was beginning to taste awful, but she was determined to learn this. She worked her chew with her tongue, and before long a load of juice was swishing around in her cheeks. Sputt! It flew out some four inches in front of her.

The men watching her had a great laugh. "There you go, Mrs. Wells."

The corporal spat again and whacked another fly. "Ma'am, you got to develop a touch." "Yuck," Laura said, "the taste is awful!

"It is, isn't it?" one of the men answered. "But no smoking—Indians can smell smoke a long distance."

Someone over by the supply wagon looked up and yelled, "Scout riding in. He's low in the saddle!" The group ran to see the rider running hellbent toward them. In seconds, the horse was spooked to a stop and the Army scout fell from his mount; he had been shot. Laura knelt down next to him and checked his pulse. *Weak.* She observed a huge wet, dark stain on his blue shirt—lots of blood lost. She tugged open the shirt and pulled back his longjohns. Sure enough, a hole in the fatty tissue between his right arm and socket. "Put a blanket around him and get me some water!" Laura shouted. "Roy! Bring me the first-aid kit!"

As Laura cut away the scout's shirt, he mumbled, "Jayhawkers."

Corporal Peterson heard this, looked up, and shouted, "Rifles, five boxes of shells for each man!" The patrol only had trapdoor 45-70 long guns and .45 Colt peace makers.

"How many?" Peterson searched the injured man's face.

Between labored breaths, the scout said, "Thirty at least."

"How far back?"

"Right behind me, corporal."

Sure enough, dust was rising in the direction the scout had come from.

Laura told a trooper, "Hold these wads of cotton, tight, front and back." She puckered up and spit a big wad of juice, wiping her lips with the back of her hand. "Roy!"

"Yes!"

"AK's. Two drums each."

"Yes, ma'am!" Roy jumped toward his and Laura's horses, took an AK-47 from each of the horse-rifle scabbards, lifted two drums out of the saddle bags, and snapped a drum on each AK. He ran to Laura; she took one and the extra drum. Roy kept the other.

Time seemed to stop, except for Laura and Roy.

"Roy, have you ever shot anybody?"

"No, ma'am."

"Me, neither. Roy, do you remember what Mitch read us about the Jayhawkers and what they did here in Nebraska at this time? You're going to have to kill today."

He nodded solemnly.

"Roy, we can't die here," Laura said firmly.

"But what if we kill someone that is supposed to become important later on?"

Laura paused thoughtfully. She chambered a round, looked at the cloud of dust that now revealed horses and men. She returned her gaze to Roy. "Roy, we're here, we don't kill anyone important. These men will kill us if we don't stop them."

"We can't die here," she repeated.

Roy chambered a round. "Yes, ma'am."

"Roy, keep your AK on semi-auto and you just shoot to kill the horses."

"I can shoot the men if I have to." She flipped her selector from semi to full auto.

The men in the dust cloud were beginning to spread out into a single front of thirty men wide as they charged the little patrol.

The corporal cussed. "Goddamn it! If they just had stayed in a group we might have gotten lucky."

Laura looked at her great-granddad. "It ain't over till the fat lady sings, corporal."

She looked around at the men raising their trap-door Springfields, ready to defend themselves. "Men!" Laura yelled. "What you will see in a few seconds you must never, ever talk about. Understand? Tell no one."

Two incoming bullets hit the supply wagon, shattering the board siding. Laura yelled, "Roy! Educate those men!"

Roy opened up on the line of men coming at a dead run. All of his bullets hit in front of the horsemen. He corrected and pulled the AK's trigger again. The sound was deafening. Men and horses began falling. Some of the men reined back. Laura opened up with her AK, and men and horses began falling all tangled together. The roar of exploding AK rounds in rapid fire had every trooper transfixed, staring at Laura and Roy. A trooper touched off his 45-70 and dropped a rider trying to head back away from the fight. That one shot distracted the troopers back to their job of defending their stand. Roy's drum was empty, but it would not eject from the trigger housing. He took out his .45 semi-auto model 1911 and popped yet another rider. Laura dropped her drum and snapped a second one in place. She chambered a round and began taking care of the last few men. A few 45-70 Springfields went off and then it was just dust and the sounds of dying men and horses and the scent of expended powder.

Dust was still visible in the air around the dead Jayhawkers. Not a single survivor lay among the tangle of dead horses and men.

The smell of black powder and smokeless powder from the AK rounds burned in their nostrils as they surveyed the carnage in front of them. The hot wood and oil from the AK's permeated the air.

"Corporal, do you think those boys learned anything?" Laura asked.

Not a word from him, or anyone else. They were spellbound, in a fixed stare at Laura's and Roy's AKs.

Laura spoke up again. "Remember, corporal and the rest of you, you are never to talk about what Roy and I used today."

One of the men picked up an AK shell, there were a couple hundred littering the ground around Laura. He turned it around in his hand and mumbled, "This did all that?"

"Yep!" Laura spat again.

A trooper commented, "Not only can ya chaw and spit—you're one hell of a shooter, too." That sort of got folks a little talkative. Laura let each man take a few shots with her AK. She put it on semi-auto. The men couldn't figure out why they couldn't make it shoot like the 45-70 Gatling gun they were familiar with. She explained to the men that the AK was a military gun in development in Europe.

That seemed to help the men accept the two AK's.

"Corporal," Laura turned to him, "your scout needs help—let's get your man back to the fort so they can patch him up. Those out there need nothing. I know about the Jayhawkers and I suspect these men have killed quite a few unsuspecting souls."

Three men set out with the shot trooper back to the fort.

As it turned out, when the corporal's patrol headed back to Fort Cottonwood, it came upon the three wagons and the pioneers, all dead. The two women who had run out onto the prairie were found shot six times and trampled by horses. Six people had been burned in the wagons. The corporal's patrol buried them all. Corporal Peterson's platoon camped at the Jayhawkers' wagon killing site and left for Fort Cottonwood in the morning.

Back where the Jayhawkers had been, it was moon-rise, a three quarter moon. The coyotes arose from their daytime sleeping. Lewis saw the moon come slowly over the eastern horizon and he heard the yelp of the coyotes. In his thoughts he could still hear his men scream as they dropped, like flies they were falling all around him. Then he was knocked out. His jaw hurt like a bad tooth had flared up. He went to reach for his jaw but a body was pinning down his left arm. He couldn't raise his right arm because it was broken. He finally extricated his left arm and his hand reached for his face, but he could not find his jaw. He squinted at his hand and there was blood all over it. He felt for his jaw again and his heart raced. There was no jaw there. He pulled himself up. His heart was pounding as he realized that his jaw was shot away.

Lewis staggered a few steps before hearing a deep guttural growling. He turned and reflected in the rising moonlight were a dozen pairs of golden eyes, burning in the night's darkness. He stumbled backward and tried to say no, but all he heard was a hiss, he did not have the ability to shout. His heart raced ever faster.

A few of the golden eyes blinked and the growling took on a deeper tone. In a flash, he was pounced upon by those dozens of eyes. He heard growls, tearing of cloth, and then parts of his body were torn from him. Pain shot through his legs, his dangling right arm, then his shoulder was ripped open and began to squirt blood—blinding his eyes.

As he swiped the blood from his eyes, he tried to yell—but nothing. His left hand was caught and a crunching sound filled his ears and a pain shot through his left hand. He raised his hand to clean his eyes, but his fingers were gone. A flash of moonlight from the fangs of the attacking coyote was the last thing he saw as he was bitten in the face and that coyote began to eat his ears, his nose, his eyes. Lewis was eaten alive and the pack of coyotes slept for two days after the feast of the Red Legs.

The three troopers got the scout to the fort before he went into shock. He lived and eventually continued west, taking the Oregon Trail and living up in the Pacific Northwest. He died an old man.

Laura spent a lot of time with Corporal Peterson. As another patrol went out, she and Roy went along. Roy asked, "Don't you want to go back to North Platte after all this?"

"No, Roy. It's over and what could anyone do now anyway?" She spit and whacked a fly. Laura's eyes opened wide as silver dollars. She yelled, "Granddad!"

Corporal Peterson turned toward Laura. "Who?"

Laura stammer, "I said, Grandpa. I hit a fly!"

"Oh," he smiled. "Like your grandpa. Ha! You think that Mr. Wells will be impressed?"

"Maybe!" Laura pulled a twist of tobacco from her vest's pocket. "Corporal Peterson, reckon I could borrow your chaw'n knife?"

He smiled. "Yes, ma'am."

The patrol formed into a column of twos and headed out the Fort Cottonwood gate. Laura and Corporal Peterson were riding easy in their saddles, talking about what he wanted to do when he got out of the Army.

CHAPTER 15

SUNDAY CHURCH AND A RIDE
TO LAST FOREVER

THE MAJOR LOOKED at Traver. "Mrs. Wells asked me to tell you that there was a problem with the Red Legs, but everything is fine." The major shook his head back and forth.

"What happened?"

He studied Traver a moment. "Apparently a group of Jayhawkers attacked Corporal Peterson's patrol. There were some thirty Jayhawkers and my men took care of them all. Corporal Peterson indicates that Roy and Mrs. Wells were excellent shots."

"Are Laura and Roy okay?"

"Oh yes! None of my men were shot except for the scout. He took a Sharp's 50 slug in the shoulder—but Laura fixed him up." The major paused a second and then said, "Mrs. Wells said for you not to worry and that Mr. AK truly helped."

Traver grinned. "Good for Mr. AK!" He was concerned about Laura being in a fire fight, but having the AKs made all the difference. *But what if Laura and Roy had been killed? Losing Laura would extinguish my light. What would I do?*

As Traver was feeling these emotions, his gaze settled on Siren talking with the pastor. He saw her from the back and just a part of her right side. Her long hair, touching her shoulders, seemed darker in the tent. Out in the light of day, it seemed that fire points glistened in her deep brown hair. He remembered how warm her lips were. He sighed. He was losing her, she was leaving on Thursday. All that was left was Sunday, Monday,

Tuesday and Wednesday. He was relieved that Laura would be gone for another three days, and he felt a little guilty, too, excited to have another three days with Siren.

He thanked the major for his reassurance that Laura and Roy were okay, shaking his hand and returning to where Siren was talking with the pastor. They greeted each other warmly. "Hey, pastor, you need a lift back to North Platte?" Traver saw Siren's mouth drop open.

"No, Mr. Wells, I have to get over to Omaha but thanks for the offer." Siren's smile returned to her face.

During the religious service, Traver sat with the major and Siren sat next to the major's wife.

After church, the major's wife invited them for chicken dinner, but Traver begged off. He told her that the coffee shop was opening in the morning and they had to return.

At noon Siren and Traver were climbing back into the wagon and heading back to North Platte. They had barely disappeared over the first hill and out of the fort's sight when Siren began rubbing her hand along his thigh. "Laura will not be back in North Platte for three days."

Siren stopped. "I'll not be able to tell her good-bye." She was watching him for any emotion his face might betray. "I truly like her, Traver."

"I know," he said, slipping his arm around her and hugging her close.

The night sky was glowing with stars as they crossed the Platte River. They rode into town and he got off at the bakery. He made sure no one could see his hand as he slid it under her blouse. "I'll be down to your place early—you be ready for me."

Siren smiled, saying, "Any time, mister."

COFFEE TEN CENTS

At nearly five Monday morning, he was knocking on Siren's door.

When the door opened, she stood there naked. "I'm ready for you, Mr. Wells." They stretched out on the rug in front of her couch, and afterward they just relaxed.

"Coffee?" she inquired.

"One cup with a breast-pink rose."

"Right away." She went into the kitchen and brought back two cups, and one had a pink rose painted in the porcelain.

"You'd better be getting down to the coffee shop—there could be a lot of business. I'll come down later, and if you want we can go to the ship. We won't be disturbed in my quarters. We don't have much time left and I want all of you that I can get," Siren said with a catch in her throat.

He took her hands in his. "Traver, while we're on the ship, would you like to be enhanced? Don't answer right away—just think about it. It's a quick and easy process. Now, you get out of here and go to work!"

Traver left, Siren filling his thoughts. A few steps away from her door, he sniffed. *Cinnamon rolls!*

THREE DAYS BEFORE FOREVER

The three days that Siren had left were intense for her and Traver. They spent hours walking in the sand hills. On Tuesday, he showed her the spot where he and his group had entered the past. Her engineers were studying the anomaly, trying to figure out how to replicate the time warp.

Siren and Traver sat there together, looking down into the canyon. "It's so strange to be sitting here with you in 1860 and knowing that in a few days I'll be back in 1995 and thinking about 1860," Traver said.

Siren put her arm through his. "I'm going to miss the Edon out of you. Let's spend the night out here." She sent a crew member to North Platte to fetch some blankets and food. Her scientists returned to the ship while Traver set up a quick camp.

"So you think you will be going home soon, too?" Siren wanted to know.

"Yes, the pressure is dropping. At the first sight of clouds we'll come out here and wait for the storm and cross back into 1995. I'll never forget this spot. I'll come here and think about you." He leaned over and kissed her cheek, which was damp from tears.

They spent the night under the stars, nestled in each other's arms.

When they drove back into North Platte, Siren asked him to come into her house for just a minute. He agreed, and when they passed through her front door, she closed it, turned, and threw her arms around him, burying her face in his.

"I love you, Wells, please, please, come with me," she begged tearfully.

"I just can't, Siren," Traver moaned.

Before leaving 1860, Siren and her second in command came down to the coffee shop. They had a cup of coffee and a cinnamon roll. Will served them. Siren paid with a twenty-dollar gold piece. Siren scruffed Will's hair. "Mr. Wells tells me you want to be a vet doctor."

"Yes, ma'am, just like you."

"Well, I have opened a savings account in your name. There's enough money in it for you to go to college and medical school." Will didn't realize what Siren was saying, but his mother overheard and she understood the generous gesture. She came over to Siren.

"I don't know what to say, but thank you," Alice said, grasping Siren's hand.

"You're welcome, Alice," Siren said graciously. "Now please ask Mr. Wells to stop by a moment, please?"

Alice went into the kitchen and retrieved Traver. When he came out, his entire body and spirit smiled with joy when he saw Siren. She looked different, she had a glow about her. She was Captain Siren, Complete Woman.

Siren asked him to come with her and Monk to the wing that would take them to the ship. Traver jumped at the chance and told Alice he would be back at noon.

The coffee shop was filling up as the three left. They walked toward Siren's home. "Traver, take this envelope. It's for Bill and it has the title to my house. Tell him I'm so proud how he pulled himself up and back into life."

They walked toward the little gully where the shuttle-wing was parked. Monk walked a few paces ahead so Siren and Traver could have a private moment. She held Traver, looked at him, kissed him, touched his chest. "I love you," she whispered.

"I love you, too," he murmured back, and their lips touched gently as he caressed her breast. Slowly she backed away.

She held up her hand in parting. He waved.

"Long life, my love," Siren said lovingly.

She slowly turned away with Monk and grasped his arm. "Oh, Monk, why is this so difficult?"

Her knees were unsteady, each step tore her heart to shreds, tears blinded her eyes, feelings exploded within her. She felt like she was peering into the depths of the universe and finding only emptiness.

She didn't wipe her eyes as she and Monk approached the wing. She just let them dry on her cheeks.

"Siren, it's not too late to go to Traver," Monk told her.

She took a deep breath and exhaled. "It is too late. And it's all right."

She stepped forward bravely. One thing she had not told Traver. It was best not spoken of.

CHAPTER 16

HOW DO YOU WAVE GOODBYE FOREVER?

ON THAT NEBRASKA morning, Traver watched Siren touch her chest and the warmest of feelings touched his lips where he had softly kissed that breast, his head on her chest as sleep befell him. His fingertips tingled as they remembered tracing the serpent tattoo from her navel to her breast. He would forever recall the softness, the warmth, and the comfort he felt at Siren's breast. His heart was aching. He saw her hand lower to her stomach and the first time they shared love reflected on the mirror of his thoughts.

Siren reached out to hold Monk's arm, her head turning to speak to him. Traver's eyes watered. He realized she was not going to look back. She was leaving.

Siren disappeared over the small sand hill. In just moments, Traver saw a silver flash in the western sky. "She's gone," he whispered to no one but himself.

The next morning, he awoke to the sounds of Will fixing the fires in the ovens and cook stoves. Within the next hour he sensed the percolating coffee and sweet-smelling cinnamon rolls. Traver rolled over on the cold stone flooring, sat up, and began to pull on his boots. Bill brought him a cup of coffee.

She's gone, Traver thought. His heart ached.

"Thanks, Bill. I needed this. Hey, Bill, the doctor has moved."

"She has? I'll miss her," Bill said. "She was awfully pretty and I liked looking at her." Traver handed Bill the envelope from Siren. Bill opened it and his eyes widened. "Do you know what's in here?" Bill gasped.

"No."

He read Traver the note. "Bill, I'll be going home, and I want you to have my home here. It's paid for and I want you to have a little something to help you start your business. "Five thousand dollars in paper money. "My God, what did I do to deserve this?"

"I guess the doctor saw something in you and wanted to help. As you become successful, you can help someone else someday."

Laura and Roy showed up a little after three in the afternoon. Thunder clouds were piling up in the northwest. Laura and Traver held each other and swayed. "Say, big boy, how much did you miss me?"

Traver smiled and reached around to grab her butt. "That much!" He pulled her to his chest and kissed her passionately.

"So what did you and Mitch and Twin Bears do while I was gone?" Laura wanted to know.

Traver spread his hands. "We worked on the coffee shop. Mitch spent a lot of time at the courthouse. Twin Bears was in and out."

Laura then asked him if he and the vet had gotten together. "I certainly would like to know more about them."

Traver answered evenly, "I am amazed at how human she is. I went up to her ship and it was beyond belief."

"Where are they?" Laura asked.

"They left yesterday for their home world."

"Oh." Laura sounded disappointed. "I would have liked to have said goodbye."

"Well, honey, looks like a storm is coming. You ready to go home?"

"Ready?" Laura laughed. "Are you kidding? I haven't had a bath in eight days. I'm ready!"

The group broke camp and said their goodbyes. They headed out to the canyons. They could feel the tension in the air, and then a lightning flash followed by booming thunder shook them up. Darkness fell as electricity crackled in the air and raised the hair on their arms. They ventured on down into the valley, walking down the center with the horses. Buster scampered after Roy. They had left the wagon with Twin Bears.

After a few minutes they walked into bright daylight. The storm was gone. They were back home.

Old Buster was barking and running around. Laura put her arm in Traver's arm as they approached the truck. Roy fired up the engine and the weary travelers piled in. Laura picked up her purse from the floorboard and placed it on the seat. Her cell phone began ringing. "Jesus! We're home not ten minutes and the damn phone rings!" She grabbed it. "Hello? Yes, this is Dr. Peterson. Who? Oh, yes. No—I've been out camping and hunting." She listened intently and then gasped, "My God, no. What? Jesus! Yes, I can be there—I can leave just as soon as I get home. Oh, in about five or six hours. Okay, I'll go to the airport. No, I don't mind flying. Bye." She hung up and just sat there, stunned, as Roy bumped along the dirt road to the ranch.

CHAPTER 17

THE STRANGENESS OF EARTH

CAPTAIN SIREN'S SHIP, hurtling toward home, appeared as a flash of light. Siren looked out the huge viewing window to see the stars that had been points of light became streams of light. Only a few hours had passed, but her heart was still back on Earth in 1860. Monk distracted her. "Excuse me, captain, may I take a few minutes of your time?" Holding his report, Monk went on, "Captain, something has artificially spun the planet we just left, to cause a stronger attraction, a gravity well. Earth's liquid core is being counteracted by the cooler mantle. Since Earth is spinning faster than the molten core, the friction is producing a deep gravity well. The Star Throwers in our legends just possibly came this way and did the planetary mechanics necessary for the environment that we see today."

"For what reason?" asked Siren.

"Reason has nothing to do with it. There is one other thing I must tell you. I re-evaluated this solar system with this gravity well, or time link. This planet does not fit the system and it was not formed in this solar system. The planet is peculiar, the densest body in the solar system."

"Denser than the average density of their stars?" she queried.

"Interesting, isn't it?" he answered her question with a question.

She tried to understand his statements. "Stars exhibit deep gravity wells and oftentimes are assumed to exhibit a harmonic feedback wave because of a density less than the size or weight ratio of a planet. That's what keeps a balance of planetary orbits."

"That's correct. But it's just too bizarre. How did this world get into this system? And the rubble two rings out from Earth. That's got something to do with this. This world has somehow come through time!"

"Through time? How could a world this large get through time?"

Monk shrugged his shoulders.

Siren sighed. "Forward or back. It's a heavy question."

"Yes. Up the time scale or down the time scale. Interesting, isn't it, captain?"

Siren withdrew into silence. Then she whispered, "The Star Throwers."

"But, captain, that's only legend."

"It is!" She spread her hands to represent the Earth on which they had stood as proof.

"But, captain, what about the question we have struggled with in theoretical time travel? Time travel is impossible due to not having directions."

Siren got up and walked around, thinking. "Monk, this abnormality on Earth is tied to the day—both times traveling together. So how is that possible?"

Monk raised his eyebrows. "I suspect, captain, that we will discover something as we monitor and search the area as we go home. And there is another anomaly showing up. You remember the stories told on Edon about the Rivers of Heaven? Sometimes they were described as whorls and at times as hoops. Let's just for a minute consider these planetary orbits as rivers, hoops, or whorls. Scientists consider space as a complete void—except for debris. Void, I suspect, means nothing human occupying it, except on worlds that occupy the void. Space in the myths, then, is a medium and a world's orbit path is observable as rivers, whorls, and so on in that medium. In the old view, the Rivers of Heaven leave a wake behind them. Yet, look at this system through this gravity well as it makes an orbit."

Monk activated a huge screen. A view of the solar system came into focus and there seemed to be iridescent wakes that illuminated the planet's orbits.

Siren lips formed the word heaven—and she exhaled. She looked at her teacher. "Heaven! It cannot be this system!"

"I don't know, captain. But look at the rivers—as they say in the legends, seven rivers take out this world from time, and that leaves seven bodies. But look at the last body, the one farthest out, it exhibits no wake and the debris field in orbit exhibits no wake colors."

"Are you saying that those two bodies are not from here either, Monk?"

"It's too early to tell, captain."

"Heaven," Siren said softly. She remembered all of the old stories of Heaven and the Star Throwers and how the myths were connected.

Siren turned to Monk. "Do you suppose the crew from Edon, all those millennia past, realized all this about this world?"

"I thought of that. It's only due to the planetary observations of the time anomaly here that have given us the mathematics to understand what we now see. It all may be true but not provable."

"But, Monk, there is a time link on Earth, and no other planet in our history has ever been discovered with anything like that." Siren sat down again and leaned her head back. "A way between two times on a planet out of time. What does it all lead to?" She looked at Monk. "A way to heaven, but where is the door? This star system is not Heaven but a sign that points to Heaven. You know, of course, the Star Throwers were from heaven."

"No, I didn't know that. But you are a 'Way' traveler and know more than most of us."

"Monk." Siren struggled with her words. "Monk, I have changed. I know love now." She studied Monk's face. Neither one spoke.

The lines of star traces remained as patterns of lines on her window. Looking back from the window, she faced him. "Monk, you have never mentioned your choosing. I do not mean to pry, but being the captain and being in love is getting impossible."

Monk touched Siren's hand and smiled. "The woman you are has finally blossomed. You will know how to balance being captain and the woman in you."

"Monk, I carry the seed of life. Two spirits will come forth."

Monk's face glowed with joy. "Your mother will smile with love for you. But how could you leave Mr. Wells?"

Siren dropped her eyes.

Monk inquired, "Does he even know?"

Siren glanced up at him. "No, I don't think so. It seems so wonderfully bizarre, a Star Mother and an Earth Father and time in a jumble."

"Will Mr. Wells ever know?"

"I pray so," said Siren.

The Star Ship reached Edon with two new crew: a girl, De Laural, and a boy, Kenneth.

CHAPTER 18

AN AIRPORT IN DISASTER

NEITHER ROY NOR Traver said anything after Laura had ended her phone call. The three of them just rode along, until the suspense got too much for Traver. He asked her in a demanding voice, "Laura, what happened?"

She shook her head as though not believing and said, "There has been a horrific plane crash at Eppley Airport in Omaha. A UPS freighter was landing and a small plane hit the cockpit. The UPS DC-9 kept coming in, but began a slow right falling turn until it crashed into the Blue Terminal. Three planes on the ground fully loaded with fuel and passengers exploded. The terminal is destroyed along with the three to four hundred passengers waiting there, and along with all those in the planes, that makes about a thousand fatalities. That was the coroner from Sharpie County. They are needing coroners to process the remains. I'm going to be flown to Omaha."

"My God," Traver exclaimed. "That's like a war zone."

In silence they drove on to the ranch and parked in front of the ranch house. Roy had called ahead to Thelma, and his wife was out front to greet them. Laura, Skip's dad, and Traver went into the house. As Laura headed upstairs, she yelled to Skip's dad that she would drop him off at home but that a shower was first for her.

When she came down the stairs, fresh and clean, to find Traver and Roy in the kitchen. Roy said, "Traver and I are going to look for that cache of Henry rifles hidden by the army before the troopers were killed by the Indians. You won't have to drop off Skip's dad. He'll help, too."

As Laura and Traver headed out the front door, they kissed deeply. "I can drive you to the airport, honey," he told her.

"No, that's fine. I'll stop and see Sharon and then leave the crew cab there, so I can drive it back next week." She turned and headed for her truck. As she drove out the gravel road, she waved and Traver waved back.

After she left, Traver felt overwhelmingly fatigued. He climbed into bed, his eyes fluttering even before his head hit the pillow. It seemed just minutes later that he heard the phone ringing, he was somewhere between wakefulness and sleep. He reached over to pick up the receiver. It was Laura's voice. "Honey, are you all right?"

"Yes, I am—what time is it?"

"It's 4 a.m., honey, I'm in Omaha."

Traver shook the sleep out of his head and talked to her. She told him about the devastation at the airfield and that she would have to stay for at least six days.

When they had a kissy-kissy goodbye, he got a light wool blanket and tossed it over himself. He dropped off dead asleep again.

When morning came, Traver awakened with the covers twisted under his chin. His left foot, hanging out from under the sheet, was cold. Outside it looked cloudy, and he rolled over to look at the barometer. It was falling. *A summer storm.* He began thinking about 1860. He pictured Siren waving goodbye. *How many light-years from here is she this moment?*

He tried to get up out of bed. "Ooowww," he moaned. His back was killing him. Probably from sleeping on the floor at the bakery. More likely, he mused, it was from the athletic sex he had had with Siren. *I shouldn't be complaining.*

He tossed off the covers, stood, and stretched. Somewhere outside crows were cawing. When he got downstairs, Roy was sitting in the kitchen his eyes glued to the live televised reports coming from Eppley.

"Traver, more than twelve hundred dead," Roy said sadly. "Did you hear from Laura?"

"Yeah, she called about four this morning. She's tied up there for almost a week."

"What a tragedy for all those families," Roy said quietly.

The guys sat drinking coffee and watched TV until they had filled up on bad news.

"Let's take the metal detector today to look for the rifles and the remains of the wagon train," Roy suggested, "even though I think I know the exact spot. The area hasn't changed all that much. It's not far off from the power diverting channel."

Traver sipped his coffee. "A cinnamon roll would taste good right now!"

"Yeah, 1860 sure could grow on a person," Roy agreed.

Skip's dad agreed, also.

"Okay, let's go dig." Traver drained his coffee cup and stood up.

They walked to the barn, getting two shovels and the metal detector into the truck. The three men got into the truck.

Traver yelled, "Buster!" The ol' flea bag came running, just like a pup. The trip across time must have done him some good.

Traver gunned the engine. "Well—where to?"

"Go out the south canyon road, north up to I-80, then down to Brady. Take the Little Platte exit. Go south—I'll tell you where to turn."

They turned off the gravel road and onto the rutted clay road for some miles.

Roy instructed, "Go off the road over there and head over to that side of the canyon wall."

When they parked, they took a short hike up a gentle rising sand hill. At the top, Roy began scanning the horizon with his binoculars. This here is an old river bed canyon. Probably a portion of the ancient Platte Course. Look here—you can just make out the old road. See the ruts just barely visible now?" He handed the glasses to Traver.

"Roy continued, "I'll bet the ambush took place just as the wagon train entered this wide spot. It would be better for the raiding party in the open. Look real hard and see if there're any grave-like ridges."

They concentrated, and then Roy pointed to slight rise land. "Let's look thereabouts first."

They rode over to the spot, got out the metal detector, and began scanning the area. The buzzer went off right away—a horseshoe. Traver tossed it away. Nothing else excited the detector. They sat down for a rest and to examine the lay of the land some more.

"Why not just walk the road?" Traver wondered. "Maybe the wagons had never left the road before they were attacked?"

Roy shrugged. "Good as any place to start. North or south?"

"My gut tells me south," Traver said.

"Nah, the canyon gets too tight—no room to fight."

"Well, let's go in a bit."

"Okay," agreed Roy.

They started going south with the metal detector turned on. There was just a faint trace of the old road. The detector buzzed strongly before they had walked a hundred feet, and the detector was bursting with noise around a fifteen-foot semicircle.

Skip's dad looked at Traver. "Bingo"

Traver piled pieces of wood around the circumference of the find, and they began to dig in the center. About eighteen inches down, Traver's shovel struck a hard object. He scraped away the sand and a piece of bone was exposed to the noon sunlight. "This is it for sure, this is a human leg bone. Let's not dig anymore. Let's go call the University of Nebraska and get a historical site going here."

Their curiosity satisfied, the men headed back to the ranch. "Let's go by the canyons," Roy suggested. Traver explained to them about his instructions to Bill to leave gold coins in the middle of the southernmost canyon. "I'm curious to see if he followed through with that," Traver said.

"Well, if he did, and the business was successful, and it went on for twenty to thirty years, there are going to be one hell of a lot of coins there."

"Yep. One hell of a lot of coins—and all should be in mint condition!" Traver was jubilant at the thought.

"I wonder if Bill buried the bags in the same area—or did he just dig a hole and dump it in?"

"Well, we're gonna find out soon enough."

It was around one o'clock when they pulled into the canyon area. At the south canyon they fired up the metal detector. Right away it sounded off. Traver got a shovel and began digging. There was a rotting leather pouch down about a foot below the sod. He gently pressed his shovel down next to it and levered back. He put the soil and the rotten bag next to the hole. The leather bag split, and a handful of big, beautiful gold coins twinkled, reflecting sunlight for the first timed in decades. There were twenty-dollar gold pieces and silver dollars—all in mint condition.

"Look, Roy, 1867!" Traver smiled excitedly. "There are going to be even more years of deposits."

Roy picked up a few coins and examined them. "Mint," he said in awe.

When the detector found another burying place. Traver pulled out his shovel. He found another rotting leather pouch in the hole. This stash was a little larger and had a few loose fifty-dollar coins and the rest twenty—with silver dollars.

"Holy shit!" Traver exclaimed. "Look at these silver dollars."

Roy hefted one. "Looks beautiful—so what's the difference?"

"They are C.C.—Carson City, 1889."

"What's so special about that?"

"These just happen to be the most rare. There were tons struck but most all of them got melted down. These could be worth in the six figures."

Roy whistled. "You're shittin' me"

"No! These Carson Citys are as rare as hen's teeth. We better be drawing a map of these holes."

"Yeah," Skip's dad agreed. "We should go into town and get a topographical map. Blow it up and put a checkerboard grid over it and then check out each square so we don't miss anything. That way we could clear a piece of land and not worry."

"Good idea. But let's see what else we can find now."

They unearthed another bag of fifty-dollar gold pieces, these with a New Orleans mint. Another pouch yielded coins dated 1856, 1859, and 1860. *The first year's profits*, thought Traver, marveling. There were 275 of them. That meant a little more than a thousand dollars was made from coffee and cinnamon rolls. Not great profits, but they stuck with it.

"How long do you think they operated the coffee shop?" Roy asked.

"No way to tell—except by the dates in the bags as we hit them."

By sundown, they had created what looked like a gopher community, small holes dotting the earth. The latest years on the coins we found that day was 1893. So the coffee shop was in business for thirty-three years. The 1893 hit was a large find of at least six big bags of coins.

They had left all the bags at each hole, and Traver got out some paper and drew a rough map. Then Roy stood at each hole and yelled out the dates to him, so Traver could sketch in the time. Traver could envision Bill coming out here and digging holes and putting in the bags of coins.

When the survey was done, Roy and Traver gathered the coins and loaded them in the back of the truck. It amounted to quite a pile. As they dumped the last two handfuls, Traver said, "Tomorrow we'll make a thorough site map." Skip's dad agreed.

When they got back to the ranch, they put all the coins in the kitchen sink and washed them. Traver spread towels over the breakfast table so the guys could arrange the coins while they dried.

The phone rang and it was Laura. "How you doing, honey?" Traver asked her.

"Another six or seven days." She sounded tired. She sounded defeated.

"Okay, honey, you be safe," Traver said lovingly.

By five o'clock that evening, the men had assessed the coins they had found so far.

9,950 fifty-dollar gold pieces

4,660 twenty-dollar gold pieces

2,180 ten-dollar gold pieces

19,011 silver dollars

876 silver half-dollars

The face value was just the beginning of what they were worth.

The next day they went on another treasure hunt, but they didn't find as many as before. The dates they found went up to 1901.

Later, as they sat at the kitchen table discussing the coins, Traver told Roy, "Take an ammunition can full."

"These are yours," Roy protested.

"Nah. They're ours."

"Well, thank you, Traver. The university crew will be out here tomorrow. They're going to X-ray the ground or something."

Late the next morning the university archeology team arrived. The radar scans indicated that seventeen skeleton were buried there and eighteen cases of rifles and thirty cases of ammunition. They decided not to dig until the Veterans Administration was contacted.

On Saturday, two news crews asked for permission to accompany the archaeology team; they were filming a special on the amazing discovery. The skeletons of the soldiers were exhumed and given military burials at Fort McPherson National Cemetery. Then the excavating of the ammunition and rifles began. It was interesting to watch. The ammunition had split their casings long ago. All of the rifles, Henry repeating 44-40, were in sad condition. The brass pieces had weathered well, but the steel and wood had rusted and rotted.

Skip's dad Mitch had done some checking of the official record. "I checked on the coffee shop and bakery. It was torn down—well, part of it was torn down. The fireplace is still here. But it's now a home."

"When did that happen?" Traver asked.

"I believe in 1912."

"Amazing."

"Yes, Will sold the the place in 1912."

"No shit! Do you suppose that Will is still alive?" Traver wanted to know.

"If he was around twelve in 1860, in 1900, he would have been fifty-two years old."

Traver said, "That would be an exciting thing to do tomorrow, to find out when he died."

The phone rang. Traver answered. A moment of silence.

"Yes, this is Traver Wells . . . WHAT?" Tears blasted out of his eyes. "I'll be right there."

He hung up the phone and looked at Roy. "That was the Highway Patrol. Laura has been in an accident on I-80 at Grand Island. She's dead, Roy!"

Traver dropped to his knees on the kitchen floor. "She's gone!" he cried out, weeping.

CHAPTER 19

LAURA'S TRIP HOME

TEARS WERE GENTLY dripping from Laura's eyes as she and Dr. Oren Wolmbsley began their drive home from the air crash at Eppley Field in Omaha. Seven days of hell, Laura felt. Trying to identify bodies burned to where you could just see they were human and nothing else. Chunks of flesh, a finger, a leg. Laura buried her face in her hands.

"Laura, you okay?" Oren asked. He was upset, too, by all the incomplete and burned bodies and parts. Working in the refrigerated semi trucks brought in to be makeshift morgues had gotten to him, too. Laura had worked the terminal, where most of the bodies had been dismembered and quite burned.

"How can I help, Laura?" he softly said again.

These seven days had changed her, she knew that. She had called Sharon and Traver every night, crying that it was all so tragic. They both tried to comfort her and encourage her that she was a woman of strength and she would prevail. But surrounded by death and carnage, Laura felt her strength draining away.

Finally, she was going home. There was nothing more anyone could do at the crash site.

Laura had discovered that she was not prepared, emotionally or psychologically, for the job.

Her job was identifying bodies. The easiest were males, whose wallets were usually close to their bodies. The most difficult were females, because their identities were usually in a purse, which had been blown away from their bodies. Then, of course, the children.

Laura was continually bombarded by surviving family members, wanting information. And many times she just couldn't help them. Her hands came to her cheeks again and she sobbed softly.

This constant barrage of grief coming from the family members started to invade her sleep. The vast loss of life began to drag her energy down. She had decided to talk with Traver about his experience in the war and all the killing.

She and Oren had just pulled out from the Grand Island rest stop. She had used the restroom and walked around in the brisk air, which helped her to clear her mind.

"So, Oren, what are you going to do when we get home?" she wanted to know.

"When I drop you off at your daughter's, I plan to go home and load the pickup and go fishing a few days to try and forget all that we went through. What are you going to do, Laura?"

"I don't know . . . I don't know . . ." She was crying again, "I need to hold Traver and try to pull myself back together. I need his strength," she shivered. "I need him."

The car pulled on to I-80 and got up to speed. "Looks like there's bad weather up ahead," Oren said, as raindrops began to splatter on the windshield and race off to the sides. In minutes it was a downpour mixed with fog. The windshield wipers began their hypnotic race back and forth. A flash of lightning streaked across the sky.

Laura liked rain. She looked out the side window at the passing scene. The Platte River was coursing along. She saw geese out in the fields, and that reminded her of hunting a Thanksgiving goose with Bill. She turned her head to speak to Oren.

Boom! The crunching sound of glass. The car filled instantly with feathers, blinding Oren. He jerked the wheel. A low-flying goose had hit the windshield on the passenger side and broken through. Its force knocked Laura's head back, breaking her neck. A shard of windshield glass pierced her carotid artery. She slumped forward, unconscious. She had felt nothing.

Oren struggled to regain control, but the vehicle rolled, three times, before coming to rest in the median, tires up. Oren and Laura were hanging upside down. He unhitched his seat belt and fell down to the roof of the car. He saw Laura, still caught up in her seat belt. Blood was dripping from her neck, the glass shard still impaled in her throat. Fear shot through him. He knew this was a death sentence if he couldn't stop the blood. After much difficulty, he finally released her seat belt.

By this time a couple of cars and one semi truck had stopped to help. The truck driver helped pull Laura out and onto the prairie grass. Oren knew her neck was broken the way her head slumped at an unnatural angle when they moved her from the car. The truck driver ran and got blankets from his cab to cover her.

Jesus, Laura was going to die here on I-80. She doesn't deserve this. Oren could not locate a pulse. Tears welled up in his eyes and as they spilled over his eyelids, he placed his hands over her heart and just cried. "I'm sorry, Laura," he cried, "I'm so sorry." And he sat down beside her and sobbed.

As more cars stopped to help, sirens could be heard off in the distance. The rain stopped but the fog became thicker. That moment never seemed to end for Oren. He knelt before Laura's lifeless body, not knowing what to do. A state trooper helped him to his feet and led him to the warm patrol car.

PART TWO

Time . . . whichever way it goes, it does nothing at all that makes any difference. It just is a way of counting, anticipating, with so much living caught up in the mathematics.

In the universe there is no such event. Things just are, day in day out, sun up sun down.

Chapter 20

TWO YEARS, TWO GRIEFS

A COLD PRAIRIE wind was blowing in from the north. Clouds were streaming by as if the world had slowed down and the winds had gone out of control. Sharon's car started, but it would take a few miles for the engine to warm up. She headed east on I-80 to the Maxwell offramp. Her car was buffeted in the strong crosswind, and she saw plastic bags whipping here and there across the interstate and catching on the fences. Autumn leaves were blowing everywhere.

Sharon's emotions were building like the racing winds, "Maxwell next exit" came the green and white freeway sign. She slowed the car, her attention still centered on all the what-ifs of her mom's death. Two years gone in such a hurry.

As she exited I-80, she glanced in the rear-view mirror and noticed the freeway was practically empty. Hers was the only vehicle out this early today.

The Fort McPherson Road sign came into view. She'd been this way often, now that her mother had died. Her dad had passed twelve years earlier. Traver had insisted that Laura should lay to rest beside her first husband Bill, Sharon's dad. Traver was a veteran, and he would rest at the National Cemetery at Fort McPherson. Sharon was stopping by her mom's grave before going on to the ranch and seeing Traver.

Cottonwood leaves shimmered like flashing yellow caution lights in the blustery wind. Deep yellow, light green, dark green, all being rushed in the morning breeze.

A crack-like sound, thunder, broke her thoughts. A huge limb broke away from a cottonwood tree next to the road. It crashed to the ground a few yards in front of her. She swerved to miss hitting it and straightened back up on the road. *Jesus, a minute sooner and that limb would have landed on the car.*

Sharon pulled to a stop at the cemetery entrance and just took it all in. The wind was blowing leaves around the tombstones. Even flowers that had been left on graves were tumbling across the manicured grass. She opened the car door, which almost jumped out of her hand with a fierce gust of wind. She held her coat close around her neck and headed for her mom and dad's gravesite.

The pitch of the wind changed, and it struck Sharon as if she heard her mother singing her favorite old cowboy trail song, "Goodbye Old Paint, I'm Leaving Cheyenne."

"Mom," Sharon whispered, and she reached out to brush the pink granite tombstone. It was cold to the touch, nothing at all like her mom.

Sharon shifted her weight to her other foot and then decided to sit on her dad's stone. Smiling, she remembered sitting on his lap and her tiny young hands rubbing his whiskers. He would bend to her and rub his chin on her young pink cheeks and tell her, "Someday you'll have whiskers." Her smile broadened as she remembered wanting whiskers then. She had solid-gold memories of growing up and always became saddened that her parents had died too early in her life.

The wind kicked up again and, shivering, she thought, just a few more moments with mom and dad before she went to the ranch. She knew Traver would have a good strong pot of black coffee going on a morning like this. That two years had passed did not make it easier. Her husband comforted her, and Traver and she had grown closer in shared grief.

Sharon rose and headed to her car. She would have to find all her mom's old records and find the songs her mom had sung to her at bedtime and when they were camping. Sharon wanted her kids to know those old-time songs. Especially "Goodbye Old Paint." She turned and looked at the tombstones for that extra moment and then left.

CHAPTER 21

WHAT A BRA DOES TO A MAN

THE MORNING HAD a lazy beginning. Dreams can be bizarre and yet, at the same time, so real. Traver lay in bed with his eyes closed, contemplating his dream about climbing a pyramid and then taking a bath in a bathtub atop it? He opened his eyes, stared at the ceiling, and took a deep breath of the chilled morning air.

Yesterday, Roy and Traver had been out mending fences where he had shot that big buck a couple years ago. That buck got Skip talking at the barbecue where Traver had first seen Laura. Her form appeared in his thoughts. He sighed. *Laura.*

He got up and slowly walked into the bathroom. When he took off his T-shirt and closed the door, getting ready to shower, he spied Laura's soft blue bra swinging back and forth on the hook. It had hung there for two years. He reached up and touched the cups. His heart wanted to rip apart. He was thinking of Laura's breasts and nipples.

He climbed into the shower, letting the warm water splash over him. All too quickly he was toweling off and thinking about what to do today—it being Sunday and early still. He would make coffee and read a bit. As he was finishing in the kitchen with the fixin's for the pot, ol' Buster scratched at the back door and woofed with his "I want in" bark. Traver let him in, and he went to his water pan and drank, lapping up what seemed like a quart of water. "Why don't you drink at the creek?" Traver asked him as if the dog would understand.

The creek. Traver's thoughts went to Laura swinging at his ass as he bent over to pick up a stone from the creek, missing, and going head first in the water. He wondered if Laura had worn the blue bra that day.

"Hey, Buster, you want to go to the river today and chase sticks?"

Buster woof-woofed, wagged his tail, and went over to the breakfast table to present his head for scratching.

"Okay, when the coffee is done, we'll go." He was thinking about going to North Platte to park where he and Laura had camped when they went back in time. He wanted just to think about Laura today. Like he did a lot of days when there was nobody at the ranch.

He poured another cup of coffee, got out the Thermos and filled it, too. He left the Thermos on the table and went up to the bedroom and into the bathroom, just to look at Laura's bra hanging on the door. He lifted it off the hook, where it had hung since Laura had taken it off just before she left for Omaha to work on the airfield disaster at Eppley Field. She never came home.

Traver folded the bra, putting one cup into the other. He lifted it to his face, but her fragrance had all but disappeared. He placed her bra between his T-shirt and his long-sleeved shirt. He was going to release her bra into the Platte River today, it was a way of releasing her.

Downstairs, Traver said to Buster, "Come on, boy, let's go see Skip."

Buster shot out the door and leaped into the bed of the pick-up. They drove to Skip's for another cup of coffee.

After leaving Skip's, Traver drove up toward North Platte on 83, thinking about the trip to 1860. As he passed the Fremont slough, he looked east up toward the Dodge Hills, remembering the night that he and Laura saw the lights up there and Laura having a funny feeling about it, like someone was watching her.

He drove farther, passing the street that he was sure was the location where they had camped. Then he headed off toward the river, which was a little further north now and much less full than in 1860. He smiled, remembering Laura's comment about bathing in the river and how cold it was. When he got to what was now the Platte River, he found a log to sit on and watched the water flow past. He took out Laura's bra and let it slip from his fingertips. It fell into the current, drifted away from the bank, and sank out of sight.

"Gone," he said to no one but himself.

He remembered Siren's ship disappearing into a rainbow of colors. She, too, was gone.

Buster came up to him, turning his head from side to side, talking in his woo-woo sound. It's as if he knew Traver was thinking about Laura and Siren. *What would I have done if Siren had stayed?* Siren knew about Laura, but Laura hadn't known of the almost other-worldly passion he had felt for Siren. He felt like he had betrayed them both. Loving them both was no excuse. But was that bad? Love, not lust.

Traver stood up and reflected that letting Laura's bra go in the river was like letting Laura's spirit move on. A bit of grief lifted off his shoulders. He decided that a visit to the Prairie Flower restaurant was in order. Biscuits and gravy topped with two eggs.

Buster settled· down in the bed of the truck as Traver went inside. Doris waved; she owned the place and always seemed glad to see Traver. *I bet she would be real surprised if I asked her out instead of teasing her about dating.*

Quickly a steaming hot cup of coffee was put before him.

"It's fresh, Traver," Doris whispered.

"But is it good?" he played along.

"Made it with toilet water," she whispered again, with a conspiratorial grin.

"In that case I'm having breakfast and more coffee, and if you're quick about it I'll pencil you in for a date this afternoon."

Doris looked at him. "No, sir! It's ink or nothing."

"Ink," he responded seriously.

Doris kept her sky-blue eyes on Traver's, trying to gauge that response. He said, "You're inked in for this afternoon."

Doris burst into a radiant smile. "Great, Traver, what time can I expect you?"

"What time are you off?"

"Noon."

"What do you want to do?"

She suggested a drive over to Lincoln and a movie, and then he could take her to breakfast the following morning.

"Breakfast!".he said rather too loudly.

Her eyes sparkled. "You don't expect me to cook on a date, do you?"

"Hell, yes, I was expecting you to cook."

Doris reached over and held his wrist. "Don't worry, mister, we'll cook all right! I've waited quite a while for this."

Traver wore a goofy grin. He had always teased Doris, but now she had a different look, a little waist, great rear end, breasts just right.

She patted his hand. "I need to go wait on customers."

He said, "Ink!"

She smiled. "Oh, yes, ink for sure."

In minutes she showed up with his food and a small white bag. "The bag is for Buster."

When he finished he left two bucks beside the plate and went up front to pay. Doris took the five dollars and gave him the change. "Noon," she reminded him.

"Noon," he repeated.

He got back to the restaurant a little before noon, parked, and stayed in the truck. In the warm sun, he closed his eyes and dropped off to sleep. He woke up to a wonderful fragrance and a voice whispering, "Can a girl get a ride home?"

Doris got in the passenger side of the truck. "Glad to see you again, Traver. You know where I live?"

"No."

"Okay, then, head north on 83 to the tracks overpass and right on Jeffers. I'm a bit east, just before you get out of town, the last stop sign, go north again. When you cross 30, I'm the first place on the right. The one with all the hay binders and corn pickers." She grinned and said, "That's a description of every place out here."

"You farm?" he asked in surprise.

"Heavens no," she responded. "My husband did. When he passed away I leased out everything. Do I look like a farm girl, Traver?"

"I had never thought about it, Doris."

"So just what did you think, Traver?"

"What I thought, Doris, was just the regular ol' stuff, I suspect." He couldn't tell her that he mostly thought about Laura.

"Well, you're here and I'm here, aren't we?" Doris sighed, as if she had read his mind.

"I've always liked you, Traver. I've been interested in you ever since Laura came in the restaurant the day after the barbecue at Gary's house, when she first met you. You should have heard her talk about you. I could tell she was attracted, and it was the first time I had seen her so joyous since Bill had died. I was happy and jealous at the same time. We went to high school together. She was ahead of me but we were like sisters."

When they arrived at her house, Doris said, "Here we are, Traver, you coming in?"

He patted her hand and said, "I better stay here in the truck so I can remain the gentleman you think I am."

"I know you're a gentleman." She took a deep breath. "It's me I'm afraid of." She pinked up and gave him a seductive smile.

"You're making it hard for me to say no," he murmured.

They walked up to the front porch and Doris unlocked the door. "I was jealous that Laura got you. And I am so sorry she died like she did, but, Traver, we are alive!" She stepped up and kissed him. Her lips were on fire. Only their lips were touching, their arms hanging at their sides. Traver felt his entire consciousness was wrapped up in his lips.

Traver finally moved his hands to her rear, rubbing her cheeks. A little embarrassed by his boldness, he said quietly to Doris, "Okay?"

She squealed. "Yes!"

It was clear this collision of bodies was going to go all the way. They made their way into Doris's bedroom, where they stripped and climbed into bed, pulling up the covers. They talked quietly about sharing feelings of love, and they embraced. Traver sensed her shiver and she whispered his name. He exploded with very little provocation.

"You're good for me, Traver. Let's do this again." She looked at him. "Like every Tuesday and Thursday and Sunday."

"Well," he drawled, "we'll have to see about that, little lady."

She nestled her head below his shoulder, and he wrapped his arms around here. "Come on out to the ranch, and I'll do breakfast for you tomorrow."

"I don't feel comfortable doing that, Traver, that's Laura's place."

"It's my place now. Do you think Laura would ever want you to stay away?"

Doris considered this and then took a deep breath. "Okay."

When they got to the ranch, Roy was cutting up two bucks and wrapping them for the freezer. When Traver showed up with Doris, he said, "I brought help."

Roy grinned. "Hi!" He had known Doris for years. "You taking up with this guy?" Roy kidded Doris.

"For the moment. He promised me breakfast."

Doris got right into helping Roy wrap the deer steaks and roasts. Then they made ground deer patties and put them in the freezers.

"Doris, come over and visit with Thelma," Roy said, referring to his missus.

"Go on, I need to take a shower and I'll catch up with you later," Traver told them.

After about forty-five minutes he went over to Roy's place, where Doris and Thelma were having a cup of coffee and Roy was catching the news. Traver sat at the table with the girls. Thelma said, "Doris tells me you picked her up."

"That's correct, and not only did I pick her up, I plan on—"

Doris yelled, "Traver!"

"Hey! All I was going to say was I picked her up because she promised me a free breakfast."

"Well, it does pay to own a restaurant. Huh?"

Well, lady, are you ready to head to town?" Traver addressed Doris. "I'm all spit and polished. Maybe we can figure out something to do as we drive in."

Doris got up and thanked Thelma for the coffee and yelled to Roy that it was good seeing him.

In the truck heading back to North Platte, Doris said that Roy and she had been in the same home room in high school. Traver asked Doris if Laura and Bill had gone to school together. Yes, but Bill had been two years ahead of Laura and had left for college. The summer after Laura graduated from high school, she had a part-time job at the library. Bill had come home for the summer and he had some research to do at the library. He and she connected and started going together.

After junior college, Laura went to Omaha and the Nebraska School of Medicine, and Bill graduated and went into business. During Laura's last year of college they got married. Laura went on to medical school, and when she graduated the following year she had Sharon, her daughter. They were an exemplary family. Laura set up a practice in Lincoln, Nebraska, where Bill was a banker.

When her parents became ill she moved back home with her daughter to care for them. Bill followed a few years later, and after he got to North Platte he decided to run a tax service. He wanted a business that allowed him some time to hunt. Then Laura's parents died, about six months apart. It was so hard on her that she decided to down-size her practice, so she could run her parents' ranch.

Doris smiled. "You know, Traver, everyone still called her Dr. Peterson instead of her married name."

"Really? I thought Peterson was Bill's last name. What was her married name?" he asked.

"You don't know?" Doris looked surprised.

"No, I never thought about it and we never talked about it."

"Russel."

Doris moved next to Traver as they drove down South Canyon and out to I-80. "No kidding, Traver—you didn't know her married name till just now?"

"No, I didn't."

"Traver, let's stop at the video store and pick up a couple movies and eat hot popcorn with butter and snuggle and get to know each other more. Does that sound like a plan?"

"It's a plan," he said.

On the thirty-minute drive, Traver put his arm around Doris's shoulder, slipped his hand into her blouse to the tops of her bulging breasts, and rubbed gently. Doris moaned softly.

"Traver," Doris's tone turned serious. "I'm still having periods and I'm not on any birth control. If there is going to be more loving between us today, we need to take precautions. I'm way too old to be chasing after young'ens. I'm fifty-one, Traver."

"You mean something might have happened this morning?"

"I hope not," Doris said, but she was smiling.

Traver thought about talks he had had with Laura about having a baby.

"Doris, if you did get pregnant, I'll stand up and be a good father."

"I know," Doris said quietly.

CHAPTER 22

HOW TIME FLIES, TWO MORE YEARS

FOUR YEARS HAD passed since the trip back into 1860. The ranch house was quiet, as it had been these past years. Buster was scratching and making little noises. It was 4:40 in the morning and outside it was chilly. Traver had gone outside to turn on some lights. The workers were going to arrive at 5.

The sky was jet black and the stars were like sparkling jewels. Traver spent an extra moment just looking up at them, thinking about Siren and where she might be out there among those heavenly bodies. He looked down. What was the use of looking and longing?

Sharon was stirring and came down to the kitchen, where Traver was pouring her a cup of coffee.

"Thanks, Traver. Butch will be getting up soon. He sure likes to sleep in on the weekends."

"That's okay. Let him. He deserves it!"

Sharon sipped at her coffee and leaned back in her chair. "You going to mom's grave today?"

"Yes. Would you like to go along?"

"I went yesterday, but I think Butch will want to go, so I'll go again." Sharon sighed. "It's still hard for me to believe."

Buster got up and went to the door. Sharon rose and opened the door for him as she scratched his ears. He just stood there, looking out. Sharon said, with a catch in her voice, "She's gone boy." The pooch went back to his rug and laid back down. As Sharon walked back to the table, she said, "It's not fair!" She began crying.

Traver went around the table and stood behind her chair, rubbing her shoulders. "I know, honey. I go to the door and look out, too. Now you go and wake up Butch and I'll be getting breakfast." As she got up and left the kitchen, Traver put on the bacon. By the time it was sizzling, sleepy-eyed Butch entered the kitchen.

"Good morning, Butch," said Traver cheerfully.

Mumbling, Butch responded, "Morning . . . need some coffee."

After a couple sips, he sighed and said, ""Now I feel better."

By the time Traver started the eggs, Sharon came in dressed in jeans and a white short-sleeve shirt. Traver felt a catch in his throat. She looked so much like Laura, more and more as time went by.

"Butch," Traver asked, "are you going to move cattle from the North Range today?"

They considered all the property north of 1-80 as the North Range, when Laura's will was probated and distributed. Well, half of the estate. They decided that Sharon would receive all of the property north of 1-80, and Traver would keep the canyon ranch. The Enchanted Canyon area was in his control.

Butch sipped his coffee again. "We're going to slaughter—oh, perhaps, two hundred head. We don't want to winter such a large herd this year over there."

"You want to go to the cemetery with Sharon and me, Butch?"

"Okay. It sure is hard to accept Laura being gone."

While Sharon was out of the kitchen, Butch said that an executive in his company had moved up here from Texas. She had a couple of kids. "What if I fix you two up on a blind date?" Butch wanted to know.

Traver scrunched up his face. "Aww, I don't know. What do you think Sharon would think about it?"

"I think she'll understand. She met Rose and I think they hit it off real good."

"Okay, then, fix me up. She has kids?"

"Twin girls, twelve years old."

"How old is Rose?"

"Forty-one."

"Well, she's a bit younger than me . . ." Traver said deadpan.

Later that week Rose called Traver and made plans to meet at the country club. He drove in with Laura's 1955 convertible.

The hostess smiled as he entered and said, "Mr. Wells, Mrs. Wilson is waiting for you." She nodded her head toward the table by the large picture window that overlooked the golf course. The woman had jet black hair, put up in a French twist with a jeweled broach holding it in place. He could see a large diamond hanging from her left ear. It was huge. She turned as he approached. Smiling, she stood up. Putting out her hand for a firm shake, she said, "Mr. Wells?"

"You're Rose?"

"Yes."

She sat back down again and he followed suit.

"May I buy you a drink?" she said cheerily.

"Yes. A Pepsi."

"You don't drink?" she asked.

"Oh, sometimes."

"Well, this is rather pleasant," she said. "Nowadays most men drink far too much."

"Being drunk is never fun," Traver told her.

She laughed, her crystal-blue eyes sparkling like sapphires. She had a good tan, which prompted Traver to ask, "Do you like being out of doors?" he asked as his Pepsi arrived.

"Why, yes, I do. I love fishing.

"Butch tells me that I need to go fishing for walleye with you."

"I understand that there's a hot spot on your spread," Rose said.

"They bite real good at night," I answered, watching for her reaction.

"Night?" Rose smiled at that. "What kind of bait do you use?"

"Oh, corn dogs, Pepsi, potato chips, a blanket, and a transistor radio."

Rose looked across the rim of her glass at him. "When does the fishing come in?"

"Oh, that? Well, we stop by the fish section in the grocery store and buy the fish."

Rose threw back her head and laughed hard.

"Well, that's absolutely the best line I've ever heard to get a second date."

"It is—isn't it?" he said, smiling a little smugly. Rose is a Texas beauty. She doesn't have Laura's zing or Siren's air of command, but she has something, he thought to himself.

"What sort of work do you do, Rose?" he asked.

She wiped her lips. "Right now I'm in quality assurance. I used to work for NASA, where I did quality upgrades on old moon tapes and photos. I redigitized and enhanced old tech with new tech." She leaned back and looked up at him. "Last year I caused quite a stir at NASA."

"How so?"

"Well, on one of the moon orbits, one of the photos showed a flash. Everyone thought the reflection was a spacecraft of some kind. NASA had not sent anything to those coordinates, so they were sure it was Russian. Well, my office team did too good of a job. Shit hit the fan when we were able to pull up what was reflecting the sunlight."

"What was it?"

Rose took out a pen and pulled a napkin over to her. "It was at least thirty feet tall and eighteen feet wide. I'll draw you a picture of it." She sketched the object and Traver almost fell out of his chair. She had sketched a heart, with "SIREN LOVES T.W." inscribed on it.

"Holy shit! How did that get up there?" Siren must have left that behind, knowing it would be discovered in my time. His heart did a triple thump thinking about Siren. He ached for her.

"You should have heard how the project managers reacted to that," Rose said.

"I'm surprised that it didn't say 'Kilroy was here,'" Traver said.

Rose laughed.

"How come this wasn't in the news?" Traver wanted to know.

"Are you kidding? No one can explain it."

Traver leaned back and laughed. "I can just see those scientists freaking out. But I think it's romantic."

"It is, isn't it?" Rose agreed.

They finished dinner and headed out to the parking lot.

"Butch tells me that your wife died in an accident. I'm sorry to hear that."

"Thanks."

Rose got a faraway look. "My husband was killed in the Gulf War."

"That's rough. For you and for your daughters."

"I try to make the best of it. And I can see you are one of the best. You know, I'm not wearing any panties."

Traver gulped. Jesus, that was bold.

Rose continued, "You've had a loss and I've had a loss. And maybe tonight is a good time for a duty fuck."

Traver widened his eyes. A what?

"You know, it's been awhile, I just scream and yell a bit, and you get a good fuck. No other involvement. Does that intimidate you?"

"Uh," Traver stammered. "Well, no, but I will have to think about that one."

"Anyway, I am glad I met you," Rose said as she stuck out her hand for a shake. Traver pulled her close to him for a friendly hug.

The next day, Butch called Traver around eleven o'clock. "Hey, you must have really impressed Rose. That's all she's been talking about here this morning at work."

Traver sort of hem-hawed about what to say to Butch. "Butch, I was impressed with her looks, but there's no emotional connect for me. I had such a wonderful life with Laura, I just will not accept less."

"I understand," Butch said.

CHAPTER 23

OLDIES AREN'T ALWAYS GOODIES

TRAVER'S EYES FLUTTERED open just enough to realize the morning was at hand. The eastern sky was billowing with those cumulus clouds that produced a spring thunder shower and occasionally hail. Hail now would mean disaster for the corn. He closed his eyes again and stretched. Goddamn Sunday mornings used to be so special, with Laura in the kitchen fixing coffee and eggs, sausage and biscuits. She was gone four years now. Then he remembered Sunday dinner at Siren's place in 1860. She, too, was gone. And Rose was no match.

Traver sat up in bed. Not feeling sorry for himself but missing the shit out of both women and not missing Rose at all.

He decided to go visit Laura's grave and make sure that the spring flowers were outdoing the weeds. Finally getting out of bed, he went into the bathroom and tuned the radio to the oldies station. The station was playing 1950's and 1960's love songs. The song "Jo-Ann" came on. Boy, does that bring back memories! Traver started thinking about taking a trip back to his childhood home in Georgia. Just to look up old friends. Smiling to himself, he jumped in the shower. When he got out and began toweling off, "Gone," the song sung by Ferlin Husky, began to play. Shit! That whipped his Sunday morning but good.

Looking at himself in the mirror, he decided not to shave. He wasn't going to stop in town on the way to the cemetery. Ol' Buster met him in the kitchen, woo-wooing as if saying "good morning, let me out to piss!" Traver scratched his ears.

"Got to piss?"

"Woo-woo!"

"Okay." Traver let Buster out the kitchen door. Then he went to the refrigerator and got eggs and bacon.

As he was fixing breakfast, the birds begin tweeting and the prairie came to life.

"Woof!" came Buster again. Traver walked over to let him in, but the dog just looked at him and whined, turning his body toward the west, looking back at his master, and staring out again.

"Goddamn it, Buster, she's gone! Get in here!" Traver stood there looking west, just like Buster. Enchanted Canyon called to him, 1860 rising in his memory, and he yearned to go back. He then looked east. A squall line was forming, so the canyon should open. But he shook off the thought. Nothing's there for me.

He decided to keep with his plan, go visit Laura's grave and then find the spot where he and Siren spent their last evening. It would be a day of living in memories.

A huge flash of lightning burst across the eastern sky, and off in the distance thunder rumbled like a cascade of rolling bowling pins. Soon showers broke over the ranch house. The rain smelled wonderful, reminding him of the drink Siren had made for him.

He filled the Thermos with the last of the coffee and let Buster lick his breakfast plate and the pan the eggs and bacon were cooked in. He grabbed his yellow slicker and the truck keys and out the back door he went.

Traver let out a shrill whistle and yelled, "Buster!" The dog knew they were going riding. When he opened the back door on the crew cab, Buster sailed in. "You keep in the back seat, you ol' fool!"

"Woo-woo!"

At the cemetery it was still raining but just slightly. The storm had rolled far to the southwest. Buster jumped out and ran straight to Laura's grave, where he put his head down and was quiet. Laura was buried next to Bill. Sharon and Traver believed she would have liked that. He was going to be buried at the National Cemetery for Veterans at Fort McPherson. Laura and Traver had not talked about that, but that's how time and life run.

The wild flowers he had seeded at their graves were getting a good hold, and in a couple weeks they would bloom for sure. Traver stared at Laura's grave. Just six feet away but gone for good. Slapping his thigh, Traver said, "Buster." The dog stood up and barked once, as if to tell Laura goodbye. Traver felt a large lump forming in his throat as a few raindrops hit his cheek.

In the truck Buster laid down in the back seat, and Traver fired up the truck's engine to head back to the ranch. He pulled into the barn area and opened the door, but Buster did not jump out. He lay there, looking at him as if the dog knew where he was headed. "Goddamn it, you ol' fool, then stay!" Traver closed the door, started up the truck again, and headed over to Enchanted Canyon. Looking at his watch, he saw it was almost noon.

Pulling up to the spot where Siren and he had camped, Traver spotted twin fawns, which spooked and ran out from the cedar trees. It was a beautiful sight, and he sat in the truck to watch them disappear. He wondered if they disappeared into 1860. Traver was sure the canyon was open. He opened the doors, and Buster ran after the deer. Traver yelled, "Whoa." The dog stopped and stood looking at him as if to say, "Hey, it's my job to chase those deer."

"Get back here!" Traver didn't want him getting back into 1860 if the canyon was open and then closed quickly.

Watching where the deer disappeared, Traver visualized Siren when they rode the wagon up to this spot. He left the truck and walked around the trees. Were they here in 1860? Couldn't be. Cedars don't grow that old. Most likely offshoots from seeds.

But this was the spot, he was sure, the lay of the land was right. He climbed back in the truck, leaving both doors open. He closed his eyes, feeling the warm sun and smelling the moist earth, with all the prairie's scents on the gentle breeze. This spring was shaping up to be a bumper one. The grass was tall, the day's warmth coming early. He fell asleep.

Later he awakened to Buster whining. He opened his eyes and tried to remember where he was. Buster whined again. Traver saw that the dog was looking straight into Enchanted Canyon. His tail was wagging. Traver followed Buster's gaze, but he could see nothing.

A quick puff of wind whistled through the cedar trees. Traver looked around, nothing. But Buster continued to stare into the canyon. "Buster!" he yelled. "Get over here! No one's there. Come on, boy, let's go!"

Traver was still looking around, halfway expecting Siren to show up. It just felt like she was there. He looked at where Siren and he had slept that night a hundred-thirty-eight years ago. He thought he heard his name called out, but it was the wind playing tricks again.

Getting back to the ranch, he began the daily chores and the day flew by.

CHAPTER 24

HOW TIME TRIES TO STEAL EVERYTHING

THE WEEKS TURNED into months, and summer was slowly coming to an end. Traver had a couple cups of coffee that morning on the front porch steps. Buster was on the bottom step. The morning was silent. A tweeter now and then awoke to flutter from its night's roost to hunt for that early-morning bug breakfast.

The phone rang, and he went inside to answer it. Roy was on the other end. "Hey, boss, do you mind if I'm a couple days late getting back to work? I'm still in St. Joseph, Missouri. The kids are having fun at the water park and Thelma and her folks are only partly done with their genealogy."

"Sure, Roy. Hell, take another week."

"Thanks, Traver, although I'm tired of vacationing—this is hard work!" They both laughed.

"See you whenever, Roy."

"Bye, and thanks."

Traver poured himself another cup of coffee and went back out front. He looked southwest, toward Enchanted Canyon. He had Laura on his mind, remembering her riding her horse, with her rear filling the saddle. She turned and smiled at him, her breasts thrust against her blouse as she twisted.

His reverie was shattered when Buster raised his head, ears perked up. He faced the gravel road and barked.

Traver could see a bit of dust rising and then he recognized Sharon's car. Buster stood and stretched in anticipation. Sharon and Butch pulled up, waving and piling out. "Hi, dad!" Sharon called out.

Butch took out a cardboard box. Sharon came over to Traver and planted a big kiss on his cheek and hugged me. "Good to see you, dad. I brought fixin's—you need a big breakfast this morning." She smiled and disappeared into the ranch house, and Butch sat on the steps with Traver. In a minute she came out with the coffee pot and a couple of mugs.

"As soon as you finish your coffee, Butch," Sharon addressed her husband, "go inside and get the breakfast going. I have some things I want to talk to dad about."

"Sure, honey." The agreeable Butch drained his cup and went up to the steps to the kitchen. "I'm giving you guys about twenty-five minutes to finish this father-daughter talk."

"Dad, when mom left for Eppley Field, she stopped to say goodbye. She told me to take care of you. I thought that it was odd for her to talk like that. But she seemed to want to share more with me, like what happened on your trip to 1860."

Sharon sipped her coffee, set the cup down on the top step of the ranch porch, and she and Traver looked out on the dawning morning. Buster wandered out into the front parking area and laid down to sleep in the early sun.

"Dad, mom told me about the doctor there, who came to the camp with the boy, Will. Mom said she noticed how that doctor looked at you, and that she thought you didn't realize how the doctor felt about you. Mom finally said something that blew me away. She said that she could understand it a bit—after all, she'd had two men."

Traver looked at Sharon. "What?"

"Yes. Mom went on about how wonderful my dad was for her and how wonderful you were for her. She said that it wasn't a comparison thing. For her, she had been loved by two men, and that had enriched her life far more than she could ever have imagined. Mom called again a few days before she left Omaha for home. I think all the dead folks from the airplane crash had gotten to her. She cried about all the beautiful people who were lost, about all their plans, about how she was so lucky to have had my dad, and how fortunate she was to have met you and to have married you. She talked about the doctor from 1860. Mom hoped that you would recognize how this doctor felt about you and that you could share that."

Traver was stunned to hear what Sharon was saying about her mother. Laura was hoping that I would experience the love that Siren was offering me?

Traver knew that Laura had liked Siren, but he didn't realize that Laura had noticed the electricity between him and Siren.

"Your mother and Siren were the mornings that brought spirit to the new day. Both had the depth of love that a fawn feels, that a sparrow knows." Traver was quietly sharing his feelings with Sharon. "Siren brought the universe to me, she gave me the knowledge that we here on Earth are not alone. I never knew that Laura felt like that, Sharon. Siren and I did share our love but I could never compare her to your mom."

"That's okay, dad. I know that," Sharon said quietly.

"Sharon, let me tell you about Siren's world. In her world, there were nine times more females than males. Three women could mate with one male. But the first chosen was the most important. Honey, Siren struggled being second. She knew that Laura was first and that she, Siren, would always be less than first. I told her that in my culture a second woman is not acceptable. One evening, back in 1860, she had dinner with Skip's dad and me, and she asked me to walk her home. She looked up into the night's dark sky and pointed out her star ship in orbit. She began to make me feel that she was Laura, so I would share my love with her. But I knew it was Siren I was sharing my love with. It was my decision to love another while married to my love." Traver sighed. "Sharon, I want to show you something. I'll be right back."

He went upstairs to his bedroom and opened the top drawer of his dresser. Under some papers was a brown envelope, which he opened. It held some papers on which he had written down some feelings about Siren. He wanted to share them with Sharon.

He held the sheets to his chest and tried to remember Siren's breasts against him. But the years had stolen the softness of Siren's lips, the herbal fragrance of her hair. Time had stolen everything.

He went back to the front porch and sat down beside Sharon. "A few years ago, I wrote about my feelings for Siren. At that time I was missing Laura so much—she was gone, never again to—" His chin began to quiver. "I thought about Siren and her still being alive. And my love for Laura somehow got all tangled up in these feelings."

Sharon took the papers and began looking through them. She stopped short at the sketch I had done of Siren. "Oh, dad, she is beautiful!"

I am a stranger
Who is come from another time,
Who does not understand
Your thoughts,
But I will try.

I heard a sound today
That played upon my ears.
And in that sound,
All those distant years—
Felt all those lightning pains
Of falling tears.
I lost a sound today;
It fell from my lips,
Drifted as a ship at sea
On an ocean of tears.
Silently.

SIREN

She walks in Beauty
Like the Night, Lost in the Dark.
Love is the word I am seeking,
But touching hearts is my thought;
Love is what some say we are,
But sharing feelings and holding you
Are my thoughts.
If this is not so, why do I search it in others.
And the year flew by.

CHAPTER 25

ANOTHER YEAR IS STOLEN AWAY

TIME THE TRICKSTER IT IS

ANOTHER YEAR HAD passed since Laura had died in that crazy accident. Five years, five long years. Sharon and Butch had had a baby—a boy who was eight months old.

Skip's dad and Traver spent a lot of time over at the old Fort McPherson site, using a metal detector and hunting for anything that might show up. They found 45-70 spent shell casings, buttons, and an old square water pipe. The wagon supply train site was totally excavated by the University of Nebraska. The Army had a special reinterment cemetery at Fort McPherson for the eight soldiers uncovered. The worst of the old Henry rifles were buried with them. The soldiers had been together since 1859, and no one wanted to separate them. Traver felt good about that decision.

Bill had buried the gold coins, the profits, from the coffee shop and gun business Traver had helped get started. He made a set of coins and donated them to the Historical Society and told the curator he had discovered the coins at the Fort McPherson site.

The summer was getting along toward fall, and Roy was done with the fence mending. He and Traver would go out and drop dead ash trees up in the canyon for firewood. But they had so much firewood already that Roy was wondering if Traver wanted to sell it. He said, "Sure. Fifty dollars a pick-up load—an eight by four-foot bed."

August rolled by and September started out hot, but the days flew by. Soon the nights got colder and the winds from the north began to keep the hot sun from heating up the land. The corn was drying and part of the alfalfa had been mowed and was just waiting to be baled.

Sharon spent the last of September at the ranch helping with the haying, and Roy's wife kept Butch Jr. while Sharon drove the hay baler. That day Sharon was taking Butch Jr. to the doctor and was going to spend the rest of the week in town. The freshly mowed hay was not drying that fast, so baling was stalled.

Traver had gotten a late start. The late September morning was chilly and a frost had touched the browning pasture grasses, giving it an icing-on-the-cake look. This was the time of the year when a fire in the fireplace was fine for the morning chill. But it almost wasn't worth all the effort at this time of year. The gas heater was so much easier to turn on and off, although Traver did love the fragrance of a fireplace.

While the coffee was perking, Traver decided to boil a half-dozen eggs. Two for breakfast and four for snacking on while he was cutting firewood. He and Roy would finish cutting up in Enchanted Canyon, and Roy had to leave around two o'clock—he had a dentist appointment in Maxwell. They always cut wood together, because it wasn't safe to cut wood by yourself. Just in case you and your chainsaw got tangled up.

Buster came in from his rug in the front room and went to the kitchen's back door. He turned and looked at Traver, waiting to be let out.

"What is it, boy? You got to piss?"

Buster seemed about to say something—his ears perked up and he turned to the door and whined.

"Okay, just a minute." Traver opened the door, but Buster just stood there, his ears erect and his eyes focused west out the door. He whined again. Now his ears were twitching from left to right and forward.

"Buster, what's wrong with you—go piss!"

But the dog was intent on looking out the door, frozen in position, like a pointer.

Traver filled the Thermos with coffee and put the hard-boiled eggs in a sack with pepper and salt. He called out to Roy, and as Traver headed out the back door he told Buster to go get into the truck. The dog shot out of the kitchen like a bat out of hell. Traver thought that's why he was acting so strange, he wanted to go riding. Traver picked up his gloves, shut the door, and headed to the truck. Roy was just now starting his truck. They drove to Enchanted Canyon in tandem and parked where they had been cutting trees the day before.

When they got out, Roy asked, "Do you ever think much about our trip?"

"I think often about it," Traver said, although he didn't mention his thoughts were mostly about Siren. "And I think about Laura having the opportunity to be with her great-grandad."

"Do you think Twin Bears will ever cross again?"

"He might," Traver responded, "but, five years have passed, I just don't know. I doubt it."

They dropped three trees and had them cut up by one thirty, when Roy had to leave and Traver began to load up his truck. It was trying work—picking up the firewood, tossing it into the bed of the truck. It brought a sweat to his brow. "Done!" he said to no one but himself.

The sun was low in the western sky. Traver looked at his watch, it was about 3:15. Darkness would fall around 6:30. He sat down on the ground by the front wheel of the truck, facing the canyon, with the sun falling on him. The warmth felt good. He wiped his face again with a wet handkerchief. That was refreshing. Buster came over and lay beside him. He reached over to scratch behind the dog's ears and dropped his hand onto Buster's back. He leaned his head back on the tire to close his eyes briefly.

The sounds of early fall filled his ears—crows calling, the honks of a flock of geese flying over. He looked up to see them pumping their wings hard, heading south. He closed his eyes again and drifted off into a twilight sleep.

Rain! His brain signaled—but he didn't feel wet. His nose scented moisture but he felt only a cool breeze. He sniffed again—sure smelled like rain. Buster scratched himself, setting his dog tags to jingling. The sounds of the canyon suddenly echoed with children's voices. Traver chuckled. "Kids!"

Buster moved about twenty feet out from the truck, intently staring into Enchanted Canyon. "What's up there, boy?" Buster shifted his head to look back at Traver, who shaded his eyes to see better. But nothing in sight.

He closed his eyes again, letting his senses absorb his surroundings. Then he heard the laughter and excited, high-pitched voices of children again.

Traver opened his eyes, to see Buster a good hundred feet away from the truck. He was whining and his tail was twirling like a plane prop.

"Damn fool dog. Buster!" he yelled. "What's up there? Coyotes?"

Traver struggled to his feet, dusting the dirt off his ass. He sensed something—like he was being watched. He looked around quickly—nothing.

The sun was getting close to setting behind the ridge of the canyons. He shaded his eyes again. By God! There was a movement just at the ridge line. He wished he had his binoculars to get a good look at who was moving up there. One figure seemed to be familiar. The height, the gait. What was there about that walk? The way the hair fell, shoulder length. The way the hair bounced and was blown in the breeze. The way the foot stepped on the earth. That easy walk.

Traver's heart was quickening. He took a deep breath. No one could be in the canyon at this time of year. The closest residence was twenty-three miles west, over the next ridge.

No. No one was out there.

Buster was still wagging his tail. Traver said loudly, "You old fool, come here," and slapped his leg until Buster came over and nudged it. "Goddamn it, boy! They're gone—it's just us now." He put both hands on the truck's door. "I know, boy, it's been five years and we're both still looking for what we've lost."

CHAPTER 26

SHE WALKS IN HIS THOUGHTS
BUT SHE SPEAKS OF TIME
AND HOW HE WAS MISSED

"Traver."

It was a voice on the breeze, so soft that he didn't respond. He wasn't even sure he heard it.

"Traver."

Again, with a settling and sweet sound.

He turned, but no one was there.

Again, "Traver," but stronger. His name was spoken for sure and not in his thoughts.

He raised his hand to shade his eyes, to deflect the rays of the setting sun. Something was moving up there in the canyon and Buster was running around, barking. Yes, there were three forms coming down the canyon. Two forms stopped and stood together. The third form continued.

Traver knew that form. He opened his mouth, but no sound. His heart exploded. He recognized that form. "Siren." It came out as a whisper.

Buster ran up to her and she bent down to pat him.

He took a few steps toward her. "Siren," Traver said breathlessly.

"Yes."

"Siren!" he yelled and stumbled toward her. Tears were blinding his vision.

She stood there, silhouetted in the setting western sun. "Siren." He couldn't stop repeating her name.

He hurried toward her and stopped just about twenty feet short. "Siren."

She smiled, pearl-like teeth flashing, and her eyes sparkled. "Yes, I'm here."

He crossed the twenty feet as if on a cloud. Slowly his hand went to her cheeks to touch the tears tracing silver streams down her cheeks. The years disappeared. His hand roamed to her hair, touching the strands gently. "Siren," he breathed.

They're hands reached out and electricity flowed when their fingertips touched. Their bodies molded together, his lips whispered in her ear, "I love you."

"I feel it," she said firmly.

He ran his hands up and down her back. ""Oh, God! It's so wonderful to feel you again. It is you!"

"It is me," she said, smiling.

He pulled away and looked at her. "Siren, I've missed you every day you've been gone."

"I've been very busy, but never too busy to not think of you. Since it's my one-hundredth birthday, and we have perfected time travel with light speed. I could come to you in real time here. I have presents for you on my birthday, two wonderful presents."

Buster came over, nudging his cold nose between them. They parted and Siren scratched his head. "Did you miss me, too?" Buster began to howl. She laughed and looked at Traver. "He's still talking."

"You're here," he mumbled.

"Yes, I came back. My place is here with you, even if I am second. I am willing to give up everything. If you will have me now and then, I will stay here."

Traver looked at her in amazement. "You'll stay here? Leave your ship and command?"

"Yes, I will! I have!"

He hugged her. "I cannot ask you to do that."

"You don't have to ask me, just be with me now and then. It's my choice. I realized that being second to Laura is a compliment."

"Siren, Laura died," Traver wailed.

Siren stood there, in shock. "I did not know." Tears welled in her eyes. "Perhaps I should not be here."

"No, stay, please. I have been so empty all these years."

"But I could never take her place," Siren said emphatically.

"I know and I wouldn't want you to try. Stay, Siren, and be with me. I love you. Your place is with me!" he pleaded.

"I'll stay, Traver, but right now you need to meet a couple of souls. Come with me." Hand in hand they walked toward the two figures standing halfway up the middle of the canyon. He finally recognized Monk and waved. "Monk!"

He waved back. From behind the two men two children appeared. Siren knelt and put her arms out to them. A boy and a girl, the children ran to her. "Mommy! Mommy!" The joyful sounds of children.

Siren caught them up in her arms and hugged them hard.

"Mommy, you'll squeeze us to death," the girl squealed.

Siren looked up at Traver. "Children, I want you to meet your papa."

"My children?" sputtered Traver. "Our children?"

"Remember when you walked me home in 1860?" Her face was glowing.

"My children," Traver said, his heart exploding with a love he had never before known.

"Hi, papa," the boy said, "I'm Kenneth."

The girl said, "I am named De Laural, after my mother's friend."

"Well, children, come give your dad a big hug and a kiss." Both children came over to him and they hugged.

"Captain," Monk said, "you must share with Traver all that you are."

She turned to Monk. "That's not necessary here, Monk, this is a different world, a new world to me."

"But it is our law," Monk came back.

Eons of emotions were swirling in her. Her eyes were like nebular star clouds. She breathed in an entire universe. As she exhaled she said, "You may tell of my lineage. I will listen and the one who chooses will know."

"Traver," Monk said solemnly, "the woman before you is the mother in waiting of our home world. She is Captain of a special time star vessel. But she is more than a star captain. When her mother passes through transition, Siren inherits the position of mother of our world. Siren is part of the Royal Family whose ancestry goes to our very beginning."

Traver remembered the first time he looked upon Siren's breast. The snake from her navel to her nipple told of her position and her knowledge, the time tunnel-hole pathway to Edon. He remembered kissing that tattooed nipple, feeling the warmth, the love, the gift of the Way, the entire universe.

Monk added, "Siren has given up all to return to this world. She has given up everything to be with you because that is everything to her. What do you choose?"

Traver felt the seriousness of Siren's choice in this matter. He addressed Monk, although he was gazing lovingly at Siren. "With my heart I choose Siren. With all that I am and will be, I choose Siren. I do not choose first, second, or third. I simply open my spirit to her totally and completely. I choose equally."

Monk smiled. "Siren, do you accept Traver's choosing?"

"I, for all time, accept and honor his choosing," Siren said, tears streaming.

Monk then turned to De Laura, daughter of Siren, daughter of De Paula. "Traver has chosen your mother and you are their daughter. In a few years, I will come to take you home to be presented to your home world as Mother. It has been ordained, and I will record this choosing and this birth. Now, I must be leaving."

Monk shook Traver's hand and accepted a hug from Siren, who said to him, "You've been a worthy teacher, Monk, I shall miss you."

"I, too, shall often wonder how you are. And I shall speak well of your choosing to your mother, Siren." He bowed, and he and a younger man departed. At the top of the hill, they turned and waved, and in a few seconds they disappeared.

Traver had his arm around Siren's shoulder. "What have you given up to be here with me?"

"I have given up a title, but I gain everything that I have dreamed of. And my children will know their father."

"I am so glad you are here, and I hope you never regret what you've given up."

"I won't! Children, let's go see how dad lives."

They headed for the truck. De Laural took her father's hand and Kenneth took Siren's hand. "You kids get in the back. Siren, you're next to me." He shut the children's door. As Siren stepped up, he lifted her rear with his hands. "Woo!" she squealed.

"Children," Siren said, "tell your father all about Uncle Bill and Aunt Alice."

De Laural grinned and said in her high-pitched voice, "Uncle Bill said that you invented coffee."

Traver laughed.

Siren said, "Honey, what Uncle Bill said was that your father brought the coffee house to North Platte—he didn't invent coffee."

"Oh, yes," De Laural said.

Kenneth said, "Uncle Bill and I went camping down by the river. I had lots of fun. We roasted a rabbit that he shot."

"How is Alice?" Traver asked.

Siren said, "She's fine, but very worried that Will won't come back from the war."

"War?" Traver exclaimed.

"Yes, between the North and the South."

"Oh, the Civil War. Yes, don't worry, he comes back. I have found him in records up to 1930."

Siren sighed with relief. "I know that Alice will be relieved then when he comes home."

Alice married Twin Bears? That bit of information distracted Traver.

Siren was facing him and smiling. Traver said, "God, I just can't believe you're here."

"I'm here, Traver. Forever."

He turned to see the children in the back seat and then looked at Siren again. "I remember when you spoke of receiving my seed."

"Yes." She was still smiling with happiness at being here.

"Children," Traver said.

"Yes, Papa?"

"Come, get up front with your mother and me."

They scrambled over the seat and into the front.

When they pulled up to the front of the ranch house, Buster jumped down from where he was riding on the pile of firewood. He bounded over to Siren, and Traver could see that the old dog loved her.

It suddenly dawned on Traver that Siren and the kids didn't have any suitcases. "Hey, where is your stuff?"

"Stuff?" Siren answered.

"Clothing, personal things?"

"We had to leave everything behind. It's just the kids and me and the clothes on our backs."

"Well, you have something else." Traver reached into his shirt collar and pulled out the jeweled orb on the gold chain. Her hand went to her lips as she gasped. "The Way! You still have it!"

"Yes, I do, and I've never taken it off, except for right now." He raised the chain over his head and placed it around her neck. The sphere disappeared between her round, full breasts.

She looked deeply into his eyes and said, "You have kept the Way. When I gave this to you five years ago, I told you it was from my home world. It is—but not the home that I was born on and lived on. It is from the Great Home, whose Way is lost to us now. It's the reason for our great star ships that constantly search for the original home." Her hands came up to her chest. "Traver, I can sense all that you have had and lost—the Way feels that also. We are so joined—you and me. Tonight when the children are asleep, we will fly upon the Way." She placed her hand on his arm softly, as if to emphasize what she had said.

"Come, children, let me show you your new home."

De Laural said, "This is sure a place of good feelings." As she climbed the stone and cement steps, she added, "I like it here."

Just for an instant Traver thought he saw Laura's twinkle flashing in De Laural's eyes.

Kenneth and Siren followed, and Buster decided he was not going to let them in first. He shot through the door as it was opened and made a beeline to his rug in the front room. Siren was amused.

Entering the front room, Siren looked around slowly. "This is a wonderful home."

"It was Laura's. My home is in California, quite a way from here. It will be her daughter's when I pass on."

Siren said, "Remember, you will outlive Laura's daughter because you've been enhanced. But since your blood type is O, you can give blood to her and she'll pick up a lot of the enhancement effects in the red blood cells. She won't have the numbers you do, but she'll heal 10-15 percent faster and she will live to be 120 or so."

"I didn't realize that. I can't wait to talk to Sharon and Butch about it."

The children were playing with Buster and having a great time laughing while Buster barked back at them. On the couch were toys that Sharon had left. Siren looked at them.

"Sharon has a baby boy," Traver told her.

Siren leaned in to give him a kiss, and he peeked down her blouse. "Tomorrow, after we have loved all night, we'll have to go to town and get you-all some duds."

"What?"

"Clothing. We'll outfit the kids, too. Siren, do Kenneth and and De Laural understand stellar travel and the differences between their world and this world?"

"They do," Siren told him. "They have very intelligent parents, you know. They might create some problems by talking to others about matters beyond this world. So we'll have to keep them close until they get older. We'll home school them."

"What was that about Monk coming back to pick up De Laural and take her to the home world?"

"My mother is the supreme person on our world. I am next in line to succeed her. Because I have chosen to live in your world, De Laural is next in line and she must be on the home world to present herself and continue our royal lineage when she becomes a woman. We are invited as her parents."

Traver heard Roy drive up outside. "Just a minute." He got up, went to the front door, and motioned for Roy to come over.

As Roy came up the steps he asked, "What's up, boss?"

"How's the tooth?" Traver wanted to know.

He rubbed his jaw. "Pulled the damned thing, no more bullshit from it now!"

"Come in and see who's here."

The screen door slammed behind him as he stood frozen to the spot. "My God, Siren, it's you!"

"Yes." She smiled. "And are you well?"

"I sure am."

"Children, come here. This is Uncle Roy."

Roy stared in disbelief.

"Roy, these here crumb snatchers are my children," Traver boasted.

"Well, Goddamn! Boss, you're a fast worker."

"Roy, Siren and the children will be staying with us for a while."

The phone rang. It was Sharon, wanting to know if Traver wanted to have supper with them.

"Did you invite anyone else?" Traver asked Sharon.

Sharon dragged out her answer. "Nooooooo, why?"

"Well, honey, I have someone I would love for you to meet."

"Sure, dad. You gone and met a girl?"

"Well, sort of," he said. "I met her a long time ago and she just came back and looked me up. Where are we eating?"

"Butch wants to go to the golf club. It's seafood night—all you can eat. We'll be there at seven, okay?"

"Great." Traver hung up.

"Sharon has invited us to dinner," he told Siren.

"All we have to wear is what we have on."

"Well, let's go into town and get some new clothes now."

They piled into Laura's truck, since Traver's was still full of firewood.

Siren was excited to see North Platte 162 years in the future. They stopped at a nice dress shop. The clerk came over. "How may I help you?"

Traver said, "A couple of dresses and lots of blouses."

The kids and Traver walked down the street to a children's clothing store. He told the lady there to fix them up with at least seven outfits each. This was rather interesting for Traver. He watched his children, five years old, acting as if they were around eight to ten years old. He carried the bags of clothes back to the store where Siren was finishing her shopping.

He was dumbstruck when he saw Siren. She had on khaki pants, a turquoise western blouse, a leather belt with turquoise stone set in it. Her brown cowgirl boots set off the outfit. Her dark hair cascaded onto her shoulders.

She looked at Traver. "You like?"

"I love!"

"Oh good, I was a little afraid that I may have over done it."

"You'll be the prettiest woman in the club tonight."

When Siren made her purchases, Traver and kids helped her carry out the boxes of clothing. He was so proud and so full of love, he was still in a state of disbelief at his good fortune. "You're really here!" he exclaimed.

They prepared to go to the country club to meet Sharon and Butch. Hand in hand Siren and Traver entered the club, followed by De Laural and Kenneth. They walked into the dining room and looked around. Sharon spotted Traver and waved, and Siren glided toward her. When they reached the table, Sharon kept staring at Siren. "Do I know you?" Sharon asked.

Traver answered for Siren. "In a way you do, honey."

Sharon put her hands to her mouth in shocked recognition: Siren!

"Yes," said Siren softly. "You look so much like your mother. And I am so sorry for your loss."

Sharon took the hand Siren offered. "Thank you . . . but how . . . ?"

Siren smiled and glanced quickly at Traver. "I gave up everything to come here. But I did not think that your mother would not be here."

Sharon pressed Siren's hand further. "We'll talk later, but now I know this is the best thing that has happened to dad for a long, long time."

"Honey," interrupted Traver, "meet De Laural."

The little girl stepped forward. "I'm named after your mother."

Sharon knelt down and opened her arms. "Come here and give me a hug." Then she reached for the little boy. "And who is this young man?"

"I'm Kenneth."

Traver interjected, "Honey, these two children are Siren's and mine."

Sharon stood up and cried, "Oh, dad, I'm so happy for you." She looked at both of us.

"Sharon, Siren and the children are staying."

"Welcome to the family!" And Sharon hugged Siren again. "She continued, "And here is my husband, Butch, and here is Butch Jr." The baby was asleep in a carrier on a chair.

"Oh! Isn't new life so precious?" Siren said happily.

The meal was delicious, and as the evening progressed a bonding between Siren and Sharon occurred. As they finished dessert, Traver noticed Rose had come in from the bar. She saw Traver and headed directly for him. "Traver," Rose called out. Shit, he thought.

He stood up. "Hi, Rose."

She stopped short when she realized he was with someone. Sharon took over. "Rose, I would like you to meet a special friend, Siren. Siren, this is Rose."

Neither woman extended her hand.

Rose said, "Siren what?"

"Siren, that's it."

Rose looked puzzled and Traver knew she was going over the mysterious message she had reported to her superiors at NASA. Rose said graciously, "Good to see you all and nice to meet you, Siren." But she left the group shaking her head.

"What was that all about?" Siren asked Traver.

He took out a pen and drew on a napkin a heart with Siren loves T.W. in the middle.

"You saw it!" Siren clapped.

"No, but I heard about it from Rose. She was working in the space program, and her bosses were so paranoid about intelligent life elsewhere in the universe, they hushed it up."

"I set that up as we left orbit in 1860. I had hoped for you to see it someday before you died and you would know how much I loved you."

Sharon was full of curiosity. "What are you-all talking about?"

Siren smiled. "I got a huge heart made out of polished granite from Earth, and on it I had written Siren loves T.W. I left it on the moon. I knew someday someone would see it. It would just be a matter of time."

On the drive back to the ranch Traver turned on the heater, and it gave off a bit of a smell of burning dust. Siren scootched down a bit so her head was resting on the seat's headrest. He reached over and pulled Siren close to him. She took a deep breath, exhaled, and went limp. "The children are asleep in the back seat," she informed him.

He backed off the pedal and as they crossed the Platte River, he pointed toward the Texaco station. "Remember that?"

She looked closely. "Was that where your camp was? The place Will brought me to?"

"Sure is."

It was 10:30, and the darkness was thick. Siren asked, "How long have I been here so far?"

Traver looked at his watch. "You showed up at 4, so it's been a little more than six hours."

Siren stared out into the black night. "It feels like I never left now that I'm next to you."

He rested his arm across her shoulder and let his hand wander slowly into her open blouse, caressing her warm breast. She gave a sigh of approval. "Are you tired?" he wanted to know.

Her head rested on his shoulder, but there was no answer.

"Let's make love right here in the truck."

No response. Just a hint of deep breathing.

"There's time. A lifetime," he whispered.

The following morning he was up before dawn. It was still dark outside. He made himself coffee and drank two cups. Roy tapped on the back door and came in.

"Morning, boss. The grass feels right for baling."

"I thought so," Traver agreed.

Roy looked at him. "Traver, it sure is great to see Siren."

"I couldn't be happier about this," said Traver heartily. "C'mon, let's hit it."

Before they left, Traver placed a fresh cup and saucer on the table and snipped a red rose from a bush outside to put on the table next to the cup.

"Oh, boss, you've got it bad!"

"I sure do!" Traver grinned. "Could you and Thelma watch the children tonight?"

Roy gave a big Western grin that said, I know what you're up to.

"Sure we will."

A few hours later, the crew cab came into the field where Roy and Traver were baling hay. He got on the radio and told Roy that breakfast had arrived. As they got close to the truck, next to the field of alfalfa, Traver saw Sharon driving and Siren in the passenger seat. Both waved at the men. As Roy and Traver were eating, Siren looked over the big baler machine. She came to the back of the truck where he was sitting on the tailgate.

"Can I ride with you the rest of the day?" Siren asked.

Before Traver could answer, Sharon spoke up, "You want to learn how to run one of those? I can teach you."

So when breakfast was finished, the girls left. When Roy and Traver got in that afternoon, they learned that Siren was a natural in navigating big farm machinery. Siren smiled. "Well, after all, I was a luminal star ship captain."

"A what?" Sharon wanted to know.

"A luminal star ship is a light-speed overboost. They were the first ships to the stars hundreds of years in sleep animation, but not many got to where they were headed. The ship we were looking for in 1860 had taken off to make a crossing. That's why so much work was done in body enhancement. A combination of sleep and waking made the trip at least more bearable. The data that were recorded here at the canyon soon developed into a complementary field generator distortion acellameter. We had hoped to go in time.

"Going in time required a knowledge that we did not have. How can you go quickly to a place you've never been to? For example, we can go to

1860 very quickly now because we know about it and just where it is. We have a gravity-well signature of 1860. But we can do nothing else. In some way, we are so advanced to being stupid and even stupider in some areas. Believe me, driving a baler is nothing."

Sharon was fascinated but bewildered by the highly technical talk. She raised her hand. "I'm out of here. You guys need some time alone."

Siren looked grateful. "My heart pounds so for this man that it deafens me. It does seem like we have no quiet time." She giggled. After Sharon left, they set up the kids' beds in Sharon's old room. They tucked in De Laurel and Kenneth.

As Siren and Traver walked to their bedroom, she told him, "I love you, Mr. Wells, I will never regret coming back here—never!"

"You've been back here two days now and I feel like no time has passed since we last held each other," Traver told her.

They fell asleep around three in the morning, after long moments of emotions and bodies exploding and settling and then exploding again. With a couple hours of sleep, Traver got up and went downstairs to repeat the baling chores. Another few days and all would be ready for winter's feed.

The days drifted, one after another. Siren was very adaptive in picking up what needed to be done, running a corn binder or other equipment. The extra hand sure helped. Roy's wife Thelma kept the children while they finished up the harvest. Siren looked even more sensuous in faded blue jeans and work shirt running the big tractors.

Roy and Traver came in early the last day of haying. Four in the afternoon was early. Traver stopped Roy a moment. "Roy, could you and Thelma keep the children this weekend? I want to take Siren to Denver."

"Sure thing, boss."

"Thanks!" Traver went in the kitchen door and heard Sharon and Siren laughing and talking, so he stuck his head in the front room. They were visiting and drinking a bottle of wine. It sounded as if Sharon was telling Siren about her mother, Laura. Their voices became hushed, so Traver went upstairs, showered, and put on slacks and a Western shirt. When he went back downstairs, he heard both girls crying. He looked in and they were holding each other. "Siren," Sharon said, "I feel right now as though mom is here holding me."

"I'll never replace your mom," Siren told her.

"That's true. You're more like the sister I never had. How old are you?"

"Well, by your calendar and time, I am 100 years old."

Sharon's jaw dropped. "One hundred?"

"Oh, yes. My life expectancy is more than 200 years. In Earth years, I am about your age."

Sharon was full of questions. "Does dad know? Does that mean you can still have children?"

"Traver knows my age. In fact, he will live to 190 years."

"What?"

"He went through genetic enhancing before my ship and I left in 1860," Siren explained it all to Sharon. "Our children will not pick up that—they will live only 100 years or so. It hurts knowing we will outlive them." Siren smiled. "But I have all that worked out. As far as having children, I'm good for at least another twenty years."

Sharon was still a little tipsy. "There are a lot of mom's things still around. Dad and I just couldn't toss them. You should wear them. I think mom would like that, and it will make dad want you even more! Where does he get all that energy?"

Siren smiled. "I don't think he needs any more to excite him!"

Both women howled with laughter.

Over hearing them, Traver hollered from the kitchen, "I was going to bring you two another bottle of good wine, but I heard you talking about me."

The women giggled and came into the kitchen with the empty bottle, tossing it into the trash. Sharon got another bottle from the pantry and they left. "Sorry, dad—girl stuff."

Sharon came into the living room, where Traver was watching the news on TV. "Dad, Siren is trying on some of mom's stuff. How do you feel about that?"

Traver had been thinking about that. "Honey, the work clothes won't bother me that much, but all the dressy things will just rip out my heart." Sharon was still a little wobbly on her feet, but she waved her hand in a dismissive gesture. "Oh, dad, don't worry about that, Siren is a little too big on top for those."

Sharon called out to Siren, "Hey! Come on in here and get dad's attention, sexy!"

*   *   *

The next morning, in their bedroom, while they were dressing, Traver asked Siren how she felt wearing Laura's clothes. She came over and sat beside him on the bed. Her hand rested on his leg. "I feel a little funny. It's like I'm invading the space she had with you."

He put his hand over hers. "I understand. I don't want to forget Laura—but I don't want to compare you to her—I don't want to shortchange you, Siren. I love you so. There was a black dress that Laura loved, though, did you see that?"

"I did try it on, and it was the only dress that fit me."

"Would you try it on for me? It brings back beautiful memories."

She formed the words with her full pink lips. "I will!"

After a bit he heard a light tapping on the bedroom door. "Traver, I'm ready." Siren stepped through the doorway with her hair touching her shoulders, her neck was bare, the fluffy bodice top clinging tightly to her breasts.

He sat there staring.

"Are you okay?" she whispered.

"You are a beautiful, stunning woman—a goddess. Right now all I see is you!"

Siren told him, "Sharon told me that her mother really liked this dress. She said it was special and reminded her of a crazy night with you."

"I do see Laura in that dress, but I am filled with love for you. Let's get married," he said urgently. "I know your custom—but I want to marry you in my custom."

She kissed him.

"We have a small problem, though. You don't have a history on this planet." He explained that she needed a birth certificate, Social Security number, driver's license, and other official documents. "We'll work on that. I think Butch can help."

Siren stood up and dropped her gown.

"Why is it that we excite each other so easily? Our hearts pound with emotion for each other?"

Siren looked at him. "What else do you expect? We are the same." She touched his face. "Born millions of miles and thousands of years apart—yet still part of the same flowing river."

Her eyes twinkled, her lips arched in a smile, her cheeks reddened. "Of everything, I remember most our wagon ride on a Sunday in 1860."

"Then, woman, we shall take another wagon ride as soon as possible," Traver declared.

"Mommy, mommy!" Kenneth and De Laural came running into the bedroom. Luckily, Traver had gotten into his shorts and Siren had pulled up the top of the black gown. The children stopped in their tracks. "Oh, mommy, you look beautiful!"

"Thank you, children. Why was there so much yelling?"

Kenneth said, "Roy's cat has just had her kittens. Roy came and told us. Can we go and see them, please?"

"Yes, go see the kittens," Siren said with a smile.

The children left and Siren was still smiling. "Do you remember your first kitten?"

"I sure do," Traver said. "Siren, what do you think of us building our own home and letting Sharon and Butch have the ranch house? After all, Sharon grew up here and I would like a place that is ours."

"Building a home with you for our children and us would be so wonderful." She began to take off the black gown and get into her work jeans and blouse. "So I need to do some digging this morning."

"Why?"

She looked at Traver pointedly. "Well, I didn't exactly leave everything behind. Come help me see if Bill did as I asked."

"Where are we going?"

"Up to the canyon. Bill was supposed to bury something for me just in case I did come back."

"You mean to tell me you were thinking back then that you might come back to me?"

"Yes, I was!"

Siren went through Laura's clothes again and found a rust-colored long, full skirt that fell to just below her knees. She picked out a yellow blouse and left the bottom hanging over the skirt's waistband. She slipped on some loafer-type shoes. "There, let's go riding," she told Traver.

When they got downstairs they picked up canteens and filled them with water. Outside, he got two shovels and Skip's dad's metal detector and dumped them into the wagon. He helped her up into the seat, went around the back, and climbed into the front seat. He sucked his lips and slapped the horse with the reins to get him walking.

"Where to, darling?" Her arms came around his chest.

"Up to Enchanted Canyon—but we'll stop a moment just down the way, won't we?"

She squeezed his arm, and she began massaging his thigh, which gave him that hot and distracted feeling.

The wagon bounced and lurched, making her squeal.

Traver whispered, "Just like 1860—right?"

"This feels soooo . . ." She lost control at that point, arching her back and bursting into a flame of passion. He couldn't understand what she was yelling, but he dropped the reins.

"Traver," Siren said, leaning against him, "let's build our home here."

He took in the area. They were just below a rise in a hill just to the north. He thought the winter winds would not penetrate the house in that location. He turned east. "Siren, look at this view."

"Oh, Traver, this is beautiful!" They kissed. "Well, Traver," she said as their lips parted, "let's go dig up some science."

"Just what is it we're looking for?"

"It's a metal chest." By late afternoon they had found the box that Bill had buried in 1860.

"What is it?" Traver wanted to know.

"It's a guidance control for a survival wing. I parked one orbiting over the North Pole. This box will energize it."

"What's in the wing?"

She became a bit distant. "Enhancement treatments for six. For our children. There are also enough diamonds in there to last us forever. I took the raw ones we had on board and packed them in the wing."

"Just how big is this wing?"

"Oh, about thirty feet across. When I contact it—it will take most of the night to cycle down. It will land within a hundred feet of this box. Let's take it home. By tomorrow the wing will be down."

As Traver drove the wagon, Siren was humming a tune. She asked, "Traver, do you think the children will like moving out here to a new home?"

"I do."

"Want me to sit on your lap, honey?" Siren said, her voice husky with desire.

"Anytime—but I can see the ranch already."

"Mmmmmm," she said with disappointment.

He swatted her rear. "Don't worry, there's tonight."

"There is, isn't there," she perked up.

When she stood up, he could see how strongly her breasts pressed against her faded blouse and how her nipples made themselves known. He could smell her fragrance of loving and how her body had heated up and then had cooled.

"This feels wonderful, Traver." She wiped a stray tear from her cheeks. "I've never cried so much until I met you—I think I'm just overwhelmed at your acceptance and spirit."

Tears were stinging his eyes, he was full of too many emotions. Here he was looking at a goddess from hundreds of light-years away. He reached into his coat pocket, took out an envelope, and handed it to her.

She looked surprised. "What is this?"

"Open it."

She looked at him with those bright dark eyes. Her face was aglow, lips shiny, with a bit of wetness in her eyes. When she opened the envelope, two little tea roses fell out. She picked up the rosebuds and put them against her breasts. She blew me a kiss. She took out the pieces of paper, unfolded them, and read quietly aloud.

I looked up and you were there . . .
I called out and you answered . . .
I began to feel like a kid again
I glow allover as you smile upon me.
I catch a fragrance of your warmth
and it's so new I don't know what to do.
I sense your lip's fire like the warmth of the hearth,
like campfires that chase the winter.
I look into your eyes and see neither today
or tomorrow, for the moment blinds my spirit.
I reach to hold you, you reach to hold me
I do not know where I begin and you end.
My lips touch your lips and it's my heart that falls,
as leaves kissed with a winter's frost.
I fall like those drifting leaves of October, floating
on the breeze of November.
I touch
You touch

We touch
In my dreams from everywhere you appear
In that dreaming moment, all too brief you go.
Like a whisper, an echo in a dream my soul has
fallen and has felt your soul.
My dreams are you.
Like a winter's breeze at dawn you dance and sing.
That song that only the soul knows, my heart seeks and
My arms reach far, light-years away.
If I kiss you I fear that I will lose this dream.
Dare I
Dare I touch
Dare I love you, dare I not

Siren looked up and then back to the pages with the poetry and read them again. She folded the paper into a two-inch square and tucked it into her blouse.

"How do you hear my soul?" she asked. "Teach me to hear your soul as you hear mine."

"I don't know how, Siren," he said.

"Traver, I can teach you nothing that you don't already know. Just center your thoughts—reflecting the daily distractions—settle the noise in your head. First tell that voice to be quiet—that you want to listen to God—that you want to listen to silence. If you would like, I can show you a wonderful place full of wonderful sounds and exotic colors."

He started to leave with her. Siren said, "No. Be still. I can bring this place to you, right now, without traveling. Do you understand?"

He just looked at her.

She continued, "Make no response, no answer, for there is no answer. Just think about my words, Traver. Sit down on the earth here and clear your thoughts."

When he sat down, she said, "Traver, close your eyes for a moment. But do not stop seeing—for you can still see where we are. You just will not let the sounds distract your seeing as I speak. Breath deeply in, hold your breath so your body can absorb all the oxygen. But more importantly, so your body can absorb the spirit of the wind. As you exhale, see your breath dissipate—breathe in deeply again. It's such a delicious taste—the wind.

Breathing the wind, you know the speed it blows, the scents it carries. Like the wind, you can fly as a small sparrow if you wish.

"Traver, as you are breathing, you are flying, your spirit sees a wonderful land in the distance and you guide your spirit to it. It is the most beautiful place you have ever seen. Your spirit senses a meadow just ahead. As that meadow comes into view, you are overcome with the strongest feeling of home that you have ever known." Siren noticed the goose bumps rising on his arms and neck. "This is your meadow, Traver. Breathe in its sweetness. It's early dawn—not yet sun-up, but close. You hear birds waking with their morning songs, you see dew droplets kissing the grass.

"There in your meadow you see the dew drops explode with the sun's first rays. You also know that the sun is rising and you feel its rays touching your back and the back of your neck. Now, breathing deeply of your meadow's air, fill your lungs with its gifts. Breathing in and exhaling you feel sun's warmth and energy flow into your lungs with every breath.

"Absorb the golden rays of the sun that fall on your back and pass that feeling down your right arm, past your right shoulder, past the elbow, into your right forearm. See the sun's golden energy flow into your right hand, past the wrist, so your palm glows with golden light. Traver, your right hand is your hand of life, the hand of action. Breathing deeply, you sense the golden energy settle at the tips of your fingers. Your hand tingles. Your right hand has the strength of building, of doing. Your glowing, golden-light right hand can touch another and share the gift of light. After a time of knowing how this energy feels, begin to pass this energy from your right hand, past your wrist, past your right elbow. Across your shoulders and into your left shoulder and arm. Breathing deeply, and with more of the sun's energy, you pass that into your left arm—past the elbow—along the left forearm, into the wrist, and you see that golden sun's glow forming in your left hand. The left hand accepts gifts. It's the hand that waves goodbye and hello. The left hand is the beacon in a dark sea. It is the light of the soul. Breathing deeply, you sense the left hand's fingertips clawing with truth.

"With both of your hands now in the sun's golden energy, know the right attracts and the left rejects; the right does, the left accepts. Know that one hand cannot heal, but both together can heal the heart, the soul, and the memory. When you are healing, lighting the way, or sharing, and you are done, you simply clap your hands together—at times that sound will be of thunder.

"Breathing in deeply, you center the sun's energy in every organ of your body and into your head. Mind, heart, and hands—glowing. Mend your thoughts, your heart, your hands.

"As you breathe deeply, you return to your meadow. Take as long as you wish to move around, to touch, to see all of its wonders. As you feel like it—begin to be here."

Siren stopped speaking and let Traver begin to gather his spirit back in the present reality. "The first visit to your meadow is very important," she whispered. His face began to twitch and he moved his hand closer to his chest. His head turned back and forth and slowly his eyes fluttered open. He was quiet. Siren reached over and touched his lips with her fingers, noticing that his eyes were still distant.

He began looking into Siren's eyes. "Traver, look past me."

She clapped her hands, making a popping sound that startled Traver. Immediately, he was back.

"Siren, that was beautiful. I want to go back to my meadow."

"It's only a thought away," Siren said.

Traver was totally relaxed. "Siren, I'm so . . . what are the words? Comfortable? Secure?"

"I understand," she said. "Maybe the better response is, 'I feel!'"

"Yes! I feel! My God! How long have I lived in the 'I know' world and ignored the 'I feel' world."

Siren's hands went out palms up. He put his hands palm down.

She smiled. "Friend."

"Friends always." He let his fingers dance on her palms. Her fragrance was of fresh herbal-washed hair, and every now and then came the aroma of sexual excitement. "Siren, I love you so very much. I am so happy that you came back and I am exceptionally pleased that we have such beautiful children."

Her hands patted his back. "You're going to be a papa again."

"Are you sure?"

"Yes, I'm sure."

"You really like the wagon rides," he said. "Every Sunday okay with you?"

"I have to wait till Sunday?"

"Darling, we can hitch up the horse anytime—but someone will begin to wonder what's up."

She smiled and Traver grinned back. "Yep! What's up! And thank you for the meadow."

As they unhitched the horse from the wagon, he turned the horse loose out in the pasture. Siren commented, "You know, as you were wondering about how we have such feelings for each other, and I said we are the same? Even though I am from 106 years in the past, and I'm from light-years away from here, we are related. The people on this planet are descendants of the home world. No wonder we have the same chemistry and feelings. Nothing separates us, nothing at all but time.

Siren looked up into the late afternoon shifting to evening. "My mother is still alive out there. In a few years De Laural will stand before her to accept her Way." Siren reached into her blouse and touched the two pink roses and then held the jeweled orb. In a soft and slow voice she said, "The Way is strong! It's our Way, Traver. Just as I gave you a meadow, I expanded your sight and you began a new path."

She spoke to him as a mother teaching a child. He absorbed her gaze, and like a child he longed to suck at her breast. He had just been led by her to the wonderful land of their ancient heritage. The meadow was Siren and she was the meadow.

"Traver, the Way is the path a tear of loss takes, it is the Way a tear of love flows. Traver, the Way is the journey your seed and my egg takes."

After this serious conversation, they took each other's hands and walked over to Roy's place and knocked at the back screen door.

"Roy!" Traver yelled.

"Hey, boss, come on in. The kids are having a great time with the kittens."

Kenneth came forward. "Dad, dad," he shouted excitedly, and the boy pulled Traver over to a box. There was the old tiger cat Tiger Lilly. He reached down his hand and scratched her head and she mewed. "Got some new mouses, Lilly?" he asked.

Siren looked in the box. "Hi, girl! You outdid yourself with eight kittens—you take care. De Laural," Siren called out.

"In here, mother," came a voice from the kitchen. "I'm helping Thelma fix beans and cornbread. We're having trail food for tonight."

Siren came out onto the back porch where they had gathered.

Roy said, "I saw you-all out by Enchanted Canyon, driving all crazy."

Siren turned a bright red.

"Oh?" Traver said.

"I thought something was wrong," Roy continued, "so I glassed you-all with my binoculars. It looked like Traver was trying to teach you how to drive a horse-drawn wagon. It's not that easy to do, driving a tractor is easier.

"Roy, Siren and I are thinking of building our home out there," Traver said. "We're thinking of telling Sharon that she and Butch can have her mom's place. Do you think she'll like that?"

Roy nodded his head. "I sure do. That's a great thing for you to do, Traver. I know she'll really love that. When you-all going to start?"

"Soon," Traver said.

Siren turned to Roy. "There's a wing landing here tonight. About eleven this evening, I would say. It's not going to make any noise, but there will be a high whine of air being displaced. It's some of my stuff coming down from 1860. Could you help unload it?"

"Sure."

Thelma yelled from the kitchen, "You-all staying for beans and cornbread?"

"Wouldn't miss it for the world!" Siren yelled back.

When they were sitting out on the porch, Roy said, "Siren, show me again where your home world is, please."

She got up and went over to point into the southern sky. "Just below the horizon. This time of year, here, it's there!" she said. "Look at the bright star and then go up to the little bluish-green star."

"I see it!" Roy said, turning to look at her. "Do you miss it?"

"Roy, I'm here with my children. I'm complete with that lovely man over there. Of course, I miss my mother—I miss the things I saw at home. But my home is here for now and in this time."

It was quiet—no bugs singing, no breeze, just silence, and then one of the horses would kick the stable wall and snort.

Roy said, "Sounds like a wind coming up" A sort of distant whine could be heard.

"No. That's the sail wing coming in," Siren said. No lights, just a sound. It whooshed overhead, jet black. It was probably two hundred feet off the ground as it passed. Siren had put the homing beacon out in the pasture. They saw the wing do a stall maneuver and it slid to a landing.

She got up. "Let's go unload it." Siren, Roy, and Traver got into the pick-up and drove out. Siren got out of the truck as the wing settled down on the extended skids. Finally, it rested fully on the pasture surface. Siren went over and pressed a panel, which opened a hatch. It lit up inside, and Siren stepped in. "Here, honey, load this in the back of your truck." She began pulling out trunks that looked like they were made of aluminum. Some were heavy and some light as air. When the wing was unloaded, Siren shut the hatch. She went to the homing box and pressed some buttons. The wing raised into the air and just floated away.

"Where's it going?" Roy asked.

"Eventually it will crash into the sun. It's of no use here and I don't want it to be found," Siren answered.

When they got back to the ranch, Roy helped bring in the metallic trunks. After they were unloaded, Roy left.

"What's in them?" Traver asked.

"These two have the enhancement fluids and treatments. The three over there have Shenaas."

"Yum!" Traver smiled. "And the heavy two? What's in them?"

"You call them diamonds."

"What!" He did a double take. "Diamonds?"

"Yes. In 1860, I noticed that diamonds were a better value than gold or silver—at least that is what I read in the San Francisco newspaper." She opened one of those trunks. He expected to see sparkling jewels, but there were dull-looking stones about the size of walnuts.

"Rough diamonds." Siren said.

He took two stones from the case. "I'll get these appraised."

The children came in, dressed in their PJs. Traver held them both as they sat on the couch.

"Hey, how would you two like to help mom and me build a new home so Aunt Sharon and Uncle Butch can live here?"

"Yea!" Both children began bouncing on the couch.

"Hey, you two," Siren said, "be careful. It's bedtime. Let's go."

The kids gave their papa a kiss, and off they went to their room.

Siren slipped in beside Traver on the couch. "The children sure love you, Traver."

He hugged her. "They had better."

She snuggled into his arms and kissed his cheek. "I love you, too, Mr. Wells."

"Me, too, Mrs. Wells. Want to go for a wagon ride?"

"Oh, you're impossible," she said, giggling.

CHAPTER 27

THE WAY AND A MEMORY

WITH THE HARVEST done and the equipment put away until another season, Siren and Traver began plans for their home in Enchanted Canyon. Roy took the D-9 caterpillar and graded a road over to the building site. They brought in twenty-five loads of gravel for the road and used the D-9 to pack it down.

Traver received a call from the gem appraiser that the diamonds were the clearest and the best that had been seen in a long time. They were worth about $125,000 each uncut. He suggested that the stones be cleaved and faceted.

One early Sunday, while Thelma was keeping the children, Siren kissed Traver at the breakfast table and told him to come into the front room. She had him sit on the couch, and she placed herself in front of him. She said softly, "Close your eyes and just feel where you sit. The last time I spoke with you like this was last week. Now my voice will become your inner voice, my voice will become your path. Breathe in deeply—hold that breath—now exhale."

Traver followed her hushed orders and felt himself becoming very relaxed. She continued, "Before one begins, one reflects on where one has been. Every path is a continuation. Traver, gently see the past paths as you breathe in and exhale."

"Traver, breathe deeply and exhale."

Softly, he heard his name. "Traver, breathe deeply and exhale that breath."

He was transported to a wonderful valley—the melody of the morning was enchanting. He expected to see fairies flying about. He expected to hear . . . what was he expecting to hear?

Like an echo, he heard, "Breathe in this meadow and let its wonders nourish your life. Are you creating this valley meadow, or is the meadow directing your thinking? It is both. A path to go, a path to come from. You are the Way."

He rested upon a rock in the meadow, from where he could see a beautiful ocean, rolling waves catching reflected sunlight on azure blue diamond-crested waves. He saw a woman on the shoreline, who held a child's hand. The woman turned to look at him. "Traver," said a voice with the lilt of twinkling silver bells, "I am Eve."

He repeated, "Eve."

She smiled and pointed at the little girl holding her hand. "This is my daughter, Siren."

Again he echoed, "Siren."

He heard, as if from a distance, "Traver, take as long as you want in your meadow. I will wait for you."

He watched the shadows lengthen and felt the coolness of a setting sun. He began to be aware of the couch upon which he sat, and the familiar smells of the ranch came to his consciousness. He could hear Siren breathe. His eyes fluttered and he saw her in the waning light of day. The sun set reflecting off her skin gave it a fire-orange hue. Her hair seemed to be on fire, her eyes were dark pools that drew him close. She breathed in, her lips parted, and he felt his soul being devoured. She exhaled, but he stayed a part of her.

His eyes fluttered again. He tried to say something, but his jaw felt stiff, he could not speak. He tried again. "I . . . I . . ." His eyes remained closed, he did not want to leave the meadow. He jumped, for he heard a sharp explosion: Siren had clapped her hands.

"Traver, be here now." She clapped her hands again. His head swirled. "My God! What happened?"

Siren reached out and touched his forehead. "You have traveled the Way."

"Honey, what do you call your home world?"

"Edon."

He understood.

"And the woman you saw, she represents order, laws, and well being. She is called Eve. My mother is that order for our home world Edon."

Traver asked her, "Honey, have you read a book called the Bible?"

"No, why?"

He got up, went to the book shelf, and picked out the Bible. "Siren, this book is supposed to be a history of a chosen people's struggle and how God formed all that is. Let me read you the story of creation and the Garden of Eden."

When he got to the part about Adam and Eve, Siren's expression showed amazement. "Traver," she gasped. "The word for man in the home world is Adorn. The word for male is Adonne. The word for woman is Eve."

"Could this be an account of the stranded star ship that you have been searching for? As the crew assimilated with the inhabitants, they left tales of their home world, Edon."

"I see what you are thinking. This is very possible." She buried her head in his chest. "They survived," she sighed.

THE CROSSING, SIREN'S GIFT TO HER DAUGHTER

"De Laural, you have heard me many times speak of the great fire, and the light that radiated our world from within it. You have heard me speak that such a fire must be built when I pass into the wind from this life. As a 'knower' of life, we ride the whirlwind. And chase the Star Throwers.

"There was a great fire, De Laural, which burns no more and no less, there was simply a fire, which from its existence radiated light, life, warmth, and love. There were no stars in the space above the fire, the light and warmth flowed outward forever. One day there came a hollow log that thundered, and it fell into the great fire. As this log hit the fire, sparks flew from its existence and scattered in the space above the fire.

"The warmth and light from this great fire kept the sparks glowing. One day another thundering hollow log fell upon the great fire and sparks flew into the sky again and the heavens became as they are today.

"My daughter, when I speak to you as a seeker of light, a knower of light, you realize that you know nothing and that your position is to search. But most importantly, sharing what you search for with the people is your search.

"My daughter, this fire was the beginning. A great light went out without shape or form, a center of a circle, not black or white, no red, blue, or yellow. Nothing that you would see as color. The sound that was produced never ends but plays ever so softly.

"De Laural, when form took place, that is, when light touched the patterns, the color created was blue, the purest sky, and turquoise, the purest store of health, the coolest of water. And there was yellow, the warmest of sun, and red, the richest of feeling. These colors settled and rested. At night, they were absent, blackness. All the lights combined produced day.

"Remember strongly what you hear this moment—this is a story not only of beginning but also of an ending. Like the stone you have tied on a piece of rope, it swings away from its start quickly, reaches its furthermost point, stops for an instant, and begins its journey in the other direction, only to reach its opposite point of travel, stop a moment and return again in the opposite direction.

"This, De Laural, is the seed that contains an entire forest of trees within itself. If you can imagine such a seed that contains all within itself, you can at once know the great fire. As a knower of light, you understand that knowledge, wisdom, and intellect are the source of the fire."

"Mommy, are the ones who tended the first circle of fire the Star Throwers?"

Siren smiled. "Yes, De Laural."

"Like the Indian princess in the painting over the fireplace?" the little girl wanted to know.

"That's right," her loving mother answered, pleased.

De Laural swirled eddies of color between Siren's brilliant white light aura and Traver's purple and magenta aura. The whorls were like rainbows curling in an azure blue river.

"De Laural, you have advanced so much in these past few months. Your growth is because your father and I are together. As you know, you are chosen to succeed and guide our people. So you must understand that when you look back into the sky, at night, you see the stars. In the day you see the clouds, sun, and sky. You are all of these things. Do you understand, honey?"

"Mother, I understand that although I am who I see reflected in a mirror, I am also a part of all things."

"Yes, De Laural. There is no separation; there simply is life and spirit. As you look at such things, do not ask where you are from. Do not ask who you are. You are the universe. The universe expresses twin spirits, the man, the woman, heat and cold, light and darkness, mother and father, De Laural and Kenneth."

"Then, mother, I should be listening and feeling for what part of me I sense in all things around me." De Laural turned to look at her mother. "Many times I sense being home, I sense grandmother talking to me. I like that feeling."

Siren reached out to hold her daughter. "Honey, soon you and I shall have to talk further. But now you go and play with Kenneth and the new kittens."

De Laural jumped out of bed and yelled as she ran downstairs happily. Siren leaned over and kissed Traver deeply and long.

"Do you think De Laural truly understood all of this?" he asked Siren.

"In her own way, yes. All I hope is that she does not try to see the totality of the universe. All she needs to understand is that she is the universe and the universe is her. She should not be searching for a beginning or an ending. Cause and effect have no beginning or ending, because all is dynamic and vibrates and we all participate."

Siren stood up, getting ready to dress for the day. "The effect that we are searching for is the rhythm of the ocean waves striking the shore of time, expressing our culture and our lives. Some think the new waves of civilization wash away the old and make advances. Not so! Sometimes all is lost. Sometimes great advancements occur, but most times we simply repeat what has been done. De Laural will be an advancing wave, her spirit has waited for this point in the universal ocean. Her spirit is old to the point of being ancient—but not ancient on Edon or Earth. When she was born, she attracted a soul from the first crack in the cosmic cause."

They walked hand in hand down the stairs and into the kitchen. Siren prepared coffee, and Traver began breakfast. Siren called out to the children. Kenneth was the first in, followed by De Laural. Traver addressed his daughter, "Honey, what did you learn this morning?"

The little girl paused a moment and then giggled. "I learned that if I stood on my head the world looked different—but I knew it had not changed. It was only how I was looking at the world."

Siren and Traver laughed at their daughter's clever observation.

"Let's hurry up," Siren said. "Today is a school day—first English and math, then art and music this afternoon."

Both kids gulped down breakfast and then went into the front room for their home schooling.

At the end of school day, De Laural asked her mother to recount the story about the star throwers. Siren turned and smiled. "Honey, you remember the story for us—you tell the story."

De Laural grinned with glee. She became very quiet and very grown up. "Everyone please sit down while I remember."

Traver, Siren, and Kenneth took a seat and watched as solemnly De Laural began.

"I will tell this story many times, because it takes me back home. It creates in our memories our home world. Before I tell of the star throwers," De Laural gestured toward the Indian princess painting, "consider our silver spheres of light and their course upon the great dark. The story is of day to night to day, the natural flow of the ultimate expression. The old home was our day, before we lost the Way of the star throwers. Our Way now is to begin a new progress of discovery." De Laural looked intently at her small audience. "The end!" She bowed.

Traver looked at Siren and chuckled. He whispered, "The condensed version."

PART THREE

In the human experience and time, we are born and we pass on. That span in between is said to be our time, gone as quickly as it appeared. What happens between the two events builds the heart and love.

Children become young adults . . .

Parents become slower, that's all

CHAPTER 28

A FEW MORE YEARS DOWN THE ROAD

THE YEARS BEGAN to fly by. The children were now ten years old. De Laural was tall for her age and so was Kenneth, but she was outstretching him. The home schooling had been such a pleasure for all of them. Sharon's family now consisted of Butch Jr., who was five years old, and Laura, who was two years old.

Siren had another boy, now five years old, named Monk, after Siren's teacher, and there was a girl born just four months before. The family had doubled in five years. They had decided to let De Laural attend school in Maxwell. She had such an understanding of who she was and where she was with her history. Siren had shared the Way with De Laural early on. The two would walk out toward Enchanted Canyon as De Laural was told tales of Edon and her home planet.

It took two years to build their home that was located where Traver and Siren had stopped after their first wagon ride. He often caught Siren looking out the picture window, her spirit billions of miles away. She would turn to look at him with a sigh. She would always say, "Someday De Laural and I will walk the canyon a last time and she will leave for Edon to take her place as Eve." Then Siren would give a bittersweet smile.

This time Traver went over to hold her. "You miss your home and your mother," he whispered in her ear while he held her in his arms.

"Sure I do. But I am happy here, with you and my family."

He kissed her shoulder.

Siren sighed. "Traver, it's not like I didn't know what would occur. It's like our first ships that plied the great deep. They left the home world, knowing that they would not return to their former lives. The ships would be gone too long and the first ones traveled in a deep sleep, so upon their return they had outlived the ones who had watched them take off. Their loss was complete. But I have you and I have the children. I have the knowledge that soon De Laural will return to Edon." She kissed him. "The past five years have been so fulfilling for me. Come with me and De Laural tomorrow, please? I will be sharing with her the first ships and the first star throwers. Knowing of the travels will make you a more settled person upon the planet. I am also going to share with De Laural my first command in the universe."

CHAPTER 29

AMONGST THE STARS WE SAILED

SIREN SEEMED OFF in thought as she began telling of her first command. "I was looking down at the heavy timbers that railed the wheel deck. They had been worn by the wind and salt seas, by blazing sun and cracking ice of the high latitudes. My heart felt so strong as my fingers lightly touched the timber rails. I could feel the strength of sun and moon, cold and warmth, old ships of the ocean and new ships of the heavens.

"The blue stone set within the heavy silver ring on my right hand appeared almost pure white now, which meant it would soon be time to throw our sails and gather a solar wind. And our ship would surge in the direction we desired. The sea would grip our hull and try to embrace us a while longer in its cool wetness and it blueness. The light of the moon shimmered over the water's surface, adding strength to our movement of forward and lift. Soon we would be dancing across the great pool reaching for the dawn.

"My hands followed slowly along the wooden rails as I walked. I could hear my boots echoing on the wooden deck. I heard my heavy steps and reminded myself of my body and how heavy it seemed. It reminded me that most of us who traveled walked lightly upon our decks and our sailing ships walked lightly upon the great oceans—leaving only a brief wake of blue-white fire as our footsteps left only a brief echo of gross weight upon the planking. One by one, the ties of the ship slipped their hold. One by one the crew settled into their thoughts of home and their loved ones. I could feel the ship gently breaking from her moorings.

"We could feel the universe catching our sails and quiet thunder reported our movement. It was good to feel mother sea gently holding our ship to her breast. Soon a tearing sound signaled that the ship was leaving her embrace. While I stood still upon the deck of the sailing ship, I felt my hands reach to gather the fires of our direction. In the palms of my hands I visualized holding the suns of the island we tracked toward. In my breath I felt our ship move swiftly across the sea in that direction. As I let out my breath, the fire of the sun I held billowed our sails and pushed us away from the island upon which we had moored.

"As we moved across the great sea, being pulled and pushed and held tightly by mother sea, I brought to mind the picture of the speed our ship would gather soon. The picture of the sky with its twinkling islands of light were set deeply in the memory of our ship. As I brought up the sails and gathered greater thunder and spent great fire, the twinkling islands of light became streaks. The night sky was changing from pearls of light to patterns of light lines. Off the horizon our ship sailed straight out to the great ocean of the universe. I stood on the deck and gathered our crew and our thoughts, all strongly focused with the energy needed for our crossing. After this they all went about their designated tasks to wait out the passage of time.

"Now as I walked across the wooden deck of the ship, no sounds of heavy footsteps fell upon my ear. We were in space now, and our gross matter was accelerated to the proper vibratory state. Our ship had evolved to the matter of light, and we weighed practically nothing."

Quite exhausted, Siren ended her story for De Laurel and Traver.

"How many stories do you have to tell me?" De Laurel asked her mother.

"Let a tear of love fall from your eye, and that tear lands upon the tallest peak on Edon. When the tears have eroded that tall mountain to just desert sand, then you will know the number of stories."

Later that evening, Traver and Siren crept into bed, quiet and still. He softly touched her breast and she kissed him with passion.

"Are there two more on Edon like you?" Traver asked.

He got a whack on his shoulder. "There had better not be! Not like me!"

Then he realized she had been teasing him.

"Just kidding, Traver. There are beautiful and smart and loving women like me at home. I am going to be very proud to show you off. You are well known on Edon. All know that I left everything to be with you. Everyone will be very interested to know you and to understand what makes one leave everything for a man!"

CHAPTER 30

TEENAGERS INTO ADULTS

DE LAURAL WAS eighteen now. Siren and Traver had one more baby, which made five children. Three girls and two boys. It had been almost nineteen years since he had first seen Siren in the Sawtooth Saloon and thirteen years since Siren and the twins had come back into his life. All that was about to take a different path.

De Laural was wise beyond her years. It was obvious that she had a connection with the cosmic. It seemed to her father that she just intuitively had a knowledge of the universe. She seemed impatient that the planet dwellers, as she called the people of Earth, kept their heads down instead of up, looking at the stars.

It was all Siren could do to refocus De Laural.

"But, mother," De Laural would start.

Siren would smile and say, "That's your dad's line." And both would smile and giggle.

But De Laural would continue, "Why is there such a distraction here?"

Siren would stop and look at her daughter. "Perhaps that's why your dad and I chose each other and then married. Perhaps it's your task to awaken the sleeping planet dwellers to look into the heavens and become more focused."

De Laural would think about that. "Thank you, mother."

Not long after that particular discussion, De Laural and Traver were riding along the gravel road that branched off Enchanted Canyon. At times De Laural would get ahead of him, and he was flooded with memories of Laura.

He came up alongside De Laural. "Honey, you're getting on toward your womanhood."

"Oh, dad, mom has talked with me about the birds and bees."

Traver turned a bright red. "She has?"

"Yes, but I always knew that a bird didn't bring babies."

They both laughed.

"Isn't that stupid?" Traver asked. "To tell children a stork brought their baby brother or sister? What I was going to say was how sometimes you remind me of Laura. Especially when we're riding together."

"I do, dad?"

"Yes, you do."

She looked at me a bit puzzled. "Dad, I'm not so sure that's good. I know how lonely you were when she died."

"Don't feel that way. I just wish you could have met Laura. She was so honest. She was herself always and truly enjoyed her life. She was a lot like you, and she appreciated being part of a greater spirit."

They rode on for a bit silently. Then De Laural looked up. "Oh, a city dweller is coming down the canyon." City dwellers were always announced by a large cloud of road dust. They stopped their horses and huddled together to let the vehicle pass. To their surprise, the car slowed to a stop. A young Marine got out of the driver's side, a lance corporal. He was wearing summer khakis. He smiled broadly. "Hello!" he yelled.

Traver waved.

"I think I'm lost. I'm trying to find the Peterson place. And Traver and Laura Wells."

De Laural snapped a look at her dad. He was stunned to hear his and Laura's name paired after all these years.

The Marine repeated his request. "Do you know where the Peterson place is?"

De Laural smiled. "Sure do! Keep going as you are—oh, two miles or so. Take the west fork and you'll go in approximately three-quarters of a mile." She grinned. "If no one is home, just wait a bit and we'll be there."

The corporal said, "Huh?"

Traver, his hand resting on the saddle horn, asked, "What can I do for you, son? I'm Mr. Wells."

De Laural was watching this Marine corporal closely—not out of fear but in great interest. Meanwhile, the corporal was checking out Traver.

"You're Traver Wells?"

"Sure am." Traver's horse flinched his neck muscles. "Whoa, boy!" He pulled back on the reins. "So what can I help you with?"

The corporal came over to the horses and reached over to pet De Laural's mount, Kit. A big old dirty-white horse, Kit was in pretty good shape for not being young. Kit's ears perked forward toward this corporal and the animal took a step or two toward the visitor. De Laural let the horse have reins.

The horse and corporal acted like old friends. "Steady, horse," the corporal said in a calm voice and looked at De Laural.

De Laural took the lead by introducing herself. "De Laural," she offered. The corporal looked at her, saying, "Unusual name for a horse."

She laughed. "No, no. That's my name. The horse answers to Kit."

Traver was aware that he had just been left out of the scene. The corporal and De Laural connected easily, and the visitor stepped closer to pat the horse's neck. "He's good stock." The corporal ran his hand down Kit's right front haunch and leg. "Solid for his age." He looked up at De Laural and said, "Russel."

She smiled and he smiled and Traver still was an outsider. He cleared his throat to get some attention.

The marine glanced over at him. "So you're Traver Wells," he said again, in disbelief.

"Yes, why are you looking for me?"

"I am on emergency leave—my grandfather passed away five days ago over in Maxwell. And as my father and mother were going through grandfather's things, they found a letter addressed to Traver and Laura Wells, Peterson's Place, Maxwell, Cottonwood Canyon, Nebraska. Deliver sometime after 1999. The letter is from my great-great-grandfather."

This corporal had a familiar feel about him, and Twin Bears popped into Traver's thoughts. His emotions jumped, and he realized this fellow had Indian blood in him.

Seemingly out of nowhere, Traver asked, "Is the letter from Twin Bears?"

The corporal's jaw dropped open. "Yes, but how did you know that?"

Traver sat there in the saddle, his horse dropping his head and nibbling at the green shoots of prairie grass. He looked the corporal over good and finally said, "You do favor your great-great-granddad. What was your great-great-grandmother's name?"

Russel studied Traver for an instant before replying, "Alice. Alice Webster—until she and Twin Bears got married. I think they got married in 1863. I remember something about a wedding on Sunday at a coffee and cinnamon roll place in North Platte."

"Alice?" Traver choked. De Laural chimed in, "Aunt Alice, dad."

The corporal looked quickly at both of them. "Aunt Alice?" he repeated.

Quite without thinking, De Laural said, "Yes, Aunt Alice. I met her and Uncle Bill." And then she realized what she had just said. She put her free hand to her mouth to cover it. The corporal exclaimed, "You met her? That's not possible."

Traver tried to cover up De Laurel's gaffe. "Son, may I see the letter?"

"Yes, sir, it's in my duffel bag. I can get it for you right now."

"Wait," he said. "Go on up to the ranch and tell Siren that we'll be there shortly."

The corporal looked at Traver. "Siren, you said?"

"Yes, why?"

"Grandfather said that great-great-grandfather used to talk about a vet with that name." He hesitated. "He also said she would point to a special section of the sky. He always said she came from a distant star and returned there."

De Laural met Traver's eyes.

"Son, go ahead and we will be glad to have you for supper and perhaps help to fill in some blanks for you."

"Thank you, sir." He returned to the rental car as they spurred their horses into a trot.

"Gee, dad, what's this all about? Can he be Aunt Alice's great-great-grandson?"

Traver looked at her, "Maybe, let's go see."

At the ranch house, Siren was just stepping into the shower, thinking how glad she was that when she and Traver built their home they built it in the style of Laura's house. She turned on the shower and adjusted the water to the right temperature. As she began to soap her skin, the marine corporal drove into their front parking area. He got out of the car, walked to the door, and rang the doorbell. No answer.

Siren was humming a tune while the shower water splashed and both sounds harmonized with the doorbell. Since no one answered, Russel sat down on the front steps to wait on Mr. Wells and his daughter.

It was not very long before Russel saw the two riders in the distance—not following the road he had driven, but coming across the lush green pasture. He waved at them and got waves in return.

Russel watched De Laural ride. She was tall in the saddle and so graceful she flowed with Kit's movements. *What a woman. She's no city girl.* Russel smiled as he remembered his own days as a young kid riding bareback at his father's place.

Suddenly he remembered the letter and went to the trunk, opened it, and rummaged around in his duffel bag. Siren had just passed the window overlooking the front pasture and saw a car that she didn't recognize out front. There was a man in uniform at the car's trunk. Then she caught sight of Traver and De Laural riding in. Siren looked over at the clock on her dresser, thinking, "We still have time to get to the country club to meet Sharon and Butch's bunch for Cindy's birthday party.

Siren slipped into a plain white western shirt and jeans, and in her stocking feet, without boots, she went downstairs and opened the front door. She went out on the porch. Russel looked up from behind the car's trunk lid. "Oh, hello, Laura!"

Siren froze in her tracks. *Laura?* It had been a long time since Siren had thought of her. "Mr. Wells told me to wait here and that they would be right up." He shut the trunk and walked to the front porch.

"Come on in while I find my boots. Make yourself at home," Siren told him.

Holding the letter in his hand, Russel climbed up onto the porch and opened the screen door. He went on into the front room and found it elegant. It was rich in feeling and it was a room that he could spend the rest of his life in. He was attracted to the painting of the Indian princess above the fireplace, the same one that had hung over Laura's fireplace.

"Something to drink?" Siren yelled from the kitchen.

"Yes, a Pepsi, if you have it, please."

Siren stopped dead with what she was doing. *Why did that have such a familiar ring to it?* "Coming up!"

After a few moments Siren came into the front room, and when she saw the corporal more clearly she stopped. She felt like she knew this young man. He looked so familiar.

"Hi, I saw Mr. Wells on the road and he said for me to come up here. I have a letter for you and him from my great-great-granddad." Russel handed Siren the letter, which was yellowed and worn at the corners.

She looked at the address and tapped the envelope on her other hand. "We'll wait till Mr. Wells gets here."

"You can open it," Russel said. "It's addressed to you both."

"I'm not Laura. She died in an accident. But I am Mrs. Wells." Siren put out her hand. "Welcome to our home, my name is Siren."

Russel's hand stopped in midair. "Who?"

"Siren Wells."

"Siren—the Star Lady?" Russel asked.

After regaining her composure, she asked, "And your name is?"

"Russel." He smiled and his hand returned to reach hers for a welcome shake. "Russel Twin Bears."

Siren felt shock waves pulsating through her. Still holding Russel's hand, she said, "Twin Bears?"

"Yes. That's the family name. I'm a quarter Lakota Sioux."

"I know," she said, "but I don't understand all of this just yet."

They heard the back door slam shut. "Honey?" Traver yelled. "Have you met Russel?"

"Yes, just now."

De Laural and Traver came in and looked at Siren. "This here is Twin Bears's great-great-grandson," Traver informed Siren.

Russel was puzzled. "You act as if you know him, but that's impossible." He looked at De Laural for some sort of answer.

"Let me have that letter, Russel," Traver said.

Siren handed her husband the letter. He looked at the way it was addressed, "Traver and Laura." He took a deep breath and turned to Russel. "Russel, Laura is not with us any longer."

Russell nodded his head. "I know. Star Lady just told me."

"Star Lady?" Traver said with a smile. "I never thought of you as a Star Lady, honey."

Traver turned back to Russel. "Your great-great-granddad knew us back in 1860. But just a moment—let me read Twin Bears's letter and then we'll explain."

Traver opened the letter and unfolded it. Just one yellowing page with beautiful script writing. He read aloud, "Hi, Traver, Laura. Should you be reading this, then my great-great-grandson has done well. I never returned because my spirit felt better in my time. Again I want to thank you and Dr. Laura for saving my life. I will always be a brother to you. I married

Alice Webster. She asked me to help her with some work at her ranch. Then one day she asked if she could be my wife. We have a strong life and a deep love and a few braves. Will left for college and medical school. I think of you often. Thank you for everything. Will you and Laura tell my great-great-grandson about our adventure? I would appreciate very much whatever you can do to help him know the land and to love the people. With hearts that span time, Twin Bears."

Russel's eyes were wide with amazement. "Take a seat, Russel," Traver suggested, "and I'll try to bring you up to present time." They sat in the front room and Siren told the story of the adventure in 1860 from her perspective. Then Traver told about how his group, including Twin Bears, journeyed back and spent a little over two weeks in 1860. De Laural listened closely and watched Russel's reaction. "This is too much to believe," he said, dazed.

Soon Siren looked at her watch and said, "Traver, we have to get to the birthday party for Cindy." She looked over to Russel. "Come with us?"

"Russel," Traver encouraged him, "you're part of the extended family." "Please," pleaded De Laurel.

As they got into the van, Russel held the door for De Laural and then got in to sit beside her. Siren looked over to Traver and they exchanged mixed-emotions glances. She arched her eyebrows and Traver smiled.

The birthday party was great fun. On their way back to the ranch, the whole family was together, plus Russel. Russel and De Laural were talking in low voices. Siren scooted close to Traver and held him. She sighed. "You see it, don't you?"

"She's too young," came Traver's fatherly grumble.

Siren sighed again. "What do we know about age?"

It was getting late, so Traver asked, "Russel, can you stay the night?"

"Well, sir, thank you. I can, but I have to leave early in the morning. I have to report at Offutt Field in Omaha tomorrow by 23:59."

"A new duty station?" Traver asked.

"No, sir, just T.A.D. till my family gets settled with granddad's death."

"Where are you supposed to be?" Traver wanted to know.

"Seventh M.A.B. I'm off to Africa."

"Oh, almost like shore duty, huh?"

"No, I'm on one of the supply ships, guard duty."

When they pulled into the front parking area of the house, everyone went into the house and disappeared except for Traver and Russel. "Just a minute, Russ."

Traver picked up the phone and called the base locator and got the T.A.D. section. A sergeant major came on the phone. "Sergeant major? Warrant Traver Wells, 4th Marines retired, here. I need to pull some strings and extend Lance Corporal Russel Twin Bears's T.A.D. for emergency leave for at least another couple of days."

It was quiet. "Just a moment, sergeant major." Traver handed Russel the phone.

"Yes, sergeant major?" Russel said into the phone. "It's 7th Marines, M.A.B., Africa. Yes, sergeant, two extra days will be fine. Thank you. Yes, I will report directly to you when I return and thank you again, sir."

Russel hung up and turned back to Traver. "Thank you, sir."

"You're welcome, and it's Traver."

"Yes, sir, Traver." The young man grinned.

The two days were spent talking about the 1860 trip. Russ was fascinated with Siren's account. At one point, he interrupted. "Where was De Laural born? Earth or Edon?"

Siren said, "She was born about halfway home. With the ship I commanded then, it took about a month to get back home. She and her twin brother are star babies."

Russel began to gaze at De Laural with even more admiration. They often perched on the front porch, in lively conversation. Traver sipped at his coffee, staring at them through the front-room window. Siren came to his side. "I had never thought about this," Traver grumbled. Siren put her arm around his waist. "I have a feeling she has chosen Russel, but the culture here requires him to choose her first. I like Russel, Traver. Let's see what develops." They returned to the kitchen.

Russel and De Laural came into the kitchen and joined them. He sat down and De Laural got him a cup and poured him coffee. "Excuse me," De Laural said, "I have to get ready for school." She looked at Russel for just an instant and then left the room. Russel stood up as she exited.

Sitting back down, Russel sipped his coffee and said that he had enjoyed the two days so much. He felt as if he had discovered another part of his family. He hated to have to leave but he would be keeping in touch. As he was leaving, he seemed to stall a bit, but De Laural didn't come back down to see him off. Finally, Russel realized she wasn't coming and he got into his rental car and left for Omaha.

Russel did keep his word and wrote to De Laural once a week.

Siren and Traver never asked De Laural about her friendship with Russel.

PART FOUR

Time has a way of passing

and causing stuff to happen

CHAPTER 31

WRAPPED UP IN TIME

TWO YEARS PASSED, and Traver and Siren received a letter from Russel. He was getting out of the Marines, and instead of staying on the East Coast, he was going to come back to his parents' home in Maxwell. De Laural was now twenty, a strikingly beautiful young woman.

When Russel had gotten settled in with his parents, he came by to visit. He talked to Traver and Siren about building up his parents' herd of cattle and wanted to purchase some of their new calves. They agreed on a price, and he and Traver drove out to the drop pasture for him to pick out and mark twenty calves.

"Mr. Wells," Russel started to speak, fidgeting a little, "I would like to ask your permission to ask De Laural to come to my parents' place tomorrow for lunch. And then go to see a movie in the afternoon." He sure seemed nervous.

"Well, Russel, I appreciate your asking—what did De Laural say about this?"

"I think she'll say yes," he said confidently.

"Russ, De Laural has a mind of her own. I don't have a problem with it,"

"Thank you, sir!" Russel said, relieved.

"But it's her choice," Traver added.

They drove on a bit farther, stopped, got out, and walked over to see the calves. Traver put his hands in his pockets. "Russ, if you feel about De Laural as I do about Siren, you are in for a most wonderful life. But not here on Earth."

He glanced over at Traver. "What?"

They walked over to a low clump of cedar shrubs and sat down in the shade. Traver began the story of Siren's world, including the fact that De Laural would soon leave for Edon to succeed her grandmother. Russel listened intently and when Traver was finished Russel declared, "I would go with her. I love De Laural and would not hesitate to be with her anywhere in the universe."

Boy, wait till Siren hears about this, thought Traver.

At that instant De Laural was talking with Siren. "Mother, now that Russel is out of the Marines and home, I want you to know that I care about Russel very much. I think that he is telling dad this morning that he likes me."

"Likes?" Siren asked.

"Oh, mom, what can I tell you about love? Russel and I have just begun."

The following day Russel came over to pick up De Laural. Siren and Traver stayed on the porch as the two young people drove down the crushed rock road. Siren took his hand and held it. They turned to go back into the house when they both saw the flash in the sky. Siren held back to look again up in the high western sky, where an aurora borealis was occurring. Traver told Siren that those usually occur up in the northern latitudes. They watched the colors shift and shimmer and then came another flash. Siren tensed, her hand tightened on his—again another flash.

She whispered. "A ship!"

"A ship? Are you sure?"

The air became charged with electricity and slowly a familiar craft settled down between the house and the barn.

A hatchway opened and Monk appeared. Siren released Traver's hand and exclaimed, "Monk!"

He waved and yelled, "I was in the neighborhood. Have you got a cold Pepsi?" He walked over as Siren ran down the porch steps to meet him. They embraced.

"Yes, we have Pepsi. Come on in and let's have one," she told him.

"Captain, you look wonderful. This world agrees with you!"

Monk looked over toward Traver. "And you look well, too. Siren is good for you."

She pulled at Monk's arm. "Monk, how did you find us? I would have thought that you would have had to come through the canyon again."

Monk sipped at his Pepsi and said, "We have been able to reproduce that effect up there in your canyon. The problem right now is we can come only here or into 1860, because we have the two signatures. All this science and we can go only two places!" He shook his head and grinned. "Siren, tell me of your family."

"De Laural is on a date—she is twenty now."

"Date? What's that?" Monk cocked his head.

Siren said with a smile, "It's sort of like choosing. It's the custom here. And Kenneth is off on a hunting trip with Roy."

Monk grinned. "And how is Roy?"

"Getting older and slower," Siren said. "And we have three other children now—the youngest is five. All the children are in North Platte at a friend's birthday party. By the way, Monk, the youngest boy has your name."

Monk smiled as he was finishing his Pepsi. "Captain, your mother calls you home. She wishes to know of you since the past years have gone so quickly."

"Is mother ill?" Siren wanted to know

"No, just lonely. She wishes to hold and kiss you again. It is her command."

Siren was quiet a moment before responding. "May I bring my family too?"

Monk nodded his head. "Of course!"

Since the children were all away, they stayed at the kitchen table, bringing Monk up to date on all the happenings. When he heard that De Laural had gone to Twin Bears' great-great-grandson's home and that the two seemed to like each other, he was surprised.

Siren was not talkative, and Monk continued observing her. "Captain, you are very quiet."

She looked at Traver and then back at Monk.

"Monk, can we go back to 1860 to the day that Traver captured you and Will brought me to his camp?"

Monk thought a moment. "Yes, that is possible. Why would you want to do this?"

"I am sure that De Laural and Russel Twin Bears will marry."

"Marry?" Monk asked quietly.

"It's another custom here," Siren said. "Russel Twin Bears would like to meet his great-great-grandfather, I'm sure." She looked toward Traver with a question in her eyes. "Laura will be there also, Traver."

He was dumbfounded. To see Laura again? He looked away. "I don't know about that," he said with a breaking voice. "I don't know."

"Do we have time, Monk?" Siren asked.

He nodded his head again. "We have all the time."

"Monk, are there others in your craft?" she wanted to know.

"No, captain, the ship is parked just outside this solar system behind a tiny ice world way out."

"Pluto," said Traver.

"What?"

"Pluto is the name of that ice world."

Siren got up and put her arms around Traver's waist. "Let's go, into the front room and visit."

The three started into the other room, but Siren turned back to the kitchen for something.

The men could hear Siren on the telephone. In a brief moment, she came in with cookies and more Pepsis. She put the tray down on the marble-top coffee table.

Siren told them that she had called De Laural and had asked for her and Russel to return home, it was important.

In less than a half-hour a vehicle stopped out front and two doors slammed shut.

De Laural and Russel came in the front door. De Laural started to say something, but then she saw Monk. She yelled, "Oh, Uncle Monk!" She jumped over the couch and hugged him.

He was delighted, and Monk told her, "You have grown to be a credit to our world."

"Oh, Monk, it's so great to see you. Grandmother is fine?" she asked.

"Yes," he assured her, "and she longs to see you and your mother."

De Laural introduced Russel to Monk and they shook hands.

Monk said, "I hear your sire name is Twin Bears."

Russell said, "Yes, sir."

Monk smiled. "I knew your great-great-granddad."

Siren said, "Russel, would you like to meet your great-great-granddad?"

"What do you mean?" Russel looked puzzled. "Meeting him is not possible."

Russel sat quietly, glancing at everyone in the room. Finally he exclaimed, "Far out!"

He asked De Laurel, "You will be going back to Edon?"

"Yes, I will," said De Laurel. The ensuing silence was thick. She finally added, "You can come along with me, Russel."

She stood up. "Russel, I choose you, as on Edon a man makes a first choice. Time is always flowing and a new river begins with me. But here on Earth you must choose." De Laurel bowed her head to Russel. She held his hand tightly. "Be my river, be my course, be with me forever." She looked over to Monk. "Monk," she spoke with authority, "you hear my choice?"

"Yes, I hear and I shall record it." He looked at Russel, asking him. "How do you respond? Do you accept?"

Russel had a confused look on his face.

"Russel, it's like being married," Traver said. A light came on in Russel's eyes and he turned back to De Laural.

"I accept your choice," he said as he grasped her other hand. "Not only do I accept—I ask for De Laural's hand in marriage." Both of them began to shed tears. Their streaked faces turned to Traver and Siren, and they said "Yes!" in unison.

Monk said, "Russel, do you wish to meet your great-great-granddad?"

"I do, if you'll come with me, De Laurel," he addressed his fiancée.

Her eyes sparkled as she said, "Yes, of course!"

Siren said, "I'll make arrangements for the children while we're gone."

Monk smiled and said, "That will not be necessary. Regardless of how long we're gone, we will return so that only seconds have passed in our running time."

"Running time?" Siren asked.

Monk said, "Yes, captain, the time that we occupy from birth to death is classified as running time. Time before is only theoretical. We haven't been in the future because we don't know the magnetic signature. We are here because we know this signature. The time past has the same problem—no reference points magnetically. Right now, it's 1860 and your running time. But we can go like the wind anywhere in the universe."

"How do we go?" Siren asked.

"In the ship that is outside."

"Then, let's go!"

"Just a moment," Traver said. "Let me get some field glasses so we can look into the camp."

It was getting close to sunset. "Monk," Siren said, "just how close can we get?"

"I can get, oh, about five miles or so and then we can fly to a closer point."

Siren thought a second. "Is your ship going to set off any alarms on my ship in that time?"

"No, captain, my ship is actually a field generator. The frequency will modulate so that when the sensors begin to feel something, then our signature will change, and consequently the ship will be invisible to our ship in 1860."

"Then, let's go," Siren said excitedly.

De Laural and Russel got up and Monk motioned to De Laural. "I shall follow you."

Siren took Traver's hand and looked at him. She glanced over at De Laural and Russel before returning her gaze to Traver. "Yes, Monk, we are ready." She shifted her eyes to Russel. "Get ready for 1860, Russel, so you can meet your great-great-granddad, Twin Bears."

Monk said, "The best place to distract Twin Bears is the night when Traver caught us and had Will drive you out to his camp."

Traver heard Monk talking, but he was thinking about Laura. She would be there—what, twenty years ago now? *I can't see her again. I can't take that.*

Siren touched him and whispered "She'll be there."

"I know, I know," he said tensely.

The five of them walked out of the ranch house and over to the ship. It was about the size of a 747. They entered and not a sound emitted from the ship. It rose into the air quietly and swiftly, and then just disappeared from sight. Everything was silent, as it should be out on the Nebraska prairie.

To Monk this was a routine occurrence. To his passengers, it only seemed a few minutes and Monk was opening the ship's hatch. The dusk air smelled a bit different. Siren smiled as she said, "1860, folks!" She stepped out.

Monk said, "We're about half a mile or so from where you were in 1860—in the wagon at Traver's camp, captain." Siren had a pair of field glasses and so did Traver. In the darkening prairie they topped a low hill and saw the camp. They were only about a quarter mile from the camp on the Platte River.

Traver raised his field glasses. "There, there." He couldn't say anything more because his throat was closing up. *Laura!* Tears flooded his eyes. Siren came over to stand next to him. She picked up her field glasses and looked toward the camp. She burst out in a fright. "No!" There she was looking directly at herself standing in the camp. Siren gasped and goose-bumps popped up on her entire body.

She saw Traver there, beside Laura, holding her hand. Siren felt like she was prying. She watched Laura and Siren's heart grew leaden with the knowledge that Laura would die shortly after they came back home. There was Skip's dad. But where was Twin Bears?

There on a little hill just behind some low cedar saplings four people were standing. Siren turned to look at Traver, who was still wiping tears from his eyes. She turned again to look down at the camp and Russel reached over and touched her.

He whispered, "Someone is out there." He pointed just west of where they were standing. "Squat down."

Everyone bent low for better cover. Siren touched Traver and pointed west. All of a sudden a dog started barking happily. Twin Bears's dog Lunch came running up to them.

Traver had to laugh. "Hey, boy! Have you missed us?"

A happy bark resounded.

Traver heard the familiar turkey call of Twin Bears. He yelled out, "Twin Bears! Where are you?"

Again came the turkey call.

"Come on in," Traver urged.

As Twin Bears approached the group, they looked at each other questioningly. Twin Bears was bemused, glancing back at the camp. Siren went up to hug him. "How are you doing?" she asked.

"How can you be here and down at camp also?" he answered.

He stopped short when he noticed Russel, his words tapering off in mid-sentence. He eyed Russell and then said, "I have dreamed many nights of my future braves." Twin Bears reached out to touch him. "You feel strong, you feel wise, you are a young brave of tomorrow. Thank you for coming."

Siren touched Twin Bears's arm. "You know who he is?"

"Yes," he answered, not taking his eyes off Russel. "He is my great-great-grandson. You found my letter?"

Russel spoke up, "Yes, that is why I have come."

They hugged each other.

Traver got up to embrace Twin Bears. "Old friend, we expected to see you at the ranch now and then."

"But this is only 1860."

"Hah!" Traver grunted. "I forgot! Let's sit and talk."

Russel sat next to Twin Bears, Siren and Traver sat together, and Monk sat next to De Laural. They talked about all that had happened and how Laura had been killed. They spoke of how Siren had come back five years later with the twins. "So you are a father," Twin Bears said smiling.

"Twin Bears, when you go back to the camp, say nothing of us being here," Siren said. Then she addressed Russel. "Are you staying for a bit?"

Twin Bears, still looking at his great-great-grandson, answered for him. "No, he returns with you. To have met him strengthens my spirit and it strengthens his spirit. There is a time meant for each person. He must live his and I finish mine. Being between time is not productive and is not the way of the people." Twin Bears looked at Russel. "You understand?"

"I do," Russel said. Twin Bears reached to hug Russell again and then held the young man at arm's length. "Your blood is my blood. Your spirit is the blending of mine and of those who came after me. Like my brother Sitting Bull, you have great hearing and seeing strengths."

"Your brother is Sitting Bull?" Russel said, amazed.

"Yes, son, you know of him?"

"I know of him."

"That is good."

Traver hugged Twin Bears again in farewell. The Indian departed with Lunch. After about fifteen minutes they saw the campfire grow as more wood was piled on. With field glasses, Russel watched Twin Bears move about the camp.

The campfire was roaring, almost as tall as Laura. Traver watched through the binoculars, seeing the reds and oranges reflecting off Laura. He felt as though he could reach out and touch her. *Touch her* echoed in his thoughts. Twenty years had passed since he and Laura had touched. Her scent drifted across his thoughts and his fingers tingled as he remembered touching Laura's lips and cheeks. He remembered kissing her. He closed his eyes a moment, tears forming at the lids. He opened them again, and through tears he saw Laura standing next to the fire warming herself. She turned and looked directly at him. Their eyes locked and nothing else existed at that moment. Laura held her gaze into the south of the camp. She felt such a drawing in that direction at that instant. Her back and her legs were heating up from the blazing campfire, but she did not turn. She felt a fire coming from the south that warmed her lips and caused her to breathe in deeply and to fill her breast with love. She put both arms across her chest. Still looking south, she felt as though at any moment she would be kissed.

Traver thought he could go down there and kiss her one last time. They could share their love one last time. *Time*—the word echoed through his thoughts. But he couldn't do that. There was something about looking into the past—being in the past this time was being out of time. Seeing Laura once again did not help with the feelings of loss welling up in him. He lowered the field glasses.

Siren did not interrupt his moments with Laura. She did not know what to say or what to do—so she just waited until he said something. Traver finally turned to look at Siren.

"Oh, God! This is so difficult," he cried.

Siren reached out her hand, still saying nothing. Traver took her hand and held it. "Goddamn it, Siren, this is so fucked up!" Tears were rolling down his cheeks.

Siren slid her arm around his waist.

"I thought for a moment that I could go down there and kiss and hold Laura one last time. I wanted to, but I couldn't take the first step. Time is hell!"

Siren pulled him closer and gave him a big hug, just to let him know that she was there for him.

"I love you," he said softly.

"I know," she whispered.

De Laural and Russel watched the wrenching scene in silence. Then they turned and headed back to the ship, with Monk leaving Siren and Traver a few moment longer in 1860. The wind had kicked up and Siren was shivering. "Let's go, Wells." They walked a thousand yards further south and climbed aboard the scout ship.

"Monk, let's go home," Siren ordered. Monk energized the gravity well field and phased in the magnetic field and instantly they were home.

When Siren had said home, she meant Earth. But Monk took home to mean Edon. When they stepped out of the ship, Siren's eyes were blazing. She was home. Unexpectedly. "It's my world, Traver." She reached out her hands to him. He looked around at all the newness. The colors were soft, the land was low and rolling, and the sky was crystal-clear blue. The sun was shining brightly. He noticed a cluster of six stars, brilliant in the blue sky.

Siren leaned close to him. "My ship was named for that star cluster." He looked again. "But, Siren," he protested, "I see only six stars. Didn't you say your ship was named Seven Sisters?"

Siren smiled. "I did, and I also mentioned that this cluster was called in your world the Pleiades. We are a part of that cluster. We are on a planet of the seventh star."

"Yes, I see now," Traver said with wonder. "Seven stars!"

"Yes! And we had better not let you steer a ship. No telling where we might end up!"

Monk came up to De Laural. "De Paula wishes your presence." He looked over at Siren. "Your mother awaits you."

Siren turned to Traver. "Come, meet my mother. Then we shall return to Earth. To our home. Here you are an alien," she said, grinning, "and there are way too many beautiful women."

THE WAY CONTINUES